RIDING WITH DARKNESS

A NOVEL

TARA MAJUTA

Text copyright © 2021 by Tara Majuta
All rights reserved

This book was originally published in soft cover by Brilliantly Forged, LLC in April 2021.
Cover design by Damonza (Damonza.com)

All rights reserved. Published by Brilliantly Forged, LLC. Brilliantly Forged and associated logos are trademarked and/or registered trademarks of Brilliantly Forged, LLC.

If you purchased this book without a cover, you should be aware that this book is stolen property. It was reported as "unsold and destroyed" to the publisher, and neither the author nor the publisher has received any payment for this "stripped book."

The publisher does not have any control over and does not assume any responsibility for author or third-party websites or their content.

No part of this publication may be reproduced, stored in a retrieval system, or transmitted in any form or by any means, electronic, mechanical, photocopying, recording, or otherwise, without written permission of the publisher. For more information regarding permission, email Brilliantly Forged at Tara@brilliantlyforged.com.

This book is a work of fiction. Names, characters, places, and incidents are with the product of the author's imagination or are used fictitiously, and any resemblance to actual people, living or dead, business establishments, events, or locales is entirely coincidental.

Paperback ISBN 978-1-7366728-0-8
Ebook ISBN 978-1-7366728-1-5

Printed in the U.S.A
This edition first printing 2021

To my god parents, Clayton and Hattie Barnett. Thank you for showing me what true love looks like, so I didn't have to suffer like these two.

Contents

Chapter One: Rebellion 1
Chapter Two: Twitching 15
Chapter Three: Gavin 27
Chapter Four: Caught 41
Chapter Five: Restless 55
Chapter Six: Taken 69
Chapter Seven: Exposed 82
Chapter Eight: Taste 95
Chapter Nine: Terrified 107
Chapter Ten: Collide 122
Chapter Eleven: Sailing 136
Chapter Twelve: Excuses 150
Chapter Thirteen: Hunted 163
Chapter Fourteen: Salvation 182
Chapter Fifteen: Leverage 197
Chapter Sixteen: Broken 213
Chapter Seventeen: The Pines 225
Chapter Eighteen: Target 241
Chapter Nineteen: Interrogation 253
Chapter Twenty: Distraction 265

Chapter Twenty-One: Starry Night 279
Chapter Twenty-Two: Midnight. 291
Chapter Twenty-Three: Breakfast 304
Chapter Twenty-Four: Halloween 321
Chapter Twenty-Five: Revenge. 336
Chapter Twenty-Six: Almost 350
Chapter Twenty-Seven: Avoid 364
Chapter Twenty-Eight: Thankful 377
Chapter Twenty-Nine: Darkness 389
Chapter Thirty: Puzzles 402
Chapter Thirty-One: Aaron 414
Chapter Thirty-Two: Anders 428
Chapter Thirty-Three: Kyle 440
Chapter Thirty-Four: Barter. 453
Chapter Thirty-Five: Settler 465
Chapter Thirty-Six: The Killing. 478
Chapter Thirty-Seven: Sanctuary. 491
Chapter Thirty-Eight: Storm 503
Chapter Thirty-Nine: Truce. 515
Chapter Forty: The Beginning 521

Darkness in the Lion's Den Chapter One: Promises. . .529
About the Author 545

Chapter One
Rebellion

"Catalina Payton, we all like the darkness. The taste of forbidden, dangerous, all-consuming darkness that feels so good," my older sister, Cecilia, said to me. She's the gorgeous one.

I crossed my ankles and rolled my eyes. Typical Cecilia. I'd miss her, for sure.

Our father, Malcolm Payton, shook his head, the SUV swaying with his movements, "Darkness isn't so romantic."

"It makes Catalina uncomfortable." She tossed a long black lock of hair over her shoulder, "It's ridiculous. She's the darkest person I know."

"Well, I like that about her. She's got a good head on her shoulders, unlike you."

Cecilia hooked her long nail into my side, breaking some skin. Served me right for trying to reason with the unreasonable. My finger caressed the power window button, threatening to unleash a car full of hot air against her flawless mane.

She quickly moved on to texting. Dad turned up his golden oldies as Mother, Sally Payton, sifted through items in her purse. I winced—Dad's choice in music only appeased him. But we allowed it, just this once, since he needed the rhythms to relax during the bumper-to-bumper Labor Day traffic.

I gazed out my window. Low branches sprawled across the small, twisting highway lightly touched the roof of our truck. Beautiful greens. Tickles of leaves swept across the water pools next to the road. It soothed me. I searched the shores of each waterway we passed and didn't find a single lighthouse.

Dad had lied to me. Well, that wasn't completely true. I had dozed off quite a bit and could have missed them. But I was still skeptical about whether or not we had actually crossed the state line.

Mother and Dad whispered back and forth, capturing my attention. The conspiracies were still in full swing. Maine didn't seem like the place for us. My parents had both grown up in southern California, and neither one had ever mentioned anything about switching states until three months ago. Then, one day, they announced their intentions to move. And that's when the secret conversations started between the two. So, I spent all my time piecing everything together.

My frustration grew when I came up with nothing. I asked questions—hard, in-depth questions. Mother smiled, and Dad hushed my inquisitive nature, stating that my paranoia and conspiracy theories were considered conduct unbecoming of a lady.

Then it happened—a startling discovery. Two newspaper articles to be exact, both claiming Settlement Island's crime rate had increased by over fifteen percent in the last year. The murder rate had doubled. Why would they take us here? I went to Dad first and expressed my concerns to him, my father and protector, wondering what he was up to.

His reply was a simple, elongated sigh and an explanation of why he didn't care about what I had found. It all came down to one thing: money. He had made plans, big plans, to open up a medical facility that would, "take everyone's breath away." And that settled it—no more discussions, debates, or arguments to convince the other to concede. It didn't matter, anyway. Dad had won the battle, just like all the others. I should have felt defeated and betrayed and I swore my revenge against him for being so irresponsible. However, his lack of concern fueled my imagination. And, because I loved him so much, these articles weren't enough to stop me from moving with them.

Mother pulled down the visor mirror, checked her beauty, and then stared at her forehead for a few moments. She looked back at me with bright brown eyes. "Are you excited?" she said while blotting her lips with a tissue.

I sighed, "I miss the ocean, Mother."

"Catalina, be a good sport like everyone else." Dad took a hard right off Highway 11 and onto Country Road 124.

I frowned—misunderstood again. "The fact that you would even consider this a rebellion means you don't know me at all," I corrected him.

"Well, get over it," he hissed.

Get over it. These words were easy for him to say. Connecting with me on an emotional level was hard for him. The world revolved around him. Of course, it did. He was the only working adult in our family. But that didn't mean I couldn't show some sort of power. "Dad, we moved 'cause it was better for your medical business, right?"

"It's a better opportunity for all of us, Catalina. Especially you."

"But why here? Why not Chicago or New York?"

"This is the best fit."

"Really? I wouldn't take you for someone who would move to a place like this. Just last week, some guy named Logan was found shot to death in the middle of the forest. The cops have no leads."

Mother put her eyebrows together, "What does that have to do with us?"

"Nothing!" Dad's answer was directed toward me. "Nice try, Catalina. You almost scared your mom." Mother nodded.

"I'm not trying to scare anyone." Silence. "There has to be more to the story, right, Dad?"

He took Mother's hand and kissed it. Then it was back to me, "There's no story here, trust me. I'm just a doctor trying to help these people."

Mother turned, "Catalina, what exactly happened to that boy?"

Dad rolled his eyes. I winked at him. "It's a turf war between two rival drug dealers. So many innocent people have died already."

"Wow, sister, you need to get laid," Cecilia shouted. Mother laughed; I assumed she felt more comfortable with the whole situation. Or she was in blatant denial about the entire thing.

My cheeks flushed red, but I didn't let Cecilia see. "If there's anyone left after you," I muttered.

"Sally, Settlement Island is a beautiful, safe place," Dad said to Mother. "A sleepy little town. We'll be fine."

"I trust you." They sealed their commitment with a kiss.

"Why do they call it Settlement Island, anyway?" Cecilia motioned to the window. "Is it an actual island?"

"The lake wraps around the town, so on the other side, it looks like an island," I answered. Cecilia nodded.

Dad slowed down the truck and asked Mother to check the GPS on her phone. Cecilia continued to pick my brain regarding our new home. However, there were other more pressing issues at hand. We were lost, I guessed. Dad eventually turned down a winding road, and we got our first glance at the town below, nestled within a blanket of trees.

We could only see pointed roofs and a few buildings stretched along a black road, probably Maine Street. I looked beyond the edge of the cliff that rested only a few feet away from us. The Green Post Bluffs. The town sat below the bluffs, dangerously close to the lake. The town limits didn't go beyond a tall, white building with a brown roof—a church, I presumed. The rest of the view was trees, two large rivers, and the lake.

My head went back against the headrest and my eyes closed. I missed my ocean, but I had to make a memory of this. A first impression. I missed the few friends I had, but I knew I'd find someone to explore this place with. I wasn't interested in being a twenty-year-old new kid, however I stayed optimistic. My stomach slowly relaxed, my shoulders following.

"Catalina, you have to see this," said Mother.

I squinted at the sunrays dancing on the large lake. The proud trees hugging the water line welcomed us as we climbed up the rest of the road.

Dad and Mother were clueless about everything in life, but they had picked a great place to live. Even if they were flirting with our lives in the process. We passed the town and continued onward for several miles before reaching the Settlement Island Country Club Estates.

Country clubbers. I planned on avoiding them at all costs. Maybe I'd be lucky enough to get lost in the woods and would be forced to live off the land for several years. Then I'd be famous for my mountaineering accomplishments instead of my family's wealth. I cackled at the thought.

Being lost was becoming more of a possibility. We turned down a total of three roads, all lined by a thick forest on one side and the lake on the other. Occasionally, a mansion appeared, but not very often. We were secluded from almost everyone.

The SUV slowed down, and we proceeded up a

hidden driveway. No gate, just a large cut into the trees that led up to our new home. I kept my thoughts to myself. But the awe growing inside of me was obvious.

My parents had spent too much money on the house—peaked roof, white paint with stone settings, large windows, and a brown wraparound porch. I spotted a lounge area and built-in barbeque on the wooden deck out back. This was the dream. Their dream. And against the cascading waves of the lake, it was my dream, too.

Dad parked right at the front steps, "Welcome home, ladies!"

"Let's go see the inside." Mother quickly left the car. Dad got out to catch up to her.

Cecilia added more lush lipstick, "There better be some good-looking guys here."

"Really?" I folded my arms. "You aren't the least bit interested in exploring this place?"

"Explore what? The trees?"

I shrugged, "I don't know. Maybe you can try living beyond your superficial tendencies and become a person."

"I'm twenty-four." She checked the hem of the sexy lavender dress hugging her hips and breasts tightly. "I need to get married while I still got all this. Not sure if I can find a good plastic surgeon out here."

"If that's the case, you should have stayed home," I scoffed.

"Why didn't you want to stay in California? I'm sure Eloise wouldn't have minded having you."

"I don't mind being here," I replied. "Besides, I'll be lost somewhere in Europe this time next year. Or maybe even Greece."

"If you're gonna travel the world, you're either gonna need a man or some money."

"Is that what's holding you back from independence? Money?"

"Why make my own money when I can marry into it?" She exited the truck, leaving me to my own defeat, like a child in timeout. Dad came to the door and motioned for me to come inside. I put my index finger up. I only needed one moment, a second to sit in the middle of everything.

This was my life.

The lake and sun had come together to form a seamless flow of sparkles. Mesmerizing. It wasn't my ocean, but the humble waves of the water did greet me warmly. I wanted to touch it. Run my fingers covered in thin gold bands across the surface.

Someone yelled for me. Another time. I kissed the crisp air goodbye and made my way to the front door.

The inside of the house bore six bedrooms, four bathrooms, a library, an office, and a large, open living room and kitchen. I took the small room with a fireplace on the first floor. My backpack dropped onto the wooden floor, and I drew the heavy steel blinds attached to the three big windows along the white walls. The movers had arrived. The image of the truck and our stuff, perfectly framed by the edges of the window, seemed like a scene from a movie. A desperate tale starring a girl trying to get to know the family who would never really understand her. My phone buzzed inside my blue canvas backpack. A text from Miguel.

Sorry no call. No free time. Are you in lobster country yet?

Yes, sir. House is larger than expected.

Dr. Dad get his car?

I laughed, Yep. It should be pulling up any minute now.

Good thing it's not Saturday or else you and the car would be competing for b-day attention.

My shoulders slouched, They'll probably forget it, anyways.

What's your room like?

My eyes glanced left to right, Boring… for now. Painters are coming tomorrow.

Cool. Miss you.

Ditto.

Take pics of you and the new home.

Will do. Find time to chat with me! I need to tell you about this place!

K. Hang in there!

I threw the phone on top of my bag, knocking a tube of red lipstick from an open pocket. Cecilia. I pulled it out and walked up to one of the grayish-white walls. I thought about colors that would match the brown wooden floors.

I popped open the tube and wrote, "Deep Blue." It took the whole damn thing to make it visible. That'll show her. I smiled and went to the porch, just in time to see Dad pointing at different rooms in the house and shouting commands to the team of clueless movers.

I wondered what their thoughts were. Had they ever seen such a sight before? Or was a place like this normal to everyone else?

Dad's attention went off into the distance. He began leaping about like a grasshopper. A tow truck pulled into the driveway with the silhouette of a car under a tarp riding on its bed. Dad had told me about his new sports car, but I never believed that he would think the icy, snowy streets of Maine would be a great place for it.

I held in my comments and continued across the porch. The back of the house faced the trees and the lake. Ripples of water and birds flying above reminded me of a painting Miguel had done. I approached the railing, put my elbows on it, and my face in my hands.

California, sun, beach, culture—these things kept repeating in my mind. The dim, soft light of the sun barely felt good on top of the still air completely suffocating my lungs. Before, I didn't mind the fresh air, but now I was consumed by it. My hair stuck to my back and the mosquitoes danced in and out my ear canal. Maybe it was like chocolate to them. I moved further across the patio until I found a set of stairs leading to the beach.

The sound of trees brushing together almost drowned out the hum of sirens in the distance. My thoughts wandered back to Logan's murder. Did his untimely demise take place out here? It was hard to tell.

"Get changed," Mother said from the top of the stairs. "We're going to the country club."

I tensed up, "Isn't it a little early for that?"

She turned and went toward the house, no longer interested in having a discussion with me.

I headed back inside. Three suitcases sat at my door. I pulled the bags to the center of the room and opened them. Mother came running in, barefoot.

"Come to the kitchen! We're making a toast!"

"I'm not twenty-one yet," I replied.

"Close enough!" She grabbed my wrist hard and pulled me.

Dad had started passing out glasses. I took mine. Maybe a little liquid courage would help me get through the rest of the day.

Mother held up her glass. "Okay, everyone should say something they hope they'll get from living here."

Dad went first. "I hope to get a trove of sick, old people coming into my hospital who have full medical benefits and phantom symptoms," he said. A very thorough answer, I noted.

Mother pulled him into an embrace, and they kissed. It was cute. She raised her glass, "I hope to lose those last few stubborn pounds, so I can fit into my new swimming suit."

Cecilia rubbed Mother's back as she gave her a slight glare. Their silly weight-loss competition was still on, even though beach season was long over.

My sister cleared her throat and let out a loud screeching cry. I contained my disgust, which was harder than I thought. Dad caught me and pointed his finger. My face leveled out as I waited for her to amuse me with some vapid declaration of hope to find her long-awaited soul mate.

Cecilia hushed her tears, "Dad, thank you so much for being a strong husband to Mom and a wonderful father to us."

He pulled her into a hug, "You're welcome, sweetheart."

She continued, "My wish is simple: I'm sure you'll share it with me. I hope to finally find a man who's as strong-minded and hard working as Dad." Of course, you do.

Mother nodded, "With beauty like yours, you will." Her tone was sharp. I hid my enthusiasm toward her sarcasm. Dad seemed to brush it off with a kiss on Cecilia's head.

I stroked the stem of my glass, thinking of a half-truth to tell them. I had my own motivations. The first was to find my own space. Second, to recapture my long-forgotten independence. It lingered close by, yet I always seemed to miss it.

Everyone readied themselves for the toast but me. They had forgotten about me. I thrusted my glass into the air without a word.

Cecilia stopped everyone abruptly from taking a sip. "Catalina, darling, what's your wish?" she said with a smirk. I glared at her and paused for a brief moment.

"I don't know," I replied. "I like adventure." The corner of my lip turned upward.

"Are you on another quest to find yourself?" Cecilia said.

"I already know who I am."

Mother and Dad smiled. Cecilia nudged me—no, I didn't want to spend time with her, if that's what she was requesting. She would figure that out, eventually. I raised my glass, and we toasted.

A healthy sip of champagne went down my throat before Mother took my alcohol away. "You're not twenty-one yet," she reminded me, pouring my drink into hers.

"Close enough," I hissed.

"Besides, we don't want you to make your big, country-club debut drunk off your ass," Cecilia winked.

I took her glass away, "Same goes to you."

"Time to get ready." Mother focused on me, "Catalina, no jeans and tee-shirt, please."

Back down the hall and into my room I went. I emptied the contents of my suitcase onto the floor and moved all the historical fictions and literature books to the side. My dress collection was still in boxes on the truck, so I only had a few items to choose from. The blue dress wouldn't work. No, definitely not the green one. The lavender dress that came just above the knee was always Aunt Eloise's favorite. It paired nicely with my jean jacket and the gold beaded bracelets on my wrists. My hair went into a low, curly ponytail. Light makeup, of course.

Mother had placed a mirror in my room. I looked at my reflection, my youthful glow still very present. I was pleased; this was the most dressing up I would ever do. But I knew Mother wouldn't be content.

The relationship with these people I had fought so

hard to preserve came to the forefront of my reflection. But conceding to my family's requests wasn't in my nature. I grabbed my soft, vintage tee-shirt and ripped jeans from the floor. Then, I hesitated.

It was a trap. If I gave into my need to be original, I would fall right into my parents' estimations of me. Instead, I had to be more clever. I straightened my dress and brushed my wavy hair. My phone chirped. It was a news article about Logan's death. No time to read it.

Mother swooped in and whisked me away to the car. "You look nice," she said. "Very approving, for once."

I took the compliment, but there was no way she was going to hide her messy, dark-minded daughter.

Chapter Two
Twitching

Mother tried her hardest to convince me to be more social, but I didn't give in. But once we set foot inside the country club parking lot, I scolded myself. Men, their wives, and darling kids sparkled in their bright colors, strong creases, and polished shoes. I reminded myself to not feel inferior. *Remember, your family probably has more money than they do.*

I smoothed out my dress. Cecilia caught me and grinned. Dad passed the valet and parked a distance away from the clubhouse. We got out, and Mother pushed her hair up one last time before rolling her shoulders back. She wrapped her hand around my father's, and they walked confidently toward the glass doors.

Cecilia linked arms with me. "Did you bring any condoms?" she whispered.

Two white-haired couples passed us. I spotted a few middle-aged men examining her long legs and curves. "You're disgusting."

"I don't date married men…anymore."

Maybe she was telling the truth. Cecilia's last boyfriend was a forty-one-year-old chiropractor named Dr. Avery. He and his gorgeous wife were somewhat separated when Cecilia trapped him in her web. So, maybe there was hope for her after all.

"Who says they'll be interested in you?" I said.

A smirk crossed her lips, "Jealous?"

"You realize we're probably the first black people to ever set foot in this country club, right?"

"On the contrary, my dear, Catalina. There's another black family. Dad's been chatting with them over the phone for a while now." She surprised me. I never thought Dad would keep her abreast of his intentions and secret motives. Maybe these things were only a secret to me.

We approached the steps, and I prepared myself. Two Roman gods wearing black tuxedos opened the glass doors for us. Cecilia took notice. I thanked them and pulled her inside. White linen tablecloths, tan leather furniture, and fine china were sprinkled throughout the main foyer. The men wore slacks and blazers. The ladies wore colorful sundresses. Everyone and everything was shiny, quite a sight for someone who hadn't grown up in this world.

Cecilia ran up to our parents, chattering loudly. I stayed back, observing the attendees.

The other black couple Cecilia had mentioned talked over a glass of red wine with an older white couple. The rest of the club-goers seemed to continue their conversations, while taking an inventory of our status. A couple of smiles washed through the crowd. Timid smiles I had seen before, belonging to those who were unsure of what to say or how to say it.

Mother and Dad danced their way over to a small group and introduced themselves. My parents were accepted once everyone realized who they were. Cecilia walked around, nudging for various people to get out of her way. I followed suit. The smell of blueberry pie tickled my nose. Awe, yes, Maine blueberries. They would become a staple in my diet. That I was sure of.

My sister circled a few more club-goers before making a beeline toward a group of blonde and brunette girls who appeared to be close to our age. Within about five minutes, Cecilia blurted out that she had sung backup for a couple of new pop stars in the California music scene. They became addicted to her instantly, hanging onto every empty word that escaped her bright red lips. Surprise, surprise. Her charms were not immune to women, either.

I ventured about, looking for my people. Dad had found the golfing group. Mother had broken away from him to cackle at terrible jokes with the rich housewives. She interrogated a few women, hoping to find a housekeeper she could trust. Golf and lunch dates flew around as my family became acclimated to our new community. I had to get out.

My shoulders brushed up against the Who's Who of Settlement Island as I darted through the crowd and scouted out different corners. A few people glanced my way, but I went unnoticed by most. Across the room, I found exactly what I was seeking—a small collection of antique books on a bookshelf. I grabbed The Adventures of Huckleberry Finn and moved away from the bookshelf before any of my family members could see me. Refuge came in the form of a corner table next to a row of windows. I melted into the seat.

Another astounding view of Settlement Island Lake. The sun started setting, illuminating the trees casting long shadows across the water. I appreciated the scene for a moment before beginning my reading journey. Three pages into the story, Cecilia came stomping up to me.

"Dad told me to come find you." She threw her hands on her hips.

"What's up?" I said nonchalantly.

She reached for the book. I pulled it into my chest, "Are you seriously reading right now?"

I shrugged, "I like reading, get over it."

"It makes you look antisocial."

"I am antisocial."

She dropped down into a chair and played with her hair, "If you think sitting and reading is making you invisible, you're wrong."

"Being antisocial doesn't mean I have to be invisible. I just want to enjoy my book."

"Your loner personality is going to send the wrong impression," she huffed. "People might get the creepy vibe from you."

"You know I don't care about that." I paused to see

what she would say next. She folded her arms. No nasty comments or slights against me. I started reading again. After a while, I realized she wasn't going away, "Cecilia, why are you here? You don't feel bad for me, do you?"

She rolled her eyes, "I set up a brunch date with some really fun girls for tomorrow. Dad said I can't go unless I take you."

"Is that your way of asking me to brunch?" I smirked.

"No, I'm telling you we're going to brunch tomorrow."

I closed the book, "What if I didn't want to go?"

She took it from me, "Why wouldn't you go? It's not like you have anything else to do."

"Maybe I wouldn't go because I'm not your babysitter."

She squinted her eyes, "I don't need a babysitter. Dad's the one who has pity on you, not me."

I snatched the book back from her, "Well, it's good to know I'm wanted."

"I hate you," she replied as she stomped off.

My attention went back to reading. I didn't get very far before loneliness set in. I missed Miguel. He would have loved this place. He would have shielded me from my parents and Cecilia. I knew what they had to be thinking: "Catalina's scurried away into her own world, rejecting the rest of us." Maybe it wasn't wrong for them to get to know me…

"No one comes to a country club party to read." A guy with blue eyes and short, slightly tossed brown-blond hair approached me. Dressed in a white polo and khakis, I knew we wouldn't hit it off. But then I saw the hunk of blueberry pie he carried. My mouth watered. He pointed to my book, "What are you reading?"

I turned the book, so he could see the cover, "Huck Finn."

The pie slice was placed down on the table, so he could put his hands in his pockets. One spoon: a bold move. I waited for him to say or do something else, but he just stayed still. The spoon called out to me. Finally, he sat down, unannounced.

"Would you like to have a seat?" I said with a hint of sarcasm.

He chuckled, "I should've asked before I dropped down here, huh?"

I studied my book, then the pie. He fussed with a cloth napkin for a moment. "Do you want some pie?"

We watched each other for a beat, both eyeing the spoon. I went in first, cutting off a small piece, and gracefully devouring it. Divine, sweet bliss. I went back for another.

"I figured you were reading a romance novel." He paused and bit his lip, "Seems like your type."

Wavy shoulder-length black hair, brown eyes, and average height made me the romantic type? He cracked a nervous smile, showing off the whitest teeth I had ever seen.

"Are those veneers?"

He shut his mouth. "No, I just got them whitened today." He ran his tongue across his teeth, "I guess they did a good job." I felt like a jerk.

The guy seemed nice. His quiet struggle to befriend me was quite flattering. "They did. Your teeth look great," I said. Another chunk of pie went into my mouth.

He hid his smile from me. I had done my good deed. We went back to our previous dance of me eating and him watching me. He dug his nails into his palms.

His throat cleared, "I'm Luke Edwards."

"Catalina Payton."

Luke pointed to a man in the crowd. "My dad's a plastic surgeon." I smirked. Now Cecilia had someone to tighten up all her loose ends. Maybe she and Luke could hook up. "What kinda doctor is yours?" he said.

"General medicine."

"Oh. So, your dad's gonna take over Dr. Callahan's old practice?" he said.

I shrugged, "I don't know."

He nodded, "I'm sure he is. Is that why you moved here?"

Too many questions. And given the crime stats, I wasn't sure if I should answer. But Luke was in the country club crowd, so maybe he wasn't a killer. He waited patiently for my response. Finally, I said, "Yes."

Then came nothing. We were running out of things to talk about. I didn't mind. Luke's uneasiness made me nervous. And by this time, the pie was almost done.

He broke the silence, "So, you're from L.A.?" Luke was stubborn. Or maybe he was just as desperate to disappear as I was.

A dark-haired girl, a waitress, I think, peered over at

our table. She quickly turned around and walked back to the party. Luke remained rigid in his seat.

I motioned to the crowd, "You should probably get back. I'm sure someone's missing you."

"I'm not interested in listening to my drunk mother parade around, making a fool of herself." He fiddled with the tablecloth. "I'm boring you, huh?" His right eye gave a nervous twitch. That reaction to a woman's company had to be hard. Luke was attractive and sweet, the perfect attributes for any woman at the country club. I wondered about his history with the other girls. He raised an eyebrow in my direction.

"No, you're fine," I said. "I'm the boring one."

"You don't ask stupid questions," his elbow went onto the table, "I like that."

"Boring people don't ask questions at all."

He chuckled. I smiled. Being social did have some perks. It wasn't often that I actually amused someone else. I rested the book on the table. A two-way conversation with Luke seemed beneficial.

"Have you lived in Settlement Island all your life?" I said with real interest.

"No, I'm from Vermont. We moved up here thirteen years ago."

I was intrigued, "What brought your family here?"

"My grandparents. When my grandpa died, he left the castle to us."

"The castle?"

"He always called it that. It's a big house on the golf course."

"That's noble," I murmured.

"Yeah. I spent a couple summers up here when I was a kid, so my dad thought it would be a good transition." Luke stayed glued to the crowd again. When he noticed me, the twitching was gone. He bit his lip.

I continued, "What do you do here? Are you in school?"

"I finished college a few years ago." He rotated the plate and mashed his fingers into the pie crumbs.

Luke was being shy. I decided to pry, "What's your degree in?"

The right eye twitched, "Marine biology. I'd like to get a job closer to the ocean and do some research on whale pods. However, my father asked me to stay here for a few more years, so I can learn more about business before I go." He leaned in, "What about you? Did you go to college?"

Mother put herself into my view. She gave me a thumbs up. I leaned back and looked Luke up and down. "Did my mom send you over here?"

His eye twitched, "What?"

She motioned for me to sit up straight and fix my hair. "Did my mother send you over here to talk to me?"

"No. Your mom," he cleared his throat, "has ulterior motives?"

"She thinks I'm a dark spirit."

"Are you?"

Cecilia marched up to Mother. They spoke a few words before turning in my direction. I got up and grabbed Luke's wrist, "Let's go outside." He didn't protest.

In the warmth of the sun, I released him. We took a seat at a square wooden table with a large umbrella. "Had enough of your family?" he said.

"My sister's trying to get me to go to brunch with her and some girls."

"Where are they going?"

"No clue. Maybe she'll find something in town."

His face straightened, "You can't go there."

There was a shift in his movements. Almost like he was gearing up for a battle. "Is it the murders you're worried about? Do they happen in town?"

"Just stay here, okay?" he cleared his throat.

"How much do you know about the deaths?" My shoulders tensed up; I didn't actually want an answer.

Luke searched the area around us. "I've only read about a few things in the paper. One guy was found really close to here. A few days before him, another guy was shot to death right by Maine Street."

I froze, "Do you guys ever have issues in The Estates?"

"Nah." His mood didn't give me much faith. Luke seemed to sense that. "Most of this stuff happens on the other side of town. But a few people got into a huge fight near the turn-off about a month ago. No one got shot then, I think."

I leaned in, getting too close to him. His forehead glistened with sweat, "Why is there a country club here, anyway? You know, with all the violence?"

"The lake. Plus, the golf course is phenomenal.

Nobody from the club goes into town unless they're looking for trouble."

"Yeah, but how do people make money and buy stuff if they don't work in town?"

"Anders. It's a much larger city about forty miles from here. That's where my dad works." He paused, "If you wanna check it out, I'd be happy to take you."

"Like a first date?"

He laughed, "Or meeting. Whatever you want to call it."

I wasn't sure what to say. Luke had been a doll but dating never worked out for me. "Maybe."

"Fair enough." His phone buzzed. After checking it, he got up, "Gotta go." He searched the dining room before gathering a cocktail napkin and pen from a nearby table. "Promise to call me if you wanna hang out, Catalina." He handed me his number.

"I will." Our awkward silence reappeared. I came to the conclusion that he was waiting for me to dismiss him. I rose and smiled, "Take care, Luke. I'll see ya soon."

He hesitated before leaning in and kissing me on the cheek, "Stay close to home."

Luke was gone, so I headed to the bathroom to hide. Inside, I locked the door and relaxed into an armchair. My conversation with Luke was good, a small victory. I had insight into Logan's murder, but I wanted to know more, especially since Luke mentioned another murder. The plan was simple—I'd get home soon enough and see what else I could find out.

Home. Now, this meant Maine, not the Pacific Ocean

and the only place I'd ever called home. Yet, Settlement Island was full of surprises. I touched my cheek. Luke. I didn't expect a kiss, nor did I mind his touch.

My phone buzzed in my jacket pocket. It was a text from Mother wondering where I was.

A quick reply got her off my back. I cleared out the screen and retrieved Luke's number. Maybe I was wrong about this whole dating thing. No, it was too soon. Maybe Luke would be that one friend I needed to fit in. Or he could protect me from the murderer lurking in some shadow.

Chapter Three
Gavin

THE NEXT DAY came too soon. My racing mind had brought troubling dreams during most of the night. *New town. Murders. Violence. Dating. Luke*—I wondered if he'd try to pursue me.

The many boxes stacked throughout my room reminded me that I needed to start unpacking. I focused on the color I had written on the walls the day before. Deep Blue. Like the time of night that is darkest. Some people despise it, but I love the quiet serene feeling that comes when the sky is empty and black, full of surprises. Like a star shooting across the galaxy or a planet coming out to shine brightly. It was in those moments, trapped below the dark sky, that I found peace.

I relaxed into the soft layers of the bed, my eyes wandering around the room. The black dresser Aunt Eloise had found and refinished for me was in disarray. Cecilia had to be the culprit.

Sleeping through her invasion of my privacy proved

how tired I was. I turned onto my side and considered freeing all my possessions that were painfully packaged away, their beauty hidden. Things I had collected from various street fairs, friends' houses, and flea markets in Berkeley where my parents had sent me away at fifteen to live with Eloise, so I could attend college.

No matter how much I hated unpacking, my love for my treasures was stronger. I rolled out of bed and went to the first box. Lingerie—Cecilia! My fragile motivation came to a sudden end.

I closed the box and went to the window. The lake rolled tiny waves onto the beach. A morning swim would help jumpstart my day. I went to my suitcase, put on my black two-piece, and opened the door.

Cecilia stood there in hot pink nails, shoes, and dress. "I'm picking out your outfit for brunch. And you can't stop me."

Shit, I had forgotten all about that. "Good morning to you, too. Did you sleep well?" A warm, sincere greeting would keep her off my back. She rolled her eyes. I gave away my biggest tell by frowning.

Her eyebrows creased into a tight V-shape. "Don't embarrass me today, little girl."

"Cecilia, I can't embarrass you unless you provoke me."

"Just don't talk about smart stuff the whole time, okay?"

"Maybe I should just stay home."

She wasn't charmed by me, which was fine because I meant what I said. My feelings wouldn't have been hurt if she blew up and demanded that I stay behind. I almost expected that from her. Cecilia never pitied me, and I never needed her pity. We were different, but our differences worked for us—most of the time.

"Look, Cat, I want you to go," she murmured.

What game was this? "Why?"

"I think you'll have some fun."

"With you and the Barbie squad?"

"For being a nonconformist, you're the most stuck-up person I know." Her perfect lips curled into a smile.

"Those two things are not correlated in any way."

She paused. "You're the product of your own hate, then!"

Her sly remarks did merit a response. "Nice try, Cecilia. I almost thought you cared about me."

"Stop being a bitch and get ready."

"What am I supposed to talk about with these people, anyway?"

She blinked quietly—I had stumped her. I took my victory and went to the closet to pick out a pair of jeans and a tee-shirt. She left the room and returned, gripping a dress.

"Books, art, California, home. Things like that. You may be smarter than those other girls, but I bet they'd enjoy talking to you about that junk."

"If they're anything like you, they won't."

"Well, they…actually aren't."

"They went to college?"

"And aced it," she murmured.

It wasn't very often that my sister needed my help.

Throwing the jeans back into the closet, I took the dress as a silent acceptance to her brunch date. No one could resist the sweet smile sweeping across her face.

"Now get dressed, kid, before I leave you here!" She stomped off.

I examined the dress and suppressed the vomit crawling up my throat.

∽

The bright orange dress Cecilia had picked out for me clung to my stomach and pushed up my tiny breasts. It sucked the life out of me. Mother decorated my hair with a wave of messy curls dangling onto my shoulders. Together, she and Cecilia inspected me before I left to make sure I didn't disrupt any of their hard work. Adrienne, some girl with lacey black hair, scooped us up right on time.

"So, how are you ladies liking the new house?" Adrienne pulled her Tahoe out of our driveway, slowly crawling down the street.

"Big and expensive," Cecilia giggled.

Adrienne eyed me in the mirror, "How about you, Catalina?"

"I like my room. Can't wait to check out the lake and do some hiking."

"Where are we going?" Cecilia said.

"Into town. There's a really good café there."

Town. My stomach jumped for a moment, but I quickly hushed it. The sun was up—that was Dad's main defense during one of our battles about the violence in our new homeland. Regardless, I shouldn't fear the unknown. Besides, there were people who still lived within the city limits and remained alive. I had a chance.

Cecilia poked her head in my direction. "Adrienne, what are your thoughts on the murders?" I said just to get under her skin. Adrienne tapped the steering wheel.

"Don't mind her, "Cecilia said. "Catalina thinks we should stay in The Estates. But all the country club guys are ugly, so it's time to move on." Cecilia checked her veneers in the vanity mirror and applied more lipstick. Adrienne gripped the steering wheel tight.

"You know, Cecilia," I started, "you're just like those dumb girls in the horror movies. The ones who think some hot jock is playing a trick on her. Little does she know…"

"The creepy sounds in the basement are from the sicko with the jars of heads who slashes her to death. With any luck, your head will be in one of those jars." Cecilia pushed the visor back up. "Now on to more pressing matters." I opened my mouth to reprimand her, but it would have been of no use. She let out a scream.

A moose had meandered into the road and stopped. Adrienne slammed on the brakes, jolting us forward. I couldn't say a word. I had never seen anything so colossal in my life. A chill climbed across me. The deserted country road close to the dense forest made it impossible to make out anything in the brush. What if someone was watching?

Cecilia reached over and blew the horn, "Get out of the way!"

The moose didn't even amuse her with a blink. "Don't bother, we're on moose time," Adrienne said. And so, we waited. Adrienne started some conversation about hair extensions. I welcomed it. Fighting with Cecilia over silly things made us look childish.

A couple minutes later, the moose moved on, and we were allowed to proceed. Cecilia put on pop music, and Adrienne balanced conversing with her and keeping watch on the road. I guessed the moose was still a major concern. But not for long. Cecilia and Adrienne mulled over all the boring things I didn't care much for—shopping, boys, and of course, sex. I was a good sport and nodded occasionally.

Soon we were in town and hunting for a parking space along Maine Street. The black coal pavement was lined with store fronts, boutique shops, and tiny restaurants. Tall roofs and bright blues, purples and yellows covered almost everything. Along the brick walkways were black streetlamps and trees towering over the sidewalks. Off in the distance was the lake and a marina filled with people and trucks backing massive boats off the ramp. I checked the license plates passing by: Vermont, Massachusetts, and New Hampshire—tourists. Adrienne found a spot, and we hopped out, heading toward a small restaurant called Settled In Café.

It was a cute place, a bit cramped, but the aroma of freshly brewed coffee was what won me over. The pretty redhead waitress gave us a table by the window. She must have sensed my fear of having to rub elbows with strangers. I sat beside Adrienne who was stuck next to the peering eyes of pedestrians walking by. After a couple minutes of flipping through the menu and ordering, we were joined by another girl named Molly. Before her butt hit the chair, the gossip came out.

"Molly, you should wear blue instead of that pink dress I saw you in yesterday. It doesn't show your cellulite as much." Cecilia leaned in, "You don't wanna look like Vivienne," she said with a wink. We weren't across from each other, so she didn't see me cut her down with one look.

Molly kissed her cheek, "Of course."

"So, what are we doing Saturday night?" Cecilia struck a match to light her cigarette.

Molly, a loud blonde with perfect teeth, started giggling out of control, "Well, there's malls, movies. All the stuff they have in The Estates and in Anders."

"So, we're going to Anders?" Cecilia said.

"It's an option."

Cecilia peeked out the window at a few couples with kids who passed by. Her face came close to Molly's, "Well, in L.A. we had non-stop fun. Take me to some place like that?" I knew where she was going with her questions. Molly and Adrienne traded glances back and forth.

"She's referring to sex and coke," I clarified for Molly.

"I'm sure we could find someone to do," Molly laughed.

"If he's ugly," said Cecilia, "I'll never forgive you."

Adrienne grabbed my hand. I tried to retract it, but

her grip was firm. "So, I saw you talking to Luke," she said into my face.

My eyes widened. We had all this time together in the car and this was the first mentioning of Luke? Did socially-awkward Luke have a girlfriend? No, he seemed too sweet to be that type. This was a trap, carefully laid, so I could fail in front of our group of non-accepting females. "Yeah, he came up to me and introduced himself at the gathering yesterday. I tried to get rid of him several times 'cause he's not my type."

She loosened her grip, but not by much. "Well, that's a good thing."

"Why? Is he a bad guy?" Cecilia said.

"We used to date a couple years ago," Adrienne raised her eyebrow, "Not good in the sack. Like really bad. Our first time was horrible. And then that was it. Nothing."

Molly nodded. I was terrified of what would come up next. Knowing Cecilia, it would be… "Cat's a virgin, so she probably wouldn't know the difference."

"Virgin or not, he's just all around bad," Adrienne laughed.

Words didn't escape my lips. Only my head moved straight toward Cecilia. She winked. And that was it for me. I stood, my destination the bathroom. Never again would I do any more favors for her.

I locked the door behind me and turned on the faucet full blast. Someone knocked loudly on the door. "Can you hurry up, please?" No, I couldn't. I couldn't stand the idea of spending another a minute…pound,

pound, pound! Fine. I shut off the water and let the impatient elderly woman in. There was nowhere else to go, so I slithered back. The girls stopped laughing when they saw me.

"I'm sorry, Catalina, I didn't mean to make you upset," Adrienne said.

"Don't worry about it." I sat down and smoothed my massive hair that had been damaged by the humidity. Cecilia was drinking her coffee with a smirk. No, I wouldn't let her get away with making a mockery of me. "So, you and Luke dated? Well, I'm fine with not dating him. As mentioned before, he's not my type."

Molly and Adrienne didn't say anything; their eyes drifted about the cafe. But not Cecilia's. She was looking at something outside. I turned my head toward the rumbling that intensified.

A black car with tinted windows came roaring down the street. It sped past the café and stopped in a parking spot close by. All at once, the girls sat up straight and took notice.

Out of the car came four guys—two blond and two dark-haired. Dark jackets, ripped jeans, and shirts with vintage designs fitting them nicely. Each had clean hair that was styled and beautifully messy.

"Looks like I picked the right place, ladies." Cecilia continued gawking.

"Kyle, Mark, Oliver, and James," Molly cited. "Kyle's the longer-blond-haired one with the deep-blue eyes. He's an alcoholic and no fun to be around."

"Mark and Oliver are the ones with black hair.

They're kinda sweet, or so I've heard," said Adrienne. "They have no money, though."

"It's a shame, too, 'cause I've heard nothing but good things," Molly said.

My sister inched closer to the glass. "What about the dirty-blond one with the muscles? Buzz-cut guy?"

"That's James. He's wild." Molly licked her lips. I had a thought. How did Molly and Adrienne know so much about these guys? I smirked—something scandalous, maybe?

Cecilia and the girls compared notes on who would be better paired with whom. As the guys chatted amongst themselves, the driver door flew open. Then he stepped out. And nothing else came to mind.

He was tall, dressed in black coal boots, dark denim, and a black leather jacket. Peeking out from his jacket was a button-down, light-blue shirt. My favorite on a guy. Fingers ran through his sculpted hair casually as he slammed the door.

"Never mind, I want that one instead," Cecilia insisted.

There was a moment of silence. "Who's he?" I said.

"That's Gavin Scott," I heard Molly's breathless voice say.

The group of guys started to walk toward us. All the girls fixed their hair and pouted their lips. I bent downward, giving my empty plate too much attention. There was no one in that crowd that would be interested in me.

Cecilia knocked on the glass. Someone knocked back. There was laughter. I glanced up to say something to her when I caught him at the right moment.

Blue-gray and deep in color, I was trapped in his eyes. His face was perfectly framed with thick eyebrows, shapely lips, and smoothness. I wanted to stop staring, but I was glad I didn't.

His face tightened when he looked at me. Not a single breath escaped me. We stared at each other for a moment before Gavin winked. Kyle touched Gavin's shoulders and pulled him into a conversation. I followed him intently as he walked past the window and continued down the street.

"What's the news on Gavin?" Cecilia said.

"No one really knows," Adrienne said.

"He's been with Slutty Ronda for a while," Molly chimed in.

"I heard they broke up."

Molly rolled her eyes, "They were never really together to begin with."

"Well, if she wants him, she's gonna have to fight for him." Cecilia shot up from her seat and proceeded to the exit.

We all got up to join her. She moved the café door out of the way like it was a curtain. A high-pitched whistle turned the group at attention. I hid inside the entryway where I could see all of them. Gavin got out his phone and started texting, I assumed. The smile on my face only lasted for a moment.

"What's up with your boy?" Cecilia shouted.

"What do you mean?" James said.

She pushed out her breasts, "When's the party?"

"We party every night, baby," he replied. Oliver put his arm around James and steered him down the street.

"How about Saturday?" Molly shouted, showing clear signs that Cecilia's man-hunting had infected her, too.

"Where?" Oliver said, stopping.

"There!" Cecilia pointed to a chipped up, faded building on the other side of the street. Neon beer signs and bottles sat in the parking lot; it had to be a bar. Maybe even the only dive bar in Settlement Island.

"Bring the girls, and we'll bring the party!" James yelled before Kyle pulled him and Oliver down the street. Gavin put his phone away and trailed after them with Mark catching up quickly.

Cecilia grabbed Molly, "Get inside right now before we look desperate," she giggled. Adrienne and Molly followed her back to the table, and so did I.

Hurricane Cecilia had swallowed them up. They worshipped her. I just frowned; she knew Saturday was my birthday. The last thing I wanted to do was spend the night with her, while she secured her hookup.

"We're seriously doing this?" Adrienne said.

Molly smiled, "We've always wanted to go out with them but never had a chance."

"Girls, prepare to have your lives transformed. If there's one thing I know, its men." Cecilia applied another coat of lipstick. "Gavin, beware."

Adrienne nudged me, "Is she always like this?"

Cecilia didn't deserve Gavin. He was too beautiful for someone as shallow as her. I bit my lip, thinking about his mystery and beauty. I released the thoughts, taking a deep breath.

"I think I'll start with James," she declared. "He looks like more fun."

Adrienne's foot tapped under the table, "Are we seriously going to do this?"

"Are you afraid of fun, too?" Cecilia had directed that jab at me, even though she concentrated on Adrienne. So juvenile.

"No, not at all. It's just that with the murders and everything, maybe we should stay away from town at night."

Cecilia leaned in close to her face, "You're gonna be fine. I grew up in L.A., in the heart of violence," Cecilia began to preach. Lie. "I've seen people killing people with my own eyes." Another lie. "So, believe me when I say that nothing in Settlement Island can be worse than the horrible carnage in the streets of California!"

Adrienne calmed down, and I had a mind to tell her the truth about Cecilia's hard life in the streets. But why take away her peace? My sister slithered close to me, "What about you?"

No blinking. "You know where I stand."

"What does that mean?"

"I've done my research, and I've made my decisions." She glared at me. I wasn't getting through to her. "Cecilia, I don't think chasing after some guy in a bar is worth my entire Saturday night."

She didn't ponder my comment for one second. "Well, if you finally want to lose your V-card, you gotta get out there."

The waitress came over and brought our order, "You country club girls are too far from home."

"My sentiments exactly," I said.

Cecilia snatched her plate from the waitress and dropped it down. "I heard the steak and eggs here are to die for," she replied. "The service, not so much."

"Just get back home before the sun goes down."

She probably felt prompted to say something after watching Cecilia throw herself at James and the others. And Gavin. The wink—it was quick, but I knew it was only for me. My stomach churned. If only I could know something about him. Anything. Something that would make for an amazing adventure. I was well overdue for one. New town, new people, a chance to bring out my free spirit and be daring again.

Breakfast came to a quick close after Cecilia declared her steak to be horrid. Another try at a café one street over was the new plan. But not for me. It was time for an excuse, so I could go off on my own. "Cecilia, I wanna check out a bookstore and some places. Tell Dad to come pick me up in an hour?"

"Call him yourself," she hissed.

"Okay." I rushed out the door and was on my own adventure in no time.

Chapter Four

Caught

I MERGED WITH a group of tourists. And behold, there he was. Gavin was not only within reach, he had stopped close by. So, did the others. James riffled through boots on a display rack outside a shoe store, while Gavin waited for him to finish. The dress stuck to my body as the sweat cascaded down my back. *What was I doing?*

James pulled his head back and shouted, "Saturday's the day," into the sky. What was he talking about? His possible hookup with Cecilia? The others were unfazed by his declaration, so it couldn't have been too important. He scanned a few more boots and continued on his way. The other boys followed except Gavin.

He stayed behind, sweeping his index finger across his phone. I stood tall, slowly approaching him, wanting to start a conversation. But what would I say?

All this was new to me. The only guy I talked to was Miguel, and he didn't count. Or at least he didn't anymore. Our history was simple. He approached me during our first year of college and started the whole friendship, which ended with us dating when I turned eighteen. After waiting for three years for me to be "legal," there was nothing left. Passing the time together as friends had ruined any and all romantic feelings he had towards me.

Gavin abandoned his phone and walked back to his crew, passing another group of tourists. I paused, taking a breath from the thick air. He could be different, right? Maybe Gavin could see something in me. Something more than the painfully plain girl I was. If only I could talk to him. Just once.

"We have other things goin' on this Saturday," Kyle informed James. His comment pulled me out of my love-struck stupor. I caught up, hiding behind the pack of tourists who moved at a glacial pace.

"Porter's gang can wait," said James.

The boys stopped. James pinched Kyle's cheeks and chuckled—he seemed nervous. Kyle's expression was flat. It seemed that something was brewing between them.

My tourist group entered a seafood restaurant, exposing me. I hid in the entryway.

"So, you're gonna let them take the west side of Market Street down to Fourth Avenue?" Kyle exchanged a look with Gavin.

"I'm over this shit," James said. "There's nothin' on that block that's worth savin'." He placed his shoulders against a drugstore wall. Pulling a pack of cigarettes from his jacket pocket, he lit one with a high flame.

"It's those stuck-up country club bitches," said Kyle. "You've got yo priorities twisted."

Smoke escaped James's nose, "I don't know—my Nubian Princess wants a ride," he laughed. "She's movin' up my list pretty fast."

"And that's more important than Market Street, Brother?" Gavin's voice was deep and edgy. Perfection.

"The blonde one wasn't bad, either," Oliver said, taking James's cigarette.

"The last blonde you had made you itch," James took his cigarette back. "You've gotta be more selective."

Kyle pushed James forward and down the street. James retaliated by thrusting his hands into Kyle's chest. My heart stopped. Face-to-face, the two inched closer to one another. James laughed, patted Kyle on the back, and walked onward. I watched Gavin.

Kyle did the same, "Whatcha wanna do, boss?"

Gavin returned to his phone and proceeded down the sidewalk. The others caught up, as did I. We stayed together, for the most part, until James got a phone call.

"It's Chris," he announced. Gavin glared at him. He motioned for James to answer. Everyone stopped walking in unison. Creepy, but alluring.

"If Porter finds out Chris's been sending us info, he'll be next on the kill list," Kyle scoffed.

"Not our problem," James put the phone up to his ear. Nobody said a word as he flicked ashes on the concrete and shook his head. "Chris, you've gotta come through for us. No excuses."

"What's goin' on?" Kyle said.

James turned his back to him, "Well, that's not gonna work."

"Tell Chris that Logan's death will cost him," Gavin said in a low, firm voice. A wave of icy cold air brushed my skin, cooling the sweat pouring from my head and back, bringing on a shiver.

It was true. All of it. The gruesome deaths and "overstated" violence were indeed true. There was no reason for me to believe the deaths to be a legend, but I somehow wanted them to be. And now they were closer than I had planned.

Had I met one side of the deadly rivalry ripping through Settlement Island? These guys were just kids, no more than two or three years older than me. They couldn't be the ones Luke had warned me against. Could they be?

"Chris, Gavin's expecting you to stay loyal!" James said. "Stay focused and get yo' ass over here." The phone went back into his pocket.

"Gavin, Porter's expectin' us to do somethin'," Kyle's voice was dry.

Led by Gavin, the group continued walking. James shook his head, "Who cares? Porter's always expectin' us to do somethin'."

"We need to send him a message," Kyle stressed, spitting on the sidewalk. "Before he puts another hit on us."

James rolled his eyes, "Dude, he always has a hit out on us." He paused, "If you haven't figured that out by now, you're dumber than I thought."

Gavin stifled a laugh, "You're about to get your ass kicked, James." He turned, and we almost made eye contact. I rushed up to the first open door I saw. The door was locked. Shit! We were too close to each other—he was bound to see me. I inhaled sharply and waited.

"We're gonna take Market Street back," Gavin's voice was some distance away. Slowly, I peered out.

"You're just mad cuz he told the cops about those cars we boosted," James spoke as he lit another cigarette. "Takin' Market Street isn't gonna make Porter's wrongs right."

"Hey, we beat those charges," Oliver said. I had forgotten he existed. And Mark. They were both so quiet, taking direction from Gavin, James, and Kyle, like they were unsure children.

"Yeah, thanks to Mark's mommy." James kissed Mark's cheek.

The conversation was coming to an end. Alone, off the street a little ways, was a two-story white building with three large garage doors—their destination, I presumed. Gavin blocked the front door.

"Listen," he commanded everyone. "Shit's gonna go down soon. Get ready." Each crew member gave their support before being allowed inside.

One short walk was all it took. The intrigue brought on by Gavin and his crew kept me on the inside of the mystery. And thanks to James's big mouth, I was now in the loop regarding all the murder-related mayhem. But I still had so many unanswered questions. A whirlwind of who's and what's circling around in my head.

All this discovery led to me standing outside, alone, and with a decision to make. Should I retreat and leave my questions for another day? Go back to the comfort of The Estates and ponder what I had learned? Or, should I continue, further invading Gavin's privacy?

I walked around the chipped white building, stepping over the puddles of motor oil and rusted car parts. Passing a few opened windows, the back door was left slightly ajar. It unlatched without any resistance. I dashed to my left, not knowing where to go. Luckily, a set of stairs provided the perfect cover. Each step pulled me into a loft hidden in the darkness.

Crash! Kyle picked up several car parts and tossed them onto a metal table.

Two cars with hoods up sat in the bays with no one working on them. In a small clear area close to the door, a soiled couch and a folding chair were next to a stereo. Tools, oil, and car parts covered everything.

The guys took seats wherever they could find them. Within minutes, cigarettes were lit, and they spit information back and forth about cars and women. James went on making speculations about Cecilia. I smirked—he had no idea what he was getting himself into. But I didn't care about that.

Gavin had left the group and approached a young black mechanic under the hood of an old sedan that sat in the third and final bay.

The boy smiled as they nodded to each other, "Hey, Gavin, I don't think I put that belt on right."

Gavin stuck his hand deep into the car's engine, "You got it, Elijah. Did you put in the new alternator?"

"Yep, finished that this mornin'." Elijah wiped his

face, adding some grease to his cheek, "I heard about your car."

"Yeah?" Gavin folded his arms, "What'd you hear?"

"Chris came in here, sayin' Porter was braggin' about havin' some new Nova parts for sale."

"Well, it's a lie. My car's fine."

"Good."

"What else did Chris say?"

Elijah shrugged, "Nothin', but he was nervous. Like Porter's onto him."

Gavin pulled a twenty from his back pocket, "Text me the next time he comes in."

Elijah took the bill, "Will do," he nodded toward the office, "Pete wants to see you."

Gavin headed toward the small office. A short, balding, round man emerged from the room and patted Gavin's back. His dirty fingers touching his beautiful jacket…gross. He guided Gavin back to Elijah and the car.

"Did you get my message?" the man said as a lit cigarette almost fell out his mouth. He wiped grease onto his white shirt and blue jeans.

"Yes, all five hundred of 'em, Pete. Chris came by?"

Pete folded his arms and leaned against the car, "Yeah, but we gotta talk about the parts for the Olds first. Did you get 'em or not?"

Gavin picked up a wrench and handed it to Elijah, "Don't worry, I got a guy whose working on it." Elijah took it and frowned. Gavin pointed downward, "Tighten that."

"Will you have 'em by Friday?" Pete said.

"The box will be in today. Along with the Jaguar parts you needed," Gavin replied as he watched Elijah work.

"Good," Pete said, "I've got a guy out of New York who's comin' up this weekend to look at 'em."

"Don't forget to saw off the serial numbers this time," Oliver laughed.

Pete patted Gavin's back, again, and walked into his office. He came out shortly. "You boys plannin' somethin' this weekend?" Pete gave an envelope to Gavin.

Gavin fanned through what had to be money, "What did Chris want?" He continued directing Elijah to grab different tools, while pointing to car parts.

"Nothin' much. He asked if I'd see you today."

"Why?"

Pete flicked some ashes onto the floor. "Not sure. He was in and out pretty fast."

Then everything stopped for a moment. A quiet moment where nobody said anything but rather waited for their leader to share some insight with them. "I'm gonna send a message back to Porter on Saturday," Gavin declared with a smooth confidence that caused Elijah to straighten up and the others to stay quiet. "You're staying out of it," he said to the boy. "Can't have your blood on my hands."

A violent scream pushed inside me to be released. Had I heard that right? A message…meaning…a murder?

What did you just get yourself into, Catalina?

The evidence was there, but it couldn't be them. Gavin was way too young to be caught up in something as serious as a murder.

The look on everyone's face was too strong to ignore. Now, in the dusty darkness of the car shop loft, I questioned my decision to follow them. To be pulled in by the murderers—dangerous murderers.

Kyle got up and stood next to Gavin, "So, we're doin' somethin'? This is news to me."

James laughed, "Is it really? I mean, come on, Kyle. We do this every time."

Gavin measured Kyle up, "I'm talking to Pete." Kyle sighed fiercely before walking away. Pete tilted his head toward his office. Gavin shook his head, "No, we can talk out here." Elijah went back to working.

"What do ya need me to do?" Pete said.

"Porter find out anything on Sam?"

"Chris told him it was an out-of-state job. Kyle's in the clear."

Gavin started to walk away, but Pete grabbed his arm. "Chris is a weak guy. A kid. Porter's probably workin' on flippin' him right now."

Gavin pulled his arm away. "Relax. I've got it taken care of."

There was a knock on the garage door. Everyone froze, their hands placed behind their back or inside a jacket pocket. My arms tucked around my mid-section, painfully holding in my scream. The door creeped open. A young man came into the shop. Oliver and Mark rose. Gavin charged up to the intruder, followed by Kyle and James. The young man flinched.

"What did you tell Porter, Chris?" Gavin yelled.

And with that, all the romance I had for him was

gone. I just had to get out. But I dared not move an inch. I had to be smart and find the perfect opportunity to run—run fast without stopping.

Chris's bewildered look caused more tension. He blinked rapidly, "He asked if I had any leads on Sam's killer."

James came up next to Gavin, "Yeah?"

"I told him that…all I knew was…what you told me to tell him," he stuttered. "Nothin' more."

"So, what's he gonna do?" Kyle said.

Chris cowered. "Nothin'. I think…I think he bought it."

"He's onto us!" Mark's outburst made me jump, "We need to start gettin' our shit situated."

No more stalling, Catalina. I counted the steps to the floor—twelve. Slithering downstairs without drawing at least one person's attention was impossible. Dammit!

"When and where?" Kyle demanded. Chris didn't quite comprehend. "Porter's smart, Chris. He knows somethin's up, and you probably told him somethin'. So, just get straight with us." He came close to Chris's face. "Porter's got a hit, and we need to know when and where."

Chris's shaky confidence had eroded, not that I could blame him. He was in for it. "Saturday night," he muttered. His eyes went to the floor, "Not sure where yet."

"Perfect. There goes my fuckin' weekend!" James said.

Gavin signaled for everyone to pipe down. "Chris, let's take a walk."

He grabbed Chris by the back of the neck, guiding

him toward the stairs. Toward me. My knees scratched across the rough floor as I sought refuge in the darkest corner of the loft, behind a short stack of boxes. Chris went up against a wall, hitting the back of his head. Gavin placed himself inches away from his face.

Chris held onto the wall, "What's your problem? I told ya everything."

"No, Chris, you didn't. Because if you did, we wouldn't be up here right now, would we?" Chris gave a slight shake of his head. "Now, Porter knows you've been feeding us information, doesn't he?" He paused and waited for Chris to confirm, which took some time. "And that means he knows you helped us out with what happened between Kyle and Sam."

Chris's body squirmed. "I didn't tell him…about what ya'll are up to…if that's what you're thinkin'."

"You're lying to me."

He shook his head, "No, no, no, I'm not! He sent me to tell you about Saturday. That's it."

Gavin put his finger to his lip. One swift move, his knuckles banged against Chris's jawline. Another punch, and Chris was on the floor, less than a foot away from me. He turned onto his back, and I was sure I was dead the moment we discovered one another.

He was young. Chris couldn't have been much younger than me, maybe seventeen or eighteen. How could Gavin be so hard on him? And if he could do this to someone so young, what would he do to me? My eyes asked Chris to have mercy on me.

Gavin's shadow neared his body. "Please," was all I

could mouth to him. Chris staggered to reach his feet. With a little help from Gavin, he was up.

"He figured it out on his own!" Chris spit some blood. "I'm sorry, Gavin. Please, don't kill me!" he whimpered.

Gavin showed no restraint, "So, Kyle's next?" Chris shrugged. Gavin's hand grazed his side. Out came a gun. A blue-steel gun with brown handle. "Chris, you better come up with some answers."

"I swear, I've told you all I know."

Gavin was still. He held onto his prey.

My prayers went out for Chris and for me. For both our sakes, he needed to level with Gavin. Another punch. More blood. It was hard on him. He wanted to drop down, but Gavin wouldn't let him. My teeth clenched behind my hands that had wrapped toughly around my open mouth.

"You're staying here until this is over." Gavin wiped his bruised and bloodied hand on Chris's shirt.

Chris painfully retrieved his phone from his jeans. Gavin snatched the phone and pressed a few buttons before thrusting it into Chris's palm. He had to clear his throat a few times.

"Mom," Some spitting ensued, "I'm gonna be over at a friend's house for the next coupla days." Chris's voice was calm. "Okay, I love you," he hung up the phone and offered it to Gavin.

Gavin opened his fingers, allowing the device to land on the floor. His boot heel destroyed it with a loud crunch. He tucked the gun back under his jacket, "Pete's got a shipment coming in, and Elijah's gonna need help with the Crown Vic." Chris nodded. Gavin closed the distance. "Chris, I swear to God, if anyone touches a single person I know, I'll kill you myself."

And that was it. He left.

Chris kneeled down next to me. "Are you alright?" I said.

"Did Porter send you?" Chris said. I shook my head. "Gavin?"

"I'm new in town. I got lost and came in for directions," I said. "I got scared and ran up here."

Chris gave the room a once over and then focused on me. I wanted to say more, ask more questions, but his face was too distracting. "You need to get the fuck out of here. Now!"

I stammered to say something, but he pulled me up. Chris went to the staircase first. He peeked into the shop and motioned for me to take the back door. Into the action he went, blocking the hall enough so no one could see me.

The door was there, but I didn't rush to it. Instead, I wanted to thank Chris. But there was no time. Gavin had approached Elijah, which had put us too close. Elijah pulled out an orange rag to wipe down the greasy fingerprints on the body of the car. Gavin smiled.

I looked down at my orange dress and pushed the door open without any regard to being silent. The forest rushed into me at full speed. Branches scratching my arms, rocks kicking up into my shoes, I kept running until I was convinced no one was behind me.

CHAPTER FIVE

Restless

BLUE-GRAY EYES, PERFECT blond hair, sculpted. Gavin Scott was beautiful…and a regular part of my nightmares. He lies next to me, his cold, dark stare fixated on mine. I dare not move. Slowly, he inches upward into a sitting position, pulling the gun from his side. My hands latch onto his wrists, but I never say a word. Clearly, he can see the tears falling down my face in a constant stream. Hammer back, finger on the trigger. *Bang!* I jolted awake, trapped by the comforter holding onto my arms and legs.

I was an idiot. Why didn't I tell anyone about what I had seen at the shop? There was no reason to keep it a secret, but I did. And Gavin's nightly haunts left my body sore and tired. My eyes fell shut.

My breaths were uneven when I checked the last two newspapers for any news on Chris. Or any other fatalities. Every day that passed with no mention of any new homicides meant I could save him. Just like he had saved me. I could be a hero for that poor boy and keep him from becoming an innocent casualty of this blood battle between Gavin and Porter. Any decent human being would do that for him.

Instead, I stayed in my room, hiding behind several books, which was a bad thing. I was up to reading three a week. In between overanalyzing the entire situation, and not doing a thing to stop the inevitable, the truth had to come forward. I had to be brave, for a change. Just once. Think of someone other than myself.

But at what cost?

Gavin would figure it out. My rapid departure from the building had to stir his attention. From there, Chris probably gave them everything, including a very detailed description of me.

Lying low, keeping the secret close, was my only defense. But soon they would come for me, tearing me from the comfort and safety of my home, only to commit the most gruesome killing anyone in the state of Maine had ever seen…

"Happy birthday," disembodied voices shouted into my face.

I ripped my eyes open and pushed away my attackers. Dad grabbed my fists and pulled me out of bed. He hugged me as Mother joined in. Cecilia smiled. A martini was in her hand. I let go of the embrace to catch my breath.

"Is that for me?" I muttered.

"Yes, ma'am," Cecilia replied in a sing-song voice. She took a sip and handed it over.

I gulped a full, bitter mouthful. The kick burned the back of my throat, but I needed it.

"Honey, there's someone here to see you. And he brought a birthday surprise," Mother said.

"Who is it?"

"Someone you made an impression on the other day at the club." Dad winked.

Who could I have…I sighed in relief, and I finished my drink. "Luke?"

Mom took my empty glass, "Luke!" Cecilia gave me a smirk and then left.

"He's a nice guy, Catalina," Dad said.

Yes, he was. And that could work to my advantage. Maybe I could tell Luke what I knew. Since he was a local, and a somewhat strong guy, he could be willing to protect me. We could go to the police together. Finally, a solution I could live with. I shooed my parents out of my room and got dressed. Putting on some jeans and a soft tee-shirt, I swept my hair into a ponytail. Bracelets on. They jangled as I left the room, announcing my arrival.

Luke, twitching eyes and all, waited patiently in the living room. A pleasant surprise on what was turning out to be a horrible birthday. Hmm, how did Luke know it was my birthday?

His hand went through his hair before resting in his pocket. I examined his attire—blue jeans, black dress shoes, and matching black button-up shirt. A date outfit. We mirrored each other…no movement, just careful studying. The twitching accelerated.

"Happy birthday, Catalina," he said shyly.

I threw my arms around his neck, relieved to see a sweet, kind face, "Thank you."

Luke's muscles flexed before he relaxed into the hug. He smelled clean. I pulled my face back and smiled; the twitching stopped. Mother came tiptoeing in. She was the culprit. My fingers released him quickly.

"So, how did you know today was my birthday?" I said to him, not only to confirm my suspicion, but to put my mother on the spot.

He opened his mouth. "Luke was asking about you the other day," Mother said, beating him to the punch, "so I told him today was your birthday. And look! He's here." She squeezed his shoulder. Her hand moved over his shoulder to his bicep. His eye twitched.

I had to get him out of there. "Luke, would you like to go for a walk?" This was a good move. It would appease Mother, and it would give us a chance to talk.

"Have you eaten breakfast yet?"

"Other than my martini, no."

"Let's go down to the club. My treat."

Mother ushered us out the door and onto the porch. I ordered her back into the house as Luke and I silently took our journey toward the clubhouse. We moved closer to the water and into the shade of the tall trees. The canopy cast shadows across our faces. There was a path of wooden planks ahead. We both had space to walk in unison, but we remained apart.

"How has your birthday been so far?" Luke said.

I giggled at such a silly question. "It just got started."

He smiled, "Oh, you're right."

I fought my laughter, "So, tell me about your stay, um, day. Other than coming over to the house, what have you done today?"

"I went shopping," he said with a wink. "I'm getting a new car," he blurted.

"Congrats!" I threw my arms around him.

This hug was different. My lips brushed across his neck and jaw, enjoying the feel of his light stubble. He pulled my face back to his. We waited for one another to decide how to proceed. I didn't mind if he kissed me. Instead, Luke hunched over and lifted me off the ground, coiling his body around mine, tight. The air was being forced from my lungs. He let me go, and I staggered over to the lake.

"This place is amazing." I turned to him, grinning.

He came up close to me and shifted his view from one eye to the next, "Are you drunk?"

I thought hard and came up with a no.

"Yes, you are."

A witty remark didn't come to mind, "Okay, maybe a little bit."

He brushed my hair, "Oh, Catalina, it's too early in the morning for that."

My fingers grazed his hands until they came down, "It's my 21st birthday. I think that's expected."

"I got you a gift." A small book of sonnets came from his back pocket. "It's from my grandfather's collection. I thought you'd like it."

I fanned through it, taking in the vintage aroma. "Thank you, Luke. That's very nice of you." I kissed his cheek. My phone rang. "You made time for me!" I rushed out before the phone was up to my face.

"Happy birthday, Mi Amor!" Miguel said. "You're drunk, aren't you?" he laughed.

"Only a little bit. Guess what?"

"Huh?"

"I'm going to breakfast with someone."

"A guy?"

I cupped the mouth piece, "Maybe."

He cackled, "Trade in your V-card, sweetheart. It's been too long." I whined. "Listen, I got a huge party to cook for. Have a good night with your guy, okay?"

My bottom lip turned downward, "Love you."

"I love you more. Send me some Maine lobster!"

I laughed and hung up the phone. Luke folded his arms, "Love you? Do you have a boyfriend back home?" Twitch.

My retort was a chuckle, giving him the wrong impression. "Just a best friend, that's all."

 ❧

We walked up the steps, and the Roman gods opened the doors for us. The setup was exactly the same as the other day. A pretty blonde showed us to a table by the window. Our table. Luke pulled the chair out for me, which was a first. I hid in the menu, trying to control my drunken giddiness. It was getting worse. Luke ordered us some waters to start. Once the waitress left, he pulled my menu down.

"Everyone's onto you."

Yes, they were. "They're probably drunk, too." We snickered for a moment, then Luke turned back to finding something for breakfast.

"Got any plans for the rest of the day?" he said.

This question would have been met with a no, however it was Saturday. And I knew my night had already been planned for me. I pushed past the alcohol to pursue a much-needed conversation. "Luke, have you been in town lately?"

"No, I haven't. And I don't plan on going anytime soon." A dark shadow came over everything, "Catalina, listen to me. I know you're probably curious about what's out there. All the cute shops and stuff. But it's not worth it. The risk."

"What risk?" I paused to find my words, "What do you know?"

"People go there, and they die."

"All of them?"

"All of them."

I raised my eyebrow, disappointed in Luke's naïve nature. How could he do this to me? He was supposed to be my only salvation. I folded my arms. "You need to do more research. More investigating."

"Have you been investigating the murders?"

I nodded, "Yeah, I have. And people aren't being gunned down in the streets left and right. In fact, for the most part, it seems like a pretty nice…"

"Well, I can't tell you what to do." He sighed, "Just… be careful."

That was it? No more concern? Luke looked over

the menu, not saying a thing to me. This wasn't how I planned for all this to go.

I nodded. "Don't worry." Another pause. "I don't plan on going back anytime soon."

He smiled. A rush of relief came over me. I had won him over…and ruined my chances of getting help. Luke changed the subject to something about sailing. I remained in my position, sinking further into how stupid I had become.

∽

Several hours passed, and the sun was far behind the tree line. I flipped on the string of lights above my bed. Glass of wine, one of Mother's favorites. Expensive. She said I could have as much as I wanted today. Book in hand, a good one. And Miguel was free to text.

Cecilia came into my room with a huge announcement. "We're going out for your birthday tonight," she said with a slight hiss.

I stayed on the book, "Why? Oh, yeah, because you can't go out without me."

"Dad's new rule is ridiculous," she growled.

"I admire his sentiment, but I don't want to be your charity case."

She sat down on the bed next to me, "Listen, I want you to go. You know me better than all those other girls."

Catching onto her game was easy. "You want me to help you land a guy. Man, you must be desperate," I said with sarcasm and heart.

She grabbed the book and slammed it closed, "Just

do this one thing for me, and I'll do you whatever favor you want."

"I'm doing you a favor on my birthday?"

"It's a form of paying it forward."

Cecilia began popping her jaw and tossing her hair. I ignored her, sipping my wine and looking at all the titles on my bookshelf. Hundreds of them. She retaliated by dancing her way to the book collection on my bed.

"Maybe we should stay in and talk about our vaginas," she snickered.

I shrugged, "Fine by me." Next, I was onto my book of sonnets.

"What's the matter, Cat? You don't like guys?" she straightened up a few items in my room. This was a different side to her. The care she took in making sure things were presentable. I almost didn't know her. But I did know that when it mattered, she'd do anything for me.

Give into Cecilia. Tell your big sister the truth about Gavin. All I had to do was say a few words on the subject, and she'd understand my apprehensions for wanting to stay in. But were they apprehensions? In fact, the bar just didn't seem appealing to me. I was happy, here, in my sanctuary.

"When was the last time we actually hung out together?" Her eyes rolled, "…because we wanted to?"

"Never," I said into my book. No, that wasn't true. "When we were kids, you used to read with me."

She sat down. "Do you think all sisters are like this?"

"Like what?"

"They grow apart?"

Another long sigh. "Cecilia, we have nothing in common anymore. We chose different paths. It's only natural."

"I like tormenting each other."

"It's our thing."

"Yeah, but you're like a real adult now. Twenty-one!" She smiled. "I had the best twenty-first b-day bash." Cecilia put her arm around me. "I just want tonight to be memorable for you."

"I'm happy." The genuine smile on my lips should get her to go away.

She was silent. Then came a simple remark. "Doctors say that people who live their lives alone die young." Cecilia took the book. "I wouldn't want you to die before you even had a chance at a real life."

Me, neither. I put my finger to my lips. Carrying the weight of Gavin's problems was bound to kill me one day, but it didn't have to be today. "Fine. Let's do this," I muttered.

No, I couldn't stand her. Cecilia was way too loud. And a gossip queen. But she was my sister, and she could be a lot of fun, which was something I desperately needed.

"Great! Be ready by nine!" She ran off before I could change my mind.

Besides, from what I knew, nothing bad was happening along Maine Street. Most of the murders and mayhem took place on the east side of town. And the shops were cute. We were probably safe.

Now, to find something to wear. My birthday meant I got to wear whatever the hell I wanted. Black. Yes, I'd wear black.

∽

The bar Molly picked for my "celebration" was surprisingly normal. No mean-looking bikers, leather jackets or bad boys. Molly, Adrienne, and Cecilia were more than happy to be out. After the first three rounds of drinks, they forgot all about me.

I sat at our table with my cranberry vodka and watched them dance with each other as a group of guys ogled their curves. It was too dark for me to read, so I just waited for one of them to come talk to me. Adrienne—she would probably be the first to keep me company. Maybe I would find something interesting we had in common. Other than Luke, of course.

The girls came back. Cecilia patted her hair down. "Where are the hot guys?" she said to Molly.

Molly canvassed the crowd, "Not sure. It's still early, though."

"What about Gavin's crew?" Cecilia said. My shoulders tensed up, "I'd settle for that blond guy!" Cecilia had remembered James. Damn her.

"He'll be here. Ronda's here, which means Gavin'll be here. She always goes where he goes," Adrienne added.

I gulped the rest of my watery drink, "We should leave," I shouted. "Find some place better."

"Well, there aren't very many places around that

play music," Molly shouted above the rhythms of yet another dance song.

"Which one's Ronda?" Cecilia said.

Molly's finger landed on a messy blonde girl with combination skin wearing a super short red dress. She towered over the other three girls with her. Ronda wasn't anything special, just like everyone said.

"That can't be her," Cecilia added.

"That's Gavin's girl," Molly said with disappointment.

"Why?" I found myself saying. I knew why Ronda would want him, but why would he choose her? Ronda had to be dirty. And unsmart. Just like all the other girls who watched her, waiting for her to dictate something else. They would never make anything of themselves, hoping someone would knock them up, so they could collect a check.

Molly shrugged, "They've always been together."

"He doesn't date, so they're not together. They just have sex," Adrienne chimed in.

Ronda, Ronda. Did she know how much of a monster Gavin was? She seemed mean—they were probably made for each other. Good for her.

"I'm gonna go talk to her," Cecilia shot up from her seat and stumbled on her platforms.

It wasn't long before I was obstructing Cecilia's path, "Don't."

"Why the hell not?"

"What if you get into it with her and Gavin's crew turns on you?"

"They're not even here," she said, waving me aside. Another attempt had to be made.

Leveling with Cecilia on her level might work. "What if a hot guy comes, and you mess up your hair and makeup in the fight?"

She paused. "You're right," Two twenties came from her cleavage, "Get us another round."

Before I complied, I told Adrienne and Molly to keep her company until I got back. With this request, I pushed hard against the crowd to get close enough to order.

"Let me get you in." A pair of hands thrust me forward until I slammed into the bar. My intention was to slap his face. "Sorry, sweetheart, I didn't mean to be so upfront."

There was no response from me. I turned to the bar and nervously waited for the bartender. Did he recognize me? Dammit! Air, I need air!

"I'm Pete. What's your name?" he said. I moved further away from him. His fingertip grazed my side, "You're really pretty. I'd love to buy you a drink."

My hand waved off his compliment, "I'm fine."

"I've never seen you before. Are you new here?"

"Please stop talking to me," I yelled into the air.

"Oh, you're one of those stuck-up country club chicks, huh?"

Enough! "Just leave me alone, okay?" I felt someone brush their nail against my back. That was it! I turned around to see my sister blocking my way. Cecilia shoved Pete aside and got the female bartender's attention. I stayed close, so he couldn't tear us apart. It didn't take long for us to come back with the drinks. We had our differences, but I loved my sister at that moment.

Cecilia threw back her shot fast. Molly, Adrienne, and I said cheers before taking ours. Molly took Cecilia to dance.

Adrienne turned to me, "So, are you having fun on your birthday?" A look crossed her face. Her lips moved, but I couldn't hear. My hand was midway to my cheek when I was pulled onto my feet and onto the dance floor.

Chapter Six

Taken

His body was cool to the touch as he clenched mine. The crowd of dancers made room for us. Or I should say *him*. He found a spot and flung me around. I turned to run away, but he pulled me closer.

Screaming was useless—no one would hear. Gavin released me. I inched backward. The couple behind us did a wide turn causing me to crash into his chest. The tempo slowed. More people took up residence on the dance floor, making escape impossible. My vague plans to avoid him diminished with the curling of his fingers around my waist.

At first, Gavin danced, and I watched him like a statue. This didn't last for very long. One turn was all it took for him to overpower me and place my hands on his biceps.

His movements with the music were smooth. Smoother than anything I could ever put together on a good day. Onlookers gawked at him from their tables. And I dreaded every moment.

Gavin seemed to lose his patience with me. He put his hands on my hips and moved them to the beat. I had a mind to fight him, but eventually, I found myself moving from side to side.

His lips lowered to my neck. I could feel him exhale onto my skin. I, in return, held my breath in an effort to gain some control of the situation. His face was back up. Dark eyes and hair. It was too much, I bowed downward.

"Why are you so nervous?" His voice was soft, calm. He grazed his fingertips across my shoulders.

A burst of energy shot through me. My chest tightened. I closed myself off from the world. My nightmares were brought forth. But yet his voice was like a tall glass of water on a hot day—and I wanted a drink.

"I don't want to dance," I replied into his chest, while I concentrated on staying calm. Something wet on his jacket touched me—blood. I loosened his grip, but we remained in our positions.

"My eyes are not on my chest," he scolded me.

Reluctantly, I complied with his demands that I pay attention to him. My arms were moved around his neck, and I allowed him to lead me. My next step landed right on his boot.

"You can't dance."

"Is that a question or a statement?" I said.

"Statement."

"Then you can see why this is not a good idea."

Gavin grazed my chin, smooth motions enticing me to want more. We were face-to-face again. He touched my waist. I shuddered.

"Your main problem is your lack of confidence. Don't look down," he commanded as the smallest space between us was now gone.

Precise moves, one after the other. That was Gavin dancing. "Well, you're really good at this. I'm not," I hissed.

"Dancing takes more than confidence. You gotta have passion, too."

I took a step back, "Well, show me your passion."

He loosened his grip. A random girl in the crowd took advantage of the crater between us. Finally, freedom! There had to be a way out. Adrienne danced only a few couples away from me.

Gavin dismissed the girl after a few short moves and grabbed me again. Licking his lips, he smiled as he moved my body for me. "You were plotting your escape." I stared at him, exposing my nervousness, then pleaded for Adrienne to put everything together. She gave me a thumbs up. I mouthed the words "help me," but she didn't catch it.

I let go of him and put my hands on his chest, "I don't want to be rude, but I'd rather just sit down."

"And leave me here on the dance floor, alone?"

"You're joking, right?" My lips were at his ear, "I'm sure there are so many girls here who would love to dance with you."

He shook his head, "It's only you. I'm dancing with you."

"I don't move much, so you're not really dancing with me. You need a better partner."

There was a lonely blonde girl in the crowd. She watched him intently. I smiled and motioned for her to come over and take my place.

"You are rude," he grunted.

The girl approached us. "And I don't think you're getting the point," I said.

"Are you sure?" she said. "You don't mind?"

I shrugged, "Not at all. You can take him home if you want to. I really don't care."

He stood directly in her face, "I'm sorry to be so upfront, but I don't want to dance with you. Go find someone else." Her cheeks flushed red. She quietly left, and he pulled me forcefully into his body. His fingers walked along my waist, "Please dance with me."

The dim lights cast sweet shadows across his face. He was indeed irresistible. My hands went to their original position on his biceps. One step, then the next, I managed to move in unison with him.

And this was my defeat. Gavin was dangerous. A murderer. Chris and I both knew that. I bit my lip—Chris. I had almost missed it. So far, Gavin hadn't brought up anything regarding my trip to the shop. He didn't know me. I had Chris to thank for that.

"Stop looking down."

He was fierce. I couldn't tell if he was disappointed in me or if he was always like this. His knee parted my legs, and he pulled my body toward the floor. Our chests touched. I followed his hips, but it was too difficult. He traced my back with light grazes, "You're fighting me."

"I don't mean to. I just don't want to do this."

Gavin put his lips on my neck again. I moved back, giving us distance. He didn't protest. "Why are you here if you don't dance?"

"I don't want to talk about it."

He smirked, "Is he that bad?"

"Who?"

"The guy who stood you up tonight."

I sighed, "There is no guy."

"So, it's me? I just met you ten minutes ago, and you already hate me. Why?"

There was no simple answer to his question. At least not one that kept me from getting killed. He was still, his entire being seemed to be only on me. One slight truth about myself wouldn't hurt. "My sister drug me out here to celebrate my birthday, only she doesn't care about me. She just needed a cover to pick up guys."

He partially smiled, "So, it's your birthday?" I nodded. "Happy birthday," he gave me a spin, "How old are you?"

"Twenty-one."

"Is this the first bar you've been to?"

"So far tonight. Hopefully, it'll be the last."

He glanced over my shoulder and put his lips close to my ear. I tensed up again. "Stop being so nervous and enjoy dancing." His breath tickled my ear. He straightened up my body. "All you have to do is keep your body close to mine and just move with me."

I shook to the beat. It was ugly, but I did put some effort into it. He twirled me, and I lost myself in the motion. Like a princess on display for everyone to see. It was a new feeling for me, to be the object of someone's attention. And then the music shifted into a slow song, bringing with it my departure.

But Gavin wouldn't let go. "You can kinda slow dance," he complimented me.

I smiled, "You've tortured me enough. It'd mean the world to me if you'd just let me leave."

"Close your eyes and imagine yourself in a place you want to be."

He put my head on his shoulder. My body relaxed into him, even though I told it not to. I laced my fingers into his and attempted to move on my own. It was an open invitation. Through my hair his fingers went softly. His touch left me feeling glad that I had stayed. Everything about him was sexy. I blushed as he mouthed something to me.

"Did you come with your sister?" he whispered.

I frowned, "Yeah, why?"

Gavin drug me through the crowd. We were headed for the back door. I found Cecilia in a flash, but she didn't even notice I was leaving. I stopped just short of the entryway and let him go.

"What are you doing? I'm not going with you," I said.

He brushed past me. Freedom was right there, just beyond him, "We've gotta leave. Now!"

"But I don't know you," I muttered.

He pushed the door open, "Worry about that later."

I shook my head, "No, I'm not leaving with you." It didn't take long for him to get into my path.

"Please. Help me." I froze. "Fuck it. I'm taking you home, that's final!"

In an instant, I was out the door and headed toward his car. No, no, no, no, no, was all I could think. Gavin latched onto my arm. Fight back! He reached into a pair of bushes and pulled out something gray and brown. His gun.

The driver's side door opened, and he motioned for me to get in quickly. I held onto the roof. "Let me go!"

"Look! I'm not gonna hurt you. Just get in the damn car!"

I had about a second to decide before I found myself sitting on the seat and moving over to the passenger's side. He got in. The heavy door slamming startled me.

"Sorry to cut your birthday short, but the cops are gonna raid this place looking for me."

Blood. Chris. Murder. I pounded my fists into his shoulder. "Let me out right now!"

He subdued me easily, "I'm not going to hurt you!" I shut down again, waiting for him to kill me. "Open your eyes."

Breathing heavily, I watched him read my fear. "Just let me out!" I said. "Please," my voice was raspy now.

He cupped my face. "You're gonna be fine. Just relax." I yanked on his wrists to release me. It didn't work. His expression softened, "Don't be afraid."

"Let me go!"

He shook his head, "I can't do that."

"Yes, you can! Just open the damn door!" I was both hoarse and broken. And tired of fighting.

Gavin turned the car on. The leather seats under me vibrated wildly. "I'm sorry," he threw the car in gear.

I lunged for the passenger door but stopped just short of the handle. He pulled me close.

Swerving around people and vehicles in the parking lot, Gavin navigated the car away from the bar.

My words were a mixture of coughing and screaming, "Why take me?"

"I need an alibi. You're a good girl, so the cops will trust whatever you say." He winked.

I turned to the window. Partygoers smiled at him as we drove onward. My face had to be a mess. Clearly, they could have seen it, if they actually saw me. I needed to get closer to the door. It was no use. His fingers tightened around my wrist.

"Sit back and act natural," he said.

Two police officers made their way into bar. My heart burned. The blood on his jacket glistened in the parking lot lights. My body went completely rigid.

Gavin entered Maine Street and obeyed the traffic laws until we took a sharp turn onto a side street. In a second, he released me, shifted gears, and we accelerated quickly. Too fast for me to jump out. I furtively peered over at him. He balanced his observations between the road and me.

"Relax," his voice was steady and low.

"I can't breathe," I wiped my face.

His eyes went back to the road, "I'm sorry for scaring you."

My hands went to my lap. The trees hid the moon

as the sky grew darker during our travel. My shoulders stiffened against the cold seat. Once he stopped at a stoplight or something, I would be gone, into the night.

"Relax," he hissed again. "I'll have you home soon enough."

I rolled my exhausted eyes. "Just leave me alone, okay?"

"I tell you to do something, and you do the exact opposite. It's annoying."

"I don't care what you find annoying."

He smirked. "There. That's the confidence you should always have."

There was no sense in putting it off. The inevitable. I tilted my head, "If you're going to kill me, just get it over with."

"I'm not going to kill you!" he replied.

I pointed to his gun, which rested by his side. "I'll be sure to keep that in mind."

"You're being paranoid." He looked at me and then back at the road.

"You snatched me up, on my birthday, and took me hostage, so you could create an alibi for a crime I'm way too terrified to imagine. That's not paranoia; it's common sense. I'll be dead by morning, I'm sure."

Gavin clicked his tongue several times. "Is that what you think?" He let out a laugh, "I'm flattered, really." My nails embedded into my palms. I clenched my teeth and went back to gazing out the window.

Streetlights up ahead brought me no joy. We were approaching a residential area. I wasn't familiar with the place, but I knew we weren't in The Estates. Things were turning from bad to worse.

We passed a couple of houses and pulled up to one. The engine and lights cut off.

"Stay here. I'll be right back."

I smiled softly. Him leaving could be a good thing. My ticket to freedom dangled from the steering column of his monster of a car. I rolled my shoulders back into the seat to keep him from suspecting something. "Okay."

He moved in close to me, "I know you don't know where you are. And GPS is spotty as hell out here."

How would he know that? Regardless, this was a game of wits. "If you want me to trust you, you have to trust me."

After he pulled the keys out of the ignition, he placed them on the seat and got out. Gavin didn't check on me, not once, as he concealed his gun by his side and entered the house.

I regrouped and retrieved the keys, putting them back in the ignition. Then, I stopped. This was a trap. He wanted me to take his car; to make a break for it. I dropped my hands from the steering wheel. But why? What would he gain by having me steal his car?

Gavin was a criminal—he wouldn't go to the police. And, if he wanted me dead, he would have done it by now. So, why? Why was he playing this game with me? I sifted through my surroundings, hoping to find something that would be familiar or useful. Nothing could be made out in the dark. I looked at the house. Still nothing.

I knew I needed to get going, but I couldn't make a

clear decision. The key turned forward. I stopped—stick shift. Damn! I allowed myself another short moment to do something. Anything. I checked my phone: dead. Shit! I was a moron! I inched back to the passenger's side, brushing my foot against an object below. An envelope.

Gavin wasn't anywhere in sight, so I opened it. The moon offered very little light. My fingers grazed across the smoothness of what had to be a photograph. I squinted hard, but it was pointless. I put everything back as I had found it and dug myself into the cold leather seat.

The faint sound of a front door closing put me back on my best behavior. Gavin meandered toward me. He remained in my sight the entire time.

"You stayed?" He seemed genuinely surprised. I didn't answer, not because I didn't want to, but I had nothing to say. He fired up the engine, and we left the driveway.

"Where are we?" I said.

"Don't worry about it." We sped back down the road in the same way we had come. I shifted my weight. "I wish you would relax."

"I can't relax if I don't know where I am," my voice was low.

"You're safe. That's all that matters."

"I don't know that," I said quietly.

He smirked, "You're with me. Nobody's gonna mess with you."

Except Porter and his crew of murderers. "Yeah, but what about you?" I said.

He ignored me. Hands in my lap, I remembered the blood on my fingers and rubbed them together in an effort to rid myself of the substance.

He raised an eyebrow, "But you stayed."

Yes, but only because I had hit an impasse. Gavin didn't seem bothered by this. He shifted gears and sped up once we were back on the open road. Suddenly he was down-shifting, and we were right at the speed limit. I looked out both windows.

"Speed trap." He concentrated on the road and relaxed further into his seat.

"If you're wanted, aren't they going to pull you over, anyway?"

"They don't know they're looking for me yet."

"But you said at the bar the cops were…"

"Well, I haven't gotten word that they're looking for me, so…" he said coolly.

I nodded as my blood pressure rose. Everything was black. There was no way to tell if anyone, good or bad, was closing in on us. "What exactly did you do?" He blinked slowly as he gazed at me and then at the road. "This is making me feel worse," I said under my breath.

"Don't worry; I've got something planned that'll take your mind off things for a bit."

Judging by his attitude, I guessed we were on our way to a biker bar. My body slumped down into the seat—I couldn't survive a biker bar or anything else he was up to.

"You really need to relax," he stated with irritation.

"That's a stupid thing to say."

"Stop worrying," he whispered flirtatiously.

"Stop being secretive," I whispered back.

"I can't keep secrets from someone I don't know."

"Well, now I know one secret about you, so that has to be worth something."

He pursed his lips. I grinned to myself for my small victory. "Seriously, relax. You're worrying over nothing." I let out a loud sigh and let my shoulders drop some. He grinned, "Now, doesn't that feel better?"

"I'd feel better if you told me where we are going."

"I bet you would," his tone had attitude. I frowned. He smiled, "It's still your birthday for about another hour."

He threw the car into another gear and it roared louder. We climbed in speed as he powered on to our destination. A fast turn, and I slid in his direction. Though he was warmer than me, I climbed back over to my side. I wouldn't touch him. Besides, someone came to mind who I slightly liked.

Luke would have died right on the spot if he saw me dancing and leaving with Gavin Scott. Same with my parents.

Gavin hummed a few beats, one hand on the wheel and the other was on his lips. I wondered what he had planned for my birthday. It had to be my death.

Chapter Seven
Exposed

For a very brief moment, I was filled with joy. We had arrived at a small diner. Gavin got out and casually walked over to my door. I contemplated what to say. *Demand your rights, you stupid girl!* He flung the door open, and I said nothing. Neither did he. Instead, his hand reached for mine. I didn't reject him. The heavy door slammed, and he paused. Out came his phone.

"What happened?" He leaned against the car.

I could see the lights of the diner and a small group of people inside. Salvation. I headed away from him. Gavin grabbed my arm and pulled me back. I twisted around in different directions to break contact. He shook his head and mouthed the word, "No." I folded one arm around my shivering body and leaned close to him. Close enough to eavesdrop.

"Gavin, it's bad. Seven people were arrested," said the voice on the other end. It sounded like Pete.

"Did James and Kyle get out?" Gavin said.

"Yeah, they took off with some chicks."

"Oliver and Mark?"

"Let me check."

He threw his head back, exposing the smoothness of his chin and neck. Perfect for kissing. And his eyes…I hadn't forgotten about them. They scanned the black sky as he quietly waited for Pete to continue. My body huddled against him for warmth. Gavin took a step to the side and released me.

This was my chance. "I'll see you inside."

Over my shoulder came his entire arm. I was securely fastened against his chest. Don't give into him! But he was warm. "Pete, tell the others to lay low," he said. "We'll finish this tomorrow."

"Hey, did James give you Chris's photos?"

"Yeah. What's with these?"

"Don't know till I see them. Bring 'em by the garage in the mornin'."

"Alright." He ended the call and rubbed my back. "No jacket?"

"Didn't match my outfit," I pried my body from his, "What's with the hand holding? I can't go anywhere without you now?"

"No," Gavin walked to the front door. I followed, not because I was ordered to, but because I had to get out of the cold. He held the door open for me, which was the nicest thing he had done all night.

The smell of burnt coffee was overpowering. Unlike the café Cecilia and I had visited, this place had tiny black booths and chipped tan tables. I made a dash for a small sink in the back corner to wash the blood from my thumb and index finger. Before someone had a chance to greet us, Gavin took a seat in a booth right off the door.

And that was that—no more chances of escaping. He watched me slide into place in front of him. A tired waitress with a messy blonde bun and numerous coffee stains on her shirt bent down to kiss him on the cheek. "Honey, will you have your usual?" Great, they knew each other. Just inches away from me, and she would be of no use.

"Yes, and so will she," he advised her before a menu hit the table. She winked and went behind a set of swinging doors.

The booth was uncomfortable, but I didn't mind. "I can order my own food."

He flipped through his phone, "You're gonna love it."

"How would you know? You don't know anything about me."

His jaw clenched. The phone slid across the table. Then nothing happened—no offerings to get to know me better or commands that I tell him my life story. His next words were, "Why can't you dance?"

"Why does it matter?" He seemed to harden even further. We weren't getting anywhere. I straightened up, "No one ever taught me, I guess."

"All girls know how to dance."

"Well, I guess I'm not all girls."

More silence. No backing down from either one of us. I felt judged which was absurd. He was the criminal, not me.

Gavin blinked occasionally, reminding me that we weren't having a conversation, but rather challenging one another. I held my ground, unwavering from my stone-cold expression. And he remained…perfect. Sharp jawline, sculpted hair, fierce eyes. He was beautiful. I bit my lip.

"Stop being nervous," he hissed.

"Stop bossing me around."

His head tilted, his eyes examining me. An animal contemplating its prey. The waitress came back with two cups and a pot of coffee. She poured them cheerfully. "How's Paula?" She set my coffee down before dropping off his.

"Good," he replied. Paula?

"Tell her I'm free on Friday, if she needs me."

"I'll be sure to let her know."

"Thanks, sweetie! Your food'll be out soon," she patted his back before walking away.

Back to staring. No need to get used to that. It became clear that I had to strike up a conversation for the both of us. Or maybe just for me. I struggled to find a comfortable position inside the booth. And he watched me, placing his finger against his lips.

"How do you know how to dance so well?" I said in an effort to set him up to spearhead our next chat.

"My grandma. She was a dance instructor back in her day," he said before drinking some coffee.

I tore open five packets of sugar and added them to my cup. Without any hesitation, he picked up his spoon and stirred my coffee.

"Thank you," I murmured.

"You're not from here," he licked his spoon before putting it down. "You're not a Settler." I didn't respond. "You know, we could just sit and not say a word to each other, if you like."

A wonderful sentiment, in the beginning. But I was onto him. As my ride home, I needed to know more about who was keeping me company. "I'm from L.A. I mean Los Angeles."

"I know what L.A. is." He raised an eyebrow, "Why are you here? Vacation?"

Gavin flashed me a wicked smile and pulled my coffee away. I stopped him. "My parents decided to move." That was all I would give up.

"You didn't want to move?" His hand went to his cup.

"What makes you think that?"

He shrugged, "Just a thought. Most twenty-one-year-olds don't follow their parents across country."

"My dad thought it'd be a good opportunity."

"And you think Settlement Island is boring?"

So many questions. Did he find me interesting? Really interesting? "No, I just think the move was more materialistic than anything else."

"I've never heard of a move being materialistic." Our conversation was leading nowhere. "So," he said, "how does Cecilia feel about living here?"

I exhaled sharply. "You know my sister?"

"No, I know of her. She's making a name for herself."

His comment must have meant something. So, my response was, "That's usually how it goes." I smirked, "She demands a lot of attention, which is something I'm sure the two of you have in common."

He cleared his throat, "Listen, I know you've had a horrible birthday so far. And I'm sure you blame me for it." Before I could correct him, he continued, "So, before we finish our conversation, let me make one thing clear. I don't feel sorry for you."

"What are you talking about?" I scoffed.

"You're ungrateful. I've tried to do right by you, but you sit here, glaring at me, judging me for some factitious reason." Gavin leaned in, "You don't know a goddamn thing about me. So, you better start showing me some fucking respect."

Unbelievable. There was something about him…and it brought out the worst in me. Hatred. Anger. And fear. Mostly fear. I gripped my spoon and stirred my drink, just to give me something to do. He watched me intently. A mixture of anxiety and embarrassment erupted. Each emotion made me feel trapped by my own undoing.

I should have taken his car when I had the chance. When he was on the phone, I should have raced toward the diner and screamed for help. Both times I was a pedestrian, allowing him to dictate where I went, what I did, and now what I ate. Every foolish thought I had wasn't keeping him at bay. This thing between us was just a façade. He was onto me—I had no defense against him. I was at the mercy of his kindness. Cold, calculated kindness. That was the only thing keeping me alive.

The break from his charade would be my idea, not his. I dropped the spoon, got up, and went to find the bathroom. The door slammed hard behind me. Next, I had to calm down.

"Breathe, Catalina," I said to myself. My body relaxed. Tears threatened my eyes, but I wouldn't give him any, even if he wasn't there to see. Why? Why let him do this to me?

His faulty promise of taking me home, that's what I relied on. This was a classic mistake, but it brought me comfort. I was so weak. Why couldn't I just stand up to him? Or die trying? Why did I hide behind his untruthful commitment to make sure I was safe with him? Stupid girl. It took several minutes for me to regain some resemblance of composure. Too much time had passed. I had to return to the dining room before he got any brilliant, yet insulting ideas.

Air poured into my lungs as I opened the door. I approached the table. Not to my surprise, he was watching me the whole time. He licked his lips and relaxed into the booth—he wasn't worried about me one bit.

This is your chance. Don't rely on him. It was a nice thought. Instead, I sat down without looking up. My coffee cup had been filled and five more empty packets of sugar lay next to it.

"Do you always get upset so easily?" he queried. I glanced up at him, my demeanor rattled. "It's just a question."

I put some hair behind my ear, "It's been a long night, and I'm very tired."

"Okay, then," he huffed.

Yet there was one more thing I had to say. "You're wrong about me."

"How am I wrong?"

"You called me 'ungrateful,' but that isn't true. I put up with your demands that I dance with you, even though we both know I'm terrible at it. Then, I stopped fighting you after you kidnapped me, all for the sake of creating a false alibi for a crime I'm too scared to think of. And all this happened before I didn't take your car and speed away from the creepy, dark driveway you forced me to stay in." I made sure he could see all of me, the exhausted mess he had created. "I never asked you for much. Just to be left alone. And you've denied me that. So, by my estimation, you're the most ungrateful person I've ever met. And you owe me an apology. A heartfelt apology."

He fiddled with his fork, "You're right, it's been a long night." Gavin threw the fork onto the table, causing me to jump. His dark secret took center stage in my mind. My fingernails dug into the seat. He leaned in, "Would it help if I told you what happened?"

My breathing hardened, "Not really. I'm ready to be dropped off somewhere, so I can go home."

He pursed his lips and blinked, "Are you sure?"

The air pushing through my lungs began to burn. I couldn't stop the panic attack. A look of confusion crossed his face as he watched me fight the monster inside that stole all my breaths.

"Just breathe," his voice was calm, "Take one breath at a time." He paused, "You're okay."

I rebuked his words at first but slowly gave into them. Each breath was unable to bring comfort. I focused on him, hoping he understood my pain. He froze, like he was unsure of what to do. Seeing him in this position allowed me to catch a glimpse of his vulnerability. He was worried about me. Genuinely worried.

My breaths became more stable. My lungs and chest loosened. I let go of the table. Soon, I was calm.

"Do you feel better?" he said. I nodded, going to extra lengths to avoid looking at him directly. "I've given you quite a few reasons to hate me." I didn't reply. The silent treatment was infantile but very effective if used appropriately. "You. Are. Unique."

"Unique?"

"I misread you earlier. I figured you would have given into my every wish. But you've proved me wrong." I wasn't sure how to respond, but I liked it. "I have a suggestion for you." Great. "Stand up for yourself."

"What?"

"Your sister and I have ruined your night. We both got what we wanted at your expense. You should have stood up for yourself." He took a drink from his coffee and refilled his cup.

"Or you should have just left me alone, Gavin."

A sly grin, "You know my name?"

I blushed, "Yeah, some of the girls were talking about you."

"That day I saw you in the café?"

He remembered me. A shiver pulled itself across my skin. I hushed it at once. "Yes."

"So, what's your name?"

"Why? It's not like it matters."

"It does. I remembered you. You were wearing an orange dress. You seemed so uncomfortable."

"I was uncomfortable."

"Why?"

"Because Cecilia forced me to have breakfast with her and those girls. You may also remember my sister yelling at your friend, James, about partying tonight."

He blinked a couple times, "Well, I don't remember anything about them or that, but I remember you."

I pondered his statement and smiled. Still no mention of the garage. Or Chris. Lucky me. "My name is Catalina."

"Catalina, Catalina. That's a very pretty name." He sounded sincere. I hid my smile. "So, Catalina, happy birthday," he said as he straightened up. "I remember my twenty-first birthday," he paused, "I was in jail."

"Your home away from home?"

He laughed, "No. I'm not as bad as you think."

"Oh, yeah?"

"I'm not a killer. Get over it."

My eyes rolled. "Why were you in jail?"

"Bar fight. My crew and I beat the shit out of these country club guys."

I pointed to the blood on his jacket, "What happened there?"

"I thought you didn't want to know about my endeavors?" He had caught me. "I got into a fight with some punk drug dealers."

"Who won?" I said.

He raised his right eyebrow, "Who do you think?" I blushed, again. "You live in the country club?" I confirmed. "After dinner, I'll take you home. I promise."

I shook my head, "You can just take me back to the bar."

He frowned, "Catalina, it's not safe."

Our food arrived. Buttery French Toast drowning in syrup with crisp bacon and eggs over-easy. And a side of blueberries, of course. I was skeptical of his choice, but I picked up my fork, anyway. He cut a small piece of his toast and held it up in front of me. I reluctantly opened my mouth, and he laid it on my tongue. He winked, encouraging me to taste it. An infusion of butter and calories engulfed my mouth.

He pulled his fork back and cut a piece for himself. I licked the syrup from my lips and melted.

"Who eats dinner at eleven at night?" I said. No answer. "Do you usually come here?"

He laid a piece of toast on his tongue and pulled the fork from his mouth slowly. "Not always. I bet you've never had French Toast like this before."

I took another tiny bite, "It's good."

He reached over with his fork and cut another large piece off. The syrup dripped down to my plate as he patiently waited for me to open up. My lips parted, and he fed me, again. I didn't rush the process. The toast sat on my tongue until I chewed it with delight. What was I doing?

"That's how you eat French Toast," he said. I

opened my eyes. He took a massive bite and licked the butter from his perfectly pink lips. We were enjoying this.

"What time do you need to be home?" he said.

"What makes you think I have a curfew?" I said. More angry looks from him. "Now. Cecilia has more than likely told my parents I'm missing."

"Cecilia's with James, so you have that covered," he advised me.

If James was anything like the person I saw the other day, they were probably all over each other by now. Or he was a murderer, too, and my sister was lost from me forever. That wasn't so bad.

"So, what time do your parents want you back?" I didn't like his question. "Catalina?"

"Just to be clear, I don't have a curfew. But tonight, I'd like to get back before midnight. The bars will be closing in a couple hours, and the crazies will be out."

"Cecilia's not gonna make it home by midnight," he scoffed.

I shrugged, "Well, that's her life and her fate."

He moved his plate to the side and folded his fingers together on the table, "What fate have you chosen, Catalina?"

I loved hearing him say my name. The inflections he used made it sound desirable, which wasn't one of the key words I used to describe myself.

"I choose life. I want a long one full of good memories." I paused, "What about you?"

"I choose death," his voice was dark and seductive.

My pulse quickened, "Why?"

"Because it's inevitable."

I didn't put too much thought into his response. It was better that way.

Chapter Eight
Taste

"Hurry up, Catalina. I've got things to do." Gavin had finished his dinner.

And so had I. The smile stretching across my face had given away my glee. I took big bites and downed my coffee. Gavin shook his head, and I was certain he was amused by my sudden change in attitude. He enjoyed my caveman eating habits. When I was done, he got up, and proceeded to the door.

"Good night, sugar," the waitress came up to the table and cleared it. I held in my anger—he had left me with the bill.

I tapped her shoulder. "I hate to do this to you, but I don't have any money."

"We've got you covered."

"But he didn't pay?"

"He never pays. Doesn't have to."

Well, that was that. I approached him leaning against

the door, waiting. "You should learn to trust me." He flung it open.

Trust him? Sure, that was easy for Gavin to say. He held all the cards. As for me, I was just happy to be leaving the diner and heading home. I exited without giving him an answer. A rush of cold air hit me. Gavin stopped and took his jacket off, holding it open for me. It was a nice gesture. I put my arms into the sleeves, and he threw it up over my shoulders. The smell of him lingered. He rolled down the sleeves of his black button-down shirt and opened the car door for me.

I sat down without protest. Then, I remembered the blood. He got in and caught me looking over the jacket.

"Is the blood from your fight tonight?"

"Don't worry about it." The car roared to life.

I pulled my arms out of each sleeve, but he tucked me in. "I don't want it if it has unexplained blood on it."

"Yes, it's from the fight," he said. I parted my lips. "Don't worry, I'm sure the cops aren't gonna haul you in for questioning. You're off the hook."

Gavin revved the engine, and we soared through the parking lot and onto the county road. He put his finger to his lip. The silence bothered me. "Tell me more about the fight."

"There's nothing really to say."

I was curious, "Did you get hurt at all?" He went on to ignore me. "Sorry."

"Don't be. I don't mind your questions."

I didn't know what else to ask. We tore down the

road and my mind wandered. I thought more about my day at the garage.

"You're quiet for once. That must be a change for you," Gavin said.

"I'm normally a quiet person. I prefer to spend most of my time alone."

"When I picked you to steal, I was afraid you were going to talk too much," he admitted.

My interests sparked, "That wasn't the only reason why you picked me, right?"

"Well, you're definitely not a criminal. Or a liar. You're too nice and sweet to do anything wrong."

"You don't know that for sure." I smirked, "Besides, I could always give you up."

A sharp turn of the wheel, and the vehicle came to a stop on the embankment. Engine off. It consumed me immediately, the realization of everything. This was the moment, the end. But I dared not look at him when the icy breeze of death came over me. No, his face was not the last thing I would see.

Gavin's hands crept over to my waist. I moved closer to him, not by my choice, but by his. Fingertips brushed through my hair and down to my scalp. My breath quickened. I turned in his direction. Through the moonlight, his lips were finding their way to me. I tensed up, and I waited for him to kiss me. To taste me.

The kiss landed on my forehead instead. I blinked, letting him know that I was still alive. "You're stiff, unsure, and scared. Those are all good-girl qualities," he said.

"I'm not afraid of you."

"Good. I haven't given you any reason to be…yet."

We were back in motion before I could fully process his comment. No commands came from him for me to move. His arm grazed my lap, and he turned on the radio. Another fast-paced song.

"This is right up your alley. All good girls like cheery pop music."

I rolled my eyes, "What kinda car is this, anyway?"

"'66 Chevy Nova."

"It sounds angry."

Gavin winked. His coal black boot slammed down on the accelerator, and he switched gears. I was scared but that didn't help me. We sped across the highway, approaching the turn-off for The Estates. He will slow down, I thought. The sign for The Estates sailed toward us. My hands latched onto his bicep. No, I couldn't look. Into his arm my face went.

The brakes were applied, and I felt him downshift. "You don't think things over, do you?" he said. Slowly, I mustered up the courage to take notice of the fact that I was still alive. And he had fooled me, yet again. "If I killed you like this, odds are I'd kill myself, too."

I melted into the seat and let go of him. A tiny light shone off in the distance. I reached out for the steering wheel. He grabbed my wrist, "What?" he said.

I pulled back. "My parents would have a heart attack if they saw me in this car…with you."

He parked along the tree line and shut the engine off. "Is this good?" It was a bit of a walk to the house, but I didn't mind. He got out, and I exited the car from his side. "You live on the lake?"

"Yeah. We have a dock and everything."

"Do your parents own a boat?"

We started walking. "Not yet. I'm sure my dad's making arrangements for one as we speak."

"Your parents are millionaires?"

"I honestly don't know how much money they have," I paused, "Why?"

"Only the ultra-rich live in Settlement Island Estates."

I took in the beautiful view. On the other side of the house was the shining water reflecting the moonlight. "I'm not much for the country club, but I do enjoy the lake."

"Have you always been rich?"

I liked this question—it allowed me to play my cards close to my chest. "I don't wanna talk about that."

"Why not?"

"Because it's not important." I blushed, knowing that the delivery of my sentence wasn't graceful.

"You feel inferior for belonging to a wealthy family?"

"I never think about it. Besides, it doesn't matter because if I did, you said, 'you wouldn't feel sorry for me,' anyway."

He stopped me, "Catalina, you didn't understand the context of my statement."

"It seemed pretty clear to me," I said.

"I don't feel sorry for you, or anyone else, for that matter."

I chuckled to myself, "Okay." I continued our walk, but he grabbed my arm and pulled me back to him.

"I don't feel sorry for people, because they shouldn't feel sorry for themselves."

"So, was that the motivation behind your original 'you're ungrateful' speech, then?"

Gavin released me. "I wanted to set the proper expectation for you. If you were going to spend all your time complaining, I wanted you to know I wasn't listening."

Rudely honest—that was his best quality. But we were finally having a real conversation. Or at least a two-way discussion. I tucked some hair behind my ear and bit my lip.

"Catalina, stop biting your lip," he hissed.

I let go, only so I could speak, "I thought we agreed that you would ask me to do things, not demand them from me."

He came close to my face, "I'm fine with anything you want to do with your body. But I hate it when you do that." I rolled my eyes. "It's a terrible habit. And it makes you look insecure."

"I like being insecure."

I turned and walked toward my driveway. The grass rustled and then he was next to me.

"The nights can be a bit tricky out here," he said. "So calm and quiet. You think you're alone, but you're actually not." What exactly did he mean? Out came a moose, grazing across the driveway and heading toward the lake. A second one followed.

"I don't think I'll ever get used to that."

"This is the great outdoors, Catalina," he said. "You're surrounded by God's greatest creations. Embrace it."

"So, I should run up and give the moose a hug?" He seemed disappointed. He seemed disappointed. "I come from a huge city filled with tall buildings, smog, and too many people. Seeing an animal like this is still fascinating, okay?"

"Just don't piss off the moose."

"I'll keep that in mind."

We approached the front door. "Goodnight." I put the key in the lock and turned it. He placed his hand on mine.

"Thank you for your company."

I didn't focus on him. "You're welcome. Thanks for taking me to dinner."

He gingerly tugged on the few loose curls that remained on my head. My breathing slowed down, as I felt his fingernails on my scalp. I enjoyed the tingling sensation moving through my body, lost in the images of my first glimpses of him. Lifting my chin, he opened my mouth with his. The sweet touch of his warm, soft lips on mine. He took a step into me and my back slammed into the door. My hands were pinned against his chest. He held me tight, forcefully, but his kisses were even and very controlled. He let go, and I was left to hold myself up. I wanted more. I needed more.

"Everyone deserves a kiss on their twenty-first birthday," he whispered as he removed himself from my body.

My eyes fluttered open. "Of course."

He didn't say much or try to sway the moment. I wanted him to stay, but I felt him slipping through my fingertips. "Go inside, so I know you're safe."

I opened the door, "Goodnight."

"Happy birthday, Catalina." He smiled as he stepped off the porch and turned back to me.

Perfectly handsome and confident, he stood there, watching me while I caught myself. I waited for him to bark another order at me, but he seemed to be enjoying himself. The moment didn't last long. He disappeared into the darkness.

I went inside and closed the door. My heart ached to chase after him. To touch my lips against his again. No one had ever touched me like that before. I bit my lip to keep it from exploding into a smile.

"Is that Gavin Scott's jacket?" Cecilia said. I squinted in the dark. The light to the foyer flashed on. She wore a large grin.

My sister was safe after all. And she was nosey. "Why would you think that?"

"I saw you dancing with him. And leave. Where'd you go?" Seeing her so needy made me antsy to tell her about my roller coaster of a night.

But I refused her. "Nowhere," I replied as I scurried to my room.

"Come on, Cat! You finally have something interesting going on in your life. Now tell me!" she hissed.

I couldn't help but torture her more, "I'm gonna go to bed." Cecilia stood in between me and the door.

"Why are you tired, Catalina?" I opened the door behind her and flipped on the light. She jumped into my bed and patted the comforter next to her. "You don't look like you got laid," she said loudly.

"How would you know?"

"Your hair would be messy, and you'd be clawing at him for more."

Silly, Cecilia. She lit up. I went over to the closet and pulled out a tee-shirt and cotton shorts. I stepped inside the huge closet and changed. His jacket went onto a hanger.

"Do you think about anything other than sex?" I said.

"It's hard not to after being with James." She smacked her lips.

"I'm happy for you?" I replied.

The spot next to her was warm and comforting. Home, at last. She put her arms around me and shook my body. "That's old boring news. What's with you and Gavin?"

"Nothing."

"What's the inside of his car like? Did he try to make a move on you?" She sat up straight, "Wait, did he force himself—"

"No! He didn't even try."

She cozied up with one of my pillows, "Don't feel bad. He probably didn't cuz of his thing with Ronda."

He did kiss me, and I didn't stop him. Why did he kiss me? "Because everyone deserves a kiss on their twenty-first birthday." I quietly replied to my own question.

"What?"

"Nothing."

"Cat, this is epic! You should embrace it with all your might!"

"Embrace what exactly?"

"Hot guy who takes you away from your better-looking sister!"

"Oh, please," I leaned in to push her off the bed, but she swatted me away.

She propped herself up on an elbow, "So, what's he like? Is he all broody and mean?" She paused, "He looks mean."

"He's a jerk, plain and simple. He spent the whole evening bossing me around and evading the police."

"James told me about that. There was a huge fight. Some guys were arrested."

"What else did he say?" I said. "Did someone die?"

"It was just some beef with a rival gang on the other side of the tracks. That's it."

"We don't know that for sure," I scoffed.

Cecilia was silent for a moment, "You really don't like Gavin?"

I sighed. "To like someone, you have to trust them. And I don't trust Gavin Scott with anything." Except his constant promises to get me home safe, which he did. This all came about because he violated my wishes in the very beginning by committing felony kidnapping. Another reason to hate him. Well, maybe it wasn't hate I had for him, but I sure as hell didn't like him. Cecilia was watching me ponder the thought. "Besides, he's not a good person, so he's not worth your attention, either."

"Well, I'm sad for you, little sister." She pushed my nose, "He's quite the catch."

"Now that he's gone, I can relax, and enjoy the little bit of night that's left."

Cecilia lay on her back and laughed, "Catalina Payton, you really don't like this boy?"

I tugged at the comforter, "I can't believe you're surprised."

"He's a good dancer."

"You saw that?"

She twisted a section of hair, "If he's good at that, it means he'll be good at sex, too. You're missing out."

A subject change was in order. "So, any news on Molly and Adrienne? They make it home okay?"

Another poke at my nose, "I know what you're doing…since it's your birthday, I'll spare you the rest of this conversation. Molly and Adrienne are fine. Just a little freaked out."

"I'm surprised they even offered to go down there."

"They're not like us," Cecilia said. "They don't have the same street smarts we do. I mean if you're right about the murders, don't worry. We can hold our own." I buried my head under the pillows. She lifted them up, "It's not that I don't believe you. It's just not a big deal."

"I think Gavin and James might be involved."

She shook her head, "They're like fake bad guys. You know, the ones who dress bad, and smoke, but run the moment someone pulls out a gun."

"What if…" I paused, "What if they actually do own a gun?"

She waited a moment before saying, "Well, if he's got a gun, he better know how to use it." Cecilia kissed my cheek and got up to go to the door. I got up with her. "Don't let your imagination run away with you. Gavin and his crew are just a bunch of small guys trying to make a name for themselves." I gave her a weak smile. "If you decide to nail him, use a condom, okay?"

I closed the door on Cecilia and climbed into bed. I was asleep within minutes.

Then the sun was up. My mind was in scrambles. No more sleep for me. I exited the room and went to the kitchen. After getting a glass of water, I stepped out onto the porch to get the Sunday paper. The glass shattered at my feet when I saw the headline: Seventeen-year-old Chris Andrews found shot to death near Settlement Island.

CHAPTER NINE

Terrified

Two weeks passed before I brought myself to look at my tired reflection in the mirror.

Fresh jeans and a gray shirt from the dryer. My clean hair tickled my cheeks and neck. Gold bands on my fingers and wrists jingled when I moved. Everything but my face was good. I shook my head at the fragile, cowardly girl I hated. Enough of that. I threw myself down on my bed and admired the abstract paintings scattered across my walls. I picked up a journal and wrote a few words. It didn't help distract me. You should have told someone! I put the journal down and retrieved a book. My phone chirped.

What are you up to? This was the third or fourth text I had received from Miguel. I ignored him—how was I supposed to explain myself?

I had kept my distance from town, but I stayed up-to-date on news about Chris's murder via the local paper. Seeing his face on the front page everyday haunted me.

The police wanted information. They pleaded for someone to come forward. I had hopes that eventually the headlines would change. Someone else had to know something, right?

Nothing. Everything stayed the same. I knew I could end this and bring his family some closure, but I didn't. I couldn't. I was lucky to be alive.

My fingers ran across the dried blood on Gavin's jacket. Why did Gavin kill Chris? I had a very good understanding of what I had witnessed at the shop, but beyond that, I couldn't fathom what this teenager could have done that warranted his death. Unless it had to do with Porter.

I picked up my phone and typed in Porter Settlement Island Maine. No images, just a few articles about Porter Construction. Apparently, it was a construction company that closed down in the 1990s. Nothing else beyond that.

Dad came through the door. "Luke called and asked to come by," he said as he sat down on my bed. "I don't understand why you won't talk to him. Or go out with him."

Luke had called me at least four times since my birthday. Having Dad in my room gave me the impression that Luke was on his way over.

"I've been busy," I said with a weak smile.

Dad looked around at the piles of books teetering near my bed. "Reading doesn't make you busy."

"I'll be the judge of that."

Dad sighed, "Newly twenty-one, and you want to sit in your room and read?"

"And drink wine."

He put his arm around me, "You know, this really doesn't seem like you. I figured you'd be hitchhiking around the state, hunting for lighthouses. Having a beer with some lumberjacks in a log cabin off the coast somewhere. Where's your sense of adventure these days? Cecilia's seen more of Maine than you have."

Cecilia was out with Molly and a couple of other girls I hadn't met. She had seen James since my birthday, and it was all she wanted to talk about. I pleaded with her to leave him and everyone in Gavin's pack of murderers alone, but she didn't listen.

"You're distracted. What's up?" My father's patience was wearing out.

"I'm just tired," I whispered.

"Well, since you don't do anything all day, I can only assume you're tired because you spend too much time inside."

Not true. I swam in the lake almost every morning, but the water tugging on my hair reminded me of Gavin. "I'm fine. I'll go out this weekend, I promise."

"Hmm," Dad rubbed his face, "Well, I did have an offer for you, but if you're not willing to go outside, it's not gonna work."

I perked up. Usually, Dad's offers were good and very lucrative. "What is it? Can I move back to California?"

"No, I'm not paying for that. I thought you liked it here."

I did, kinda. "Maybe just a trip home to reconnect?"

He smiled. "If you come help me with some of my

patients, I'll buy you a plane ticket back home for Christmas. Eloise said you can stay with her."

My haven! My home! A holiday with Aunt Eloise was exactly what I needed. But there had to be something else he wanted. A catch. I cleared my throat and pulled my shoulders up. "What do I have to do? Do I get paid?" I said.

"Just a few errands for me and help with the patients. And no pay until you pay off your plane ticket."

"How much?"

"You'll be poor for a while…"

"Really? I thought minimum wage was higher than that."

"It probably is, but you're forgetting about all the online shopping. Not to mention that trip you and Miguel took last year to Mexico."

I frowned. "It was so we could reconnect with his roots, Dad."

"Still, your ledger is full of nothing but red. We'll talk more about it tomorrow."

"I think I can manage that." I sealed my appreciation with a hug.

Dad patted my back, "Good. I'll buy your ticket." He went to the door, "We leave bright and early at six tomorrow morning!"

I met him at the door, "Dad, um, I know this is gonna sound selfish, but I don't get up that early."

"That's the point." He rubbed my shoulders. "You need a routine. A little change in your day."

Mother came into view with a martini and a smile.

"Sorry to interrupt, but Luke's here," she said before disappearing.

Dad diverted from his path to the door and peered into my partially opened closet. Sitting in the middle of all my girl's clothes was the black leather jacket. The blood-stained leather jacket.

"What the hell is this?" he said.

His attention had been called there for a reason. It was as if God had given me a helping hand. Tell the truth, Catalina. Share your secret, so you'll be set free.

I walked over and closed the closet door, "I ordered it online. All the girls back home are wearing them."

He kissed my head, "Six o'clock tomorrow morning. I expect you to be ready."

I paused, "Okay."

Dad slipped out.

"Catalina, Luke's waiting," Mother said.

I slithered down the hallway and spotted Luke sitting on the couch. When he saw me, he shot up. His right eye twitched.

"And you're here. In my house," my tone with a tad sarcastic and annoyed.

He ran his fingers across his jeans and smoothed his white polo, "Hey. Sorry for coming over like this. I called you a couple times, but you weren't around."

I wanted to scold him for his efforts. Then came his amazing smile. "It's okay. I don't mind." I forced one of my own.

"How was your birthday?"

A sore subject for him, I was sure. Luke probably

knew about my night out. After all, Cecilia had the biggest mouth of anyone. However, he was here, which meant there were no hurt feelings. "It wasn't that great."

He folded his arms, "So, you didn't have plans?"

I was wrong, the news hadn't reached him yet. He didn't know about Gavin, the car, my horrible trip home, the passionate kiss, or the murder plot that kept me in bed every day. I wanted to tell him. But the truth would hurt. If I said I did nothing, he would have been hurt that I didn't call him.

"I went out with my sister and watched her friends celebrate my birthday without me." There. That was a happy medium.

"I would have kept you company," he said sweetly.

"Adrienne was there."

He recoiled at the mention of her name, "She told you we dated?"

I walked out the door to the porch. Talking to Luke about sex wasn't something I wanted to do in the presences of my nosey parents. Luke followed me, and we sat down on the swing Dad had installed a couple of days earlier.

"Adrienne just said you guys were together and now you're not," I said. "Nothing else."

He relaxed. His eyes sparkled in the sunlight, a light flow of energy and happiness surrounding him. "Where'd Cecilia take you?"

"Some bar in town." I had slipped.

Luke's entire position changed within a second, "At night?"

I had seen this flash of anger before. Gavin. I flinched. "Luke, it's okay. I was…fine."

"Catalina, it's not okay. Adrienne should've known better!" Luke was now close to my face. He gripped my upper arm, almost hurting it. "That kid got killed a couple of weeks ago!"

I was well aware of that. Luke's eyes twitched. Any confidence I had in telling him the truth was now gone. "We were…fine. We didn't see anything, and nothing happened. I was home by midnight and so was Cecilia." I bit my lip. His grip on me remained firm. "Luke, relax. I'm not in any danger. Trust me."

He took a few short breaths, released me, and then went silent. I inspected his every move. "Catalina," he broke his silence, "you can't go back there. The Settlers are no good."

"What's a Settler?"

"People who grew up in Settlement Island Township. We're The Clubbers, that's what they call us."

"Well, I'm working with my dad in town at his practice, so I don't have a choice," I answered. He shifted his weight. Luke's concern was appreciated. Much appreciated. But I wanted my trip to California more than being a hermit. "Let's talk about something else." No response. I had to try harder. The perfect thought came to my mind. "But before we change the subject, you can help me out by telling me who's the one person I should probably avoid. You know, the worst Settler." He scrunched his eyebrows together. "Who do you think is the most dangerous person in town?"

He ran his hand across his smooth chin, "I don't know," he paused, "Robert Somebody?"

I leaned forward, "What about Gavin Scott?"

"Who's that?"

I hid my elation. "Just some guy Cecilia met. What about someone named Porter?"

Luke tapped his lip with his finger. "No, it's that guy Robert. Or so I've heard."

I sighed heavily. Who was Robert? Gavin had never mentioned him.

Luke's arm brushed against mine. I could feel his muscles. He was strong, there was no doubt about that. And he was slipping through my fingers. I needed a friendship with Luke for my own sanity. "So, what have you been up to for the last coupla weeks?" I said. "What does Luke do when he's not looking after me?"

"Sailing lessons."

"Really?"

"Yeah. I'm taking the boat out tomorrow. Do you wanna come with me?"

"Sure. I have work in the morning, but I can probably go in the afternoon."

"Sounds good. Have your dad drop you off at the marina."

"In town?" I teased.

"There's only one."

"Okay, cool." I got up and so did he. Another brief and awkward silence flowed between us.

"I should get back in the house. And read."

He nodded, "Okay." Luke was halfway down the

steps when he turned and faced me, "Do you like your book of sonnets?"

Over the last two weeks, that was the only thing I had enough concentration to read, "I do. Thank you again for them."

"Anything for a pretty girl," he winked before walking up to a shiny, blue convertible.

"Is that your new car?"

Luke swiveled around, "Do you like it?"

It's just a car. Of course, Luke wouldn't feel the same way. A quick once-over and the words, "Yeah, it's very cute," put him at ease.

He opened the passenger door, "Do you wanna go for a ride?"

I got in, and he closed the door softly. Then he was next to me, starting the engine. It lacked the wild-animal roar that Gavin's Nova had. Luke put on some sunglasses, "Hold onto something."

His seatbelt clicked into place. Mine did the same. We cleared the driveway in a flash. The intersection to the highway was a good two miles. Luke put his foot down, and we climbed in speed. If he was trying to scare me, it was working.

"It's fast!" I said nervously.

"I know!"

My nails dug into the leather. The intersection sailed toward us—he wasn't slowing down. I waited for him to take the turn smoothly, like Gavin did. However, I didn't feel as confident in Luke's driving.

There was jerking, lots of jerking, but we continued

forward. Panic set in. A loud scream came from us both. My eyes shut, and I waited for Death's hand to reach out and touch mine. Several sounds hit me at once. Skidding, snapping, crunching, and then silence. The car stopped moving. My eyes opened.

I was still alive. No injuries. The car had flown through the intersection and landed in the dirt bank on the side of the road. Lucky for us, the bank was soft soil with a large clearing that allowed the car to coast to a stop.

Luke threw the car into neutral and turned to me, "I am so sorry! Are you okay?"

A group of large-eyed brown deer stood frozen in front of me. "Don't ever do that again!" I slugged his shoulder, my bracelets snapping my wrists.

Luke's shocked look morphed into a large laugh, "I got scared and tried to slow down at the last moment. Won't happen again."

"We could've died!"

His face came close, "Catalina, I wouldn't let anything happen to you." Luke moved closer to my lips.

I pointed at the deer, "What about them?"

"I'll get them during hunting season."

"That's horrible! The mere thought of you killing for sport is just disgusting."

"Relax, my family loves venison." He hushed my hysterical breathing. "That turn's impossible, I'm telling you."

"Actually, it's not, if you know what you're doing," I countered.

"Yeah, I wanna see you try." His expression was sweet. I glared at him. He patted my hair down. "Enough joy riding." Luke put the car in gear and the tires spun. He tried again, and nothing happened.

I folded my arms, "I'm not pushing your car."

He shifted the car into a different gear and pressed on the gas. Nothing. "Shit!"

"Now what are we going to do?" I said.

"Well, cell reception is bad here, so we can't call anyone." He got out and headed toward the road. Standing there, Luke waited. After a couple of moments, I joined him.

"Twenty bucks says I'll get a car before you do," he joked.

I smiled, "Game on."

A car came by, and we started jumping up and down. The driver, an elderly woman, slowed down, and then sped up.

"You got turned down, Luke!" I said.

"She wouldn't have been any help, anyway." Another car came. "It's your turn." He pushed me closer to the edge of the road.

I swatted him away and stuck my thumb out. The older man slowed down. He gave Luke a brief frown and kept going.

"What the hell?" he joked. "Friendliest town in Maine? Not!"

"You better come up with another plan," I replied, squinting to see what was around us. We were alone.

He tilted his head toward the road, "There's a car garage maybe a mile from here?"

Gavin worked in a garage. I latched onto Luke, "Or we can stay here."

He scrunched his eyebrows, "What's the matter? You afraid of old Mr. Hill?"

"Mr. Hill?"

"That ancient guy with the lazy eye who owns Hill Towing? He's nice once he gets to know you."

This was good news, but I didn't lead Luke onto my concerns. The timing didn't seem right. He walked alongside the road and motioned for me to accompany him. The wind rustling through the trees was the only thing I could hear. The forest along the rest of the roadside was dense. Dark. I turned to Luke. He seemed at home in this place. And I felt safe with him. "So, can I ask you a question?"

"Yeah."

"That murder that just happened. The kid who got shot. Did you know him?"

Luke kicked some rocks, "No. I didn't know any of those guys."

"Settlers?" He nodded. "I still don't understand why all this is happening here. It's such a beautiful, small town."

He shrugged, "It's those lowlifes, I'm telling you. I know some of the Club girls wanna hook-up with a hot greaser, but it's not worth getting shot over."

I shook my head, "But there were tourists and nice older people when I was there. Everything was fine."

"Obviously, you're itching to get out. I mean, they do have really good food in The District. Plus, the marina is the best. That's why all the Massholes from Massachusetts come up here during the summer. And Vermont, and New Hampshire." He shook his head, "I'll have to take you to Anders," was his solution. "My dad has a condo there, so we can stay over."

Luke was always trying to find ways to entertain me. And it was getting hard to resist. I spotted a truck down the road, approaching us. Yellow beacon lights flashed on. The clean-cut, mid-forties, brown-haired driver rolled down the window. I sighed; not Gavin.

"Mrs. Bradley saw you two and called it in. What do you need help with?"

Luke jumped up, "I win!"

"Don't rub it in. She didn't stop!"

He pulled me into a hug. I breathed him in. My arms wrapped around his mid-section as he scratched my back. Nice, sweet touches. "I'm a terrible driver. I can't get her out," he said while still holding me close.

"Where's the car?"

He released me, "Back that way."

The driver turned around. We walked back to the dirt patch to meet him. He jumped out of the truck and assessed the situation. Luke pulled three hundreds from his pocket and handed them to him. As the man prepared to carefully remove the car from the embankment, we sat down to watch. Luke grabbed a piece of straw and put it in his teeth.

He leaned in, tickling my nose with it. I mimicked

him. Thirty minutes seemed to pass by in a matter of seconds. Soon the car was free, and the man was approaching us. He had something in his hand. "Bet you don't wanna lose this." Luke was handed a ring with an "L" on it.

Luke looked the ring over. "It's not mine."

The man shrugged. "Keep it."

Pretty soon it was being offered to me as a token of his apology. I admired the thick silver band with Celtic symbols on the side. The "L" was unmistakable. It was unique. This had to be very important to the owner. I looked around the spot. What was it doing out here? Luke reminded me that he was sorry again, and he offered to take me home before dark.

Luke pulled up the driveway. Engine off. I undid my seatbelt, "Bye, Luke. Drive carefully." I dashed out of the car.

He rushed after me, "I'm sorry, Catalina!" I glanced over my shoulder. He folded his bottom lip, which was actually cute.

"You are forgiven!" I held up the ring. "Apology accepted, remember?"

"Consider it your consolation prize for surviving a car ride with me."

I waved him goodbye and walked up the steps to the porch. Two shadows moved across the window—Mother and Dad. I sat down on the swing. The dusty blue car sat in the driveway while Luke checked his phone. Stalling, of course. On the inside, he was probably begging for me to let him in.

Luke was allowed to spend time with me. Both Mother and Dad encouraged it. I pulled out the ring from my pocket and ran my finger across the L. It felt like real silver. I thought about putting an ad up, but that seemed too risky.

Why was I still scared? Luke was right—as long as I stayed close to home, I'd be safe. I went back to my room and pulled Gavin's jacket out. The dull dried bloodstains made my stomach cringe. It had to be Chris's blood. I shoved the jacket into a shopping bag and stuffed it into the back of my closet. No more sleepless nights. I was no longer going to live in fear.

I placed the ring on my desk and stared at it. It could be my symbol of turning over a new leaf to unleash the old me. It would be my good luck charm. I smiled; yes, it was.

Chapter Ten
Collide

FINDING YOUR FREEDOM is a strange thing. For me, it didn't mean going out and hunting for remnants of my past. Or finding a boy who could kiss away my uncertainties. It meant coming face-to-face with the things that scared me most. Exposure therapy. Looking in the dark, seedy places that led to Logan's and Chris's murders, and finding comfort in knowing who the killer was. To others, my extracurricular activities seemed grim. But to me, they were necessary.

I put down my Claudia Broadstad mystery book and sighed. It was Logan's turn.

I had been up since 4:30am, on my phone and computer, searching through Logan's articles. I had only pieced together a few facts: when he was murdered, where he was found, and where he was last seen. Logan was found in the field where Luke and I had landed. My fingers ran over my new ring. "L" could stand for Logan. I felt the ring had to belong to him.

He had been shot the first week of August. No suspects. The last time he was seen was leaving his girlfriend's house two days prior to his body being discovered.

I was no detective, but I knew things didn't seem right. He was gone for two days before his body was found? That made no sense. The turn off to The Estates is very busy; there was no way he could have been laying there for two days before someone noticed him. So, if he wasn't in the field, where was he?

Dad didn't give me much time to ponder my thoughts. He rushed me out the door the moment he discovered I was awake and dressed.

We were making house calls for his elderly patients who were bedridden. The first two patients, both men, were fighting cancer. Close to the end of their lives. I felt uncomfortable walking into their homes, invading the space of their grieving loved ones. Wives who would no longer have their husbands. Children losing their father. Both men had served in the Army and had lived well into their eighties. That thought made it easier to bear.

Dad's compassionate spirit also helped. After administering treatment, he sat down with the family members and asked questions about his patient's life. Stories and laughter filled the room. The cold stare of death transformed into light-hearted jokes and joyful memories.

His last two patients were women. Fussy women who were recovering from non-life-threatening ailments. Dad's approach in these situations was perplexing. He made sure his patients were comfortable before sending me in to chat and read to them. An honest mistake.

When he asked me to read to the women, he didn't mention the fact that both were sleeping. It didn't bother me, at first. I ended up sleeping for over an hour in a cramped armchair at the first house. But as time went on, I actually wanted to talk, just to give me something else to do.

After lunch, we pulled up to a small white house close to the lake. I prayed this patient would be awake. Dad charged up to the door with his white coat on. I followed behind in a vintage shirt and black pants, thumbing through my book. My outfit announced that I was just "the help." The patients would say, "Nice to have your daughter working with you, isn't it?" Dad beamed, and I wished I had something better to wear. Something more "medical" to give me a chance to fit in.

After knocking a couple times, a short white-haired lady came to let us in. No mention of my outfit, she just smiled.

"Dr. Payton. How are you today?" she said with glee in her voice.

"Good, Mrs. Scott. How are you?"

"I'm still dancing," she stepped aside, and we made our way into the small living room.

She was upright, which was a good sign. And energetic. I glanced around, expecting her house to be dusty and decaying, like the others. On the contrary, everything seemed to have a place. A black baby grand piano consumed most of the living room. Above it was a shelf with a collection of old family photos, mostly faded. Two oak bookcases held books and a few knick-knacks. I took a quick peek: not a bad selection. The flat screen TV meant she was probably obsessed with soap operas.

Mrs. Scott turned and lowered herself into a leather chair. After getting settled, she sweetly motioned for us to sit on the couch. We moved through the narrow space between the couch and coffee table to drop ourselves down. I fought to keep myself from being swallowed up by the cushions.

Dad put his arm around me, "This is my daughter, Catalina."

I waved at her, "Hi."

"Catalina, Catalina. That's a beautiful name."

"Thank you."

"Mrs. Scott had a hip replacement about eight weeks ago. I need you to help with some things around the house," Dad informed me.

She clapped, "Great! My friend, Marcy, usually comes over, but she's been working double shifts at the diner."

"What can I do?" I said, a weak smile following.

Mrs. Scott pulled the lever on the chair and lounged back. "Honey, can you go to my room and get my slippers?"

"Okay, sure. Which room is it?"

She pointed down the hall behind her, "The one on the end."

I pulled myself up and entered the hallway. There were three rooms in total. My first stop was a bedroom door that was slightly ajar. I pushed it and examined the contents inside. Just a bed with dark blue comforter, a black dresser, and closet. Nothing interesting to see. The couch cushions squeaked—Dad was on the move. The slippers came back to mind.

Last door on the end...I gasped—Mrs. Scott was a hoarder. A closet hoarder, at that. A stack of newspapers covered a lounge chair in the corner and towered over a heap of black garbage bags. Clothes dangled from an open ironing board and poured out from an armoire. She was in dire need of my help. I stepped over the small knitting messes on the floor, following a path to her bed. I had to rummage for a good ten minutes, but I finally found the slippers.

On my way back, I noticed the first bedroom door was closed. I rushed into the living room. My first sight was Dad dancing with Mrs. Scott. They weren't moving fast, but she was doing a good job for someone with a recent hip surgery.

"It's great to see you're moving better than last time," Dad gave her a gentle spin.

"Dancing is my life. I can't wait to make a full recovery."

I put the slippers in front of her chair, careful not to disturb them. Such a sweet moment. My arms went around my waist as I watched. Dancing: something I'd never be able to do. But I admired how Mrs. Scott showed her appreciation for the art. Each beautiful move, careful, yet passionate...

"She can really move, can't she?" Someone else was in the house. And I knew that voice.

I didn't want to turn around, but I had to.

Gavin stood in the hallway wearing a tight gray tee-shirt and his hands in his jean pockets. He looked over at me. No smile.

Fear. Unhinging fear overcame me. I didn't move. Breathe. I froze in my position, except for my heart hitting my chest violently.

"You have to say that. I taught you everything you know!" Mrs. Scott said.

It all came together. She was his grandmother. Dad gave her a twist and leaned her back into a dip. They were talking, but I couldn't concentrate.

Gavin folded his arms. I eyed the door. Sure, I'd have to run down Dad and Mrs. Scott, but it was worth it. Anything to get away from the killer who stood within a few feet of me. Dad ended the dance.

"Gavin, this is my doctor, Mr. Payton. And his daughter, Catalina."

"Catalina, Catalina. Such a beautiful name."

Dad came up to Gavin, and they shook hands. I shyly waved at him. I closed the gap between myself and my father. Gavin's eyes didn't leave me.

"Well, it's nice to meet you." Dad turned and bumped into me. "Catalina, can you please move, so I can do my job?" he joked.

I stood still, staring at Gavin. Eventually, Dad had to guide me to the side in order to walk by. I stayed on his heels.

He turned to me, "What's the matter with you?"

"I'm just not sure what to do," I stammered. "Do

you need me to do anything for you, Mrs. Scott?" She shook her head.

"Well, I need to have a private conversation with Mrs. Scott," Dad said. "You'll have to step out for a moment."

A moment wouldn't be long enough. "Can I borrow your car, so I can go get some coffee?" I put out my hand and waited for his keys. It trembled, but I managed to steady it.

"Catalina, I can take you for coffee," said Gavin.

"Thank you, Gavin." Dad walked me over to the door. I heard Gavin's heavy boots against the wooden floor behind me.

We stood in the small yard. The smirk on his face made my stomach hurt. I wanted to scream and run. "Nice to see you again, Catalina," he said with his low, sexy voice.

I was stunned. I knew our town was tiny, but… "I didn't know this was your house."

"Now you know," he said. "Still interested in coffee?"

I shook my head, "No, I'm fine."

The sun only amplified everything that had me lusting after him the moment I saw him for the first time. His hair was a mix of grayish blond with brown undertones. His eyebrows matched perfectly. The skin covering his blemish-free face enhanced his sculpted pink lips. If he lived in L.A., he'd get picked up for a modeling gig in no time.

"How have you been?" he said. I didn't answer right away. I was preoccupied with his dark, murderous presence and his undeniable beauty. Like a majestic predator. "Catalina?" he sounded annoyed.

"Someone was shot the night of my birthday," I blurted out. "And killed."

His eyebrows narrowed, "You heard about that, too?" His response was both confusion and irritation.

"Yeah. It's all I can think about."

"He had it coming." That comment summed everything up. Gavin smiled. Run, Catalina. Save yourself. "Anything else happen on your birthday?" he said.

"Did you know the guy?"

"I know everyone in this town." He stared. "Don't worry about what happens around here. The country club's pretty safe."

"That's not what's on my mind," I said. He didn't ask for more details, so I continued, "I just think it's a coincidence that someone died…" I paused, hoping he'd stop me. He kept his focus on me. "You were in a fight that night."

"They were unrelated." He smiled, "So, you didn't do anything fun after I dropped you off?"

I cleared my dry throat, "I'm fine."

He frowned, "No, you need to get out more. You're skinny, I'd take you for a hiker."

Gavin wasn't going to answer any of my questions. It would take more digging on my part to continue the conversation surrounding Chris's death. And Logan's for that matter. I needed more time, which seemed like something Gavin was willing to allot me.

I shrugged my shoulders, "I like being alone."

He folded his arms, "Yeah, you told me that last time. Why?"

"Why what?"

"Why be alone so much?"

"It makes things easy. And uncomplicated."

Gavin circled me, "Well, Catalina, if that's what you want, you're welcome to it."

Away from the house I went. In front of me was a small path that followed the lake which was now visible through the trees. Once inside the tree line and on the path, my eyes shifted over my shoulder. No Gavin. Relief. I walked further into the foliage until the water brushed against my Converse shoes.

I sat down on the damp shore, tucking my feet under my body. Gavin's coolness regarding Chris's death…

"Why do you hate me so much?" Gavin said behind me. I stayed still, breathing as shallow as I could. "Catalina, I hate it when you don't answer my questions," he growled. There was silence. I could feel him staring at me.

I stood upright and faced him. Leaning against a tree with his arms folded, his short temper with me had gone beyond his control, "Answer my question, Catalina." I remained as I was. He approached me. No, do not back down. No matter what, do not lose your ground. Gavin stopped inches away from my face. "You're afraid of me. Why?"

I bit down and chewed until I hit some blood. He placed his thumb on my chin and pulled until my lip was free. "You never answer any of my questions," I choked.

He examined my face, "So, that makes you afraid of me?"

I crafted my next words carefully. "There are people being murdered, and I don't know who's killing them. Wouldn't that put you a little on edge, too?"

"I've already settled that with you. There's no reason to be afraid of me."

"You're kind of an asshole," I said. Gavin was taken aback. My lips turned into a slight smile. "You keep avoiding the subject, even after you promised to tell me more about your fight the other night. I thought you'd get the hint by now, but I was wrong." In with a deep breath. "I'm not giving up until I get some answers from you."

He put his hands on his hips. A laugh escaped his lips. The irony of the situation must have hit him. "Fair enough. But not yet." Gavin looked at the water and then back. "I don't know you, either. Regardless, I find you interesting. Is that so hard to believe?"

"Actually, yes. Guys like you don't find girls like me interesting."

"Don't think so little of yourself." He paused, "it's beneath you." Gavin's eyes softened. I read his emotions and intentions. A slight breeze kicked up my hair causing a few strands to cover part of my face. They were swept to the side by his fingertips. "I'm not going to hurt you."

The trees began to rustle as dust blew onto my cheeks and forehead. I didn't blink. A small part of me believed him. To my surprise, it overpowered the dominant part that was telling me to run like hell.

We needed distance between us. "Give me time to figure that out on my own, okay?"

He folded his arms and sighed heavily, "If that's what you want, I guess I can give that to you."

We were silent for a moment. During that brief break, my mind came back to its senses. Enough talking. Time to head back. He dropped his eyes from mine and started looking around at the trees. I watched him carefully.

"You can ask me one question about myself," he said. "Something personal. But no murder or crime talk."

I was mortified. But then I realized this could be fun. Maybe I could ask him something embarrassing. Like when was the last time he had a gay dream about James? "So, do you go out dancing often?" I said instead.

He shook his head, "That wasn't too personal, Catalina."

"Well, that's as far as we're gonna go today." Game, set, match. I had my first victory over him. And it felt good.

He leaned into my ear, "You can ask me anything."

Night after night of fretting over this moment, and here I was, without a single thing to say. "Let me think about it."

Dad yelled something about lunch. We had already eaten, so this was a grand gesture to win the Scotts over. Gavin watched me, contemplating my next move. I had nothing. Absolutely nothing to say to him. I regrouped and took the first step toward the house.

He took one of his own. I kept up with him, so he

wouldn't fall behind me. Dad came into view. I was relieved.

"Your dad's nice."

"He is."

"It's a miracle that your parents are still married." I waited for him to say something about his parents. He didn't.

Dad stood at the grill. Great. Grilling in our family meant the person cooking was on a mission to do some fact finding. Mrs. Scott came out the back door with a pan of cut vegetables. Gavin grabbed it from her and gave the pan to Dad. I helped her sit at the gray patio table with soft green chairs.

I sat as well while Gavin gave my dad some tips on his car. Then he kissed Paula's cheek. He was so caring to her. Very sweet. And then we held a moment together, his care for her being transformed into a silent acknowledgment of me. I nodded at him, still caught up in the mystery behind his fixation with me.

My stare lingered longer than it should. I didn't care. This game was necessary, if I ever wanted to get inside his head. Trap him in his own web.

"Your father tells me you like books," Mrs. Scott said to me.

"I like old books. Mark Twain, Edgar Allen Poe, and Jane Austen are just a few of my favorite authors. I've also started reading murder mystery books."

"Catalina's our dark, antisocial child," Dad informed everyone. Here we go.

"There's nothing wrong with that. I find that people

who enjoy reading are far more interesting to talk to," Paula said.

"I think reading is a necessity if you want to be cultured," Gavin added in.

"Not when you read too much." Dad cleared his throat, "Maybe you can take her out and show her some things?"

"Love to," Gavin said gave me a wink.

"Dad, I hate to cut you off, but I've gotta meet someone." It was a poor subject change, but I had nothing else. "We should go."

Dad glanced at his watch, "Luke, right?"

Gavin pressed his finger to his lip. I was intrigued to know what was going on in his mind. "Will you be back next week, Catalina?"

"I'm not sure," I said shyly.

Dad raised his eyebrow at me. "Yes, she will."

"Good. I'll see you then."

My father excused us from the table, and we said our goodbyes rather quickly. Once we were in the car, I patiently waited for us to move on.

Dad put the key in the ignition. "Catalina, maybe you should spend more time with Gavin. He's really popular in town, his grandmother says. And you're the same age."

"For the final time, I'm fine, Dad," I scoffed. "There's no need for me to make more friends. I have Luke."

"Well, if Gavin's very well-connected, he might be able to help you get more acclimated."

I shook my head. "He doesn't seem that nice." A

thought came. "You wouldn't mind me being friends with someone like him?"

Dad laughed, "No. He seems like a stand-up guy."

"How do you know?"

"I got a feeling about him." He patted me on the shoulder. "Well, if you don't hit it off with Gavin, at least you have Luke."

Dad's phone buzzed. He checked the text. There was a look I'd never seen on him before. "What's wrong?"

"There's been another murder."

CHAPTER ELEVEN

Sailing

LUKE'S BOAT WAS massive. The tall white sails pierced the sky, offsetting the dark cherry body swaying along the rolling ripples. It was heavenly against the open, mossy green water with lily pads edging toward the shore. Sailing was something I hadn't done before…I was thrilled to do new.

It put things in perspective. I wasn't going to think about the new murder. Dad insisted that I didn't, especially since it took place in Anders. But I could tell he was rattled a bit. That seemed to vanish once he saw Luke and the boat.

"Catalina, you're one lucky girl," he exclaimed. Waving enthusiastically, he got Luke's attention. I thanked God for his busy schedule. It wasn't a "date" in my eyes, but time alone with Luke seemed refreshing.

He jumped off the boat and met us halfway, "Hi, Catalina. Dr. Payton."

"Luke, she's a beauty!" Dad said.

"Thank you, sir. I just finished up all my training last week."

"It truly is amazing," I said. My comment was sincere. All his effort and care were worth acknowledging.

"Well, I'm off to my appointments. Bring her back by eight. We're having a late dinner."

Dad left us to each other. Luke's fingers laced into mine. His warmth felt nice. We walked down the dock, and he helped me onto the boat. I took a seat and scanned the water. Two or three boats sped across the lake. There were five pontoons in total and three of them had a few swimmers bathing in the sun. Everything else was quiet. Sort of romantic.

"How has your day been so far?" Luke fiddled with the ropes.

I could deflect the question, but I charged head on, "Horrible and good. But mostly horrible."

"Wow, what happened?"

A small truth sufficed. "Had to go into town to help out with my dad's sick and lonely patients."

"So, you don't like working with your dad?"

"No, it was just a rough start. I hope next week will be better." This was a wishful thought. Gavin would be there for sure. And we would continue on with whatever it was we were doing.

"Well," Luke cleared his throat, "I hope this is more fun than that."

Dear, sweet Luke. The aspect of the adventure seemed enjoyable. Beyond enjoyable. I tucked some hair behind my ear. "It's really pretty out today." The wind kissed my face, blowing the musty scent of the water in my direction.

"Wait until the sun starts setting."

He continued to move things around. Arms up. His muscles flexed under his skin-tight blue shirt. Cut-off jean shorts positioned right at the base of the infamous "V." My eyes lingered for too long.

Luke was rich, handsome, and super nice. There was also a question of whether or not he was going to kiss me. Hmm, a kiss. Gavin's beautiful, dark essence pierced my fragile composure. Regularly comparing the two wasn't good for me. Gavin's motivations and murderous tendencies were enough to keep me at bay. And our frustrating interactions kept me guessing about everything else.

"Are you okay?" Luke said.

"What?"

"You didn't answer my question."

I paused, "What did you ask me?"

"I asked if you wanted some cake?" A small chocolate cake had appeared on the deck. Where it came from, I did not know.

Then I realized it was for me…for my birthday. "You should stop buying me things."

"It's homemade, woman!" Luke worked on the sails while giving me intermittent smiles. No more insecure eye twitching. Now, I only saw a fun spirit. A full human being.

I jumped into the action with him. "Homemade, you say? Did your housekeeper make it?"

"I put the frosting on…does that count?" I pursed my lips. He considered my point, "It was made in a house, so it's homemade."

"Okay, if you say so."

"No cake for you!" he swooped down and gathered the cake in one impressive move. Over the ledge it went, dangling above the water within his unsteady hand. A loving tickle from my fingertips brought the cake back to me.

Now to try it. I dipped my finger into the frosting and gave it a taste. "You did good, frosting man." He bowed.

I returned to my seat, and he regained control of our vessel. We moved further into the lake. Soon enough, Luke sat next to me to celebrate. "Happy birthday, Catalina Payton!" Then came the kiss—a soft peck on my cheek.

This made me think of a familiar conversation. "What was your twenty-first birthday like?"

"I travelled across Europe. My grandfather's from London, so my cousins hit me up to come over for a visit. It was probably one of the best trips I've ever had."

"How old are you, anyway?"

"Twenty-five," he paused, "I'm old."

"Not at all."

He cut off a piece of cake with tons of frosting and proposed I dig in. My first bite prompted me to take another. And another. I didn't slow down until half of my slice was completely devoured. I coughed hard, searching for air.

"Oh, my gosh! Are you alright?" He slapped my back until my airway cleared.

Once I controlled my breathing, I couldn't stop laughing. I regained myself. "It's so good!"

"I'm happy my frosting job did the trick," he said. I cut off a piece of cake and motioned for him to open up. He wrapped his lips around the fork and waited for me to pull it out, slowly. "Yep, the frosting definitely makes a huge difference."

I teased him with some frosting on his nose. Then came the food fight. Frosting went into our hair, on our clothes, and across various arms and legs. We were like children, unable to express exactly what it was we felt for one another. The boat rocked, and I fell into his arms.

"I really like you," was his reply.

"I know." My body stiffened, and I moved away.

He put his whole hand in what was left of the cake and took another bite, "You have this warm sweetness about you."

I straightened up, "You're a lot nicer than me."

"You're an introvert," he smiled, "I get it. That's what I like about you. You're very thoughtful. And honestly, I think you're far better-looking than Cecilia."

This was new for me. Everyone in L.A. was always so exceptional. I barely stood out. I would have been flattered, but I was probably the only girl who talked to Luke after Adrienne told all those stories about their sexual mistakes. "Well, thanks for noticing."

He shook his head, "I was a little wrong about you, though."

"How so?"

"Well," Luke looked over my entire body. "You have this bohemian vibe; kinda California, surfer girl. Like you're open and ready to explore. I felt intimidated. But, once I talked to you, I realized that you're shy and sheltered. And unsure of yourself."

His remarks were insulting yet warranted. There was more to me, even if I had forgotten it. The water sloshed back and forth against the boat. Luke's face had a mixture of intrigue and caution.

I pulled off my shirt and pants. Luke grabbed me. "That water is freezing."

I chuckled. "Where's your sense of adventure?"

"Trust me, it's not worth it."

He turned around and gave me a chance to put my shirt and pants back on. "I've lived, you know," I said, sitting down next to him.

"I didn't mean it as an insult."

"What about Luke?" I said. "You seem like the sweet, boy-next-door type who's never had a beer. Takes his grandmother to church on Sundays."

Luke flashed me another smile. He dipped his hand in the cake and licked off the remains of the frosting, "Well, it sounds like we still have a lot to learn about each other."

I smiled and took a deep breath. The wind picked up. Luke tied the tiller and then rose and approached the bow of the boat. Putting one foot on the deck, he opened his arms, and let the sun hit him. I couldn't resist my desire to do the same. The waves crashed into us, making my journey to join him a slow and unsteady one. I managed to get close enough.

"I love sailing!" he exclaimed. I was happy for him and the new freedom he had found. Luke pulled me up next to him. "Put your arms out and let the wind hit you. It's the best feeling!"

His hand remained tight around mine. I raised my arms and let the wind embrace my body. The sun and water caressing my skin. The bright feeling grew inside me.

I screamed loudly, and he joined in. The release was what I needed. The good things were coming back to me. I was alive.

∽

Luke and I chitchatted during the drive home. I peeked over to his side of the dashboard; he never rose above the speed limit. As we pulled into the driveway, he turned the car off and positioned himself in my direction. My shoulders tensed, and a lump grew in my throat. Was this it? The kiss?

"Sailing was good or bad?" he said.

"Good. You get the seal of approval." My thumb went up.

Another awkward silence. He turned his head toward the window which was pointless. It was after eight and pitch black. I released my seatbelt.

"Okay, well, I'll see you soon," I opened the car door. Within a minute, Luke was out of the car and next to me.

"Let me escort you inside." He jetted for the front door.

"Okay," I called behind him.

Luke turned, "What are you doing tomorrow after work?"

Nothing, but he didn't need to know that. I bit my lip. Stop biting your lip. I abandoned the flesh as I tried to come up with something that would sound busy. Mother met us, interrupting the conversation. Having her there brought immediate joy until I remembered that she was pro-Luke and overly-involved.

"Come in, come in! Your dad's cooking steak!" She reached her arm around Luke's bicep and gave it a squeeze before entering the living room.

I retreated to my room, avoiding another conversation. I needed just one minute, a moment to myself before having to coach my family into not asking me any questions about my date. But it wasn't a date. However, I began to think that maybe I wanted it to be.

"I like your room," Luke stood in the doorway, a towel in hand as he removed remnants of frosting and cake from his body.

"Thanks." I left him there.

He took the hint and didn't linger. I closed the door and quickly cleaned up before joining everyone outside.

Mother did a great job setting up the patio with a pumpkin-spiced-colored lounge area. "Fall colors," she reminded us. The grass was fading into its own fall display. Dad and Luke talked over beers. Steaks sizzled on the grill.

Mother and Cecilia talked with some tall guy. He noticed me first. He wasn't James. Of course not. His entire look was dark: jeans, shirt, eyebrows, and hair. I headed over to pick up on what they were discussing.

Cecilia turned him in my direction, "Catalina, this is Aaron." He brushed her off and gave me his attention. She didn't know he knew I was there before she did.

"Hi, Aaron." I glanced over at Luke. He was completely occupied and seemed to be enjoying himself.

"Aaron's going to start working with Dad in his office." Cecilia nuzzled up against his arm and planted a kiss on his cheek. He enjoyed it. And there it was. My sister was showing her true colors. I felt bad for James.

"What kind of doctor are you?" I said.

"General medicine, like your father."

Aaron's stiff reply was all I needed to sum him up. Boring. Absolutely, completely boring. Cecilia had chosen him for this linear quality. A dull boyfriend meant she could lead him on.

Luke came up next to me, "Hey, Aaron, I didn't know you moved back."

"Yeah. Just last week."

I turned to Mother who hadn't said a word. She was observing us, which never meant good news. "Wow," I said. "I had no idea Dad was going to expand his practice so fast."

Mother offered me a glass of red wine, "He wasn't at first, but with his growing client base, he has to."

"Your dad's the only doctor in the county who's accepting new patients," Aaron informed me.

"Well, good for him," I said to Aaron. "And for you, too. It must be exciting to be in charge of the office."

"I'm not an office manager," he snapped. "We're gonna partner with some people in Anders. Your dad will be the head of the practice, and I'll be his number two."

"Enough about work!" Mother gulped her wine, "Your sister has been kind enough to help Aaron get settled in. Something I wish we could have had when we moved here."

"Really, Mother? What exactly could Cecilia share with Aaron about Settlement Island that he doesn't already know?" I scoffed. Cecilia glared at me.

She guided Aaron to the lounge couch. I accepted my victory. Luke and I took a seat across from them. Now I could study her new fling without seeming too obvious.

"Dad tells me you went sailing today." Cecilia flopped her hand down onto Aaron's lap, her pinky too close to his crouch. He shifted around, but she showed no interest in moving it.

"Luke took me." I didn't elaborate. A mixture of expressions crossed Aaron's face.

Cecilia winked, "That's so sweet."

"You got the boat?" Aaron said to Luke.

"I've had the boat for over a year. I just needed the lessons to get me out there." He put his thumb into the opening of his bottle and flicked it out.

"Good for you, man. Nothing like being on the open water."

Cecilia perked up, "I'd love to go sailing, too."

Aaron grazed her face with his fingers, "Absolutely. A beautiful woman always makes things better." He was struggling, I could feel it. My estimations were wrong—Aaron was bored with her. Perhaps he was using her for something. Maybe an instant win with Dad.

Cecilia planted an opened-mouth kiss on him. I held in my contempt. Luke looked over at me and motioned toward them. His gestures made me laugh. I moved closer to him. He put his arm around me, but it felt slightly staged.

"How have you been adjusting to Settlement Island, Catalina?" Aaron said as he broke away from her.

"Good. Luke and Cecilia have been helping me stay occupied when I'm not reading."

He sipped some of Cecilia's martini, "Your dad tells me you can finish a book in one day."

"That's true."

"I have a library back at the house with tons of titles," he said. "You should come over and look through them. I'd love to get your opinion on my taste."

Luke seemed uncomfortable and for good reason. It was undeniable, this interest Aaron had in me. Almost borderline. And I had no idea how to address it, either.

Cecilia laughed, "Aaron, don't encourage her. She needs to get out of the house, not stay in." If she was jealous, she hid it well. But there were a few cracks in her demeanor. At last, her baby sister was no longer invisible.

Aaron turned to her, "What have you been up to

lately? I called you three times yesterday, and you didn't answer."

She shifted her glances between him and me. "How did you two meet?" I said to help her out.

Cecilia grew a smile, "Aaron came by the house last week looking for Dad. I convinced him to go for a swim with me."

"Your sister doesn't swim," said Aaron.

"Yeah, I know." I turned to her, "Why did you lead him on like that?"

She grinned, "I thought he was cute, and I wanted to see what he would do."

"Well, that's kinda desperate," Luke said. A snap from an unlikely source. Cecilia didn't have a chance to retort.

"We went for a walk instead," Aaron said.

"And you didn't find that boring?" I couldn't resist the question. Time to think on your feet, darling.

By this time, Cecilia was onto me. "Not at all, Catalina. Aaron had a lot to talk about, and I listened."

"She listened after she serenaded me with one of the many songs in her collection," Aaron stroked her long mane.

"So, when's the wedding?" Luke quipped.

Neither Cecilia nor Aaron laughed. Luke had made one of my dreams come true. I almost loved him in that moment.

Cecilia gave Aaron a kiss. Luke rubbed my arm with a nice graze. We made a good team. I could use this to my advantage. I contemplated telling Aaron about

James but decided against it. Too risky—Cecilia knew of my interaction with Gavin on the night of my birthday.

Aaron motioned to Luke with his beer bottle, then me, "What about you two? When did you become an item?"

Luke rubbed my shoulder again, "Catalina and I are just friends." No twitching or nervous gestures followed. I was shocked. Cecilia smirked.

"It's a shame, Luke. She's a very pretty girl."

I bit my lip, then a mouthful of my wine went down my throat. Who was this guy?

"Careful, Aaron. Someone might think you have a thing for her, too," Luke's voice was even but slightly stressed.

"I mean no harm, brother. I'm just getting to know everyone."

I waited for Luke's response. Nothing. Dad came over, "Food's done!"

We went to the large glass table with gold place settings and candles. Luke pulled out the chair for me. Mother addressed us, "This is truly a beautiful night," sniff, sniff. "I've wanted a moment like this for so long." She was drunk.

I laughed to myself. Luke leaned into me, "My mom's the same way."

We tapped our glasses together. "I had a great time with you today," I said. Things were much better with him around.

He smiled as he moved in close to me, "Me, too. We should go on that date soon."

"Sure." My head felt light. Like mother, like daughter.

Aaron caught my eye. He continued to study me. Dark eyes and perfect black hair; he had his own mystery. I remembered what Gavin said about not giving into people so easily. I didn't want to think about him. I took a deep breath and killed my wine.

CHAPTER TWELVE

Excuses

Cecilia drug me into the house to retrieve more alcohol. "What the hell is going on with you and Luke? And Aaron?"

"Nothing's going on with me and Luke. And I don't even know Aaron." I paused for a second. "What happened with you and James?" I said. "I thought you were dating him."

She checked the rest of the kitchen and leaned into me. "I wouldn't call it that."

"Gross, Cecilia." I made my way to Mother's wine cellar in the basement. Floor to ceiling, cobble stone settings in the walls, it was larger than her cellar in our old house. And it wasn't even finished yet. "You need to re-evaluate your choices."

"Look, just keep your hands off Aaron, okay?"

"Ce-ci-li-a," I shook my head, "I don't want him. He's all yours." I looked at the bottles, even though I knew nothing about wine. "Why do you like him, anyway? Because he's a doctor? Or is it because he's completely bored with you, and you need a challenge?"

"You don't like Luke. So why are you going out on dates with him?"

An interesting assumption on her part. Unfortunately, she had a point that needed to be addressed. "Luke's nice. And he's a ton of fun. I guess I haven't really thought about what I want."

"There's also Gavin Scott," she said. I didn't respond. "Look, you can deny it all day, but I know you have a little thing for him."

I settled for a red wine. "Gavin's not a part of this."

"So, you're gonna go for the Wonder Boy?" She pursed her lips. "Luke's a lost cause, sister. Pursue Gavin instead." Her phone buzzed. "Hold on, it's James."

"Great," I scoffed.

"Hey, lover, what's up?" She licked her lips in my direction. My index finger stabbed her gut. Cecilia's face flashed from teasing me to concerned. "Wait, slow down. What happened?"

James's voice was audible, but I couldn't make out the words. Cecilia's racing breaths bothered me. "What's going on?" I said, putting my face in her view. No answer. I reached for the phone.

She grabbed my wrist. "Well, hold on, I'll be there soon." She cut off the phone. "James almost got killed over something Kyle did. I've gotta go pick him up."

Cecilia moved quickly upstairs to her room to grab a coat. "No, Cecilia, you can't," I said after her. "What about Aaron?"

"What about him?" she snarled.

"You can't ditch your rich boyfriend for…your poor one."

She paced a few steps, kicking a stack of dirty clothes as she went. This was my first trip to her room. I felt like an intruder. "What am I supposed to do?" she said.

The silence between us was enough for Cecilia to get her things together and head back downstairs. I could hear the voices of Dad and everyone outside. There wasn't much time. "Maybe you should, um, find another way to help him. Do you have Gavin's number?"

"Gavin's with Ronda right now."

I could taste the vomit in my mouth. "Look, I know you want to help, but this isn't your problem. Just let them work it out."

She took two steps toward the front door then back to me. "I know you can't understand what it's like to love someone, but I do. I'm not gonna just leave him out there to fend for himself."

It took me a moment to bring all the clues together. Cecilia knew more about James's backdoor dealings than I did. She cared for him, despite seeing his true colors. That sentiment alone would have been enough for me to help her, especially since I longed to know more about the murders. However, James's potential involvement with the deaths gave me reason to pause. "Cecilia, you have to listen to me. Gavin and his guys are into something we don't wanna come anywhere close to."

"James is a drug dealer. He sells a little here and there. Nothing too bad."

"People are dying!" I grab her into a hug. "Don't get caught up in his drama."

She brought her face in front of mine, "Catalina, I'll be fine. You just have to trust me."

Aaron entered the kitchen. His timing was almost too good. "Cecilia, are you okay?"

My sister had tears smudging her mascara. She wiped them away. "Yeah. I'm just worried about a friend back home. I'll be out in a minute." He kissed her forehead and returned to the patio.

"Calm down, Cecilia," I said.

I spent the next minute coming up with something to fix the situation. It was of no use.

There was no stopping her. I left her in the kitchen to ponder her choice. Mother and Luke were clearing the table. She dismissed him once I came into view.

"So, I guess I should head out," he said. I didn't say anything to sway him to stay or leave. I hoped he wouldn't pick up on my uneasiness.

Luke said his goodbyes to everyone, and we went out the front door and onto the porch. Cecilia had left the kitchen, so I didn't have to cover for her. Not that it mattered. I'm sure Luke was happy to be rid of her.

I gazed up at the sky. The moon was large and beautiful. I glanced over at the spot where Gavin had placed his lips on mine. Ronda. He was kissing and making love to her at that very moment.

I stopped at the swing and sat down. "I need a moment to enjoy the air."

Luke didn't hesitate. He dropped down next to me

and laced his fingers in mine. "Aaron seems to like you a lot."

My head leaned onto his shoulder. "I don't think that's the case."

"Well, you're blind," he said. "I hope you don't take this the wrong way, but he's gonna have to try harder if he's thinking about taking you away from me."

"You know, I'm not one for the jealous type." I moved to the other side of the swing, but he caught me. He knew he had crossed a line.

Luke's thumb rubbed mine. I positioned my face inward and pulled my head up. We were face-to-face, eye-to-eye. Cecilia was right—Luke would never make a move. I needed to go in for the kiss. But that wasn't how I wanted it to happen.

"Catalina, I should get going," he whispered.

What little confidence I had was destroyed. "Okay. I'll see you later." I released his hand and walked over to the front door.

"Wait!" He approached me, "I just don't want this to be our first kiss." He bit back a smile, "You deserve better than some bad porch kiss."

I chuckled. "That's shallow, but I appreciate it."

He leaned in and kissed my forehead. "I'll call you tomorrow."

"I'm gonna hold you to that."

Luke gave me one last smile and headed for his car. I rushed to my room before Mother could quiz me about my status with her golden boy. I threw on my pajamas and hopped into bed, book in my palms. The day had been long. I fell asleep before finishing a few pages.

Shuffle. Pound. Shout. Various curse words. That is what I heard next. My eyes yanked open. It was still dark. The next crash helped me comprehend everything. Someone was at my window.

It was 2:30 in the morning—the perfect time to break in and take a rich family hostage.

"Cecilia?" a voice said. Really?

I made the brave move to get closer to the window. A shadow, only one, crossed my path. I pulled back the blinds and cracked the window enough to make contact. "What are you doing here?"

He climbed inside, stepping on my thigh, and almost taking us both down to the floor. "I'm looking for Cecilia," James said. "She lives here, right?"

"Really, James?"

He smirked, "I'll take that as a yes." He walked over to my door, "Which room is hers?"

I blocked his path. "Listen, I'm not gonna let you drag my sister into some stupid vendetta you have with a fellow drug dealer."

He placed his index finger to his lips to shush me. "I've had a very bad night. Kyle started some shit he can't handle with Porter. I need to lay low for a few days. Cecilia said it was okay."

No excuses. Yes, Cecilia had drug the rest of us into her sinister love triangle, but what James didn't understand was the fatal error in my sister's stupid plan. I was going to murder him, slowly and without mercy. And I'd make Cecilia watch, just to teach her a lesson.

"Cecilia's not in her right mind, James. Whatever it is you're into, you can't put my family in the middle of it."

He raked his hair and embraced me in a firm hug. "Baby Sister, I know what you're thinkin', but I'm not that bad. Trust me, I just need a day or two to get things straight and then I'm gone."

"You need to leave now."

James clenched me tighter. "I can't! Porter's the type of guy who'll kill me just to make a point. Then he'll come after everyone I know. He's sick, Baby Sister."

I rubbed my temples. "James, everything you're telling me is not helping your case. If that's true, you should know better than to get me and Cecilia involved."

He abandoned me and locked my door. "I'm sure this is fuckin' up your life. And I'm sorry for that. Believe me, I wouldn't be here unless I had nowhere else to go." He hushed my attempt to challenge him. "You have a heart! You're reasonable. Just cut me some slack and let me just stay."

"What about Gavin? Aren't the two of you best friends?"

He pulled his phone from a pocket. "He hasn't gotten back to me yet. But even if he did, my chances would be better here, anyway."

"And why's that?"

"Cuz Gavin's not interested in breakin' up the

family. Kyle's like a brother to him, so I can't put him in that place. And even if I did, he'd side with Kyle." James grabbed my hand, "That boy's crazy, twisted. Cold-hearted. Gavin's gotta have a guy like that to have his back."

"What about you? Wouldn't Gavin do the same for you?"

"I've got too many priors. I've burned too many bridges with him over the years."

I sighed, "I'm sorry your boy crush isn't working out…"

"Baby Sister, this is serious!" James's hand went tighter around mine. "If I can't get him to reason with me, I'm dead." I pulled my hand back and paced the room. "You know you wanna help me!"

I worked myself up into a heated frenzy. James seemed mesmerized by my struggle to reprimand him and keep my voice down. A few taps on the window brought our conversation to a pause. James put me behind him. I felt the gun against his back. He reached for it.

"You can't do that!" I whispered.

His hand didn't move.

His leg came through the window. Then his body. I didn't have much time to ask any questions. James ran over and threw his arms around Gavin's shoulders. Gavin didn't buckle under James's strength. He didn't mind the hug, either. The closeness of their friendship made me miss Miguel. Gavin pulled James from his body.

"What did you do?" he said.

"Kyle," James sighed, "talked to Adam today. So, I

got on the phone with Adam to find out what's what. He told me about Kyle takin' Oliver and Mark over to start some shit. Cameron got smart, and Kyle killed him. Then Adam came back to finish Kyle, but I talked him down. Porter should be good, too, now that Adam's good with us."

Gavin raised an eyebrow, "He's cool?"

"Yeah, I gave Adam a few of my regulars to seal the deal."

"A few hundred more a deal can't trump murder, James."

"I know!" James paced around the room. "I had to do somethin'. Not like it helped. Kyle got in my face, talkin' about how I need to stay out of his shit, and we got into it."

"Where's Kyle now?"

"Don't know. Mark said he thinks he went to Anders, lookin' for me," he said. "I wanna know why in the hell would he think I'd go to Anders?"

"Kyle got something on you? Something I don't know?" Gavin said. James shifted his weight several times but didn't say anything. He had balled his fists up at his side. "James, listen to me. Pete's got a place set up for you. But I'm not gonna let you go until you start answering questions."

"I ain't keepin' nothin' from you, brother. Kyle's off it, I'm tellin' ya. We need to mobilize or somethin'."

"I'm not putting a hit on Kyle!" James and I jumped at his voice. "I need time to figure some shit out. But if you're being straight with me, I'll help you."

James sighed. He kissed my cheek. "Thank you very much for your hospitality. Tell your sister to call me in the mornin'." I watched him climb back onto the porch and disappear.

Gavin stepped one leg through the window.

I made sure my next comment was both thoughtful and intriguing, "Kyle's going to kill James, isn't he?"

"Don't worry about our business. It no longer affects you."

I took a step toward him. "That's the thing," I said. "If he's half as scary as James has made him out to be, we're all in trouble."

Gavin stuck his head out the window, said a few things to James, and pulled himself back inside. "Do you have anything to drink?" I frowned. "I'm sure there's wine in the kitchen." He unlocked my bedroom door.

I trailed behind Gavin as he waltzed through the hallway and into the kitchen. He flipped the light on, illuminating a large portion of the downstairs. I held his hand on the switch and turned the light out. "You can't be in my house right now. You haven't been invited in."

Lights on. "I know that." Down to the basement he went. He rummaged through my mother's collection as if he knew exactly what he wanted. I watched him for a bit. Every sound heightened the nerves in my body. Gavin found a bottle of red and a clean glass. He filled it to the top. Back upstairs to the kitchen. He leaned against the counter. "Out of all the shit James has pulled, I can't believe he thought coming to Cecilia for help would be a good idea."

He sipped his drink slowly. It was too much tension for me. I scanned the room, expecting each shadow to be my parents. Gavin took another small sip. I grabbed the glass. "Okay, you made your point. James is a moron. Now take him and get out of my house."

Gavin leaned in, "Everything you heard tonight was just an exaggeration." He took back his drink.

I grabbed onto his arm. "Gavin, please don't do this," I strained. "My dad will kill me if he finds you here."

He dropped down onto one of the stools at the kitchen island. "Truthfully, I'm sick of this shit. It's the same thing every week with no end."

My gut twisted up. You have control over this. "We all make bad decisions. And me being in this kitchen with you is one of my own. Just turn the light off when you leave, please." I didn't hesitate. One step, then two, each carefully planned to make sure no one woke up.

"Why did you ask about Chris?" he said. No more steps. "He died on your birthday, and you made sure I had put two and two together. Why?"

The time had finally come. "I think you know why."

"Don't worry about what happened to him. It won't happen to you, if that's what you're afraid of." His finger swirled around the rim of his glass. Such an odd thing to say.

My forehead was damp with sweat. "What is it that you do? Are you a killer?" He didn't acknowledge me. His eyes drifted over to the front door. I scanned the windows.

Gavin amused me by staying tuned into my actions. "Is that what you think about me? Why you're terrified of me?"

"I don't know." I dared not tell him about my trip to the shop. "Yes, I'm scared of you. But for good reason. I mean, let's look at all the facts. James is here, in my house, because he's scared that someone you know is going to kill him. And you have blood-covered jackets…"

"One. I have one blood-covered jacket. And that was from a fight outside the bar. No one died, Catalina."

I sucked in a few breaths, "You're not a good person. None of the people you know are good people."

"I know you." He sipped his drink.

I leaned in close to his face. "You don't know me!" my voice was a whisper. "You think you do, but you have no idea who I actually am."

"Okay, obviously you're gonna need a little more comforting." Gavin put his hand on mine. "I don't expect you to trust me." I looked away. But then I found his eyes again. "I don't expect you to believe that everything is going to be okay." He paused. "But I hope you'll drop all your inquiries into Chris's death and anything you heard about James and Kyle."

Somewhere during his speech, I figured it out. His true reason for coming to scoop up James and whisk him away from my house. Gavin was protecting me. Or at least trying to. For what reason, I wasn't certain. But it was there, in between the lines. He was pleading with me to let it go for my sake, not his.

"Are you a bad guy, yes or no?" I couldn't help

myself; I had to know for sure before I could make any movement toward opening up to him further. He looked away. "Please, I just need to know."

He finished his wine and stood. "Yes."

Gavin didn't wait for me to ask any additional questions. Soon after his admission, I was alone in the kitchen with an empty glass.

CHAPTER THIRTEEN

Hunted

IT WAS THURSDAY, so Dad took me back to Gavin's house to work. *No more questions about him being a murderer.* That was the arrangement we had made. And it was smart. I needed to stay away from this murderous mess, anyway. I wanted to.

Dad and I pulled into the driveway. I was relieved—no black demon car. Paula let us in. My first task was to discreetly search for him. After invading every room, I was at peace. No Gavin. But hiding under a car magazine on his desk was something. The envelope. I opened it without hesitation.

There were photos of someone meeting with a man. From my research, I knew that face. It was Logan. He was with another man, someone I didn't know. I couldn't make out his features against the grainy background.

I flipped through the photos quickly, examining each finger on Logan's hand. And there it was, the ring. I had his ring. A part of me was happy to know that my hunch was true until I realized I had a dead man's jewelry.

Dad called to me. I put the photos back, even though there were a few I still hadn't seen.

Paula put me in charge of rearranging her cupboards, which was the mundane task I needed to sort through my discovery. I started with the obvious question: why did Gavin have pictures of Logan? And why was his ring in the field by my house? Did the other man in the photo have something to do with his death? All these questions would take some time to get through, and I didn't have any easy answers.

Dad relieved me of my duties early, so he could go into detail with Paula about her situation. She wasn't dying—Dad wouldn't have been in a good mood if she was. I didn't pry and followed his orders.

I took a walk down to the water front. I checked the distance between myself and the house—I wasn't far enough away. The sky was overcast. Black shadows covered the only path leading further into the trees. I continued west for a while, resolved to take a hike to clear my mind.

Dark thoughts entered immediately. The papers said they still had no new leads on Chris's murder. And now the photos. The jacket sitting in the back of my closet was calling me. Every morning when I woke up, I pulled it out and ran my fingers over the dried blood. What was the matter with me? Why wasn't I charging up to Gavin and demanding to know more about the deaths? Did I even want to know more?

My foot landed in a puddle, swallowing my shoe. I rolled my eyes as I yanked it out of the edge of the lake. There was no longer a path. "Great!"

No more adventuring for me. I turned to go back the way I had come, but nothing looked familiar. No houses were in sight. I surveyed the tree line and a small hill to my right. That could work. While on the move, I fell back into my thoughtful inquiries.

There was no reason for Gavin to have those photos. They seemed like surveillance shots. I bit my lip but stopped immediately. What if the photos had something to do with James? Gavin had accosted James for keeping secrets. Maybe the photos were attached to that. But that didn't seem strong enough.

In each photo, Logan was talking with the other man. So, why would James be in trouble over something so meaningless? My pace slowed. There was the possibility that I had missed something. Maybe the other photos told more. I had to see them. I made my way back, determined to get to Gavin's in record time.

The grassy hill quickly became a rocky cliff. I wouldn't be able to climb it. West became my only option. Maybe I could find a road.

I travelled along the rocky terrain and kept thinking. There was no allegiance between Gavin and me, so I had to do this. I had to see those photos and confront him. Delaying the truth wasn't going to keep me or anyone else safe. He had to take responsibility and fix all the trouble he had caused. Just then, something paused my considerations. I heard something. Whoosh. A car!

I had made it to the road…and a jagged cliff.

Head up—it was only about a twenty-foot climb. I hiked up my jeans. First hand went to a sturdy rock; up I went with a lot of effort. This would be harder than I thought.

A tree was embedded into the side of the rock face. Bingo! I latched onto the steady branches. Then I pulled up with my hands and pushed with my feet. The process was repeated. I could see the road. I had made it to the surface in one piece.

With no phone service, ride, or sense of direction, I was stuck there until someone drove by. I didn't fret. The precious daylight was ideal for reading, if I only had a book. Yet nothing could hold my attention except my need to see those photos. But then what? I picked a rock close by to perch on.

What if there was nothing extraordinary to figure out? Would I be saved? Unlikely. And I would be left with more questions. Besides, what would I do with all the information I had learned? It was a never-ending cycle, one I couldn't control.

I would get up the courage to take a peek inside Gavin's murderous world, and then I'd run away once I found something new.

More and more frustration mounted in me. Was I even brave enough to find something else? I was surrounded by this temptation to look under the bed to find the monster hiding down low. "Just don't look!" I screamed at myself. The hysterics were bound to tie me up like they always did. My head peered up to the heavens, hoping God would give me some sort of answer.

The trees wrestled together above me. Clouds were rolling in, bringing another chilly breeze. I looked down at the road. Leaves of brilliant oranges and yellows brushed against the asphalt. I closed my eyes and took a few deep breaths. My shoulders dropped. More deep breaths.

Dad always said my anxiety over life's problems could easily be solved if I just stayed inside myself. If I just focused on my own energy and breathing. Another deep breath. Then another.

That's all it took to bring me back.

I got out my phone; still no reception. A pleasant excuse to just savor the moment. I was free, for once. Free from Gavin, my parents, Cecilia and her love triangle. Enjoy it, Catalina. I admired the un-manicured lake being swallowed up by the grass and lily pads. Another thought of hesitation erupted. I would have to go back, eventually. It was inevitable. The idea weighed me down, but my change in luck didn't have to succumb to reality this time. I didn't have to fret. I loved where I was, and I wanted to make the most of it.

The next hour or so was spent playing in the wind and dancing with the leaves. My head went back as I sang a few notes out loud for no one to hear. Seclusion. Comfort. Peace. Serenity. This prompted a story I could write, something that would be dark and twisted, just like what people thought of me. Well, what some people thought. If only my family knew of the boy I had met.

The stand-up guy my dad claimed him to be. Then they would know the true meaning of dark and twisted.

Instead, my story would be different. What if I were some strange foreigner in a new land? Not a Settler and not really a Clubber.

The notion wasn't far off. There was so much I wanted to know about Maine. So much to do. To take the road forgotten by travelers who had more important things to do.

I took the road in front of me, eager to see what I'd find on the other side. The long road with trees leaning over it. I'd create a daring story like I had devoured before.

Everything remained quiet except for the wind and my feet. The world seemed far enough away.

I made plans, like my dad. Gone was the pity party I would throw for myself. If James and Gavin wanted to kill each other and everyone else, I'd leave them to it. The road called, and my response was a sweet smile.

Now, back to the plan. Where do people start when they make these types of arrangements? Dad was always the one doing these things for me. But I could begin, somewhere…anywhere.

The sun came out, which was a good omen. And along with it came a sound. A slight rumbling. A car.

I could hear it for a while before I could see it. Once I recognized it, I threw my arms around my chest and waited. No, he wouldn't take this peace away. He'd have to fight me for it.

Gavin pulled up to the side of the road, and got out

quickly, slamming the door hard. "What the hell are you doing out here?" he said as he stomped toward me.

"I went for a walk," I replied.

He raised an eyebrow, "From my house?"

I had been caught. "What are you doing here?" I said with genuine surprise.

"I just got back from Anders." He paused, "You know you're like miles from town, right?"

"It's nice out here," I said sternly. "Kinda quiet."

"It's quiet," he emphasized, "because this is the back road to Anders. Only loggers and hunters take this road."

"Oh," I sounded disappointed, even though I wasn't. "Well, it's a change of pace."

"From Settlement Island?" He raised an eyebrow, again. I didn't have a quick answer.

"Get in, and I'll give you a ride."

No, not a chance. "I'll see you later." I headed west again.

The skin on my neck burned as I waited for him to attack me. Be confident. Still, I drifted down the road. Swift footsteps approached me as he caught up.

He got into my path. "Catalina, I'm sorry about the other night. James shouldn't have barged in like that."

I shook my head, "Don't worry about it."

"So, you're just gonna be rude to me? Even though I apologized?" he scoffed.

"Whatever. Like you said, it's not my problem."

He stroked his bottom lip, "Oh, I see. You're hung up on our conversation about me not being a good guy."

"You are who you are." I continued forward.

"And you don't like me because of it?" he said

Each question brought me closer to a stalemate. But I wouldn't give up. "Gavin, we're two different people. We'll never get one another."

His tongue rolled across his teeth, "You think you're better than me. You, some stuck-up rich bitch, think you're more valuable to this world than I am?"

I was surprised by the amount of restraint it took for me to stay calm. He wasn't. His expression was amusement. No, not today. I wouldn't back down. "I've never given you an actual reason to think that you were garbage next to me…until now. Because Gavin, the only way you would feel like you were nothing is if you believed you were nothing. That's on you, not me."

Gavin took a step back. "Just get in the goddamn car." No more looks or advances from him. He didn't stare, either. I had never done that before…crush someone.

There was no time to feel guilty. He grabbed my arm and pulled me back to him, this time our faces were closer than before.

"When I kissed you, you kissed me back, so you forgave me for that. And the way you look at me doesn't have a hint of hate in it. It's your fear that makes you weak and rude."

The blood boiled in my veins. "I don't like you because you make my life unnecessarily difficult. And you're always bossing me around. It has everything to do with your personality."

He scrunched his eyebrows, "I was being honest with you. You could have been understanding with me."

"Your honesty doesn't wash away your sins."

"This is about Chris, isn't it?" I couldn't hide anymore. Gavin shifted his weight, "Chris died because he was an idiot. He got in with the wrong people, and they killed him. Same with all those other idiots. I had nothing to do with what happened to him or anyone for that matter."

I didn't want to believe him. A truck approached, signaling for us to get out of the road. "There's no way I'm going to just start trusting you like that. Remember, I don't even like you."

"Fair enough." He paused, "But I've got you figured out, Catalina. And deep down inside, you want to believe that I'm this horrible monster, but you know I'm not."

"Then prove it," I said. The truck honked again.

Gavin backed off, "Fine." We stood there looking at each other for several seconds. "But first, let me take you back to town."

It was getting late. I had to go.

We walked in silence. I approached the passenger door, and he opened it for me. He joined me inside, slamming the door loudly. The engine turned over. Once the car was in gear, he put the pedal down, and we flew.

We were back at his house in less than ten minutes. Dad met me in the driveway.

"Oh, good, you found her," Dad said to Gavin who

didn't stick around. "Next time you run off, I'm docking your pay," Dad said to me.

"You have to start by giving me a salary, first."

"Anyways, Paula wants you to stay for dinner. I'd stay, too, but your mom and I are meeting Cecilia and Aaron." He kissed my burning cheek. "Gavin said he'd drop you off. Be back by seven." Dad charged off to his car before I could rebuttal.

"A curfew?"

"Murders, Catalina, remember?"

Unbelievable. Abandoned, angry, and confused, I charged into the house. Gavin wasn't in the living room. I went to his door and pushed it open. Lying on his side, car magazine in hand, he glanced up at me and then back down. "Yes, Catalina?"

The envelope had vanished. I folded my arms, "You're giving me a ride home?"

He turned a page, "After dinner."

And with that, I was back to being a prisoner, again. His prisoner. I left the room and sat down on the couch. Where was Paula? I wondered. Neither she nor Gavin appeared. I resorted to counting my breaths to pass the time.

My thoughts ended up where I knew they would go. He thought I was conflicted about him? A ploy, that's all this was. I only had one feeling toward him—indifference. At first it was fear, then anger and terror, but now I was firmly rooted in indifference.

Gavin came into the living room and went to the front door. "I'm going to the store to pick up some stuff for dinner."

Finally, something to take my mind off things. I got up from the couch and followed him out to his car.

"I thought you only ate at eleven at night?" I said to make conversation.

He opened the door for me, "Paula doesn't eat that late."

We both got in the car and rolled down the windows. I enjoyed the breeze on my face as we headed down the street.

"What's your favorite food?" he said.

"Pizza."

"Pizza it is."

꿎

We pulled down Maine Street. It was late in the afternoon, but tourists were still all around. This was our first trip into town together. I glanced over at the *Settled Inn Café*, remembering our first interaction. Smells from a bakery made my stomach hurt. Yeah, I was hungry.

Once inside the market, a cashier and about four other people said hello to him.

"You sure are popular," I said.

"It's a small town."

Gavin headed over to the produce aisle. I grabbed a cart, wondering what to say to him. The ride over had been quiet. He seemed to give me space. And I was exhausted from our constant fighting. This trip would be civil. How much could we have to fight about over food?

Mushrooms, bell peppers, olives, onions, spinach, and tomatoes—he examined everything with a watchful eye.

I was impressed. "You're making pizza from scratch?"

"Paula only gets fresh food." He walked over to the meat aisle and ordered pepperoni from the deli.

"Did she teach you how to cook, too?"

He shook his head, "No. My grandfather was a chef." We moved on to cheeses: mozzarella and parmesan.

"Your grandma was a dance teacher, and your grandfather was a chef," I smirked, "You're the perfect guy for any girl."

He laughed, "I wouldn't know." I frowned. "Come, Catalina, we need to pick out some wine."

We entered the refrigerated area, and he sifted through the different brands of pizza dough. "No crust from scratch?" I said.

"Not enough time."

Our last stop was the alcohol section. We passed by the hard stuff. Tempting. He turned to me, "Which is your favorite? Your mom's got a great selection at the house, but hopefully this will do."

"How did you know the wine was my mom's?"

"I just have a knack for these sorts of things."

A knack? More like a lucky guess. "I don't have a favorite wine."

He examined the bottles before grabbing a red. We headed to the checkout stand. Some stringy brown-haired teenage girl perked up when she saw him.

"Hi, Gavin." She leaned forward on the counter, pushing up her well-rounded chest. The bag boy started unloading the cart.

"Stephanie." Gavin pulled out his phone and tapped on the screen.

I didn't mind him ignoring me. My weakness was situated right between us: chocolate. Dark, creamy chocolate, sitting next to an assortment of taffies and candy drops. Yummy caramel and chocolate chips. My mouth watered.

"Your total is forty-five, ninety-eight," said Stephanie.

He handed her some money, "Keep the change." Now he was next to me. "Catalina, is there something you want?"

A line grew behind us. I shook my head and looked at Stephanie, "No, I'm ready."

He gave a small smile, "You look like a child contemplating the perfect candy bar. Very cute."

"Well, I wanted something sweet, but I can't choose," I stammered.

"You know which one you want, but you're over-thinking it, just like everything else."

"I don't over-think everything," I hissed.

A wave of huffing from those behind him sped up the process. I grabbed a dark chocolate bar and put it on the counter. He dropped a dollar onto the register.

"Good choice." He winked.

"It was hard to make under all that pressure."

I helped him carry the groceries in. Everything landed in the kitchen. Out came two wine glasses, one for me and one for him, which were filled immediately. I took a sip.

"How is it?" he said.

I sighed in relief, "Good."

My back went against the counter as I watched him chop vegetables and prepare everything else. Bits of chocolate hit my mouth as he smiled at me before returning back to work. I broke the silence.

"How old are you?"

"Twenty-four."

"Where do you work?"

"I'm a mechanic." He looked up from his chopping, "Why do you still live at home?"

I shrugged, "I don't know."

"You should get your own place."

"Why? So, you can come over?" I joked.

"I make a mean lasagna...we could watch old movies." He wiped his hands on a dish towel.

I liked old movies. He grinned, and I cleared my throat. "Do you have a best friend?" I said.

"James, I guess. I have a crew, which is all I need."

"You mean your band of brothers who are trying to kill each other?"

"We're not trying to kill each other." He stopped his cooking and pondered something.

"What is it?"

"Maybe you're the good influence I need."

I didn't have a chance to answer. Next thing I knew, he placed a spoon full of sauce in front of my face. I opened my mouth, and he rested it on my tongue.

"Mm, it's good," I said as I licked my lips.

"I'm happy you like it." He dressed the pizza and popped it in the oven. "Let's go outside."

We sat on the steps. The lake shimmered before us. Nothing was said for a long time, just sipping of wine, and admiring the view. He looked good contemplating whatever was on his mind.

"Can I ask you a question?" he said.

I knitted my eyebrows together, "What?"

"Tell me something you have never told anyone else."

"That's not really a question, so I don't have to answer."

"Why not?"

"Because I don't have to. Besides, I can't think of anything."

He shook his head, "I have trouble believing that. You're a quiet girl. You have to have something." One thing came to my mind. Well, it kind of was something that fit the description of what I thought he was looking for. "You're just as secretive as I am," he said.

"I guess we have more in common than I first thought," I said.

He licked his lips, "I figured."

Change the subject. "So, how did you get your car?"

"It was my grandfather's. He drove it every day until he died."

"I'm sorry you lost him."

"Don't worry about it. It was over ten years ago."

"I don't really know my grandparents. My mom's family lives in Florida, and my dad's parents died when

I was young." I turned to say something else to him, but he had gotten up.

He left me and pulled the pizza out, serving us both. We sat down next to each other at the patio table. I held up my piece for a bite, blew on the cheese, and tore into it. Completely divine.

"Are you a selfish person?" he said.

"I don't think so."

"Do you lie?"

I nodded, "Only when I'm nervous. But I'd never lie to hurt people."

"Have you ever cheated on a boyfriend?"

"I've only had three boyfriends in my life: one in junior high and one for like a month in high school." I laughed lightly, thinking of Miguel. "And one in college."

He stared at me, "Did you cheat on any of them?"

"No."

"There has to be something," he murmured to himself.

"Why? Trying to find some dirt on me?"

He didn't say another word.

In fact, we finished our dinner in silence and remained that way until we pulled into the driveway of my house.

My hand caressed the door handle until I pulled it. Gavin did the same. Our footsteps were in unison. "What are you going to do tonight?" he said.

We stopped in front of the door. Our kissing spot. I shrugged, "Listen to music and stuff. Read."

He sighed, "That's boring."

"Boring is predictable. I like it."

"You're a lot less predictable than you would think."

My teeth grazed my lip. No biting. I opened the front door and stepped inside. He didn't follow me in, or demand that I be a polite and warm host. "Do you want to come in?" I offered.

Gavin's boots clicked against my mother's freshly polished tile in the entryway. I turned the lock behind him.

He looked over my parents' cream color sofas, tan rugs and the fireplace that was still burning. A deer head had been mounted on the tile above the fireplace. "Didn't see this part of the house." I rolled my eyes.

We walked down the hall to my room, out of habit. I turned on the light and motioned for him to go in first. He eyed the pictures of me and my friends and family. He then moved onto the abstract paintings scattered over the walls. I sat down on my bed and watched him examine my things.

"Did you paint these?"

I shook my head, "My Aunt Eloise did."

He picked up a few books from my deep green comforter, "You love being here. I can tell."

"It's my sanctuary."

He sat down on the bed next to me, "You should spend time outside, too. Get to know Settlement Island better."

"I'd like to. A few summers ago, I hiked up the Pacific Coast with some friends. We did a lot of camping. I imagine Maine has a lot of good camping spots."

"It does." He turned toward me. "What would your ideal day be?"

This was easy. "My best friend, Miguel, his family owns this amazing Mexican restaurant. I'd have breakfast there before heading off to teach a class."

"Teach a class?"

I nodded, "Literature. Then, I'd head over to my aunt's house and chat with Irving, her partner, about politics and the complexities of human life." I could see their faces. "And things would make sense." My eyes closed. "And then there's the beach. Tiny sea creatures tickling my toes the moment the sun sets. Seagulls stealing food from unsuspecting couples trying to enjoy a last-minute picnic."

Gavin moved on the bed. "It's like you lost a good friend when you moved?"

I opened my eyes. "California's all I've ever known, really. It was my home. But I've travelled a lot, met a lot of people. Mostly wander-lusters seeking some place to belong."

"I've never missed anyone or anything like that before."

The sadness crept over my heart, but I wasn't going to lose it. "I hope you never have to."

His phone vibrated, he quickly pulled it out and checked the screen. He sat up with the phone in both his hands. As he sent a text back, his presence grew dark. "I have to go."

Don't ask questions. I brushed my hair back into place, "Thank you for taking me home."

"You're welcome." He waited until I got up before heading out my bedroom door.

Now alone, one thing came to mind: blood-stained jacket. No need for me to keep it. I retrieved it and met him at the door, "Goodnight, Gavin."

He threw it on, blood and all, and turned to me, "You're a good person, Catalina. I hope you stay that way."

"I plan on it."

"Lock the door, okay?"

He stomped off to his car. The darkness in his eyes bothered me.

Chapter Fourteen
Salvation

Dad came into my room that Sunday, reminding me that we were going to church. He seemed excited, and I couldn't really blame him. He had been working Monday through Saturday, all day, and Sunday mornings to get all his patients sorted. Today was the first day he had to spend with Cecilia and Mother.

I, on the other hand, had spent tons of time with him. He had me volunteering overtime, helping him set up his new client folders and inputting information into his patient software. I didn't mind. I longed for something to do that would keep Gavin out of my thoughts.

I wondered where he had gone after dropping me off. There were no new murders in the papers, so I figured James and the rest of the crew were fine. Including Kyle, who had started most of this mess. Maybe they had worked it all out…

A knock at the door summoned me to appear before Mother for another inspection. But I had bested her with the perfect outfit. I waited until she meandered off to the kitchen before I darted out the front door and hopped in the car.

Settlement Island Christian Church wasn't separated. Clubbers and Settlers attended the large, white cathedral that sat on the outside of town, just off the lake and close to the Lazy S River. We passed the less-desirable part of town, only to be met with more tall trees in the distance. It was another beautiful place, no doubt.

Before the church service started, Dad convinced the pastor to allow Cecilia a performance. I took my seat next to her. A pretty yellow piece of satin tied around her neck hid her indiscretions.

"Nice scarf," I said.

She leaned in, "I couldn't keep James off me."

I knew for a fact she had stayed with Aaron just two nights earlier. I shook my head. "So, he's okay? Nobody killed him?"

"Apparently Gavin made him work it out with Kyle. They're fine now."

This had to be good news for everyone involved, including me. But there was still the Aaron issue. "Seriously, you need to choose one and get on with your life."

"I can't let go of Aaron yet. He makes me look good."

"That's selfish." I turned away from her and spotted him heading our way.

Aaron said hello to a couple of people and came to

sit next to Cecilia. I moved over and gave him my seat. Cecilia put on a fake, floozy smile. He pulled her into a kiss. I put my shoulders and back to them, thinking this would keep Aaron from talking to me.

"You look nice, Catalina," he said. Too late. Secretly, I was flattered by his comment.

Mother had pleaded with me to wear something acceptable. I complied without any protesting. You never know who could show up on the church steps, full of sin, desperate for forgiveness. I smoothed out my violet dress and pumped up my hair. I liked looking all dolled up, which was a surprise to me.

My eyes drifted across the sanctuary. No Gavin. I was curious to know if he'd come. If he did, I planned on being nice to him in an effort to keep building trust. Maybe that would bring him back to the light.

Why couldn't he be good for once? For me? For the friendship he was so adamant to pursue. And most importantly, for the fun he had promised me. I had spent the entire weekend in my room typing away, crunching numbers, and drinking wine. An adventure in the great outdoors would have been more than appreciated. I giggled at the thought.

My glee-filled anticipation cascaded into fear. A lump settled in the bottom of my stomach. Then came a feeling of delight at the thought of his face. To see his eyes look into mine, and his mouth curl into a smile at the sight of me. I bit my lip. No, I shouldn't be so excited to see him.

I needed to let him go. But I just wanted to be around him. That's all. It was harmless. Just a healthy curiosity.

My eyes floated up and around the congregation. There he was. Staring at me. He had just arrived with Paula on his arm. His beauty made me speechless. Black boots, slacks, tucked in white button-down shirt and a black tie loosely wrapped around his neck, I couldn't help but watch his muscles flex under his rolled-up sleeves. They took their seats on the other side of the church.

I put my face down into my Bible and studied the book of Matthew. Blood filled my mouth—I had been chewing on my flesh. Another glance back over at him. He put his finger to his lip and stroked it. Staring deeply at each other, I wanted to look away, but I didn't. His stern eyes didn't blink as he gave me a small smile. I reminded myself that God was watching and went back to studying.

Cecilia reached across Aaron to swat my leg. Luke had taken a seat next to me.

"When did you get here?" I said in a panic.

"Earlier. I saw you and decided to come down." He put his arm on the back of my chair, "You look beautiful."

I smiled, "Thank you."

He straightened up his black suit and blue tie, "It's so hot outside."

No, it wasn't. "You look nice."

Luke shook his head, "I'm sweating a river over here."

Poor, silly boy. He was always on a mission to impress someone. Or maybe it was a country club thing. Everything was a competition that couldn't be won. No one could out do the rich doctor and his elegant family. Mother was absolutely pristine in Chanel, Jimmy Choo, and a handful of designers only found on the streets of L.A. and New York. Cecilia had her fair share of celebrity favorites adorning her closet. Then there was me—ripped jeans, dresses fished out of some hippie's shop in a back alley located deep within Telegraph Avenue.

Why, Luke? Why put yourself through the agony of competing with a family that welcomed you with open arms? And the girl who would consider a stick of gum a reasonable dinner on a date night?

I frowned, "You don't need a full suit and tie to have a one-on-one with God."

"I figured you'd look nice, so I thought I'd look nice, too."

"Luke, don't be a conformist. It's beneath you."

"In that case," he took off his jacket, "I think I'll leave looking gorgeous to you."

My attention drifted back to Gavin. More staring. The pastor said something, and Cecilia grabbed my hand to pull me to the front. I had almost forgotten about her world debut.

She yanked the mic from him, "Hello, everyone! I'm Cecilia and this is my sister, Catalina." Tears fell from her eyes, "You know, it's so hard to be a young person and a Christian these days." I fought the laughter brewing in the back of my throat. "But every day, I hold on to my Jesus and walk out into the world to be the best person I can be."

Dad clapped, "You're doing a great job, sweetheart!"

Cecilia continued, "Thank you, Daddy. Today, I want to sing a song that will encourage you all."

She handed me the mic, and I took a deep breath. My job as her backup singer was to follow her lead. Nothing hard. Cecilia caught on to the tempo of the piano and belted out her meaningless, empty song. Her voice was truly heavenly. The audience was taken by her. But Gavin never broke his stare from me.

The song was over, and the audience roared into clapping for her, not me. Gavin sat still. A few rows behind him was Ronda. She looked at him and then at me. I slithered into my seat next to Luke and he threw his arm around my shoulders. This would keep her at bay.

After church, a group of volunteers set up tables and food for a church picnic. Kids clad in their swimming suits started running toward the lake. The water was much too cold for me, but they didn't seem to care.

Luke conversed with an elderly couple. His grandparents. He mentioned introducing us, but I told him it was much too soon for that. After all, we were still figuring each other out. And there was no need for me to muddle things with my long, complicated answers.

Someone crept up behind me. "You should go talk to him."

I sighed, "Dad, I know you wanna play matchmaker, but these things just need time."

He folded his arms, "Oh, really? Why's that?"

"Because…" I didn't have an answer.

"He's been nothing but nice to you. Stop turning him down."

"I'm not turning him down, Dad. It's not proper for the girl to chase the boy."

"Hmm," he said. "You did a great job up there, honey."

Something was up. But I was soon too distracted to investigate. I found Gavin in the crowd. He was about twenty feet away and coming in my direction. I was worried. Who was watching us? Ronda, Cecilia, Aaron, Luke, and others I didn't know. Great, this was bound to get the people talking.

"Good morning, Dr. Payton," Gavin put out his hand, and Dad shook it eagerly.

"Good morning, Gavin."

"Hi, Catalina," his voice was seductive, but Dad didn't pick up on it.

"Hi," I tucked a few curls behind my ears.

"Did you enjoy listening to my girls' beautiful singing?" Dad said.

"Catalina sings like an angel," Gavin said.

"Yes, she does. I'm gonna go find my wife," Dad turned to me, "Be social!"

Gavin smiled at him. I laced my fingers together to keep them from fidgeting, "You should be telling Cecilia that she sings like an angel."

Gavin shook his head, "Cecilia's overrated." I grinned. That meant a lot coming from him. He started walking, and so did I. "I wanted to tell you that I enjoyed our night together," he said while looking at me. I bit my lip but quickly released it. He smiled, "Good girl." I wanted to say something more but couldn't find anything fitting the mood. "So, have you made up your mind about me yet?" he said.

No, I hadn't. I checked to see who was still watching. Ronda. Her stare pierced into my skin. I had to do right by her, "You should go to her. Ronda. She's your girl and all."

"I don't have a girl."

I exhaled sharply. An arm slide across my shoulder. Luke. Gavin stroked his jaw. "Luke, this is Gavin."

Luke seemed baffled but finally put out his hand. They shook loosely and proceeded to look at me, like they wanted me to choose between them.

Luke's expression lightened up, "I think I know you. You drive that loud black car, right?" Gavin nodded. "And you went to the preparatory?" he said with intrigue.

"I did freshman year."

I giggled. I couldn't see Gavin at an upscale school, wearing the stiff uniform. Creased shirt, slacks, perfect hair…it didn't sound too bad after all.

"What happened?" said Luke.

"My grandfather died, and I lost my scholarship." Gavin's face fell.

"Dude, I'm sorry to hear that." Luke shook his head. Gavin didn't respond. He continued, "I think I remember your grandpa, too. He owned that five-star restaurant in the club. Oh, what was it called…"

"Persuasion."

Luke grinned, "Yeah, that's the one. Man, I wish that place was still open."

Gavin cut him off with a question, "So, are you two a couple?"

I blushed at his forwardness. Luke turned his attention to me. "We need to set up another date." I knew where this was going. Just as I had expected, Dad was watching us from afar.

Gavin patiently waited for my response. "We'll figure something out," I said.

Luke smiled, "No pressure, sweetheart. I meant when we get back from The Pines."

I put my eyebrows together, "The Pines?"

"Yeah, your dad's planning a trip there for the festival this weekend. He invited our family to go." His eyes twitched.

"You should go," Gavin chimed in. "You'll have fun."

Really?

"See, you should go," Luke said.

"Sounds interesting," I replied with a touch of fakeness.

"Good. It'll be nice to get out of town. Did you hear about the other murder that happened a couple days ago?"

My heart dropped. Another murder. I looked over at Gavin. "I think I might have heard something," Gavin said calmly.

"Well, I didn't hear anything. What happened?" I said to Gavin.

"Some townie named Cameron," Luke said. "He was stabbed." This was news to me. And it shouldn't have been news since Luke said his father had alerted my father of the situation. So, why didn't Dad bring it up?

Cecilia charged into our group. "Luke, your mom needs you," she announced.

"I'll see you Friday." He kissed my cheek then paused and took a deep breath, "It was nice to see you again, man." He and Gavin did a quick shake before he went off.

Cecilia was too close to Gavin. "I'm Cecilia, Catalina's sister," she put her hand in his before he offered it. He gave her absolutely nothing. They had no reason to be well acquainted.

I latched onto her wrist, "Let's go, Cecilia."

"I know who you are," he said.

A parade of different sultry looks crossed her face. I should have been embarrassed, but I knew this was all a show. Kind of like when a man is vying for the attention of a beautiful woman, only Cecilia was more persistent than any man I had ever met. "Well, it's nice to know James told you about me."

"Or Gavin's in tune with the town gossip," I said.

She ignored me, "Why isn't James at church?"

"Cuz James doesn't go to church."

"Tell James to call me," she insisted.

He folded his arms, "Before or after you're done with Aaron?"

I winced at his words. Cecilia's focus narrowed. Boy, had he done it. "Come on, Cecilia!" I tugged on her hand, but she was immobile.

"Excuse me?"

"Before or after you're done with Aaron?"

Cecilia wasn't one to back down from a fight. And this wasn't the fight to have. Her hair flew back, and her chest puffed out. "Listen, Gavin! I don't care who the hell everyone thinks you are. Don't you ever talk to me like that, again!"

Gavin remained silent as Cecilia called him numerous obscenities and threatened him with bodily harm. I was most impressed by how well she defended her actions. As if she wasn't doing anything wrong. Once she finished, I braced myself for the backlash. The epic battle between the most-worthy contenders on the church grounds.

"Hmmm," was all he said before walking away from us both.

"He needs to get laid," Cecilia hissed.

I was tempted to shake her senseless, but I let her go. "I'll go talk to him," I said.

Gavin had disappeared down a small path covered by dense trees and grass. I hunted him. Instead of fear, I focused on my curiosity, hoping he had some information on Cameron's death or what was really happening with James and Kyle. It didn't take long for me to find him in an old cemetery, leaning against a tree, waiting for me.

"I knew you'd come," he said as he straightened up.

"No, you didn't."

"I did." He walked forward, and I kept up with him. "You have questions about Cameron's murder, and naturally, you think I have something to do with it." His smile drew me in, throwing me off-guard.

"No, I don't." I paused. "You didn't kill him, right?"

It slipped out. I had been asked not to bring up anything regarding James and Kyle, but I figured Cameron was still fair game. I waited for him to bark some order for me to not inquire about his business. Instead, he stopped.

Leaves began to rustle. Footsteps. Gavin's attention was no longer on me. My skin grew hot. We weren't alone.

"What the hell are you doing out here?" It was someone I didn't know. A man. He seemed angry.

Gavin turned me around and positioned himself in the intruder's view. A tall, red-haired man in a long, dark coat and sunglasses. Not someone from the church. Gavin's arm prevented me from moving forward.

"You need to leave," he said to the stranger.

"I've got business to take care of."

"Ralph!" said another voice. I turned my head. James. "We put you out of business last month," he said.

James, Kyle, Mark, and Oliver walked up the path leading into the cemetery. Nervousness set in. I swallowed the vomit climbing up my throat.

"Call off your dog," Ralph said to Gavin. "I'm outside the boundary."

"There are no boundaries in Settlement Island. Or did Porter forget to tell you that?" James responded.

Gavin's crew was standing next to me. I felt small and inadequate. And Gavin's arm holding tight around my body didn't help.

"Stop selling in our town," Gavin said.

Ralph eyeballed each person. Everyone except me. "Which one of you bastards killed Cameron?"

"Who do ya think?" Now Kyle was taking the reins of

the conversation. He pulled his shirt up, exposing a shiny gun tucked into his jeans.

I dug my nails into Gavin's arm. Ralph drew his gun. Kyle and James were the first on our side to do the same. Oliver and Mark shuffled looks between themselves and me. I cowered behind Gavin.

"Let's talk!" said Ralph.

Kyle and James clearly had the advantage. Ralph had to know this by now. Gavin spoke next, "It's simple. Stop pushing dope here. You stop, and we'll all walk away."

"I've got my orders."

"You've got a death sentence." Kyle pulled the hammer back on his gun. He worried me the most. Unsteady on his feet, angry. Quick to pull the trigger too soon.

"You kill me, and Porter kills all you. Not my rules. You know that."

"Nah, I don't think anyone'll miss ya," James joked.

Stay alert! This was the difference between his cockiness and my death. I couldn't afford to give into the churning in my stomach or the pain crawling throughout my body and into my heart. I latched onto my lip, almost biting through it.

I took Gavin's hand. "I need to get out of here."

"Calm down. He's not going to hurt you," he whispered.

My body shook, but I didn't cry, "Gavin, let me go."

"Looks like your little girlfriend's got the right idea," Ralph said. I had hoped he didn't notice me.

"Last chance, bitch," said James to Ralph. "Get out of here, or I'll shoot ya myself."

Ralph whistled loud. Two more men approached from behind him, guns drawn, eyes on the six of us. We were outgunned until Mark and Oliver stepped forward with their weapons in hand. That left only myself and Gavin.

"We can do this all day," James said.

My fingers were embedded into Gavin's flesh. "I don't wanna die," I muttered.

"If we're gonna settle this now, I'm gonna let the girl go first." Gavin didn't look back at me. A few long seconds ticked by and no one objected. "Run," he told me. "Run and don't look back."

My feet pounded the ground. All the fear I had since the day I stepped into that car shop flooded through me. My first fatal mistake was the root that got tangled up in my shoe. I landed on my knees. I stalked forward, realizing my second mistake. I had gone the wrong direction. There was no path—just the lake to my right and low hanging branches ahead. It had to do.

I dove into the trees, ripping up my arms and legs. No gunshots yet. I still had time. Snapping, tearing, and bleeding, over and over, this continued until I made it out of the thickness of the trees and into the sun. My salvation was a small field. I leaned against a tree and caught my breath. The tears burned, but I didn't give in to them. To my surprise, Aaron rushed up to me.

"Catalina, are you okay?" he examined my arms.

I grabbed onto him and cried, "Run!"

He searched my body, "Who did this to you?" I

pushed away from him and headed forward. "Catalina, what's going on?" he looked behind me.

"Aaron, I can't tell you," I got out. "Can you just… trust me?"

He shook his head and started to walk down the path I had torn through. I reached out to him. Not knowing what else to do, I put my arms around his shoulders and wrapped him into a hug.

"I'm okay. Aaron, please just trust me!"

He pulled himself away and put his hands on my shoulders, "Why are you protecting that asshole?" He eyed the path.

I put myself in his view, "You have to let it go!" I quieted my voice, "If I were in trouble, I'd let you know."

He looked down the trail, "I'll give you this one time. But if he comes after you again, I'm breaking his face." Aaron sighed as he took off his suit jacket and threw it over my shoulders. "Let's get you cleaned up."

He led me down a dirt road and into a back entrance to the church parking lot. I held onto him, grateful for his unspoken interest in me.

Chapter Fifteen
Leverage

AARON MANAGED TO drive me home without raising suspicions from the others. I wasn't sure how he did it, nor did I care. He gave me the courtesy of peace during our ride, even though I could tell he wanted to say something. The moment I walked through the door, I shut him, and the rest of the world, out. The next days that passed were agony, filled with nightmares and constant sleepless days. My physical wounds had scabbed, but my emotions remained fractured.

I had seen Aaron a couple of times around the house and had successfully avoided him. And everyone. Then Thursday came. Bloody, cursed Thursday.

Dad and I pulled up to Gavin's house, and my heart stopped when I saw his car out front. I lightly smoothed my white long sleeve shirt and black leggings, pretending to be preoccupied as Dad spoke to me. I couldn't talk to him. I couldn't even look at him.

He opened my door for me when I didn't do it for

myself. For a moment, I tried to come up with an excuse, but he was starting to pick up on things. Tomorrow was our trip to The Pines, and for the entire week, he kept asking me about my relationship with Luke. There was nothing to report, of course. But Malcolm Payton was a persistent man.

Luke had called me at least twenty times since Sunday and had stopped by the house three times. This was Dad's doing. But Luke wasn't invited in, either, no matter how much I wanted him to hug me. I had to handle this on my own, otherwise more people could get hurt.

"Come on, Catalina. We've got work to do," Dad admonished, interrupting my thoughts.

"Can I have a day off?"

"We're going on vacation tomorrow."

I leaned back. "I've been cooped up in the house, working on your patient books all week. I'm tired, and I just want to go home and sleep."

His nostrils flared. "Look, I don't know what's going on with you. But whatever it is, I'm sorry, you're just gonna have to get over it. This is the real world. And in the real world, we work, whether we want to or not."

I shook my head, "I don't mind working. I just don't want to do this today."

The tail of his Doctor's coat flew back as he placed his hands on his hips, "Oh, you don't wanna work today?" Here we go. "Catalina Rose Payton, let me tell you something. I've been patient with you and your exceptional aptitude for far too long. All this moping, argumentative, reclusive behavior stops today!"

I had to cut in, "You just don't get it. You have no idea what I'm going through."

"What you're going through? Ha! You and Cecilia have lived on Easy Street all your lives, and it's just not gonna cut it anymore. You're twenty-one years old! Get off your ass and do something with your life!" Dad caught his breath.

My face ran red, not from anger, but from embarrassment. Was I truly that pathetic to him? My own father? Traitor—he was supposed to be on my side.

"Why won't you just let me have this?" I cried.

He grabbed my hand, "Get out of the damn car."

Gavin caught my eye. This gave Dad the advantage. Out of the car and down the driveway we went. Gavin met us halfway.

"Morning, Dr. Payton," he turned to me, "Catalina." Dad quickly released my hand. Gavin raised an eyebrow, "Is everything okay?"

"We're fine," I said with no energy in my voice.

Dad darted his eyes at me, "Son, it's been a long day. If it's all the same to you, let's go check on your grandmother."

"She's inside." Gavin's eyes went to me, "Catalina, Paula had me take care of the kitchen this morning for you." He smiled.

"Well, look at that." Dad chuckled with a sarcastic snicker, "Guess you'll just have to hang out and do nothing all day." He patted Gavin on the back and proceeded to the house. I knew I'd have to apologize to him later.

On to more important things. I pushed my hands into Gavin's chest.

"You murderous bastard!" I didn't waste any time tearing into him, taking him head on.

He put his hand over my mouth, "Stop talking."

My teeth sank into his palm. He recoiled. I took my chance and jetted down the street. His arms went around me, and we went down to the grass. We wrestled for a few minutes until he got the upper hand.

"Let me go," I screamed.

His hand went over my mouth again. "You're overreacting," he said calmly, "I'm not going to hurt you, Catalina."

"You killed Chris!" my words were completely muffled, but I knew he could hear me. "And Ralph! I saw it with my own eyes."

Gavin's attention shifted from the street then back to me, "You're gonna end up getting us both killed."

I glanced around and saw nothing. But I proceeded with caution and remained quiet. He released me and stood.

I looked like the crazy one, not him. By the time I got up, Gavin was several feet away from me. I wiped my face with my grass-stained shirt.

He slowly walked over and pulled some grass from my hair, "I'll give it to you, Catalina. You're stronger than I thought."

"Oh, you're full of jokes now," I scoffed. He started to talk, "No! You don't talk to me unless you have some answers."

He sighed, "Well, that's obvious."

His eyes were kind again. He brushed the dirt and

grass from his gray tee-shirt and dark jeans. The bulges of his muscles peeked out.

"Tell me what you did," I said firmly.

"Not here."

"I'm not going anywhere with you."

"Chris was shot, right?" He pulled off his shirt, exposing his bare chest and back. Turning around in a circle, he stopped, staring fiercely at me, "I have no gun." I bit my lip and the blood lightly saturated my mouth. He put his shirt back on and handed me his keys. "You can drive, if it makes you feel better."

I raised my eyebrow, "Are you kidding me? I can barely drive automatic."

He smiled as he took his keys back, "Well, that's settled."

"Nothing's settled. I'm not getting in the car with you."

"Will you just trust me?"

I got up close to his face, "No."

He blinked, "I told you I won't hurt you. Now, it seems like you're hoping I changed my mind—just so you can be right."

"Gavin, I don't…"

"You can hate me for the rest of your life. And I'm sure you will. But let me do this one last nice thing for you. You deserve to know the truth."

Mother always told me that if someone hurts you and gives you the chance to leave, you should go. Dad told me that if someone hurts you, and wants to make it up to you, let them have that one chance to make it right before you walk away. Since I still had questions, I went with Dad's advice.

※

Our destination was about twenty miles outside of town. Too far for anyone to hear us argue or fight. *Smart choice, Gavin.* Poking out from the ground was the foundation of an old building overgrown with weeds and grass. A waterfall cascaded into a pool next to us. Gavin sat down on the broken steps.

"What is this?" I said.

"The original Settlement Island Church. It was the pillar of our community when it was founded in 1865."

I looked around, "It's a beautiful place to die, I guess," I scoffed.

"You read old books, so I figured you'd like it." He picked up a stick and drew circles in the dirt, "Now onto more pressing matters." He paused. "I didn't shoot Chris, but I did cause his death."

"Why couldn't you just tell me that when we were back at your house?"

"There's nowhere for you to go here."

I folded my arms, "You mean run?"

He nodded slowly, "I respect you and how you feel about me. That's why I arranged this field trip." The stick traced the mud. "You're one of the only people I can talk to about this without catching heat."

"What do you mean?"

"My crew has their opinions on things. And I don't have anyone else who can listen to all this shit and give me their take on it. Everyone I know has a tainted version of who I am and what this is about, what I should do. Everyone except for you." A compliment, no doubt.

I was flattered and swayed to listen. "Tell me your story, so I can prove either you're right or wrong. How are you involved with the murders?"

He smirked, "Let's not jump ahead. We have to start at the beginning."

"What's the beginning?"

He shifted around a little, getting more comfortable. "My mom was a junkie. She died when I was six. My dad's a trucker who's been married four times. He's got at least two girlfriends that I know of. I was raised by my dad's parents after my dad lovingly dropped me off at school one day and didn't come back to pick me up." He looked up at me, "I was nine."

"I'm sorry," I murmured.

"After my grandpa died, I had to transfer from the rich school to the public school because my grandma couldn't afford the tuition." He licked his lips and ran his hand through his hair, fidgeting.

"Gavin, you don't have to tell me all this."

He put his arms on his knees, "You need to know it."

"Why?"

He sighed, "Because if you know where I've come from, you'll know where I'm going."

"What do you mean?"

"Catalina, I've been fucked since the day I was born."

I walked up close to him, "I don't wanna sound

insincere, but what does this have to do with Chris's murder? Or Ralph's?"

"Everything. My life changed after my grandfather died. Public school was hard, but it was nothing compared to the ass kicking I got at private school." He paused as a smile crept across his face, "I remember coming home with two black eyes and a busted lip. My grandfather met me at the door with this look on his face. Pure anger. That night he taught me how to fight. I went from being this scared little bitch to never losing."

I chuckled at the thought of Gavin being a scrawny little kid, "And you've grown up quite a bit since then."

"I had to. High school came and went, and the next thing I know, I'm twenty-four and still living in Settlement Island."

"So, what have you done since graduation?"

"Make a living. I work at Pete's garage," he leaned into me, "boosting cars."

"You steal cars?"

"Occasionally," he replied. "Before you start judging me, I'll let you in on a secret—the cars belong to drug dealers, or they've already been stolen. We do this, so we'll stay out of the courts and jail. No one wants to report a stolen car they stole."

I laughed. "That's pretty smart, I guess. But eventually, you'll get caught."

"The cars are gutted and stripped, sold for parts."

"Got it."

"Everything we do is all about survival, nothing else. I don't sell drugs. I don't kill people; I've never really had to."

"Kyle?" I whispered. He nodded. "Why would you allow him to murder all those people on your behalf?"

"I never told him to kill anybody. Sure, we knock guys around, but he's been into all this shit on his own."

I could see that he had more to say. He was held captive by something.

"You don't know how to stop him, do you?" I said. He looked down. "And you're not innocent, either."

"I'm not absolved of all of Kyle's sins, but I haven't even come close to killing anybody."

That was a lie. I sighed; it was time for a truth of my own.

"I, um, saw you threaten Chris before he died." The darkness coming over him frightened me, but I couldn't stop. "The day I was in the diner. The day you saw me for the first time. I followed you back to the garage. And while I was there, I overheard your conversation with Chris."

His expression turned to a combination of fear and confusion, "Where were you?"

"I hid upstairs in the loft." I swallowed, "You drug him up there to ask about his deal with Porter, and it ended with you pulling your gun out and beating the shit out of him." All of Gavin's bravado was gone. "When you left, he warned me to get away from you."

He remained still for a moment. "That's why you've been terrified of me."

I nodded slowly. "Chris died, and I assumed you killed him." Another inhale. "Plus, your erratic behavior and deadly temper didn't help anything."

He stood, "Catalina, what you saw was just a scare tactic."

I stepped closer to him, "Then there were those other murders. And the thing with James and Kyle. Now Ralph. I couldn't ignore the overwhelming amount of crushing evidence that ascertained all my theories about you and the evil you had done."

Gavin shook his head, "Chris was connected to Porter, a heroin dealer in Anders. Porter's the one who originally started this war with us. Chris set us up for a fight, blows were thrown, and he vanished. Then he was dead."

I paused, "Who killed him?" Gavin waited for me to work it out on my own. "Porter?"

"Robert Porter killed Chris. He killed my friend, Logan, too."

"Oh," I said. "I'm sorry." Logan's name brought about another admission of truth from me. "I think I have Logan's ring at my house." I told him the story about Luke and I getting trapped in the dirt embankment and my trophy for not getting killed by his bad driving.

"Can I have it?" Gavin said.

"Of course." I hated to bring up the next murder, but I had to. "And what about Ralph? He's dead, right?"

"Kyle stabbed Ralph." A deep sigh escaped his perfect lips. "He killed him."

I thought for a moment, "Oh, my God." I quieted the panic inside. "He's a murderer. And he's free."

"You're not in danger, Catalina. Kyle knows I'd kill him if anything happened to you."

My stomach clenched. "Will he listen to you?"

He looked surprised, "Why wouldn't he?"

"Well, he's kinda off the rails. And a bad omen. All his killing will catch up to you. People like that don't take direction very well." There was something else, though. Something terrifying that I hoped Gavin already knew. I nodded my head. "If Kyle is killing people for sport, then he must not have much to lose."

Gavin searched my eyes. My words seemed to scare him. Never before had I been so afraid, and so comfortable, in my life. He finally knew all my secrets, yet I didn't know if I would ever be safe with him.

"You're right. I should've known he'd cause so much trouble in the family." His thoughts went deeper. "You're really smart. I didn't mean for you to go so far into all this. But you figured it out."

"You just wouldn't leave me alone," I corrected him. He tapped his lip.

The sunlight threw shadows on his face as he stared at me. A marvelous view for the dark story he was telling. However, I felt relieved after telling him what I knew. Both full of light and free.

"Catalina, I…" He didn't blink. Nothing else came after.

"You never lied to me," I said. "Is that what you were going to say?" He didn't respond. It was becoming easier to understand everything. The epiphany behind it all. I smiled, "You never lied to me."

"So? It's only a matter of time before I'll have to."

"That might be the case, but you've always been

straight with me. Even when you didn't want to be." Gavin started to say something, but I put my hand on his arm. "It's almost like you wanted me to figure it out. But why?"

He shook his head. "I never wanted you to tie all the murders back to me and my crew. I just wanted you to stay out of it. But it was like you were circling around everything, all the time. Consistently there, always being you, prying and bringing everything back to the surface."

I wrapped my arms around my waist. "I'm sorry."

No more words from Gavin. At least not for a while. We watched each other carefully. I longed for him to say something. When he did speak, the conversation had changed.

"You know, I did leave Settlement Island, once. I went to Anders for a bit. Paula was still a dance teacher, but she wasn't making enough money. Then she got hurt, so we sold the studio to pay for her surgeries. I moved in to help out with the bills. And that was it." His head dropped down. This had taken its toll on him. I had a mind to ask a question, but I allowed him his time.

"All these murders are on me," he said. He went back down to the steps, "Porter's had it out for my family this entire time, Catalina. It started with some shit that my dad got into with his dad. Then came the threats, and my dad had to leave. I went to my grandparents and things died down." He let out a long sigh. "Then I found out Porter's dad was the dealer who shot up my mom and killed her. So, I took the fight to him in Anders, and Porter brought the heat back here onto me."

"How did you find out about your mom?"

Gavin brushed his arm across his face. "James. He had gotten out of jail and was dealing again. He got high with Porter one night, and the truth came out."

"Why did Porter tell James? Are they close?"

"James is the kinda guy that just gets along with everybody. Porter didn't think anything about it."

I sat down next to him. Our legs brushed together. "So, what do you do now? If you and Paula left Settlement Island, and started over, would all this stop?"

He sighed, "No, it wouldn't change anything. Porter's got Kyle to deal with for his hand in the murders, and James is gonna do everything he can to get revenge for what happened to Logan."

"When I was spying on you at the shop, I heard James talking about being done with fighting Porter."

"Yeah, James is tired of fighting, but he won't forget what we're fighting for."

I softened my eyes and my fingers laced together. "What are you fighting for?"

"World peace," he laughed. I nudged his arm. "Settlement Island meant everything to my grandfather. His family was one of the founding families. And my grandmother loves it here." Gavin was on his feet. "It's like your allegiance to California. All the things and people you love are there. Well, all the things and people I love are here."

I nodded and accepted his truth. His need to fight. It was a sad, twisted tale that had bruised my heart. But we were even now. I knew about him, and he knew almost everything about me.

"My parents had a storybook wedding. My dad grew up and became a rich doctor. My mother's a beautiful housewife, and my sister's dating two guys at once." I approached him as a friend, "I've never met a person like you before. Not even in my dreams. Someone with this toxic past that commands everyone to stay away. But you're alluring. Like a beautiful tragedy that beckons me to know you more."

"I'm not the guy for you, Catalina."

Gavin took a step away. I had invaded his space. Little, defenseless me. I moved my hand into his, and we laced our fingers. He held onto me for a moment before letting go.

"Well," I said with a smile. "Tell me nicer things about you."

He raised an eyebrow, "Nicer things?"

"Yeah, like, do you like music? Do you read?"

Gavin gave me a smile and told me more about himself. His favorite subjects: history and psychology. He told me about his cousins who lived in Anders and how much fun they had as kids. His adventures camping in the forest and swimming in the lake. He was…normal.

We were the same. Our cards were on the table, and we both bared our soul to the other. I no longer feared him—I didn't feel sorry for him, either. We were creating something else; a true, endearing friendship. Something that made us equal. A genuine smile spilled across my face.

"I want to do something nice for you," I said. "Make you something."

He laughed, "Why?"

"Because the entire time I've known you, I haven't done anything for you. And you've done a few good things for me. Selfless things."

His hand ran over my cheek and moved some hair from my face, "You're a sweet girl."

"I'm too nice."

He looked me in my eyes, "Yes, you are."

∽

We stopped by the store, and I made good on my promise. I carried the bag with a box of cereal and milk into the kitchen. Paula took one look at the both of us and scrunched her eyebrows.

"What have you two been up to?" she said.

"Catalina's attempting to make me a meal," Gavin told her.

"What's on the menu?"

I smirked. "Cereal."

"Oh, that's nice." She watched me as I poured the marshmallows and oats into a bowl. "Catalina, your dad left and will be back in an hour," she informed us.

"Thank you, Paula."

Gavin took a seat at the kitchen table, and I placed the bowl down in front of him. I eye-balled the milk, making sure the serving was full. His first bite warranted a smile. "Thank you."

I sat down next to him, "You're welcome."

The whole time he ate, I watched his lips moving. I wanted to kiss them. I fought the urge. My focus went around the kitchen and then onto Kyle.

Chapter Sixteen
Broken

Gavin stood. Kyle's eye shifted from him to me. I was afraid of Kyle and for good reason. He was a killer, plain and simple. And Kyle looked tough, like a scrappy animal that fights aggressively for food.

"Hey, brother. What is she doing here?" Kyle said.

I was on my feet now. "I should be asking you the same question," Gavin replied.

"I called you," he explained, "and you didn't answer. It's Thursday and…we got business to settle."

"Kyle," Gavin nodded toward me.

I figured everything out immediately. Then I was disgusted by his willingness to just let Kyle remain free after what he had done. "Maybe I should go," I said.

Kyle agreed.

Gavin sighed loudly as he folded his arms, expressing his bravado for Kyle to see. No more nodding from him. Gavin seemed to restrain himself for a moment.

I took a few steps toward the living room. "No need to leave, Catalina. This won't take long."

I hid my shock. Did he want me to stay in the house while he and Kyle hashed it out? Yes, I was working up the nerve to be his friend, but that was too much. Kyle wasted no time taking a seat next to him at the table.

Instead of reprimanding him right off the bat, which is what I wanted him to do, Gavin looked Kyle over. Kyle leaned in to whisper something to Gavin.

"Seriously," I uttered, gathering their attention, "I can find my way home."

The front door opened and closed. Dad appeared in the doorway. "Catalina, time to hit the road." He wrinkled his nose at me. It had to be the grass stains covering my clothes.

I had never appreciated the sight of my father so much before. "Bye, Kyle," I whispered. This was deliberate. The last thing I needed was Gavin's crazy best friend, murderer, or whatever he was, coming after me.

"So, how was your day? Did you enjoy your afternoon off?" Dad said as we both got in his Porsche. It took me a moment to remember our last interaction. When I did, the perfect response came.

I clicked my seatbelt, "You know, you were right. I'm a very selfish and entitled person. I've taken advantage of you, and I'm sor…"

"Whoa, wait a minute. Are you actually telling me that you're sorry for taking advantage of me?"

"Yeah, pretty much," I paused, allowing his perplexed look to linger. "And you're right, I need to be more appreciative of you. And the work you have given me. I'm gonna start pulling my own weight."

He smiled. "This is all I've ever wanted from you. Just to take responsibility for your life and make an effort."

"I know. And I'm on board."

He started the car, "Did Gavin talk some sense into you?"

"No…I came up with all this on my own."

※

`Luke waited for me on the porch swing. Dad said hi and strolled into the house.

"He didn't call me over here, if that's what you're wondering," Luke said about my father. Was I that predictable? Yes, more than likely.

I took a moment to really study Luke, from top to bottom. It had been a while since I had last seen him. This was, of course, my fault. Or Gavin's fault. After examining him, I wrapped my arms around his body and held on. He reciprocated the hug.

"I missed you," I mumbled into his chest. His body shook from laughter, I assumed.

"I've been worried about you." He released me, "Is everything okay? You're all dirty."

There wasn't a simple answer to this question, and I didn't overanalyze it. "Yeah, things are fine. I was doing some yard work."

"So, you've been really busy?"

"Yeah, working with my dad and stuff."

"Well, here's what you missed, while you were away,"

he sat down on the porch swing and patted the space next to him. I joined him, "So, there's this Halloween festival coming up soon, and I wanted to go with you."

"Are you asking me out on a date?"

He took my hand, "Yes, but not just any date. I'd like you to go as my girlfriend."

Gavin. That was almost my first answer. "Hmm," is what I came up with next.

"Listen, I know I don't have killer hair and a slick black car, but I do care about you, Catalina."

"Luke, it's not…"

"He likes you. It's pretty obvious. And according to your dad, you two spend a lot of time together."

I fidgeted with my dirty shirt, "I only hang out with him when my dad and I work at his grandmother's house. We're kinda friends, but that's it."

Luke's eyes twitched. "So, it's not him, then? You're just saying no?"

His observations were sharp. Maybe even sharper than mine. And in that moment, all my defenses were down. I could see Luke clearly. He was a good person and an even better friend. Not complicated like Gavin or anyone else I knew.

What was my answer? Luke shifted his weight. "Maybe I should have waited."

I laughed. "No, Luke. It's not your timing. I'm just being awkward, like always." More twitching. This time, he seemed to have no way to make it stop. Poor Luke. "I'm more of a take-it-slow type," I said. "I don't want to rush into anything."

Luke nodded. "Let's talk about something else," he cleared his throat. "I've decided to follow your lead and get a job."

"My lead?"

"Well, yeah. You seem to be working all the time, so you gave me the idea. There's an opening for an administrative assistant position at this marine life company in Anders. I'm pretty much a shoe in."

"Good for you."

Luke popped his knuckles. "It's a virtual job, so I'll still be in town. You know, in case you ever want to hang out."

Our fingers intertwined. My head went to his shoulder. "Yes, Luke, we will hang out."

His chin grazed the top of my forehead. My eyes went up to his. "I better get going." Luke stood. The moment was ruined, mainly because of me and my stiff, uninviting responses. We got wrapped up into another hug. He smelled amazing, which was a bonus. "Have a great night." And with that, we parted ways.

Mother greeted me at the door and marveled over my disheveled clothes and hair. "Luke waited for you for a while." She coughed, "Too bad his first glimpse of you was this one."

My arms wrapped around my body and into a fold, "Have no fear, Mother. He's still interested in me."

"Well, it's nice to know he gets to spend time with you. I feel like I don't get to see you anymore."

Funny thing was, I felt the same way. "Dinner? Tonight?"

"Your father's already at the grill."

"Will Cecilia be joining us?"

She escorted me into the kitchen. "She's staying the night at Aaron's. He's gonna swing by tomorrow morning to pick you and Luke up from here."

"And what about you and Dad?"

"We're going up early to get situated. Apparently, your father's meeting some potential business partners from Anders, too."

Typical Dad. I poured myself a glass of wine. "Did Dad tell you about our fight today?"

Mother got some wine for herself, "Catalina, he's just worried about you. We both are." Knowing that she cared was all I needed to feel better about my day.

I nodded and changed the subject. "What exactly do you think of Luke?"

That comment brightened up her mood. "He's a really nice boy. One of the nicest boys I've ever met. And strong." She lingered for a moment.

"He asked me to be his girlfriend." I gulped down my entire glass, "And I know you want me to say yes, and I'm probably going to say yes, but not yet."

This was a test…a way to get her to perk up and cure her somber mood. To see how she would respond. But something else remained. It was subtle, but I could tell she wasn't herself.

She wasn't as ecstatic as I thought she'd be. But she was happy, nonetheless. Mother's arms came around me, "If that's what you want, I say go for it."

The doorbell rang. Mother asked me to get it. The

door opened, and his hand went over my mouth, so I wouldn't scream. Mother asked who it was. He motioned for me to come up with a lie. I informed her it was a package of books for me, and I'd be right back. He walked into the house, me stepping backwards, my feet tripping over one another. The intruder knew exactly where my room was.

The door closed. "James!" was all that came out.

"Hey, Baby Sister. Got a sec?"

My fingers balled into a round fist and connected with his shoulder. He yelped. "You're a deranged man!"

James checked my windows. "I'm sorry to come over unannounced like this, but I need to talk to you about something."

"No, James. No talking. My parents are here, and your beloved Cecilia is not. Whatever it is can wait until never."

His hands cupped mine. "Do you remember what happened in the cemetery on Sunday?"

I could feel the color run out of my face, "Don't tell me where this is going."

"Listen, Kyle killed Ralph." I didn't let him know that I already knew this. "There's some blow back comin', and I wanna make sure you get the story straight from me."

"What are you talking about?"

James was raking through his pockets now. "He's up to somethin', and Gavin won't believe me."

"Believe what?" I said. His eyes darted over to the window and then back. "Who are you looking for?"

James ran his fingers vigorously across his short hair. "Don't worry about it. It's nothing."

Things moved around in his pocket. We were getting nowhere. I stopped him. "James, you're confusing the hell out of me. Who and what are you talking about?" James didn't seem to see my desperation to get him out of my house. He didn't seem to see anything.

A knock at the door made us freeze. "Dinner's ready!" Mother said.

"Porter's gonna kill Gavin," he whispered to me.

My arms released him. First, I had to answer Mother, "Thanks!" Then to James, "I thought they've been trying to kill each other this entire time!"

"It's different now. Time's up. Gavin's out of cards."

Nonsense. "James, Gavin told me about his past with Porter…"

"Kyle's on Porter's payroll now."

This was bad. Another knock at the door; she wasn't going away. "We can't talk now." I guided James to my window.

He latched onto me. "Baby Sister, too much has happened. We've shed too much blood, and now Gavin's got two people after him. Kyle being so close, he could kill him at any time."

"Look, I believe you, James," I reminded him. "But if Porter's sending Kyle to get Gavin, it won't take Gavin long to figure it out."

"If he wants to! Gavin's got to get out of Settlement Island. Fuck, he can't be in the whole state of Maine." If James was right, I had to help.

I put my hand on the knob, "I'll put something together. Now go away!" Deep breath in, and I left my room.

※

Dinner was rather uneventful, not that I would have noticed if it were. Mother and Dad talked over their plans to take some time off during Christmas. I could understand Dad's need to relax, but Mother? She mentioned joining a yoga class, which was somewhat entertaining. Or at least I pretended it was, so I didn't have to fall back into the nightmare that had become my life.

What was I going to tell Gavin? Last I knew, Kyle might have still been at his house. Shit. At least Gavin seemed to hold his own with Kyle. I needed an escape. Someone to talk to. My eyes drifted over to the clock—8:30 pm. I grabbed my phone and called the last number in my call history.

"Hola, mi amor. How's lobster country?" Miguel said. My mouth opened to reply, but I choked. "Catalina?"

"Miguel, I'm in deep..." I slithered into my bed.

"Deep?"

I didn't cry, even though I wanted to. He waited. I rubbed my fingers against my face and cleared my throat. "I've made a mistake."

I told Miguel everything. Gavin. Chris. The murders. The cemetery. Luke. Miguel knew about the lies and my feeble attempts at handling everything on my own. He comforted me with a very long and deep sigh. "I'm coming out there!"

"Wha...Why? You can't do anything about this."

"Catalina, if you keep jumping back in with Gavin, he's gonna put your name on a headstone soon."

Classic domestic violence talk. Miguel would know—his sister was a survivor. I should have called her instead. She could have told me why she held on for too long. "Miguel, I gotta get him out of here. Somewhere safe."

The phone shuffled, "Go to the cops."

And betray James? That wasn't an option. If something happened to James because of me, it would come back on me. There was no telling what Gavin would do.

I felt myself regretting the decision to tell Miguel anything. "I'll be fine. I'm just being overdramatic."

"No, you're not. Listen, I know guys like Gavin too well. I've got three cousins just like him. They run around in these gangs, shootin' up places, causin' all sorts of problems. And in the end, they wind up in jail, and draggin' the rest of us through their shit." He paused to say something to his mother in Spanish. "Catalina, my love, you're smart. I mean, come on, you graduated college light years ahead of the rest of us. Do the math."

A light flashed across the driveway. A car. It pulled up close to the front steps. Lights off. I parted the blinds enough to see who it was. Aaron stepped out and walked around to the passenger door. Cecilia emerged. They jumped into making out.

I cringed. "They're not a gang. They're just a bunch of twenty-something-year-old white guys who are running around killing each other. That's it."

"Why are you making excuses for him?" Miguel was losing his patience with me. I didn't blame him.

Cecilia released Aaron and walked toward the front door. His eyes met mine through the window. I ducked. "It's complicated. Cecilia's got her hand in this, too."

"What's she doin' runnin' with these people? I mean, she isn't the most virginal person I know, but she's not known for hanging out with poor street trash." Another few words in Spanish. "I've gotta go. Please, please, tell the police what you know."

Footsteps neared my room. I tucked myself into the comforter. "I'll think about it. I love you. We'll talk soon."

"I know, it's just I want to check in with her for a minute." Cecilia. I killed the lamp close to my bed, but one final light stayed on across the room. I grabbed a book and placed it open on my chest.

Miguel shouted a few swear words into the phone… he didn't hang up. I put my head in the pillow. Eyes shut.

The door opened. "Cat?" Cecilia said.

"I think she's asleep," said a man's voice. Aaron.

"Let's go upstairs."

One set of feet trailed away. I heard Aaron sigh. Instead of leaving, he ventured further into my room. Into my privacy. My eyes threatened to open. A breath of air grazed my neck. Then a finger brushed a few strands of hair from my cheek. What are you doing, Aaron?

His soft lips kissed my forehead. My soul clawed to get out of my skin. "Goodnight, Catalina," he said.

A few moments passed, and I could hear his footsteps leave. Eyes open. I rushed to the door and locked it.

Chapter Seventeen
The Pines

AARON DIDN'T HINT at anything regarding our last interaction. I wasn't going to bring it up, either. His eyes drifted in my direction several times. Cecilia never caught him. I felt the kiss he had placed on my forehead brushing against my skin. Things were bound to remain awkward between us.

What did that tender touch of affection mean? I didn't know him well, but Aaron seemed like a faithful guy. So serious. He would never trick me into liking him, as Cecilia had done with so many guys before. His eyes went back to me. My focus went to the car window.

More dense trees, which was worth noting since we already lived in a vast forest community. The Pines were described to me as an oasis in a valley of trees. Some flat land that would appear from nowhere. I cringed at the boring, mundane metaphor, but I didn't correct Aaron when he explained this fact to me and Cecilia. No, I wouldn't dare do that.

I did, however, appreciate the potential seclusion this trip promised. I craved it. And each mountain pass that brought on more and more trees made me antsy. Just get there already.

Luke pulled his ear buds out and put his hand on my shoulder, "For a person on vacation, you sure look depressed."

Finally, he was speaking to me. After our last exchange, I was certain Luke would never say another word to me again, even though he never hinted at it. Having his ego bruised so many times had to take a toll. "I'm not depressed. I'm deep in thought."

"About what?" he said.

Cecilia sighed, "She's always like this, Luke."

I shook my head, "You're just jealous because you have no thoughts."

Aaron laughed. Cecilia hit him on the arm. "Sorry, babe," he teased.

Cecilia pulled out her cigarettes. Aaron grabbed the pack. "There's no smoking in my car," he said.

This was not going to play out well. "I thought I was the exception." Cecilia's cute and playful defiance would surely turn things for the worst. A fight was brewing, for sure.

He shook his head, "Besides, all that smoke is gonna make you ugly one of these days." Cecilia folded her arms.

Luke looked at me, and I leaned over, "I think they're fighting." He nodded.

I knew they were fighting. Aaron was becoming

suspicious of Cecilia's intentions with him. Or so she had told me before we got into the car. The last love bite James left on her neck was hard to hide. Aaron was coming to his senses, and I was happy for him. My shoulders tightened—I hoped I wasn't his next conquest.

Cecilia looked him over and puckered her lips, "Aaron, honey. I'm really stressed out and could use just one, little, harmless cigarette." He threw the pack behind him, nearly hitting Luke. Luke didn't budge. Cecilia threw her arms together into a fold, "This is bullshit!"

Luke leaned forward, "My grandpa died of lung cancer. It wasn't pretty."

She turned to him, "Catalina, tell your boyfriend to stop lecturing me."

I pulled myself up to the front of the car, "Luke's not my boyfriend, Cecilia."

"Yeah, Catalina doesn't want that," Luke said. "Apparently, I'm not good enough." Ear buds in.

The front of the car was silent. My hand went onto Luke's shoulder. He didn't respond right away. I nudged him. Luke's eyes stayed fixed on the scenery. Passive aggressive behavior was my main line of defense, but I never knew how to handle it on the receiving end. Maybe I should make a joke and brush it off. No, that wasn't me. Forgiveness was what I had to seek.

If I wanted him to forgive me, I had to at least show some compassion. "Luke, I'm sorry. It's not you, it's me."

"You're gonna have to do better than that," Aaron commented. How would he know?

Cecilia turned around to me, "Sex will make it

better." I rubbed my temples. Why, God? Why did you make her my sister?

Aaron laughed, "Calm down, tiger. Sex doesn't solve everything."

"I think it does."

"You're not helping, Cecilia," I pleaded.

"You're right. Sex isn't Luke's strong suit."

I smacked her arm. Too late. Luke's body slumped down into the seat. Aaron concentrated on the road. Cecilia mouthed the word, "Whatever," in my direction. Now it was up to me to smooth things over…again. I took the easy route and watched the endless tree line.

After about thirty minutes of silence, the oasis amongst the trees emerged. Still no snow. Aaron passed the cute little houses and stopped outside a white building with a tall, sharp black roof and long windows on both floors. A lighthouse stared out into the lake which was a quarter of the size of Settlement Island Lake.

There, I had finally seen my lighthouse! It was a silly but prized moment for me. "Aaron, is the lighthouse real?" I said with a smirk.

Aaron laughed, "Nope, it's fake." Eyes up at me, "The next time I clear my schedule, I'll take you to the coast, so you can get your fill of them."

Cecilia passed a look between us. I thought of Ronda. The way she glanced between me and Gavin. I wasn't afraid of Cecilia like I was Ronda, nor did I have any reason to be. I had done nothing wrong, and I intended to keep it that way.

"Cecilia, come with us," I said before realizing how ridiculous my request was.

Aaron kissed her hand. "I can't forget my girl. There's this cute bed and breakfast I'm gonna take you to." She nibbled into his neck.

I pursed my lips. The real lighthouses could wait.

Dad had reserved a cabin with six bedrooms and a tremendous view of the lake. Not too different from the situation at our house. Cecilia and I shared a bathroom, but we were pretty much alone on our side of the property, except for Aaron. He stayed with her. Dad allowed this.

Luke's room was across the kitchen, next to his parents'. Mother set the tone, stating that it's not proper for a man to share a room with a woman unless they had an established relationship. Not that I minded, but I felt discounted. Like a child who wasn't allowed to make decisions for herself. Besides, Dad and Mother were a bit premature with their assumptions. After all, they didn't know about Luke's "inabilities."

Once we got all settled in, we gathered in the living room to plan our weekend. Luke and his parents were absent due to a phone call from his grandmother. Apparently, it took three people to walk her through a scare at her nursing home. Or so Luke mentioned before giving me the cold shoulder on his way out.

I didn't really care what was going on with him, but I was grateful to be free of the shame and guilt creeping into my heart. Cecilia curled up next to Aaron as he threw his arm around her. Why couldn't something like this be easy for me and Luke? All seemed to be forgiven on their front. They did look cute together, all snuggled up, but it didn't seem right since it was all a lie. I sat down adjacent to them.

Mother thumbed through the travel brochure, "Let's do the wine tasting! We get to sample seven different wines paired with appetizers and a full-course dinner."

"Sounds good," Cecilia chimed in. Her mouth went to Aaron's. They kissed for an extended time.

"Better get ready." Mother went out of her way to kiss my forehead. "Dinner starts at seven." She made a dash for her bedroom to fix her hair and makeup, which wasn't needed. She was glamourous, as always.

Dad and Cecilia followed her lead, each disappearing into their parts of the house. Now, it was just me… and Aaron. I eyed my bedroom door.

"Catalina, we need to talk about what happened the other day." He shifted further into the couch and patted the seat next to him. No, I wasn't doing that.

"Don't worry about it," I said.

"You were really upset. There were scratches on your arms and knees." His fingers clenched into a fist, "Who attacked you?"

For a second or two, I took in all the frustration and anger on Aaron's face. So different from the sweet kiss he had placed on my forehead. Tread softly, I told myself. "No one did anything to me."

"Okay…so what did he try to do?" By now the skin around his knuckles was white.

"Aaron, this seems personal to you." I paused, wanting to describe how he was making me feel. I decided against it.

He slouched forward in my direction, laced fingers rested on his knees. "My older cousin was raped. It changed her life. I'll never let that happen to another woman I care about."

A sigh escaped my lips, "I'm not in that kind of trouble."

Aaron moved in closer, "I saw you running for your life." I shifted my weight. "You were scared to death." He didn't take long to ask, "What kind of trouble were you in?"

Shit, how do I get out of this one? "Did you follow me?" I said.

"Tell me what you know, and I'll share what's on my mind."

Something sinister had taken ahold of Aaron. I could feel it on him. "Well, if you did follow me, what did you see?"

Aaron shook his head and paused, "It's not what I saw, but rather a hunch. Did you find someone out there?"

The trap had been laid so carefully. And I was already in it. His eyes were now dark, black. He knew. I glanced at the clock. "I've gotta go get ready." I raced to my room and locked the door.

I pressed my head against the wood and allowed my

body to slide down. No breathing! He could probably sense that I was still so close. But I did scold myself for admitting that someone was with me. What if Aaron saw Gavin and this was the last piece he needed to figure everything out? Did he hear anything about the murders? Now, I couldn't breathe. Two light knocks, almost taps, hit the door right above my head.

"Catalina?" It was Luke. No sign of him talking to anyone else. I rose and opened the door a bit. His eyes twitched. "Can I come in for a moment?"

I didn't move. "I'm sorry about everything that's been going on between us," was my reply. "But I need to get ready."

"It's the sex thing, isn't it?"

So bold. I accidently stepped back, opening the door with me. He took advantage of my shock and invited himself in. "I can't believe Adrienne. What a bitch."

I closed the door, "Luke, don't worry about her." He could see how uncomfortable I was. Each eye twitch gave it away. I tried to think of a clever way to bring up my problems with Aaron and his damn intuition. That would bring Luke some solace.

"Catalina," his voice replicated his bruised ego, "if having sex with me is something you're worried about, let's talk."

He was more courageous than I could ever be. "It's not that," I said. Now, time for a subject change. We both needed it. "Luke, I gotta ask you about Aaron. Is he a trustworthy person?"

Luke's head rolled back. "You're into Aaron now?"

"Luke, no. Not at all. I just need to know if you trust him."

"He's a doctor, so I think that kinda makes him a trustworthy guy." He dropped down on the bed. I imagined all these mind games and emotional runs were bound to get old. "Beyond that, I don't know much about him."

I sat next to Luke. Now, how would I bring up the next part? The important part? "There's something about Aaron that just doesn't feel right to me."

His contemplation focused on me. "Like how?"

A very good question that I didn't have an answer for. But I couldn't accuse him and leave it at that. "He just seems like he's got something on me. Like he's trying to blackmail me."

"What for?"

Sitting there, having this conversation with Luke, reminded me that I couldn't go any further without pulling him into my real troubles. "It's just a hunch. He's probably trying to use me to get my sister to love him or something."

Thankfully, someone knocked on the door and opened it. It was Dad. He looked at the two of us and smiled. Great.

"Catalina, your mom's ready for the tasting."

I leaped off the bed. "Let's go." Dad vanished before I could excuse myself.

Luke was already up and close to me. My throat closed. "Catalina, um, I'm sure that Aaron's probably being nice to you because your dad's his boss. And in a place like Settlement Island, he's got a pretty good job." I nodded. Luke's conclusion made sense, which would not probe for any more questions from him. No eye twitching, yet I knew there was more. "Listen, I don't mind helping you and being your friend, but I gotta make something clear; I don't play games. So, I need to know whether you like me or not."

Luke had no idea who he had become. That unsure guy I had met no longer stood before me. He had found a confidence somewhere inside himself that was no less than…sexy. And that's when I knew. I actually liked Luke.

A smile appeared on my face. I liked Luke! This revelation brought a calm sense of control to my life.

"Catalina?" Luke said.

I fluttered my eyelashes a few times and focused. "Luke, I like you," I paused, "and I'm open to the possibility of us dating. But," there was always a but with me, "not yet. I don't think I'm ready."

He chuckled, "So, you're interested in dating me?"

"Almost," I said. "Not quite."

"What more do you want?" he said. His eagerness was borderline needy.

I didn't want anything more than to have my feelings push me completely over to him. But that would never happen. It was sad, really. I had to be true to myself.

"I believe that a relationship can only work if there's trust and honesty. I want to be honest with you, however, I can't. There are things I just can't tell you yet. So, until that changes, nothing can change between us."

He wanted more, that was obvious. One foot closer to me. A smile. "I appreciate your honesty and your maturity. It's better to be sure than to lead me on." He smiled, and the drama was all over. "Are you ready for this whole wine-dinner thing?" I nodded.

He locked his arms with mine. We walked into the living room where everyone was waiting. Mother noticed us first, her eyes drifting to the position of our arms. She was happy, which would make dinner a breeze. We left the house and headed down the gravel road to the other side of the resort.

Luke placed his arm around me and smiled wildly. I guess I was forgiven, even though I didn't deserve his kindness. We were not together, but I gave him this touch. The closeness. And I was okay with it. At least I knew Luke wasn't going to end up dead center in someone's murder plot.

The restaurant rested at the edge of the winery and orchard. Apple wine was a thing in The Pines. While waiting for our table, we learned all about the history of The Pines and the resort's rich wine production. The Seafood and Wine festival would help us pay homage to the summer months and the robust apples it had provided. I imagined that the orchard would look more like a graveyard once the frost set in. Most of the apples had been rescued from the chilly nights and mornings. Any apples that remained were bound to bear the elements on their own.

The leaves were already changing color, a reminder to the residents of Maine to prepare for warm fires and bundling up. My first blistery-frigid winter was on the way. My yearning heart prompted me to think of my trip back home. California ocean breezes, that's what this winter would mean to me.

We sat at our table, and the first course of appetizers came out. The first wine we tried was an expensive red. I drank my glass without savoring the taste. Then came a glass of the next wine. Thankfully, dinner followed soon after. The roasted duck served with a dark red was a good mix.

I took a break from drinking and surveyed the restaurant. Everything was so romantic. A live band was setting up. Dad cleared his throat. Another speech, of course.

He held up his glass, "I'd like to toast to Aaron, my new partner! He's been a terrific addition to the practice and the overall vision of the hospital. I look forward to seeing what you can do and learning a thing or two from you."

Everyone raised their glasses and said their cheers. Aaron stood.

"Well, I feel honored to be working with you, Dr. Payton. You have a great family, and I'm so happy to be here with you all today."

Cecilia jumped up. I could tell this wasn't planned, but no one said anything. "I'd like to thank my parents for blessing me with this amazing life. And to Aaron for being such a great boyfriend!" She leaned down and kissed him. Everyone cheered, a light roar of approval.

This was our life. Simple, expensive, and safe. I put my glass down as I contemplated her last word. Boyfriend. The position Luke vied heavily for. Something I couldn't give him.

If I were to choose someone to be with…but I couldn't. I wasn't able to summon my heart to do anything of the sort. My love had been chosen for me. It was dark and unpredictable, just like I needed it be. And it was strong and stubborn, exactly how I wanted it to be.

The only necessities in this life, my life, were the things that truly mattered. And somewhere, and in some small moment, I mattered to him. He had probably met so many people, known some of them intimately, but I mattered enough to share his life and destiny.

All the reign of terror had consumed me. The elegant, yet fearful dance that we had shared moved us to and away from each other. Gavin had taken me, and because of him, I would never be the same.

Luke put his hand on my shoulder, "Are you okay?"

Then there was Luke: the safe friend who would never get it. He would never hold my affections, no matter how hard he lobbied for them.

I felt the moment come over me. The feeling of relaxing into the truth. The choice had been made, and I could no longer ask myself to deny it.

A smile to Luke. "I'm gonna go get some air." I was up before he or anyone could ask me questions.

The sun had ducked below the tree line which settled perfectly with my mood—hopelessly dark. I put my elbows on the railing and gave into the broken feeling that had consumed my heart.

I never thought I'd fall in love this way. I imagined that it would be a happy occasion that was solidified by a tight embrace and meaningful sex. But I stood there, alone, not knowing what to say or do next.

"I can tell something's bothering you," Mother said behind me.

"What?" I replied, my voice slightly low.

"Catalina, things are going to work out for you, too. Just be patient."

She ran her fingers through my hair in an effort to comb it. I couldn't reject her comfort. "Mom, why does life have to be so hard? Why does it seem like darkness takes over everything?"

Mother leaned against the railing and faced me, "Honey, what do you mean?"

"I'm on a dark roller coaster ride, and I have nowhere to go. The darkness rides with me, and I have no way to stop it."

Riding with Darkness—I had never thought of it like that. Gavin's darkness. We were connected, attached in a way that tore me from the warm relief of everyone I knew. I hated the suffering I continued to endure by just knowing him. Yet, I couldn't stop myself from craving him.

"It doesn't have to be complicated." I rested my head on her shoulder, "Catalina, I don't think Luke has a dark side. He seems like a nice guy."

"If he wasn't rich, would you still feel the same way?"

She sighed, "Of course…I think." I rolled my eyes, "Honey, people can change. We aren't stuck with being the same person all our lives." She smiled, "When I was your age, you and I were a lot alike. I was an antisocial soul, just like you."

My eyebrow raised, "Really?" Mother nodded. "So, you understand me? And you never said anything?"

"I never needed to. I know you pretty well, better than you might know yourself." I started to contradict her. "So, let it go. Whatever it is you're holding on to, let it go. Just be in the moment and feel whatever it is you want to feel."

"That doesn't help me."

Mother stroked my hair. "I'm sure it will, if you try it." She kissed my forehead. "You are far too smart and too beautiful to be held captive by anything."

This was the nicest my mother had ever been to me.

Cecilia joined us, "Here you two are!"

Mother smiled at me, "I hope you'll always remember that." She would never know this, but I would never forget her words.

"Dad's had a good amount of wine already," Cecilia interrupted, "And he needs your assistance with the check."

Mother patted my back. I nodded as she walked away and inside.

Oh, Cecilia. "You have to apologize to Luke," I said.

"What are you and lover boy doing tonight?" she said with a light lisp.

My brow raised at her obviously tipsy self. "I'm not sure if you can handle tonight."

"Of course, I can! Come out with me to the bar, and I'll prove it."

"You have to apologize to Luke first," I said.

"Nah, I'm fine." Luke came up to me. Cecilia scurried away without making eye contact. Not that it mattered. He didn't seem concerned with her. "So, uh, we're getting ready to leave." His voice was sweet.

"Right. I was just talking to my mom," I was rambling. "And Cecilia—she wants to go out tonight."

"Yeah, she and Aaron have the whole weekend party scene planned out for us."

A shiver ran up my arm, not because of the cold, but because of something else. "Aaron doesn't seem like the partying type."

Luke laughed, "He's not. Took me by total surprise when he brought it up."

Another intrigue for me to follow, yet again. All the mystery and secret motives were driving me crazy. "We should stay in."

"Normally, I'd be all for that, but I wanna go out and get wasted."

This was my doing. My fault. "Okay, but only for a little bit." A thin smile followed.

I turned toward the tree line for one last view before complete darkness set in. A few straggling vacationers walked back to their cabins. A man, dressed in all black, walked briskly past them. Short blond hair. I knew him. My hand clasped over my mouth. It was James.

Chapter Eighteen
Target

I lost James in the crowd of diners heading off to various eateries. Luke ushered me inside, and we finished up dinner without any more interruptions. I wanted to ask Cecilia about James. Did Cecilia invite him here? She couldn't be that stupid, right? There was the possibility that he came on his own accord. Maybe to talk to me, which I was open to.

That idea stayed with me as Cecilia drug us out partying. Like many other nights out, I expected her to dance the night into oblivion as I watched. But at least the resort had several bars and restaurants to choose from. I huddled close to Luke as he held the door for me. Music, blasting loud. Very little lighting. And tons of young people. Yes, I should have stayed in my room.

Cecilia pushed past me, Aaron in tow, and took up residence on the dance floor. He seemed uncomfortable, trying to control her body as she slammed up against him, hard. Luke pointed to the bar, "I'm gonna go get us some drinks."

I looked in that general direction and found my mark. My hand latched onto Luke's arm, "No, I've got this round."

My shoulders went back as I stomped toward the bar. "James!" I said over the music.

"Baby Sister!" He grinned. "I thought I saw you on the deck earlier, but I couldn't come by and chat. How are you this evenin'?" So cool and unsuspecting.

"What are you doing here?"

"Workin'." James handed off a few beers to the man next to me. He gave me a wink to stay put and mixed another drink for a girl with thick eyebrows. No flirting from him, just a nice compliment. "Cecilia wants to get together tonight. Cover for us?"

I leaned into the bar, "James, we need to talk about our last conversation."

"Not now." His body moved to the music as he sang the words and made more drinks.

"When?"

"Give me some time to figure that out." He popped open a beer, "Didn't expect you to be here or else I would have planned something."

"Like what?"

He shrugged, "I don't know. Kidnap ya, Gavin style."

James poured me a rum and coke and him a shot, "You gotta get Gavin to know the truth about Kyle. All you have to do is drop the idea in his head."

"He won't listen to me."

James disagreed and held up his shot, motioning for me to grab my drink. We toasted, and I sipped it. Before the alcohol could touch my tongue, Luke grabbed the glass from me and downed it.

"What's going on?" he said to James, aggressively.

James downed his shot, "Nothin', man. What's up with you?"

"Are you flirting with my girlfriend?" Really, Luke? He had to know I wouldn't approve of this. But his interaction with James would help me see his limits.

James looked at me, "Nah, man," he paused, "I'm gay." He winked. I rolled my eyes.

"You serious?" Luke was both angry and perplexed.

"Yeah. Got a boyfriend with these blue-gray eyes. He's dark and mysterious with a soul as harsh as the black, angry car he drives." James's description of Gavin was spot on. Impressive. Then his eyebrows narrowed. "Got somethin' against gay guys?"

Luke put his hands up, "Nah, man. Didn't know you went that way."

"Where's your boyfriend right now?" I said to James.

"Don't know. Maybe he's makin' plans to leave town." His eyes flashed up to Cecilia and Aaron. He ducked into my line of sight.

Now, James was busy keeping the crowd of angry partiers from jumping over for a free sip. Luke got another bartender's attention, and we had another round to take back.

Luke howled, "What the fuck did you put in her drink?"

James laughed, "You'll see." He turned to me, "We'll continue our girl talk later." He poured me another shot. Luke took it, too. "You're a good person, Catalina," said James, "Don't forget that." His gaze went away from me for good and onto other patrons.

Luke grabbed my hand, "I finally have you away from Gavin Scott, and you're hanging out with the bartender?" His eyes twitched.

I put on a smile. "Luke, there's no one else out there I'd rather be with than you. You're my best friend."

"Let's dance."

"I don't dance."

I was pulled onto the dance floor, anyway. Keeping up with Luke's swaying was the first challenge. We tilted back and forth. His face came into mine as the song lyrics spilled from his lips. Drunk Luke could sing pretty good. I let him guide us through the rhythms, my body holding onto him. The mixture of alcohol and pheromones was the next challenge. My fingernails brushed down his back as I steadied him against me. He moaned.

We were getting closer. This isn't what I had planned, but he didn't seem to know that. I knew he would kiss me, even if the moment wasn't right. I bit my lip, nervous about what was going to happen next. Luke's foot stomped down on mine.

He pulled my face to his, "Feel the music…" a pause. "What's…" His fingertips dug into my shoulders. We began to topple over.

My heels planted down hard as I shifted Luke's weight on me. I thought it was a joke until his head flopped forward and then up. Pain crawled through my chest. This was bad. "Cecilia!"

She, alone, rushed over to me.

"I think he's had too much to drink," I said to her.

His weight was giving in, along with my back. She put her strength into helping us both up. It was no use.

"Luke, you're gonna have to stand. We can't hold you," my voice was straining as my body slipped into fatigue.

Cecilia came around and grabbed his arms. Seconds later, I was upright. Hands supported my back. Cecilia's face held both shock and appreciation.

"We need to get him outta here," said Gavin. He came around and threw Luke's arm over his shoulder. Cecilia and I followed, bracing him on the other side.

She patted my back, "Don't worry about him. I'll make sure James pays for this."

This wasn't a threat, but rather a promise of rough sex. "Where's Aaron?" I said.

"Dad texted him. There was some sort of medical emergency or something." Good. I didn't need him around, too.

The doorman stopped us. Cecilia put on her charm, but he still didn't permit us to leave. A short conversation with Gavin, and we were on our way to Gavin's car.

Gavin opened his door, and Cecilia hopped into the back without protest. She grabbed Luke and placed his head on her lap. Seat in position, I slid in next to Gavin.

✌

Gavin and Cecilia helped me sneak Luke into my room. They tossed him onto the bed. I checked for a pulse: still alive.

"James is a dick," Gavin said as he folded his arms.

"Why would he do this to Luke?" Cecilia said.

"He thinks it's funny."

I said nothing to the contrary. But if they ever learned I was the intended target, I would allow them to seek their vengeance on him.

Cecilia sat down on the bed next to Luke. She stroked his hair, a gesture of care and support for someone who meant absolutely nothing to her. "Gavin, what's the deal?" she said.

This was going to be interesting. I never really saw any exchanges between Gavin and my sister. If it went well, I could learn something from her.

"I'll sort it out," he said. "Did James tell you anything?" She nodded.

"I'm sorry," I cut in, "what are you talking about?"

They motioned for the other to answer. "James can't stay in Settlement Island for long," Cecilia said. "Neither can Gavin. All the drama between Kyle and James is starting a war."

I already knew that. "What are you going to do? Are you going to convince James to leave?" I said to Cecilia.

The bed moved. Luke swatted to get up. "I'm gonna hurl."

"Come on, honey," Cecilia said, "I'll take you." She

put one of her arms under him and helped him to the bathroom.

Gavin said nothing to break the silence, so I went first, "I didn't know you'd be here." My statement wasn't accusing him of anything. It was the truth.

He contemplated my words, just for a moment, but not for too long, "I can't leave you like this with a sick golden boy on your hands."

"My dad's a doctor. He'll be fine." I cleared my throat, "But that's not what I mean. You're here…at The Pines."

"It's a popular place to go."

Normally, I would shout orders for him to stop crowding my space or to leave me alone. But now that I had chosen him to be my crush, these behaviors didn't seem appropriate.

Cecilia summoned Gavin to help her pull Luke up and place his body back on the bed. She tilted Luke's head to the side, making sure he could breathe.

"You're really good at this," Gavin complimented her. Not a slight at all.

"When you party all the time, you've gotta take care of the lightweights." Cecilia glanced at me. I nodded. She then wrapped Luke in a blanket. "I should get to my room before Aaron comes back in."

I gave her a hug, "Thank you for everything."

She kissed my cheek, "Be sure to wrap it up in a condom." One wink, and she was gone.

Gavin sat down on the bed next to Luke, "When did she grow a heart?"

A laugh tickled my lips. "I'm not sure."

He looked down at Luke, "I've always wondered what it'd be like to be him."

"What? Having a rich family?"

He paused, "It must be easy, you know?" I nodded. "He just gets up in the morning and lives. No worries."

"You could find a way to have that life, too."

Gavin pressed on before I could ask anything else. "He's a nice guy. You don't want that?"

"No." I wanted to tell him more. "I, uh, just need some time to sort through all this stuff. Him, you, the murders."

"Smart. Did I ruin Settlement Island for you? Did I kill your chances at a normal life?"

That was a worthwhile question. One that I wondered about myself. I took a deep breath, "No," I paused, "This is my home now. I like it here."

The fierce look returned, "If I were you, I'd get the fuck out and never look back."

This is what James had hoped for. A pathway in to level with Gavin and tell him Kyle's motives. "Maybe you should take your own advice." His eyebrows furrowed. "James wants you to go before Kyle gets you killed."

"Really?"

I nodded and then caught myself, "But, it's up to you. I know you don't think Kyle would ever disobey you, but James is pretty sure about his estimations."

"What do you think?"

Luke muffled something and opened his eyes, "Catalina?" His timing couldn't have been less appreciated. I put my hand on his arm for comfort. He panted some, "I feel like shit," two big gulps of air, "How much did I drink?"

Gavin's lips turned upward into a smirk. Jerk. "Luke, you should get some rest," I said.

"No!" he wiggled into a sitting position, "I've been… waiting for this…weekend…with you…for so long."

"You should be sleeping," I pleaded.

Luke looked over at Gavin, "Hey, what's up, man?"

Gavin just stared at him. Luke snapped his fingers in my face. "Catalina! I'm sorry I…your…weekend… is ruined."

Keep your patience. "Don't worry about that. It's not your fault."

He put his sweaty hands on my lips. I looked over at Gavin who couldn't stop the grin from crossing his face. "Things! I want to say things…"

I pulled my head from his hands, "Come on, Luke. Go back to sleep, so you'll be more you tomorrow."

My upper body hit his chest as I pushed him down. He tried to tangle me up into a hug, but I scrambled out.

"You know about them, don't you?" Luke said.

I shrugged, "Know about what?"

"The murders?" Luke said. He shifted downward into the bed, his eyes closing.

Gavin and I made rapid movements to get Luke to keep awake.

"Whose been murdered?" Gavin said.

"Aaron…" He shifted again on the bed. We pleaded with him to continue. "Aaron said you'd know."

Luke closed his eyes and started moaning in a mixture of pain and confusion. I shook his arm. Gavin motioned to the door. I got up, and we stepped out onto the porch together. I peeked in at Luke before focusing on Gavin.

His black button-down shirt, dark jeans, and black boots made his appeal hard to fight. Hard to pay mind to anything but how much I wanted to kiss him. But I resisted.

"Is he talking about Aaron White?" he said. I shrugged. "Cecilia's boyfriend." His arms folded.

"Probably."

"Why would Aaron know anything?"

I started to bite my lip but didn't, "James is attached to Cecilia, and she's dating Aaron. Maybe he found out through her." Believable, but totally untrue.

He walked up to me. I took a step back. "Why are you lying to me?"

I was afraid again. "I can't say for sure." But he didn't seem angry but rather taken aback by my lie.

Gavin shifted his weight. "Catalina, I can't protect you if you don't tell me the truth."

"I'm not the one who needs protecting."

I took another step forward, and we were close. He nodded, "Do you think I'm scared of Kyle? He was at my house, yesterday, counting his sins. Asking for forgiveness for everything."

"That won't keep him from killing you," I said. Gavin's eyes were dark. "You have to be smart. This isn't a game. If he's coming for you, he's not gonna listen to reason."

"That's not who I am," he said. "You know that." He received a text message. After a quick view of the screen, he came back to me. "Let's talk about it tomorrow."

"Tomorrow?"

"I would like to see you."

A sweet tingle ran through my stomach. I had to make sure it was warranted. "You want to talk about James?"

He blinked slowly, "No, I just want to spend time with you." No more space between us. Gavin grinned, "I owe you for always putting up with me. And you owe me an opportunity to pay my debt."

This unexpected twist had me stumped. A debt he had to pay me. Some sort of score he had been keeping. My next move was simple, just a nod. "Until tomorrow, I guess." He turned toward the door, and I muttered, "Is it that simple? You don't want anything else from me?"

His lips caressed my cheek before he kissed it. I refrained from touching him. "Where shall we meet?"

"The main building. Nine o'clock." He looked in at Luke, "Take care of him."

"I will."

"Goodnight, Catalina."

I watched him go. Back to Luke.

"Who were you talking to?" he said as I touched him.

"No one. Now go to sleep." I tucked the blankets around him.

And we were intertwined together. How did he manage that? A tinge of alcohol and sweat brushed my nose.

"I love you," was the last thing he said before everything went completely silent.

My intentions were clear—grab a pillow and blanket and head to the floor. However, Luke felt comfortable with his torso parallel to mine. His breath on my neck as he breathed heavily.

Was this what marriage was like? A man and a woman, their bodies woven in between each other and the sheets. The stillness. The anticipation of drifting off to sleep. For Luke, falling into a dream seemed so easy.

I laid there, feeling him breathe. Rhythmic breaths. I didn't mind it. He could have my body as his pillow. But my heart wasn't his for the taking. It was consumed by the torrid mysteries of Gavin Scott. Yet, there was something Luke had over Gavin. He was my key to figuring out Aaron's real reason for befriending my family. And that made him my next target.

Chapter Nineteen

Interrogation

"Cat, are you still in there?" Cecilia whispered into my door. But it was a loud whisper that I'm sure Luke had heard.

"What time is it?" he murmured. Eight o'clock. Too early for my sister to be up. Luke grabbed his head, "Tell her to stop, please."

My feet touched the cold floor. Each step made me want to turn back. I cracked the seal a few inches for her to see me, "Hey, Luke isn't feeling too pretty right now."

Her eyes dipped into the room and then to me. "How was your night? Did Gavin go home?"

"Yeah, last night. Will you help me get Luke out of my room?"

"Sure." She leaned in, "Aaron and the parents have plans to hit the festival in an hour. After breakfast."

"Luke's in no condition for breakfast. Or more alcohol."

"Well, Dad made it clear that he expects you and Luke to be ready to have the vacation of your lives."

"I'll do what I can." Luke had joined our conversation. My head turned in his direction. No shirt. Just tight chest muscle ridges.

"Just, um, take it easy," Cecilia stammered. "And take your time." Then she vanished.

"Luke, where's your shirt?"

Sexy, sleepy grin. "I got hot."

I rolled my eyes, "Come on, you've gotta get ready."

"Before I go, tell me what happened last night."

"You drank a little too much," was all I said. He didn't ask for additional details, which I appreciated.

At the start of the festival, Mother did pry into what had happened the night before. Luke's obvious condition gave us away. She knew nothing about Luke staying the night, but she did question why I was rushing off so early in the morning. The solution was easy—I had left my ID at the bar. Enough said.

When I walked through the doors of the empty bar, James was so focused on the twenty-dollar bills flipping through his fingers, he didn't notice me slip into the seat across from him. He went about his tasks, still ignoring me. A song overhead inspired him to sing. He had a nice, deep voice.

"Good morning, James."

His eyes shot up, "Hey, Baby Sister! Don't scare me like that!"

"Oh, it's the least I can do after the stunt you pulled last night!"

He threw the money into a bag and put it in a drawer, "Relax, your boyfriend took the drink, so no harm done."

I shook my head, "James, why did you try to poison me?"

"I'm sorry, baby. It wasn't gonna hurt you, I promise."

"James…"

He nodded, "I figured you'd get sick and dizzy, and Gavin would come in and save you. Then, that would create the perfect front for you to tell him." His hand landed on mine, "Sorry, darlin'." James winked at me and pushed himself off the bar. "What are you drinkin'?"

"Nothing. You couldn't possibly think that poisoning me would make Gavin believe the Kyle thing?"

"Well, if you've come all the way down here for an apology, you've gotten that, so…"

I leaned in, "I told Gavin."

James looked at me with a slight grin, "Did he listen?" he poured a mixture of rum and coke together.

My eyes drifted down. "I'm not sure."

"Well, that settles that." James sipped the drink. Back to more work. I figured he would have an endless stream of things to say, but he didn't.

Had I missed something? Was the urgency to get Gavin to understand his fate no longer an issue? If so, what had changed? I didn't ask at first; his answers probably wouldn't help me understand his position any better.

But this was a great opportunity for me to pry. Ask him another question that had baffled me for far too long.

My intrigue took me away for a moment. "James, if Gavin believes that Kyle is trying to kill him, what will he do?"

"Leave," he scoffed. It was a simple answer, almost an immediate reaction.

"Leave Settlement Island and go to Anders?"

"No, he'd leave the state. If Porter and Kyle are runnin' around fuckin' killin' everybody, and Kyle's on the wrong side of the crew, Gavin can't stay here. He'd have to go." Another sip, "Us Settlers are only so loyal, and Kyle has lots of ways to get people twisted on Gavin. So, to save his life, and to keep the peace in the streets, he'd find somewhere else to stay."

"James, what are you talking about?" I paused, "Are you saying Gavin has more enemies than just Porter?"

"We're like trophies. We've put a lot of people out of business. Lots of people would like to cash in Gavin's card, I'm sure. They might not be as motivated as Porter…but, they will." He shook his head, "If you told him flat out, and he didn't believe you, there's nothin' we can do."

James didn't stay tuned in for too long. His eyes wondered around the bar, looking for something to do. Easily distracted.

"If you care about him so much, why aren't you trying harder to get him out of here?"

He sighed, "What am I supposed to do, kidnap him?

Use that chloride shit on him to knock him out, then drag his ass out of town?"

"Chloroform."

"Whatever," he snapped. "Gavin still thinks Kyle would never go twisted." He shrugged, "I'm outta ideas."

My hand went into a fist. "So, it's done? All that trouble for nothing?" I shouted.

"No…not nothin'," he said. "He's gotta see it for himself."

"The only way…" I bit my lip. My throat went dry. "The only way he'll believe you is if Kyle put a gun to his head. Is that what you're telling me?"

James's back went into the bar, holding himself up. "Baby Sister, I'm tired of all this shit. Been tired of it. Just cause I wouldn't leave him doesn't mean I have to follow him to the grave. The crew's divided: he doesn't think Kyle will turn on him, and I do. I fuckin' hate Kyle, and Gavin probably thinks that's why I'm throwin' all this heat around. So, fuck it. If he wants to take Kyle's side, that's on him."

I didn't want to admit it. And I'd never admit it to anyone. But I understood exactly where James was coming from. He had done his job, just like I had. We were kindred spirits by this fact and ready to go our separate ways.

"So, how long have you been in love with him?" His angry exhaustion turned into a smirk.

His words caused a shiver to run down my skin. "I don't love him. I'm worried about what's gonna happen.

His death would only be the beginning of a downward spiral. Or so it seems."

"This is cute." And with this remark, his mood was uplifted. "Are you one of the millions of girls in town who wants to tame his wild heart?" He took a large drink and waited for me to answer. I looked down. "You know, he probably loves you, too."

"Why would you say that?"

He leaned against the bar close to me, "I've known Gavin since the 3rd grade, and he's never gone out of his way for someone as much as he goes out of his way for you."

"Does he talk about me?" I was trying to stay coy, but I'm sure James was onto me. "Just trying to find another angle to help Gavin see the truth."

He leaned in further, his breath on my face, "You know, Porter has spies all over the place."

I pushed him back, "You think I'm working for that guy?"

He straightened up, "No, but you have to understand, we try to keep our personal lives to a minimum. Anyone who's attached to us can become collateral damage."

A laugh should have escaped my lips. A chuckle or cackle. His conclusion was ludicrous. "Gavin is collateral damage to me," seemed to be my best defense.

"And you like it. You love the suspense. The drama."

"He scares me sometimes."

James sighed, "Yeah, I can see that. But don't worry, he'd never hurt you."

Nothing was said for a few minutes. I'm sure James wanted me to ask more questions to prove that Gavin loved me, but I believed him. Or I hoped I did.

I moved on and dug down deep to find something else worth his attention. "How much of this does Cecilia know?"

James grinned, "That is not up for conversation today. But I've got a few questions for you about this Aaron asshole."

"What do you want to know?" I said.

He shook his head and killed his drink, "Tell me about him."

James poured himself another rum and coke, this time with a lot more alcohol than soda. Something was going on…I could feel it. "Why do you care about Aaron? Other than the obvious reason."

His eyes lost their normal carefree color. "I don't trust him."

"He's been nice to me…of course that could all be a show." I chuckled, "I think he's secretly lobbying for the fair Cecilia's heart, which is disgusting." James opened himself up to say something but seemed to pause intentionally. Almost like he wanted me to guess his next statement. "My friend Luke says Aaron might know something about the murders. Is that it?" I said.

"I've lived in Settlement Island all my life. I know everyone. But I've never met this motherfucker before."

"He's attached to the country club," I reasoned. "That might be why."

"Baby Girl, I used to live in the club. My dad's ex-girlfriend was a black widow."

I put my hand on my chest. "No way!"

He nodded, "Bitch was loaded and crazy. I hated her."

James always knew how to surprise me. "So," I said, "you don't live there anymore?"

"Right now, I've got an address in the trailer park on the other side of Maine Street. You've probably never been down there."

And I intended to keep it that way. "Well, I can't see you living in the club." I smiled, "We couldn't handle someone like you."

James finished his drink, "Catalina, I don't trust Aaron. Stay away from him."

More orders barked at me. Yet James's warning seemed genuine. I brushed it off with a smile. "Look, you're a good person," he continued, "and I know you think I'm just bein' a dick, but I'm not. I've sold all over theses blocks, both in the club and in Settlement Island, and I know when things aren't right. And there's somethin' not right 'bout that guy."

What an admission of truth. I liked James in that moment, but Aaron was now part of my family. How could I tell James that? He would never understand. "I'll see what I can find out."

"Good."

James seemed to be done talking with me which was mildly disappointing. That was the thing about him; he was highly addictive. His nonchalant approach to life—he made it seem like he was cool and aloof, but James was neither. He could make you believe anything you wanted to, no matter what it cost you. No wonder Cecilia loved being with him.

I had a mind to tell him the true nature of his existence to my sister when he said, "You spy on Aaron for me, and I'll make sure our boy stays alive."

I wanted to agree, but I had to be careful. Yes, Gavin was in danger, and a pact with James to keep him alive would make me feel better. But before I accepted his arrangement, and stepped further into the plot, I had to settle one last thing. Confirm one more truth. "James," I sighed. "Did Gavin kill Chris?"

"No."

"Has he killed anyone?" I said.

His tongue lightly licked across his lips, "No. Neither have I. Kyle and Porter kill people." The relief was too much to hide. "You thought Gavin killed people? And you love him?"

"He's just kinda intense. The only things I know about him are what I've seen, and unfortunately, they're not good. All the violence and everything." An image came to mind. It was big and bright. I liked it. I liked it a lot. "What if you and Gavin came up with a truce?"

"What kinda truce?"

"Between you and this Porter guy." He tried to cut me off, but I didn't stop, "Settlement Island is a war zone, and I don't want Gavin to have to stay on the run. Besides, he's not gonna move, and I wouldn't ask him to. So, a truce could end all this and save everyone." I looked him right in the eyes, no blinking or second guessing my ask, "And you would be able to stay, too."

He nodded once. James then danced around the bar—a nervous kind of dance. He looked like someone getting ready to box. Then he stopped. He remained frozen, eyes trained on a corner of the bar. My head turned to the side, but he motioned for me to stop moving. Was it Gavin? The overwhelmed look on James's face said no. Time to go. I shifted my weight in the chair, slowly putting one foot on the ground.

"If you move he'll see me," he whispered.

"Who is it?" I whispered. His hand disappeared behind his back. He was reaching for something. "No, not here, James."

"Stop talking."

My teeth gripped onto my flesh. Things were evolving rapidly, and I only had James's contradicting facial expressions to gauge how we were doing. A smile seemed to indicate that someone of no harm was near. I could see the shadows cross the bar next to me and fade away. Once they had vanished, his eyes trained on something to the side of me again.

"You know, this really isn't fair to you," he said.

"Please tell me what's going on."

"It's better you don't know." Sometime during our interchange, he went back to bartending.

"James!" He put his hand on mine and shook his head. I huffed a sigh, "Can I go?"

James nodded, "Yeah, the coast's clear."

I had half a mind to scold him for being so vague,

but I desperately needed to go. "I'll find out what I can about Aaron. But please leave me out of the rest of this for now."

He scanned the bar again, "Catalina, I can't call a truce."

Wishful thinking, I knew it. But I still had hope. "Why not talk to Gavin and the others about it? Maybe they would agree."

He pursed his lips and sucked air in through his teeth, "It's just not who we are."

"But you haven't even tried. How do you know Gavin won't consider it? I mean, he's got a sick grandma at home. He would do anything to protect her."

"Look, this war is beyond us. People have been fightin' over turf since we were kids. We inherited the battle from them. That shit doesn't end overnight. Or because I put my life on the line to try to reason with the unreasonable. That's just a straight-up fairytale."

James had gotten too far under my skin. "You were the one who told Gavin about what Porter's dad did to his mom. You have to take more responsibility, James."

"That's only part of it. Before Gavin found out about his mom, we had a beef with Porter for tryin' to run our town." He beat his chest. "Settlement Island is our town. And no one owns us. We're not stepping down." I gave him a sad nod. "Sorry, baby, I'm not you're hero." He tilted his head toward the door, "Now get out of here."

"I'm disappointed in you, James. Really."

"Sweetheart, pride is pride," he said. "If you stick around Settlement Island long enough, maybe you'll get some, too. Settler's pride would look good on you." He winked and tilted his head toward the door.

I hesitated but relented to his request. My feet hit the floor, and I glanced over to the area he had watched so closely and found nothing.

Chapter Twenty
Distraction

My conversation with James left me disappointed. But I didn't have much time to ponder things. Dad and the others had lined up along the beach, in jackets, to soak up the mild sunrays that were shining. I plopped down next to Cecilia. She had intertwined her body with Aaron, who kissed her forehead. His eyes split from her and onto me. I gave him a short smile, but that didn't seem like enough.

Cecilia leaned over, "I'm so cold."

I looked between the two. She had to know what James had told me. But before I could mention a thing, I had to tread lightly. Sure, things couldn't have been too serious with Aaron, but he probably didn't know that. Plus, sharing my thoughts with Cecilia could make things worse. A lot worse.

"And you're back," Luke smiled and sat down next to me.

"Yeah, I went for a walk."

Luke narrowed his eyebrows, "Why didn't you ask me to come?" Cecilia waited for my response.

No more lies, I told myself. Luke deserved the truth. "I went to go talk to someone."

"Oh," he scoffed. Then he cheered up. "So, tonight I want to thank you for taking care of me last night."

What? No more inquiry into my disappearance? Cecilia turned her head to Aaron who was laughing at something she said. They were making fun of me, for sure. Aaron giving me a quick wink proved my assumptions. I chose not to get mad or be the brunt of their jokes any longer.

"Cecilia, Aaron. What plans do you have for the day?" I said.

Aaron placed a finger over his lips, "It's a surprise."

She smiled, "A surprise in the engagement department?"

Too soon. Way too soon. Aaron didn't respond but rather made a few faces that weren't very good. At least not for Cecilia. Luke mimicked a gun shooting him in the head. I didn't laugh. Instead, I said, "I'm sure Aaron would want to make sure he's the right guy for you first."

"Yeah, babe. It's only been like a month."

"Well, if you're gonna do it, don't wait till Christmas. Catalina's going back to Cali, and I'd hate for her to miss out on the celebration," Cecilia said.

This caught Luke off-guard. "You're thinking about leaving?" he said.

"Only for the holiday. My best friend and a bunch of

my family still lives there. We've got all these goofy traditions we do. I'm super excited."

"You should stay here," Luke muttered. "A Maine Christmas with white snow and good, home-cooked food could be pretty awesome."

"Nah, I'd trade in all the snow for the beach any day," said Aaron. "Hey, why aren't you going home for Christmas?" His question was for Cecilia who had moved on to looking at engagement rings on her phone. Large, expensive rings.

"Eloise and her boyfriend don't like me."

"It's not that they don't like you," I corrected her. "You never spend time with them. And when we go to visit, you're always trying to hook up with some…" Her phone no longer held her concentration. Aaron was a smart boy—I was sure he had filled in the blank.

"Well, we'll have to compare notes when you get back," Aaron said. He put out his hand for his girlfriend's, "Come on, let's go find some trouble before lunch."

Now it was Luke's turn to give me his assessment of how bad that whole conversation went. He laughed, hard. "You have this terrible habit of saying the wrong thing to the wrong person at the right time."

My lips curled into a smile, then I let out a laugh of my own. The irony. Cecilia was the one who took care of him, yet he still hated her. But I wouldn't say anything.

Luke climbed up to his feet and put a hand out for me to grab. I took it. "Wanna find some trouble before lunch, too? I know just the place."

꼬

Hiking and exploring were on the agenda. Dad and Mother were fine with this, based on Dad's visual assessment of Luke's clearly hungover face. But he didn't judge us, which made things easier for me.

Luke pushed himself to be present in the moments with me, even though I could tell he was still upset over our "status." I smiled at his efforts and ignored the feeling of guilt creeping into my stomach. No one should try that hard to please anyone, especially me. My apprehensions didn't last long. Luke's warm fingers wrapped around mine as he helped me over a few boulders that peaked above ground. Our destination: an overlook next to a shoreline. A swift drop to the lake below, if you weren't careful.

"Where are we?" I said.

"Other side of the lake." He pulled me into a hug, "It's very romantic at night."

"I'll bet."

A group of tourists climbed the boulders behind us. I moved away from Luke. Tight smile. Eye twitching.

Then we were alone, and I had a chance to soak in the quiet.

"Catalina," he spoke, "what am I to you?"

I could understand why he would ask. "You're my best friend."

"Yeah, but I think you should reconsider that. You told me you're not really looking for a boyfriend, but that doesn't mean you don't have feelings for someone else."

God, why did he have to keep bringing it up? Our relationship didn't need definitions or parameters. Why couldn't he just leave it at that? Keeping the balance between inviting Luke in as a friend and pushing him away was beginning to teeter toward the direction he wouldn't want it to go.

"Luke, don't make this something bigger than it needs to be."

"It's just," he paused, "I remember some things about last night. And I'm almost certain Gavin was there."

I nodded, not giving too much thought to what my answer should be. "Luke, Gavin is not my boyfriend. He's just a friend, like you. And Aaron."

"Like you and I are friends?"

A sigh. "Not really. I like you more than him," and I also love him, "because you're more of my style of friend. You bring joy and happiness to my life."

"And he doesn't?"

"Gavin's…well, he's kinda like the friend you have who's a work-in-progress. That one person who you want to believe in, but they have to take responsibility for their own life." Luke didn't respond. "With you, I don't have to worry about that. You've been great this whole time." Still nothing. "And, since you've been great, I'd like to spend more time with you, while we get more comfortable." A smile emerged from him. This was good. Gaining Luke's trust meant I could bring his Gavin point home. "You remember seeing Gavin last night, right?"

"Yeah, bits and pieces."

I backed away from him, so I could get a better read off his puffy face. "Well, he was there helping me, and Cecilia, get you home." A brief pause. "And right as he was leaving, you said something about the murders and Aaron. What did you mean by that?"

He shrugged, "What did I say?"

"You said Aaron told you I'd know about the murders."

Luke scratched the rough edges of his chin. "I don't know. Maybe it was a conversation that he was having with your dad. And your dad said something about you doing research or something." I sighed. "Why, is there more?"

"No," I stammered. "I was just taken aback by your comment. That's all."

"Have you been doing research?"

For this question, I had to buck up for a long conversation. I sat down on the ground and he did the same. Neither one of us spoke for several minutes. We just looked off at the scenic view. Below was the lake and what seemed like a few boats on the water. I needed this break to formulate the right plan to tell him. To open the door and bring him in on my secrets, the secrets that had driven us apart.

But I kept everything simple: not too much about Gavin's role in the murders. Instead, I focused on the ties I had made to my discoveries. The murders, bits of what James had told me about Porter, and a few things about Kyle. The tethers that held me close to the murder plot without giving away all the key players.

"What if Aaron did know something about the murders?" was Luke's response after all my admissions. I turned my attention back to him. "There's this thing about him and you. This quiet strength that's kinda rebellious and sorta caring. You guys shove people away, but deep down, you really do care."

"What does that have to do with the murders?"

He looked back out, "I think you're just kinda…" Then he stopped.

I shook my head, "Luke, I'm struggling to follow anything you're saying right now."

He stood, pacing, "I don't know how…" he rubbed his face. "You have, uh, put yourself in a very bad position."

"How?"

"I've been doing some research of my own," he said. My shoulders tightened. "The murders, actually." Luke's eye twitched. "I think Gavin might be killing people."

I wasn't sure how to proceed forward. "I know him," I said. "He's not a killer."

Luke pulled me up. "A few of the people around the club have been talking…"

"He's not a killer, Luke," I stressed.

I couldn't tell if he wanted to buy it. Regardless, Luke had moved on from me. Then he was still. I took a step back as a joke to see if he was looking at me or past me. My foot stumbled, and I broke away from him completely. I kept going, all the way to the ground. Embarrassment, complete and total embarrassment. I rolled over to my side to position myself, so I could get up. The goofy smile on my face vanished. I didn't move, nor did I breathe.

A foot was lying next to mine, within a few inches. There was brush covering other parts of her body. No blood. Or at least none that I could see.

Luke crouched down, "Catalina, is that…"

My fingers touched his cheek and turned his head down to the ground. He shot up and pulled out his phone, abandoning me. I didn't close my eyes. That would have brought nightmares, for sure. And I couldn't look away, she was too mesmerizing.

This was bad. I had to let Gavin know. He'd know what to do. But he wasn't here. I didn't know how to find him.

Luke stumbled through the call. He asked me a few fragment questions, but I had no answers. Then he appeared again, getting me up to my feet. "The authorities are on the way. We need to stay close by until they get here." He pointed to a rock a yard or two away. "But we're gonna go over there." I gave him a nod.

He held onto me. We were both cold. "Gavin didn't do this," I said into his chest.

Luke's grip got tighter. I felt his heart hitting me. I didn't blame him; I was scared, too, and still. Completely still, like I was honoring her.

Rosy red hair, hidden by the bushes, but still flowing, it stuck out. I didn't look at anything else but her hair.

If I was the praying type, I would have given in to God. Pouring out cries of help to someone bigger than I would ever be. Yet, I was held too tightly by my disbelief to plead with anyone.

Finally, a uniformed officer met us. He ushered Luke to one side and me to the other as more officers came in to control the scene. Most of the questions were directed to me, as I was the one closest to the discovered body. Luke tried to provide support, but we were kept separate.

I had nothing much to help with their investigation, but the officer assigned to question me wouldn't let up. He asked about everything—why was I at the resort? Who did I come with? How long had we been here? Had I been on this path before? Then something slipped. "Did you know her?"

Her? The body? I shook my head, "No, I just tripped and landed next to her."

He grazed a finger across his lip, "What about your boyfriend? Had he been up to this location before?"

Luke had to know of the lookout point, but the officer didn't need to know that. "He's not my boyfriend, and I don't know."

"Hmm." He was unimpressed as he scribbled a few things on his notepad. I wanted to offer something more. Give him a key piece of information that would make all this better. He thanked me for my time and dismissed me before I could get to that point.

Luke swooped in, securing his arm around my shaking body. "We're free to go."

We exited on the far side of the path. She came into full view. A half-dressed figure laying on top of the brush. No shirt, dirty white bra, a pair of jeans, and marks covering her back. Stab wounds. Luke pulled my head into his chest.

I protested his advances. "I'm fine."

He rubbed my shoulder, "I know," his hand dropped down from me. I liked the space. Luke did keep a close eye on me as we climbed down the boulders and found the path again.

Once we were on the path, we stopped. I leaned against a tree. Another officer walked by me. That's when Luke came over. He said some things, but I wasn't paying attention. I was still hung up on our last conversation. Instead of humoring him with empty responses, I built my agenda.

"Aaron," I said. Luke was perplexed. "I have to talk to Aaron."

∽

I searched all over the house for Aaron. Mother told me I had just missed him. Before she could start another Luke-inspired conversation, I fled to my room and changed clothes. I stayed inside for an extended minute, waiting for her to leave. Then, I poked my head out of the door frame. Luke was standing in the hallway. No words, just a hand out. I grabbed it and pulled him inside.

"Did you find Aaron?" he said.

I shook my head. "No, but I'm not giving up until I talk to him."

"You think he had something to do with that girl's death?" I gave Luke an overview of my conversation with James without revealing my source. "I just don't think he's doing any of this," he said.

Careful. Be patience. "I don't think he's killing people," I clarified. "He just knows more than he's letting on."

"But Aaron doesn't even live in Settlement Island. He's got a house in Anders."

"Where does he spend most of his time?"

"I don't know. I haven't seen him around the club much, so maybe he's just busy working?"

Hmm. "That explains why he's not well-known." This satisfied James's point. "But why is he working with my dad in town? Why not focus on the practice in Anders?"

"Cecilia. She lives in Settlement Island. He told me," Luke said. I asked for more. "Aaron was going to head up the new clinic in Anders, but he fell in love with Cecilia, so your dad put him in charge of this clinic."

"Where does he stay when he's working?"

"At your house."

I should have known that answer, so why didn't I? It was a lie. But Luke didn't know that, so I didn't tell him otherwise. He put his hand out.

"Let's table this until later, okay?" I said. Luke nodded, and I took his hand.

We headed to dinner and met everyone for the walk to the restaurant. Dinner was at a club along the beach line. I ordered chicken alfredo which made Luke's face turn up.

"That's one of the most boring things on the menu," he winked.

"Well, I like boring food," I whispered. He was alarmingly calm, and I was trying to follow his lead, which was easy. No one else in our party knew of what we had seen.

Cecilia fed Aaron a piece of shrimp. A goofy grin crossed his face. No looks at me.

What did he know? After my talk with James and Luke, I was more alert than ever. If Aaron was up to no good, I'd find out.

"Here, have some wine. It'll take the edge off." Luke poured me a glass of red. His lips grazed my ear, "But don't drink too much." He was becoming fun. I hated admitting it, but being around him was making dinner manageable.

"I'm okay, Luke. But I guess I'll be good, for your sake," I scolded him.

Aaron sat up straight, "What have you two been up to today?" As if you didn't know.

Luke shrugged, "Not much. Just getting to know each other better." Under the table, his fingers laced into mine.

"You seem a little tense, man," he said. I stared Aaron in the eyes, and his discontent was hard to hide. It was like the day at the church all over again. I took in a sharp breath.

"Aaron, Luke's trying to woo my darling little sister. Give him some space," Cecilia chimed in.

Aaron chuckled. "You're not the only one."

"What are you talking about?" I said.

"I hear you've been hanging out with Gavin Scott a

lot lately." Aaron tilted his water glass toward me before taking a swig. His comment left me completely still.

"Who's Gavin Scott?" Mother said.

"He's my patient's grandson," Dad uttered. "Nice guy." Mother nodded.

And then my hand was bare. Luke cleared his throat and moved closer to Cecilia.

"That's boring news, Aaron," said Cecilia. "My sister's nice to everyone…well, kinda nice to everyone… she can tolerate most people. So, being friends with Gavin probably fits in there somewhere." She winked at me and then gasped. Out came her phone, "I found some rings I like." I made plans to extend my gratitude to her later. Aaron didn't look in her direction.

"Careful, Aaron," Luke said, his knife pointing to Cecilia's phone, "you might want to see what you're getting yourself into." A smile went to Luke for his chivalry.

"Aaron…Aaron?" Dad got his attention. "There's new patients coming in for exams…" Dad said.

Aaron stared at me in his usual manner. He was good at berating me in this way. I didn't let go. Eyes forward, no ducking. He wasn't going to win this one.

"Aaron?" Dad said.

We both looked at him, "Yes, sir," Aaron replied.

"So, I've got your load up to twelve for Monday." Dad turned to me, "Catalina, you're gonna start helping Aaron in the office."

What inspired this? Perhaps Aaron had made the request. And I was right. "I'm sure you enjoy the house calls," said Aaron, "but I'm getting swamped. Your dad says you're good with paperwork." I nodded slowly, careful not to seem eager at all. "Well, I can use you."

This was part of the plan. His plan. Normally, I would bow down, but not this time. I smiled at Aaron. This would be my chance to finally catch him at his own game.

CHAPTER TWENTY-ONE

Starry Night

AFTER DINNER, WE all retired to the cabin, so we could warm up for the festival. I lied, saying that I needed to stay in after the hike. Luke came to my door, which was exactly what I had expected.

He looked good. Ready to go out. My outfit was hiding under a robe, and I was running out of time. I needed to get rid of him, so I could run off into the night with the enemy.

"I'm just gonna take a bath and read," I said to him.

Luke didn't come through the door. He folded his arms, a very military-style stance. "You shouldn't be alone right now."

My throat went dry. "I just want to give The Pines a break. Take a vacation from my vacation."

He rocked back and forth on his heels. "Well, I'm not gonna make you do something you don't want to do."

I felt the guilt and released it. "I'll see you in the morning."

"Goodnight, Catalina." The doorway remained empty for a few moments. Not too long. I grabbed a gift for Gavin, tossed the robe, and went out.

⚜

It was four minutes until nine o'clock. I peered in at everyone in their beautiful clothes, dancing as the lights grew darker inside the ballroom. A wedding. The bride and groom smiled at each other. I watched them, turning and swaying to a slow melody. By my dress alone, they could tell I was an outsider crashing their big day. But they welcomed me.

My pink cashmere sweater, dark jeans, and boots were warm enough to keep me comfortable. Pink. Not my favorite color, but Cecilia had given me this sweater for Christmas one year. A little bit of brightness to lift my mood. A chance to try something new, that's why I had packed it. I knew he'd be intrigued after seeing it on me. My teeth clenched down on my lip, but they soon abandoned it. Instead, I pondered the body hiding in the brush. Cold, dead, no need for a sweater. No jacket.

When would all this end? Never, that was James's estimation. And Gavin's. It followed us around. To be completely accurate, it followed me the most. No one else was tripping over dead people or being caught up in a volley between all these suspected people. Maybe I was the bad omen, not Kyle. It reminded me of a story I had read once of a man who started a war over his love for a woman. A single woman. Someone unimportant, but extraordinary to him.

If only I could be so flattered by this notion. But instead of fighting over me, they were fighting around me. Their blood dripping from each other's hands.

This dark turn in my thoughts made my shoulders tense. My gaze focused on the wedding party. Everyone was so damn happy. Sure, up the hill in the darkness, a body was being brought down the mountain, but no one concerned themselves with this. The lights on the cliff illuminated parts of the sky. I could see red and blue flashes. The uniforms weren't done yet.

Back to the wedding party. There was nothing I could do now, or ever, for that poor girl. I didn't know anything, and my convictions lay heavily in staying out of it. No more trouble, at least not for tonight.

Gavin sauntered toward me. How beautiful he was.

He wore a white V-neck sweater, dark jeans, and his coal black boots. Leather jacket. Perfect hair and skin, of course. I dug my hands into my back pockets and contemplated his observations of me. They were somewhere between being content and highly-annoyed. I hadn't said anything yet, so it couldn't have been me.

"Nice sweater," Gavin said. Off his shoulders went his jacket and onto me. Sleeves rolled up. Now he looked unforgettable.

Gavin reached behind my back and retrieved a hand. I knew where we were headed, yet I allowed him to guide me into the group of dancers. We were face-to-face, him leading me to move this way and then that.

"Dancing?" I said.

"It'll make it easier for us to talk."

Smart. "I found a body today," I snapped, a small whisper. "But I don't want to talk about it." I hoped this would be a bizarre comment, but given our history, that was unlikely.

"Cops interrogate you?" he said. I nodded. "Give me a description of her."

"Red hair, skinny, dead."

His eyes floated around the room. "Sounds like Rachel, Cameron's girlfriend."

I felt my head throbbing. Very mild at first, but then the sensation built into a constant pound. Why do this to myself? It didn't have to be this hard—not for him or me. My body drifted away from his firm grasp. "Can we not talk about it, for once?" I said. He respected the distance between us. That move gave me courage. "This has been the worst vacation I've ever had. And I know you guys are gonna handle it, so I just don't want to go there tonight."

"That's not how it works." He moved closer. "Decisions need to be made. I'll have to talk it over with the crew and see what they think."

I wasn't sure what to say. We were close again. His touches were soft, not demanding. A sense of ease flowed over my body. I was safe. Safe enough to say the next thing that needed to be out in the open.

"Listen, Aaron and Luke think you have something to do with the murders." Someone bumped into my back. Gavin pulled me closer. I waited for a comment. Nothing. "And it sounds like Kyle is up to no good. Whatever it's worth, I trust that you'll do the best thing for the situation."

"Catalina," he said in a low voice, "you talk like a textbook."

"No, I don't." I brushed hair away from my forehead.

"Just say it from your heart."

I rolled my eyes. "No matter what, I trust you."

His expression brightened at my response, "So, you're not breaking up with me? Cuz if you are, that's kinda awkward since we aren't together."

A small smile was on my lips. It was almost undetectable. Then it was gone. "So, you owe me something? You want to do something nice for me, right?"

He put out his hand. I looked it over and tried to decide whether or not to take it. "There's this small part of you that still isn't sure about me," he said.

"No, I just don't think we've said everything we need to say." I paused, "Besides, you annoy me when you say mean things to me. I want none of that tonight."

"Is that what you want? More truth? Distance?" I didn't answer. This was a shock to me, but not so much for him. "And I'm keeping you from that?"

"I don't want distance, I just want to be a normal kid again. And you should be nicer to me."

"You see yourself as a kid?"

"No, of course not."

A dangerous game had started. He smirked, "I'd like something from you."

I raised my eyebrow, "Really?"

"Let's just enjoy ourselves until midnight. Then I'll let you decide what to do with me."

My heart started racing, "Gavin, this could be dangerous territory for you."

"I'm only asking for one night. You and me together for one moment without any fighting or drama."

I searched his eyes—stern and concerned, like I thought they'd be. We only had less than three hours to enjoy the peace. The aftermath of every decision he had made was still close, as always. But we could have tonight. Then, we'd be left with the uncertainty of what to do with the deadly details. I put my hand in his, and he closed it firmly.

"Let's get into some trouble," I said.

We entered into the darkness. Only moonlight lit a path before us. Shadows and lights danced across the water. But all was still and quiet.

"You seem more confident tonight, Catalina," he said. "I like it."

"I'm not pathetic, you know."

He smiled, "I never meant to insult you."

"Of course, you didn't."

I had a second to breathe until the images returned. My head went from right to left, searching, hunting for anything that seemed out of place. A simple task that was pointless. What should I expect? Then, we were there. I was taken away when the red and white riverboat came into view. A sweet gesture, indeed. Gavin took the lead, and we travelled down the dock.

"This is our ride?" I said.

"Not tonight." He leaned into me, "There's more to come."

I nodded.

A man came off the boat, "Gavin, here's your order." He retrieved the items. "You should come back here, we miss you."

Gavin patted the man's back, "I know."

"Come back?" I said.

He put a bill in the man's hand and said goodbye. "I used to work here."

"As what?"

"A chef."

These were the things I liked about him. His hidden artistries and ways of bringing beauty to things. "Why did you stop?" I said.

"Paula. I can't be here and in Settlement Island at the same time." No more talking. We were on the move, close to the trail Luke and I had taken.

My fears had subsided by now. Gavin stayed close to me, his hand in mine. Imagining our next adventure brought great delight. Apparently, this unexpected stop to collect dinner was a common occurrence for him. "I've got an even better place for us to go…"

Gavin continued pulling me forward and into the tree cover. There were no orders for me to do one thing or another. Just us being together.

Twinkling lights hovering slightly above the ground was our next destination. There were blankets laid across the grass in a small clearing. No other couples, just us. I turned around. The lighthouse towered over the cabins below. I sat down, and he joined me. He took back his jacket. Apparently, it was too cold, even for a Mainer like him. Around my shoulders went a soft, fleece blanket.

"What's in the bag?" I said as I snuggled in.

"Too early for dinner," he pulled out a small round cake, "Let's have dessert first."

"Hmm. Looks good."

A fork was placed in my hand. Then came a glass of wine: apple wine. He held his up, "Here's to Catalina and her beautiful, open mind."

"Open mind?"

"You have not fought me once this evening. I appreciate it."

We toasted and took a sip. The wine was smooth, delicious. I remembered to pace myself. On to the cake. I reached down and sliced off a piece, and he wrapped his lips around my fork as I offered it to him. "This is really good." Now it was my turn. He played me for a fool when the fork was dropped at the last minute. My lips landed on his.

I'm not sure who kissed who first, but the sensation just pulled us together. His hands smoothed my hair, my arms wrapped around his shoulders. Neither one of us wanted to stop. His lips were warm and surprisingly soft, his hands were rough. They gripped my hips as he pulled me closer. I could feel his heart beat faster. But his hands didn't wander, like he didn't need to take it further. We were embracing, exploring, not growing tired of each other. No thoughts, no complaints, just him and me, living in the closeness.

I held myself there for a moment, just kissing him,

not thinking about what else I should be thinking about or doing. He broke first, rubbing his jaw, and moving away from me. I waited for him to say something about slowing down, but he didn't. He just stared out into the space in front of him.

To lighten the mood, I swatted his arm with a good deal of strength. He snuggled next to me, waiting. I cut another slice and devoured it. Blended dark chocolate touched my tongue first, then the strawberries.

"You like it?" he said.

"Yes," I muffled. "It's beautiful up here, too. Like a night-sky painting."

He put his wine down, "Lie back."

The opaque sky—stars in front, blackness in the background were soothing. I breathed in the cool air that burned my throat. My eyes fluttered close.

"Tell me more about your life in California."

I could see it. The rolling water in the bay. Miguel. Shops and tents up and down Telegraph Avenue. The sunshine warming my skin. A trickle of ice cream running down the corner of my mouth. "You'd love it in Berkeley."

"I thought you were from L.A.?"

"I am. I went to college in Berkeley. It was the best four years of my life."

"When did you move away to college?"

"When I was fifteen." I widened my eyes, "Oh, no." There was no point hiding the truth any longer. Not like it would hurt anything. "I'm a child prodigy."

He laughed, "Yeah, I kinda figured that. You talk

like a textbook and all. And you're the most sheltered twenty-one-year-old I've ever met." Again, I let my fist sink into his shoulder. Then he settled down. "When I was a kid," he said, "my grandparents and I used to come out here and have picnics. It was our thing, you know?" I nodded. "Grandpa would tell me stories about his time in the Navy."

"Sounds nice."

"We were just normal."

"I'd like to go to Florida and get to know my grandparents. Maybe they're a lot like me, too."

"So, there was some tragedy in your life? A bit of brokenness in your family?"

Other people would have taken this as an insult. A slight. But I knew what Gavin meant. "Not like you've experienced. Families separate, but it wasn't that bad for me. I'm more curious about them more than anything."

"Yeah, I can imagine." He traced the constellations with his finger, "Your dad's parents died when you were young?"

"Pretty much."

"And you weren't close to them, right?"

"I saw them a few times," I said. "But not that many. They didn't like my mother much, apparently. My dad's parents wanted him to marry someone like them…someone really smart." I felt bad for referring to my mother as inferior to my father. Gavin didn't comment on this.

We both took a drink. More cake. "I had a lot of trouble when my grandpa died," he said. "And when I lost Logan." I allowed him a minute to let his shoulders sulk. "He was part of my crew, too."

"There were six of you?"

"I knew Logan longer than anyone. My dad went to high school with his dad. He helped me be tough, you know." Gavin ran his hands over the blanket.

"Was he your best friend?"

"It's hard to say." He laughed, "James is the most loyal person I've ever met. But Logan wasn't loud like James or a dick like Kyle. Wasn't worried about being seen. But when I got into a bind, he always came to rescue me." No more talking. Just looking up at the sky.

I reached into my pocket and pulled out the ring. "Well, I'm sure this will help you remember him."

Gavin took the ring and slid it onto his right ring finger. "Thank you."

My small gift, token of kindness, warranted another kiss. A sweet, soft kiss that was placed on my lips very gently. I liked kissing him a little too much. He broke again to answer a text message.

"Sorry." His voice was almost inaudible, his eyes shifting around. I could feel his concerns and smiled at him. The trees rustled behind us. I slid closer to him.

"Relax," he said. "James just asked me a question." He put his phone away, "I swear he always knows when I'm talking about him."

I touched Gavin's arm. "He's worried about you."

"He tried to convince you to get me to leave Settlement Island, but I'm not going anywhere." He leaned his shoulder into my body. "You'd miss me too much."

"Whatever," I scoffed. "My life was perfect before I met you."

"So, all the drama and murdering is my fault?" I nodded. He grabbed his chest. "Ouch! That really hurts, coming from you." It was truly strange, the fact that we could joke about death like it was a hot topic during anyone else's night out. "I wish…" he took my hand, "I wish we could have met under different circumstances."

"How would it be different?"

"Like how other guys meet girls. At a bar, in class, through a friend." His head went back up toward the stars. "I wish we could be normal." He pondered something for a minute. "If we were normal people, what would we be doing right now?"

I crept up closer to him, "I have something in mind."

CHAPTER TWENTY-TWO

Midnight

"THERE ARE PROBABLY clothes all over the place," I warned him.

"Where's Luke?" Gavin said.

I shrugged, "Let me check the house before you come in." This task was completed in under five minutes. Having a few more seconds, I tossed various items into my suitcase and shut it. The bed was freshly made. Good. No sweat or scent from Luke.

Another deep breath, then I opened the door. Gavin came in. "You cleaned up…for me."

"No." I said, hiding my smile. Then I proceeded to find something for us to do. There was nothing except TV or conversing. Books were also promising, but I wouldn't be able to concentrate.

Gavin sat on the bed. He turned his phone off and flung it onto the nightstand. An invitation. I rushed to the bathroom to look at my reflection. Too many emotions filled my heart and mind. Nervousness was the biggest one. I changed into flannel shorts and a long sleeved black tee. My fuzzy bathrobe went around my cold body. Pulling the door open, I caught Gavin leaning against the wall.

"I'm not trying to get you in bed," he said.

"And I'm not trying to get you into bed, either."

He turned on me when he asked, "Waiting till marriage?"

That subject was not up for discussion. "So, what shall we do?"

"Do you believe in love, Catalina?"

This was ironic, coming from him. For a moment, I was reluctant to reply. But I had to say something. "Yes, I do, but it's not easy. I believe that love brings pain and suffering. And if you love someone, you have to prepare to withstand that white-hot feeling of fear that comes with losing yourself and your control."

"Did you read that in a book somewhere?" he grinned.

"It's over the top, I know, but it's how I feel," I responded.

Back to silence. I had never had a guy in my room like this. Having to entertain him after making that first move was harder than I had thought. This was more of Cecilia's territory.

"And you wanted to be a teacher when you grew up?" he said.

I thought the answer was obvious. But Gavin didn't know me that well. "Yes, even before I went to college."

"Do you like kids?"

"College-level, yeah. Any younger than that, and I'm not interested."

He approached me, "I have a son, is that okay?"

I paused, "Yeah…" My skin burned.

"And a daughter…" He put his hand over his mouth. I cleared my throat.

Dating someone with two kids. Yeah, I could learn to like them…I hoped. My arms tightened around my waist. Should I ask about their mother? Was it Ronda? The disgust and disappointment on his face was a reaction to my silence and the subtle shock over yet another secret from him. He removed his hand from his mouth, a big smile now present.

I shook my head and hit him again. "You jerk!"

"Sorry, I had to see what you would say!" He shielded his arm from me. "I love kids, though. And I do want some one day."

"Well, you'd be a terrible dad!"

Gavin couldn't stop chuckling. Really, it wasn't that funny. He continued to enjoy himself at my expense. He probably needed a good laugh; I was happy to give it.

I peeled off my robe and sat down on the bed. To my surprise, he took off his shoes only and joined me. My head relaxed into the pillow. This would be my first night's rest after seeing the body. I pulled him over to my side, and he laid down on the pillow next to me.

We were far enough apart to see each other comfortably. I could feel his hand stroking my arm.

"I can't make all this go away like you want me to, Catalina. I can't take it back now."

My intentions didn't include Gavin fixing things. I was well aware of the sad truth surrounding all the events of the last several months. But I no longer blamed him.

He wasn't the one to be feared. It was Kyle. And Porter. "So, can I ask you one more question about Kyle and Porter?"

He shifted around in the bed, slightly, "It's already midnight, so you can ask me more about that, but I don't feel like answering."

Oddly enough, I didn't mind his request. Eventually, I would have to close my eyes and try to sleep, so a break from the mayhem was a good thing. Sleep seemed like a wonderful sentiment, but there was always something. An unexpected twist or person would come and disrupt my peace. My face went upward, not by my doing, but by his. His skin was beautiful, and his lips were perfect. Gavin stared at me. Another kiss was inevitable. I watched his chest rise and fall instead.

"Catalina, I have to tell you how I feel about you."

"Here we go again," I sat up. "Luke already 'feelinged' me today."

He laughed. "Is that even a word?"

I shook my head. "He wanted to know where we stood, he and I." Gavin sighed. "He thinks you like me. So, does everyone else, apparently."

He smiled, "Well, I, um, have a lot of respect for you. You've got a good heart. And I'd fight for you any day."

"Of course, you would."

Gavin's eyes were now more serious. "I've never really had this talk before. But you need to know."

"Okay." I didn't brace myself for anything. Everything needed to flow naturally.

"You're really important to me."

"I know," I whispered.

"And I appreciate everything you've done, how you've handled all this. No one has ever been so kind to me. So, thank you."

I nodded. Silence. "Is that it?"

"Well, you don't want to be feelinged, do you?"

Point well taken. My intrigue did go a bit further. "James said you never date. And you don't like girls." He rolled his eyes. "That's not what I mean." I grinned, "But you like me?" He nodded. "That's good to know."

I ran my fingers through his soft hair. A small act that meant a lot to me. To touch something of his that was so personal. His most distinguishing feature. I wanted more of him. He pulled away.

"So, what do we do?" he said.

Rejection was something I had gotten used to. The moment was already broken, and I didn't feel the need to revive it. "Are you hungry?"

"What do you have in mind?"

I grabbed the room service menu and tossed it to him, "Order whatever you want."

He flipped it open, "Dad's paying?" I stammered for a response but came up with nothing. "Crab cakes and more wine," he handed me the menu.

I dialed the front desk. Once the food was ordered, my attention went back to him.

Gavin pointed to my PJ's, "Do you usually sleep in that?"

"Yeah, or some variation of it."

"You look adorable."

Another compliment. It was becoming funny to me—Gavin's softer side. I always wanted to see it. It wasn't what I expected; I welcomed it. "Shall we watch some TV?"

"Is that what people normally do at a slumber party?"

I shrugged, "You usually do whatever you want."

He laid flat on his back. "I've always wondered what it'd be like to sleep next to another person."

"Really?"

"I've never slept over at someone's house before."

"What about girlfriends?"

"I've never had a girlfriend, remember?" Gavin propped himself up on one arm.

Now Indian style, I faced him, "Not even Ronda?" He shook his head, "Why not?"

"I didn't see the point."

My shoulders tensed up, but I had to ask. "So, you just sleep with her?" He raised an eyebrow at me. "Sorry."

"I haven't slept with Ronda in over a year. Or anyone, for that matter."

"I saw how she looked at you at the church on Sunday."

His thumb rubbed his chin, "She's still got a thing for me, and she can tell that I'm into you." Gavin had to enjoy the look of relief on my face. "I don't spend too much time worrying about girls."

"But you're into me?" I joked. A sinister grin. "And you worry about me?"

He smirked and sat up, "Let's play Truth or Dare."

My heart raced, "Nice subject change."

"Don't worry, I won't touch you inappropriately." He sighed with boredom. I laced my fingers and placed them in my lap, "Truth or Dare, Catalina?"

"Truth."

"Have you ever had a boyfriend?" His stare was blinding.

"Yeah, I told you that," I said with confidence. That was a great question. An advantage I had over him.

"You said something about a few middle school crushes. I'm talking about a real boyfriend."

I told him about my Miguel, my favorite of all my boyfriends, and the only one who really counted. Memories of him brought a smile to my face. Gavin looked jealous. If only they could meet, I thought. Miguel wasn't keen on Gavin after everything I had told him, but he would appreciate this version of the boy who was ruining my life.

"And you dated for about 3 months?"

"Yeah. I love him more than anyone else in the world." Except for you. I bowed my eyes and then came back up to look at him. Gone was the light-hearted, whimsical smile on his face. "He's my best friend now." He stared at me. It was my turn. "Truth or Dare?" I said.

"Dare."

Coming up with the right dare would take time. I wanted something good. Satisfying. Something that would have made all my hell worth it. "I dare you to," I paused. The only things that came to my mind were inappropriate.

"Don't be shy, Catalina," he said. "I'll do whatever you ask."

"Can I reserve a dare?" I said.

"A reserved dare?" he raised his eyebrow.

"Yeah. Something that can happen in the future."

"If you like. What's your dare?"

I became brave. The only thing that came across my mind was his skin and eyes. I stared at his beautiful lips. I had to go for it. "I dare you to leave Settlement Island… no, wait…I dare you to leave Maine one day. Just go out on your own and experience life somewhere else."

"So, what makes you think I'd agree to this now?"

"You said it yourself," I grinned, "If you could leave, you would. You would get as far away from here as possible." My face no longer held any happiness. "I want you to go. I want you to experience life, the good parts." A desperate yearning grew inside me. "You don't understand, Gavin. No one ever told you this, but life isn't supposed to be this hard." His face became serious. "If I could have anything in this world, if I could make any wish come true, it would be for you to know what it's like to sleep easy at night. To have something for yourself that you don't have to share with anyone else."

One slow nod. His fingers then ran across Logan's ring. "I will do my best."

"No, that's not enough. You have to do it, not for me, but for you."

"Give me time to think it over." He leaned in close to my ear and whispered, "Truth or dare, Catalina?"

"Truth."

He licked his lips, "If I did believe in love. And if I wanted to date. Would you date me?"

I had nothing to say after my big, gushing, heart-felt truth. This question seemed juvenile. The man that I first saw, the one staring at me through the café window, was my dream. That man, I would have dated without question. But I never got a chance to know him. I had no idea what type of person he would've been when we finally stepped through the glass and found each other.

He danced his fingers against my scalp, "I'm still waiting for an answer."

"If you don't date, why did you wink at me?"

"When I first saw you?"

"Yeah."

He seemed to weigh his options, "I honestly don't know."

"No, you do. You're just afraid to admit it."

Gavin ran his hand through his hair. It remained perfect. "I've been a Settler all my life, and I've seen every girl in this town. I just thought you were beautiful…different."

He thought I was beautiful. My demeanor and attitude remained steady. "But it doesn't matter because you don't date."

"Maybe one day, I'll make an exception for you."

And I hoped he would. "Truth or Dare, Gavin?"

"Hmm," was his response. "Dare."

I had made one brave move and contemplated making another. "How come you never pick Truth?"

"Why would I? I've already told you the truth about everything in my life."

"Yeah, but there has to be something."

His arms folded. I knew this stance. "What do you have on your mind, Catalina?"

"You gotta have a secret that you're hiding."

"I don't have secrets. If I don't want to tell you something, I won't."

We could argue this fine point of semantics for hours, but I didn't want to spend our time together going around in circles. Gavin was still, accepting his defeat. I had seen this look on him every time he demanded I stand up for myself or do whatever he asked of me. No, he wouldn't get this victory over me.

I tried to come up with something that would put him in a trap. My lip went into my teeth.

"Stop biting your lip, Catalina."

"Why does that bother you so much?"

He ran his hand through his hair. "My mother used to do that when she was craving a fix."

"Is that the only memory you have of her?"

"Can we get on with the game?"

His irritation put me in good spirits. I had found my something. "The only thing I can think of is to dare you to tell me the truth. So, I dare you to tell me about your parents."

"Can we talk about them another time?" Gavin started to say something but paused, "Maybe tomorrow?"

My stomach flipped. I didn't want to think about what the next day would bring. "We still have tonight." I put his hand in mine, "and I think this slumber party is going really well."

"That's good to know. Cause you're stuck with me."

I hugged a pillow, "You could always stay with James."

"I'm starving to death. Where the hell are my crab cakes?" Gavin got up and started looking around my room.

"What's wrong?" I said.

Gavin winked and opened my room door. He came back shortly with a plate of shrimp. I sighed knowing these were someone's leftovers.

"Slumber party snack." He locked the door and got back on the bed.

"So, what are you doing tomorrow," I snagged a shrimp, "when you are no longer in my good graces?"

"Damage control. I still have to sort out all this shit with James and Kyle." He paused, "What did your dad want you to do when you graduated from college?"

I sighed, "Something that would pay me a lot of money."

"What about your mom?"

"She was a model. She wants me to marry well, like she did."

"Someone like Luke?"

"Yeah."

"Is that why you like him?"

"Luke's more of a friend than anything. He's a lot of fun to be around, which makes things really easy." I looked over at the clock. It was going on two. "We should go to sleep." I started getting up and Gavin pulled me back down and into his chest.

"Shall we play more truth or dare?"

I had a better idea. "I want to know more about you. What do you want out of life?"

Gavin placed the plate of tails on the nightstand. "You know, I didn't think I was gonna live this long." He pulled himself closer to me, "Now that I have, I should go back to school or something."

"What would you study?"

This darling grin stretched across his face. "Maybe I'd be a doctor, like your dad."

It was a joke, but we were making plans for things that probably wouldn't happen. With that, I was ready to move on to sleeping. I got up and turned off the light. The lamp on his side switched on.

"If I left town, I'd have to say goodbye to you."

I tucked the blanket around me, "And I would have to let you go."

His eyes were on mine, "Would you be able to do that?"

Like I had a choice. Gavin called the shots in his life, and if he couldn't, his enemies would. So, his question was irrelevant. But he wanted an answer.

"If it made you safe, yes, I would."

My head nestled into his chest. The kiss on my forehead was sweet, "One more request." My eyes were heavy. His skin was warm and soft. "When I'm ready for a girlfriend, can I choose you?"

I woke myself enough to respond. "But you'll never be ready, so don't get my hopes up."

He laughed, "Okay, I'll keep my sappy comments to myself."

Sleep was creeping up on me fast. I was at ease with everything. A strength was growing in me. It made me excited. "Yes, you can choose me," I muffled. "But only if you are strong enough and brave enough to date me."

He shifted again, but I didn't move. "Catalina?" he said. I growl at him. Almost asleep. "You make me strong and brave."

Chapter Twenty-Three
Breakfast

My head on Gavin's chest. My arm laid comfortably across his body. I regretfully woke up and saw his eyes watching me, "When did you wake up?"

"A few minutes ago. Did you sleep?"

Yes, I did. Very well, despite everything that went on the previous day. I nodded, "Yeah, a little too well."

"Is there such a thing?" he said. I nodded again. He adjusted himself upward and into a sitting position. "Let's go somewhere."

The adrenaline in my veins almost overpowered me. "Last time I went somewhere, I ended up tripping over a dead body."

"This is a place with other people, if that helps."

"I'll get dressed."

Gavin put on his boots and walked outside, to give me privacy, I assumed. I took my time to get ready: brush my teeth, apply fresh makeup and bundle myself into another pair of jeans, a sweater, and some boots of my own. Bracelets and rings on. When I opened the door, he smiled.

"Beautiful."

I pointed to him, up and down. "Are you wearing that?"

He nodded. "We probably don't have much time." I couldn't believe it; he still looked good, even on next to no sleep. It truly wasn't fair.

Gavin put out his arm and I wrapped mine in his. It was earlier than I thought. I looked at my phone: 7:00am. "Do you always get up early?"

"Yeah," he said. "I don't sleep much. Never have."

"Like a vampire…"

He shook his head, mocking my silliness, "Like a person with insomnia."

I moved my body closer to his to block the cold. No snow, still, but the sky looked threatening. We walked a ways and landed at another set of cabins. Out front was his black car.

"This is where you stay?" After he nodded, I asked to see his room.

"There's not much to see. But I do want to brush my teeth, if that's okay with you."

"Please do."

I didn't go inside with him. Instead, I walked up to the Nova and ran my finger along the driver side door. Clean. Everything about him was clean. When he returned, he tossed me the keys. "Take her for a spin." I threw them back and headed to the passenger door before he could notice my nervousness. "Do you even know how to drive?" he said.

"Yeah."

"But not stick?" I didn't confirm or deny his observation. He bit back a smile, "So, that's why you stayed with me that night? You had no way to get home."

"You're overthinking it…"

He went to my side and opened my door. "And here I am thinking you actually trusted me."

We didn't go far, but we did leave the resort. About four or five miles down the road was a small town, maybe a couple of hundred people. It was a mountain community, higher in elevation than The Pines. A large river ran through it, a few snowy rocks peeking out from underneath the river bed.

There was a row of boutique restaurants, which told me this was also a tourist town. Gavin pulled up in front of a very busy diner.

"So, The Pines is a great destination spot for people coming down from Canada," Gavin said as he opened my door. He looked toward the diner and smiled. "You never know who you might meet." I turned in time to see a girl with long, blonde hair crash into him. Her hug was so tight and secure.

I didn't have time to hate her. The hug was onto me next, tight, warm and full of love. She smelled like campfire and adventure.

When we parted, she held onto my hand. Gavin

placed his hand over his mouth, something he did when he knew I was nervous.

"Well, are you gonna tell her who I am?" she said.

Hand down, "Catalina, this is my cousin, Brianna."

"I'm more than your cousin," she punched him in the arm. Brianna was a strong girl, an athlete. She seemed like she could take him. "I'm his moral compass."

"Brianna was up in Canada this past week, so she asked to meet up before she headed back to Anders."

Brianna's hand tightened around my fingers. Her eyes went to mine. She was full of energy. Very full of life. I gave her a smile, even though I was completely overwhelmed. "Gavin told me he was bringing someone to breakfast, but I thought he meant James."

"Nope, just me…little old Catalina."

Brianna shook her head. "You should be more confident…" she leaned into me, "it's sexy." Gavin pointed at his cousin and nodded. "Let's go in. Matt's got a table, and I think Julia and Rick are parking the car."

Matt, Julia, and Rick were friends of Brianna's. They looked like lumberjacks or models from an outdoor catalogue. After Brianna introduced me, Matt and Rick jumped into a conversation with Gavin about hunting and snowmobiling. Apparently, it was a huge thing for them. Julia and Brianna had no interest in that. Instead, they only talked to me. And the conversation led to where I was from and what I did. Julia was happy to know I knew of Telegraph Avenue.

"I make it out that way once a year," she said. "Love the ocean and the California vibes." I told her about Aunt Eloise's shop, and she thought she may have moseyed in there on a few occasions.

Brianna was different. Unlike Gavin, she left Maine regularly, heading up and down the East Coast. She was a wilderness guide and a biologist. I told her about Luke and his hopes to do something with his marine biology degree. She raised her eyebrow at the mention of another man's name on my lips. If she knew her cousin at all, she should know that I had to keep my options open.

When the food came, I realized I hadn't ordered anything. However, my plate was full of sausages, bacon, some type of biscuit with gravy, eggs, and stuffed blueberry pancakes.

"Sorry for intruding," said Brianna, "but if you're not a Mainer, you'll never know what to order."

It had to be a Scott thing: ordering food for other people. But Brianna's taste was better than Gavin's. I ate everything and drank the apple and orange juice I was poured. Then I sat back. Brianna had joined in on a conversation with the boys about winter camping. Julia was helping Rick, her fiancé, figure out where his phone went. And Gavin stayed in tune with his cousin and Matt as they fired back details about when to set up their trip.

He didn't notice me once, which was a first. I pushed my plate aside and watched him laugh loudly and be… excited. I had never seen him excited before. Throwing his head back and laughing as Brianna and Rick fought over who was stronger than whom. The light in his eyes as he put his arm around Matt who had agreed with him about something so trivial as which hunting trails were the best. And the look he gave me when I smiled at him the moment he remembered that he had invited me here as his guest.

"So, you're coming, right?" said Julia. "To the big camping trip?"

I stammered at first, but Gavin nodded. "Yeah, she'll be there. Catalina needs to learn what it means to be a Settler."

Brianna threw a sausage at him. "No, she's not! I'm not gonna let my new best friend here go so low." She smiled at me. "I'm gonna turn you into a Mainer. Trust me, it's better than being a Settler."

He threw the sausage back. "You're a Settler, too, Brianna."

"Only by geography!" Back to me. "Seriously, Catalina," her expression had turned slightly more serious, "I hope to see more of you."

"Me, too."

Matt announced it was time to go. They had to get down to Anders before noon, so he could check on his dog. When I asked why he didn't bring her, he mentioned something about Tex not getting along with Rick and Julia's dog. "She'll learn, though," Matt said. "She hates being left behind." I knew the feeling.

When we got up from the table, Gavin put his hand in mine. Brianna winked at him before twisting around, her long mane hitting him in the face. Out to the parking lot, and more hugs were placed around my body. Brianna got her phone out, and we captured each other's phone number.

"I should give you mine, too," Gavin said.

Brianna narrowed her eyebrows, "You're in love with this girl, and you don't even have her phone number?" Another punch to his shoulder. This time he groaned. "Did grandpa not teach you anything?"

"We have a way of finding each other," I said to help him out.

She gave me one more hug, "I love you, Catalina. It was so nice to meet you." Then a hug for Gavin. "Stay cool, punk, and take care of my girl, okay?"

"Love you," he said.

"Love you, too." Brianna blew a kiss our way and hopped into the SUV next to Matt who was driving. Windows came down and Julia, Rick, and Matt waved until we could no longer see them.

Gavin threw his arm around me. "Still want my number?"

I rolled my eyes, "Sure."

Luke came to my door an hour later. When Gavin dropped me off, we didn't linger on our goodbye. It was almost like we knew we'd see each other again, really soon. No kiss, either. I simply thanked him for breakfast and exited the car. When I did, he told me to be good before heading toward his part of the lake.

Back to Luke. He found me in my room, completely packed, a book in my hand. I looked him over and tried to think of the right way to greet him. A warm, soft hug felt appropriate. He held me for a moment. It was nice.

"How are you today?" he said.

I nodded, "Great! Happy to be going home." It felt like an eternity since I had slept in my own bed. I threw some things in my suitcase, a few bottles of apple wine and a leather notebook that Luke wanted me to have. Luke helped me get everything to the door.

"Have the cops come and talked to you?" he said.

Oh, wait, there was that. Rachel's murder. "No. You?"

"One guy came by this morning. Asked me if I saw anything else."

I had to be very careful in my next response. It had to be enough to drop the subject. "Well, if they need to get a hold of us when we get home, they have all our information. Until then, no more drama, or murders, or anything like that. I'm sick and tired of it."

His eyes twitched violently, "Okay, I'll drop it." My bags were picked up and his arms flexed. "Catalina, I, uh, want to talk to you about something."

I didn't want to go into the conversation blind, so I imagined what he'd have to say. We hadn't spent much time together since the body. A wild idea came to mind, "It wasn't Gavin. He didn't kill her."

"I know."

I slowly nodded. "How did you know?"

"Because you said he didn't."

"So, you trust him?"

"I trust you." His eye twitched. "You're my best friend, and I'm really sorry that my feelings for you got in the way of that."

No, that wasn't right. He was entitled to his feelings, even if I didn't accept them. "Let's just move forward, okay? Maybe we should see a movie. This week?"

"Are you serious?"

I happily nodded. "I'd love to."

He piled all my suitcases under one arm, "Well, alright then! But I'll have to give you a rain check."

"Why? You've been trying to set up a hang-out since I moved here."

"I've got my own adventures planned."

I opened the door and let him out, "Good, for you. It's always nice to have a change of pace." Sunglasses went to the bridge of my nose.

"You sure are in a good mood today."

"Life is short. And we're too young to be stressed." We were at the SUV. Aaron walked around back and popped the hatch. I threw my bags in, with Luke's help, and proceeded to the rear passenger door. Aaron followed me.

"Ready to go home, Catalina? Start working in the office with me?" he said.

"You got your wish, Aaron. I'll be your slave." I grabbed the handle, and he stopped me.

There was always more to discuss when it came to Aaron. He looked over his shoulder. Cecilia and Luke had already gotten into the car. "I'm on your side," he said. "I'd never hurt you."

"Was that something I had to be worried about?"

Cecilia's window came down, "Aaron, I'm tired! Let's go!"

He left. I reluctantly got in. Cecilia put her mirror down, "Catalina," she said, "you look good."

Luke put his arm around me. Aaron whispered a few things to her but didn't pay any attention to me the whole way home.

Dad gave me the whole week off. Two of his terminal patients had passed away, and Paula was off the list for the next several weeks. He also didn't need me to work with Aaron until the following week, either. "Just enjoy yourself before things pick up," is what he said.

And so, I did. I helped Mother clean around the house and sat in the audience as Cecilia went through her wardrobe to ditch the clothes she no longer liked. Aaron mentioned selling them online, and Cecilia jumped at the opportunity for a new business venture. Within a few days, she had netted over $2,000 from just a purse and a scarf.

While remaining present with her, and relaxing in my room with books and wine, I refrained from thinking too much about Gavin. We still didn't talk, even though we had each other's number. It just didn't feel right to have so much access to him. Brianna, on the other hand, sent me pictures of her and her friends as they went out on their adventures. She also kept up the conversation with me regarding my interests and what not. She truly did want to be my friend, a genuine friend.

One thing I liked about Brianna was she didn't pry into my relationship with Gavin. "He's complicated and private," she said over the phone. "But give him a chance to grow into his feelings. Don't give up on him, even though I know you might want to." She did ask more about Luke, wanting to know if I'd ever date him. "Seems like a nice guy, I wouldn't blame you. But I gotta root for my dark and twisty older cousin. He needs love, even if it kills him."

Luke was out of town visiting family in Vermont, so when Mother came to the door saying I had a visitor, my thoughts went blank. There was a short list of people, some good, some bad, who would want to see me. Today, it was Aaron.

The moment I saw him in the living room, I looked for a quick exit. But Mother was still in the area, hovering between us. She asked him a few questions before disappearing into the kitchen.

Since Gavin and I hadn't seen each other, I didn't have any tabs on what was going on with James and Cecilia. Was this about her? Cecilia had been a ghost for the last two days, which was for the best. No more drama. At least not until now. My attention went straight to Aaron.

"Hi, Catalina," he smiled. Dressed in his blue scrubs, he looked too young to be a doctor.

"Aaron," I said stiffly.

He motioned to the couch. I declined, "I'm gonna sit." Once settled in, he sighed, "I've already done 60 hours this week."

"Well, my dad gave me the week off, so..." No bullshit, that was the best tactic.

"I'm sorry," his elbows were supported on his knees. He looked tired. "You and I have not had a good relationship so far. And that's mostly my fault. I love your sister, and I'm going to continue working with your dad, so we need to clear the air."

I was unimpressed with him. "Aaron what exactly is it that you want from me? You and Gavin…" he motioned to the kitchen where Mother was still close. Smart. "I still don't trust you," I whispered.

"I watch people die every day. It sucks because it's my job to keep them alive. So, when I see you throwing yourself at Gavin Scott, my instincts are to keep you from getting hurt."

"Well, Gavin's not your problem, he's mine, so don't think about it." I sat across from him in one of Mother's new white leather chairs.

"It's been real quiet around here lately; maybe it's because of you." He seemed content with my comment. Surprisingly, I felt the same way.

The newspapers were boring now. Everyone had moved on from Chris's death. There was nothing mentioned about Ralph. I believed Gavin when he said he would take care of Kyle. As the silence grew, so did my confidence. Things could get better…maybe.

Mother came into the room. "I'm off to Susan's for some Bridge." She came over and kissed my cheek. "Aaron, it's nice to see you." With her gone, I could leave, too.

"Well, I'm happy we had this talk." There was nothing else to discuss. At least not for me.

"Catalina," Aaron cleared his throat, "I thought I'd ask you directly to work with me and my patients for a while, so I could keep an eye on you."

Dad had announced my new work duties while we were on vacation, and Aaron was there. I supposed Aaron felt the need to make the formal invitation. Whatever the case, my answer was pretty obvious.

"Like I have a choice." The gloom in his eyes made my reaction harder to stand by. It would have been better if he was mad. "I think we have a lot more mending to do before we can really move forward, you know?"

"You don't like me, I get it. But there's more to the story…"

A cackled, "In what universe…"

"Porter's my brother." This was interesting news. "He's actually my half-brother. Same mom, different dad."

The moodiness. The need for me to stay away from Gavin. Aaron's strange behaviors made sense to me. "Um, you…" It crashed into me at once. There was no getting away from the obvious. "You know about Gavin and your brother?" Aaron nodded. "And you know about me and Gavin, so you have something on me?"

"No!" Aaron said. "I would never let my brother know about you."

"Who else knows about Porter being your brother? Cecilia?"

"No one. And if you know anything about my brother, you'd understand why I want to keep this to myself."

"He's a monster, Aaron. All those people he's killed!"

"Look, I only know a few things about his dealings, but he's been quiet for the last week. I think things are gonna blow over."

"Blow over?" A slap in the face, "Aaron, he's free. He's able to go out and kill more people. And no one's stopping him."

"He was only killing people in Gavin's crew. They provoked one another. No one else has gotten hurt."

"That doesn't make it right!"

"No, it doesn't, but I haven't figured out how to stop him yet. Someone like my brother is well-connected and heartless. He's not gonna let anyone take him down, including me."

Point made. Oddly enough, I appreciated Aaron sharing this with me. Something so personal. And deadly. This kind of information was invaluable. With Gavin and Porter's position, I had to be smart. Not upset Aaron too much. "Listen, I don't want any trouble," I said. "Gavin's been trying to keep me out of all this. And it sounds like working with you will put me back in your brother's crosshairs."

"He would never do that. If you're not lying to me about your situation with Gavin, you'll be fine. I can help you."

No, it wasn't enough. There was no incentive large enough to change my mind. "I don't want to work with you. I don't like you, and I still don't trust you."

"Well, if you decline my offer, we can't come up with a plan together."

"What kind of plan?"

"Something to keep you hidden from my brother, while we get some dirt on him."

Bringing down Porter would keep Gavin safe for good. I wanted that, but not with Aaron's help. "We can do this without having to work at the clinic together."

"Catalina, your dad's already set it up. I just came over as a gesture."

"So, I'm stuck with you?" he nodded. "Fine," I said.

"Great." He paused, "I honestly thought I'd have to fight super hard before you'd agree."

Take it easy, I thought. No need stirring the pot. I sat quietly and waited for him to release me. Instead, he said, "Things will get better around here. They always do."

"It's fine," I said. "No need to explain it to me."

"Okay," and he was up. "I'll see you at the Halloween party, then."

I almost forgot Halloween was coming up. It was going to be my first real friend date with Luke. We were going as Mark Antony and Cleopatra. Halloween wasn't really my thing, but I knew I'd enjoy it. I smiled at the thought of the endless supply of alcohol.

"Catalina, I'm happy you're gonna give me a chance."

"It's not a chance, Aaron. It's a hostile takeover." Something came to my mind that was important, "What if Porter figures it out…what we're up to?"

Aaron didn't waste any time responding. He said he knew his brother well and calculating his actions would be simple. Getting the truth about the murders would be hard.

I wasn't intimidating. Nor did I have anything to hold over Porter's head, except for maybe Gavin. Gavin leaving town wasn't a threat to Porter, since in some ways he was already gone. But playing with Porter, telling him that I knew something about his enemy, would only lead him into whatever trap Aaron wanted to lay. Yet, that would be incredibly unfair to me. Why did I have to lose Gavin? And for once, I had a moment to decide what I wanted instead of having this problem thrust upon me. So, I told Aaron that. I explained why I didn't want to just fall into his plot. Instead, I wanted to come up with another plan that wouldn't put me or Gavin in harm's way.

"Just let me know when you've got an idea," he said. "Remember, I try to stay out of my brother's affairs, so we're gonna have to be slick."

And that's where we left it. He got up and was at the door. I didn't bother walking him out.

"Are we starting at six tomorrow?" I said.

He smiled, "Nah, I wanna sleep in. We'll start on Monday." I clasped my hands together, silently waiting for him to leave. "I've got a ton of books at my house. You can always come over and check them out."

"Too soon," I said.

He nodded. "Take care, Catalina."

The moment Aaron opened the door, Mother appeared. "I forgot Susan's casserole dish." She let him out and grabbed the dish. I was on my way to my room when she stopped me. "Don't forget to take Luke to the Halloween event, Catalina."

"Okay." Tension gripped my stomach and shoulders. I bit my lip. It had been so long since I had done that.

My mother kissed my cheek: she smelled sweet. I remembered being a kid and holding onto her, breathing in the same smell. She patted my back and mentioned something about being back before Dad got home.

Then the house was quiet. No one but me. I grabbed a book from my collection; sonnets and poems from Luke. I flipped through the pages and picked one.

The Lost, The Forgotten

Before you go, you must know, the hunted will soon fall

And in my heart, I've been torn apart, I must heed the call

Destiny's broken, my love has spoken, it's all that I know

The lost has wandered, the forgotten been
laundered, and you'll never let me go.

I got a text from Cecilia. A picture. Gavin was in town and he was talking over things with James. In the background, I saw someone else. He looked upset, ready to strike. The next photo was of Kyle, in broad daylight, holding a gun to James's head.

CHAPTER TWENTY-FOUR

Halloween

LUKE AND I hitched a ride with my parents to the massive Halloween party put on as a joint effort between the town of Settlement Island and the Country Club. Settlers and Clubbers. I was told that this was the only time the two communities came together, other than church. Supposedly, it was a tradition.

The city center had been converted into a bar, dance hall, and haunted house. It was nice to see the kids running about in their costumes. Their imagination was really inspiring.

Luke grabbed my hand, "You look so beautiful."

That was all Cecilia's doing. She loaned me the dress and dolled up my face to look like Cleopatra herself. Luke didn't look bad, either. I had told him this earlier, but it didn't seem to sink in. He had been acting strange, but I didn't have the heart to ask what was going on. I wanted a fun, exciting night. Nothing less.

Cecilia had told me not to worry about James and

Kyle. She was convinced that it was a prank, a minor brawl brought on by James's constant badgering of Kyle. Apparently, their relationship status was falling apart, but it was still on the mend. Neither one felt intimidated by the other any longer. Fine. However, that wasn't my concern.

Why hadn't Gavin told me about it?

Luke opened the car door, letting in the cold air. Too cold. Mother offered me one of her fur coats, and I took it without any debate. Luke tucked it around me.

I smiled, "Thank you. You look muscular."

He flexed for me a bit and extended his arm. We proceeded into the building. Once inside, I could tell that this was a big "To Do" for the town. Luke pushed past a veil of spider webs. A tap hit my shoulder. I turned. A zombie swayed closer to my face.

I laughed, "I'm on your side. Plastic surgery is so overrated."

The zombie growled at me and moved on.

"We should go find the bar," Luke commented.

I nodded. Hand in hand, we fought through the crowd until we made our way into a large room with a dance floor and a bar along the wall. Luke approached it first. I looked for anyone I knew, primarily James. With Cecilia around, he had a way of finding her. Not seeing him, I got comfortable with whatever Luke had handed me.

"Did you have a good couple of weeks?" Luke said.

His turnaround trip to Vermont right after The Pines would have seemed odd if it wasn't for our gruesome discovery. A break from the Settlement Island drama put him in good spirits.

I didn't need such a dramatic change of pace to smooth things over in my mind. No new murders meant a world of opportunities. And on nights like this one, that's all I wanted.

"I'm happy you're back," I said.

The D.J. came over the loud speaker, "Good evening, gals and ghouls. Prepare yourself for a night of food, fun, dancing, and games. Not to mention things for the kids to do. It'll be to die for!"

Corny, very corny. But it put a smile on my face. I tasted my drink: rum and coke. Luke went with a beer which was probably a smart choice. A cheesy Halloween song came on. Luke sang off-key to me. He gave me a twirl.

"Thank you for the lovely serenade," I joked. Luke pulled me in for a kiss on the cheek.

Cecilia, Aaron, Molly, and Adrienne approached us. Cecilia and Molly were dressed as Victoria Secret models. Adrienne was a nun. She and Luke did a once over and then averted their attention to the room.

This was the first time I had seen her in a while. And the first time I had ever seen the two of them together. She had no idea Luke and I were such close friends, unless Cecilia had told her. I doubted that since my sister and I were actually becoming friends ourselves. My secrets seemed to stay with her these days.

Aaron was a vampire which was no surprise to me since Cecilia always made her dates dress up as vampires on Halloween.

I nodded in Cecilia's direction, "So, what are you guys up to tonight?"

"Well, Baby Sister, Aaron's throwing a party at his house after this one ends," she said.

Aaron nodded a little too much. He went in for a hug. I couldn't escape in time, "Looking forward to working with you, Catalina."

Alcohol was on his breath. No wonder he was allowing Cecilia to destroy his house. Otherwise, I'm sure he would have been looking for a chance or two to corner me again and plead with me to get my sister to calm down. Or there was the option for another talk about my feelings toward him.

Surprisingly, after our last little talk, I didn't mind Aaron as much. We were on level ground, and I intended to keep it that way. But once time was up on our understanding, I would find a way to stay ahead of him. That seemed to be the nature of the game in Settlement Island.

Cecilia clapped to get everyone's attention, "Alcohol run. Let's go to the bar."

Luke and I held up our drinks in unison. I smiled—same page.

She didn't press us to follow her group. Aaron didn't linger. Now it was just Luke and me. Adrienne looked over her shoulder at us. I felt bad for not clueing her in on what had developed between her ex-boyfriend and me.

Luke wasn't bothered by Adrienne. He continued dancing and singing to various songs he knew. I delighted in his light-heartedness. Soon, we were off drinking, talking, and checking out the rest of the hall. The rooms grew darker. I downed my rum and cowed closer to Luke.

Strobe lights blinded me. Luke darted around through the decorations until he ran across a guy he knew. I couldn't make out what they were saying until he pulled me through the darkness and pulsating lights. We stopped at the entrance of the haunted house.

Introductions were made, but it was hard for me to get the name of his acquaintance over all the music. Luke placed his hand at the small of my back and put his lips to my ear, "I'm gonna go get another drink."

"I'll wait here."

Luke's hand went to the side of my face. His eyes were trained on me. This was it—that kiss he had been saving for far too long. Out of instinct, I closed my eyes. It took a few seconds for his lips to find mine. They stayed together. No open mouths, just two pairs of lips planted firmly on one another.

I was relieved when the kiss ended. Luke grinned and walked off with his friend to retrieve more alcohol. If we were going to kiss again, I would need it. This whole time, he had held onto our friendship for that kiss. Now that we had experienced it, the magic was gone.

I didn't like Luke. This was another win for Gavin. I loved him more than I thought, or at least I had my own version of love for him. Love was complicated, which went right along with everything else that was complicated about me and him.

Couples rushed past me to enter the haunted house.

I decided to follow. The first step was up. I almost missed it. There were countless giggles bouncing off the floor and walls. I had lost the group ahead of me.

I wasn't afraid. Safety was my biggest concern. The constant flow of strobe lights was making me sick. My hand latched onto a railing, and I continued upward until the steps stopped. A light flashed on. The chainsaw sounds were silly but effective.

I thought about going back before I tripped over some stupid decoration. "Awe, honey, don't be afraid," said someone. The man holding the chainsaw pointed to the left.

I had to keep going. Now the path was taking me downward. My soft slip-on shoes hit a puddle of water. Great! I hiked up my dress to preserve my costume. Lights on. A bathtub scene with a woman covered in fake blood. She screamed for help as a dark shadow came up from behind.

I screamed and turned to retreat. Something stood in my way. A person.

"Catalina."

We couldn't talk there with all the silly attractions. He put out his hand, and I grabbed it. The rest of the house was a maze of ups and downs. Before long we were at the end and in a corner behind a stage.

My hand smacked him out of habit. "Why haven't you called me?"

"I've been working on something," Gavin said.

I should have been happier to see him, but I wasn't. He looked good—his regular outfit of a dark button-down shirt, dark jeans, and black jacket. Same boots and same killer hair. It hadn't been long since I had last seen him, but I had forgotten how beautiful he was.

"What are you doing here?" I said.

"I was looking for you." He surveyed the blackness and then focused on me, "I needed to see you."

I didn't fight the joy that was so prevalent. He needed to see…me. My happiness was short-lived. Gavin was restless. "What can I do to help you?"

His hand came out again, "Come with me."

A few minutes later, I was climbing into his car. It smelled familiar. Gavin put the car in gear, and we rushed out of the parking lot. I soon realized I had no idea where we were going. However, I didn't question him or his motives.

"Where have you been?" I tried not to sound bossy or too excited.

"Brianna's in Anders."

"She never mentioned anything to me."

"I told her not to."

"And James? Kyle? Cecilia sent me a picture of their brawl in the street."

His hand ran across his entire front section of hair. No answer. We had passed several city landmarks and were headed for the open darkness ahead. Before, I would have been clawing at the door handle. I would have counted the seconds that passed, convinced they would be my last. Tonight was different, for us both. But there were still secrets between us—mainly his.

I kept my mouth shut, hoping that he would trust me enough to let me in again. But he didn't. Or at least he didn't until we had arrived. Our destination was a clearing off a deserted road. I got out the moment the car stopped. The moon was hauntingly bright in the sky. Cars could be heard close by, but their headlights could not be seen. This had to be one of the safest places for us both.

Gavin put his jacket around my arms and took my hand. I thanked him, seeing how I had left my mother's fur coat on some rack back in town. He put his hands on my hips and helped me up on the hood of his car before he slid up to join me. We lay down against the windshield, both of us admiring the stars above.

"Aaron came to see me," he said.

I held in my reaction. It wasn't a good idea to give anything away. "When was this?"

"Thursday. He came by to check on Paula. Said he was following your dad's orders. But I had talked to your dad earlier about Paula's improvements, so I knew Aaron was lying."

Now I couldn't keep quiet any longer, "Gavin, I had no idea…"

He placed his hand on my leg, "It's okay. I'm not accusing you of anything."

"What did he want?"

"He's Porter's brother." That I already knew. But I still remained silent. Gavin got closer to me, our bodies touching. "He told me because he wanted to bury the hatchet between us. Said he might be able to help out the crew."

What a ludicrous idea. "He's like thirty. And a doctor. And his brother is really, really bad. Why would he be so reckless?"

"Porter's activities are creating an issue for their family. Apparently, he wants to get him thrown in jail for life."

"I had a conversation with him, and he wanted my help with getting something on his brother."

"So, you knew they were related?" There was no patience from him.

"Well, if you had called me…" I said.

"You could have told me," his voice was strained, not quite angry.

He sucked in a deep breath and bit his lip. I corrected this terrible habit by pulling it out and moving on with the conversation. "Are you gonna let Aaron in?" I said. "Help him, I mean."

"I'd never let a member of Porter's family help me or my crew. That would create more problems than it would solve."

"You guys are so fickle: Kyle and Aaron switching sides."

"It's about loyalty and trust. Regardless, I still need to know the truth about Aaron's motives. What the fuck is he up to? And why would he think Porter wouldn't kill him?"

I understood Gavin's need for answers. However, the solutions were right in front of him. He could leave our town for good. All he had to do was tell Aaron he was out, and stay gone, and that would be enough to put everything in motion. It would help me and Aaron come up with a plan.

The earliest I could get Aaron alone to ask more questions would be Monday. Gavin didn't have that much time, probably.

"Well," I finally said, "you can't get answers without asking him directly or waiting to see what happens."

"That doesn't work for me, Catalina. This is my life we're talking about. Porter's a sneaky bastard who'd do anything to kill me."

"Yeah, but he hasn't been successful yet. Maybe you have more time than you think."

He was quiet. "Maybe you're right." His eyes were kind, "But I'm not a cat. I don't have nine lives."

"You don't need them. Leave Aaron to me. We'll figure something out, I promise."

With these new developments considered, Gavin and Aaron would be a great team against Porter. It was perfect—the illusive nemesis and the wronged brother secretly plotting behind Porter's back. After all, Aaron was good at staying hidden, even in his brother's sight.

That was it. I mulled over everything I knew, and the final inquiry came up. "Gavin, Luke knew who Aaron was in high school. James said he never knew Aaron existed. So, how can that be?"

"Aaron's family is beyond rich. He probably stayed in the Club." Gavin sighed. "James doesn't know everyone as much as he thinks."

"Did Porter ever live here?"

"Porter's never set foot in Settlement Island. He's got a whole network of guys who filter in and out."

"But Porter always seems to have the upper hand?"

Gavin sighed, "He doesn't have the upper hand, Catalina."

I placed my index finger on his lips. "Aaron's being used. Porter knows that no one would ever suspect anything because Aaron's the town doctor. He lives here, at The Estates. And no one has ever seen Aaron's brother in town, so Porter's identity will always remain a mystery. So, he's got the perfect cover. Aaron can live his life under the radar, not drawing any attention to himself, and Porter can use Aaron to be the face of his operation. It's genius."

Gavin didn't say anything. I almost thought he hated my idea until… "You might be onto something," he said. "So, if Aaron gets smart about his plan, he can spy on Porter and get away with it. Porter wouldn't know the difference because he might think he's using his brother."

Then came the big bold move. My effort to save him. "I can talk to him about it on Monday. Mention that he should get closer to his brother and dive further into Porter's business, so he can turn on him."

Gavin reached into his pocket and pulled out his phone. Ronda. He shot her a quick text. All I caught was, "It's been over for a while."

He caught me glancing at his phone. His lips locked onto mine. That warm, sweet taste I had missed. So much better than Luke. I broke away. He persisted, his lips massaging mine, making me forget things. That was the way a kiss should be. But it was wrong, slightly tainted. An apologetic gesture after his old, dirty flame begged him to come back.

"You don't have to kiss me to spare my feelings," I said, blocking him from getting another kiss.

He moved some hair from my face. "I miss kissing you."

"And what about Ronda?"

Gavin seemed to seek the right words. "I've known her for a really long time. Since middle school."

"And you never loved her?"

"No," he scoffed. "Ronda and I were only together out of convenience. She made it easy." I gagged. "Don't worry, I've been tested for everything, and I'm good."

"It's not that…" I put my hand through his hair, "you're just so beautiful. Like a dream. And she's…"

He kissed me again, this time slow. "You're the most beautiful person I've ever seen…inside and out." I smiled, taking in the compliment. Another kiss from him made me appreciate him more. Gavin kissed my forehead. "I better get you back." He helped me off the hood, and we got in. "You know, I should have taken you up on your offer. To run away with you."

"I never invited you to run away with me, per se. I meant for you to go find your own adventure."

"Without you? I thought you loved me or something…"

"I never used those words."

"Maybe you should…some time."

"We'll see," I said. And then we did it again. Another

kiss. It was becoming a habit. A sweet habit neither one of us wanted to kick.

∽

When we arrived back at the community center, Gavin pulled up right at the door. I climbed out without saying goodbye.

I didn't have to travel far to find Luke. He was drunk and talking to Adrienne. She noticed me first. "Where'd you go, Catalina?" she said.

Her face was soft and charming. Soft, like she wanted him to enjoy his time with her. Luke, on the other hand, seemed relieved. Or maybe it was guilt. I hadn't received a single call or text from him during my absence.

He put his arms around me, "She just came up to me and started talking," he whispered. "I'm not trying to rekindle anything, I swear." He stumbled backward.

"How many drinks have you had?" I said.

"Too many. Aaron wants us to hit him up." Now his back was to Adrienne.

I shook my head, "Nah, let's just call it a night."

My hand went around Luke's to guide him toward the door. He said something, his other hand motioning toward Gavin talking to Molly. The distance closing between them as Molly tried to pull him onto the dance floor. I was uncomfortable until I remembered what he said about missing kissing me. Part of me wanted to march up to them and take back my Gavin. My beautiful muse. Yet something stopped me. A hooded figure appeared. A man, rushing through the crowd. A loud bang could be heard over the music. My ears rang. Molly slipped to the ground, Gavin kneeling down next to her. Then came James, Mark, and Oliver.

Panic ensued. People grabbing their kids. Hanging decorations were torn down as various costumed people ran in every direction. Aaron and my father rushed to Molly.

Luke managed to pull me back away from the scene, but it took much effort. Cecilia had tried to move me before, but I released my arm from her. She grabbed Adrienne and shouted something to Luke about our mother. He reluctantly complied, leaving me alone.

"Run!" my sister said to me.

I headed outside into the cold. Miraculously, I was the first one out. The snow fell down on me. A brush of cold hit my skin, making me long for Gavin's jacket. Gavin. I had to find him. As I rounded the corner, I saw Molly being carried out by my father and Aaron. She was crying, holding her arm, blood spilling down to the snow.

They were close. And I...I was slipping away. My arm was caught in someone's hand. The hooded figure.

He pressed his finger to his lips. His body smashed against mine as my back hit the wall. I couldn't stop from shivering. My breathing slowed to help me stay calm. There was no fighting him; he was too strong. He had too much to lose.

"If you don't leave now, you'll get caught," I said. His face had been obstructed by the hood, so his features were completely unknown. The gun went into his pocket. Closer and closer, he came. "I'm not worth it," I said, staring into the blackness covering his face.

Sirens…I could hear sirens.

"I'm not worth it…please, I'm not worth it."

He was gone before I could say his name. Kyle.

Chapter Twenty-Five
Revenge

I wasn't allowed to leave, that was the deal I made with myself. Kyle had slipped by, and I wasn't going to be his next victim. Molly was alive; that was something I had to deal with. I didn't have to go to her funeral, which was a good thing. And the police were upset that I didn't have any information they could use to find her attacker.

In the midst of everything, I harbored a secret. But I wasn't afraid. Kyle had a chance to shoot me, and he didn't draw his gun. In fact, he put it away.

His behaviors were inconsistent: shooting Molly and merely approaching me. Putting out his hand to touch me without really causing any harm. He had me, right there, yet…nothing. With all this, only one thing could be true: he was planning on taking me. He needed me to remain unharmed just long enough for his plan to work out. I had to know why.

The newspaper had been crawling with stories about

Molly's unsolved attack. Every time I saw her face, I tried to force myself to feel something. Nothing.

I didn't know Molly. And she probably wasn't someone I would have been close to.

Yet, the nature of her attempted murder stayed with me. She was probably hurt because of me. I was the target, even though I couldn't believe it. And if I wasn't the target, was Gavin?

Oh, Gavin. I hadn't seen him since that night. He was safe, according to Cecilia. Due to the nature of Molly's attack, he had to lie low; lie low and leave me to my own devices. What a way to protect your one, true love. And I was now working with Aaron, so there was no need to go over to Gavin's house anymore.

I looked at the clock. It was six. My phone rang. "Hello, Aaron." My voice was still sleepy.

"Good morning! I have coffee and doughnuts, and I'm heading to your house." He was more excited about my new job than I was.

I rolled out of bed, "What should I wear?"

"Skirt or dress. You'll want to look nice."

I picked out a dark blue dress and gray leather jacket, "I may need you to iron my clothes when you get here."

He laughed, "I actually know how to do that."

I yawned, "How long till you're here?"

"Ten minutes…you better get a move on."

I hung up on him and went to the bathroom to brush my teeth. My outfit felt comfortable and warm. Hair went up into a ponytail. It was snowing outside and had been for the last two days. Pure white snow. Fresh. Unspoiled.

Warmth was more important than anything else. I added black leggings and a matching parka. The door shut behind me. Whistles of cold air breezed past my face and hands.

Aaron pulled into the driveway. I jumped into the SUV without hesitation, "Hey."

"Good morning, Catalina!" He had passed being chipper and entered the region of annoying.

A steaming cup of coffee was handed to me. One sip and the hot poison did its magic, "Thank you."

"Welcome to your first real job!"

It wasn't my first real job, but I'd give him this. Instead, there were other things on my mind. I wondered how exactly I would be able to pry into Aaron's life without setting off any alarms. This seemed easy. After all, he was being nice. But why? Was it something I had said or done? Not possible. Actually, my behaviors were the exact opposite, so there was no way his happy demeanor was attached to me. Yet, here we were, together, frosty relationship and all.

I had to be warmer to Aaron. Stop being so rude and strive to make an honest connection with him. "It's one more step towards independence."

He nodded, "Very true. At your age, you should be clawing your way out of your dad's house."

"I'm happy at home. Dad gives us plenty of freedom, so it's not too bad."

"Cecilia seems to have a lot of freedom."

I knew it was best to leave that be. "What are we going to be doing today?"

"Well, I have a couple of patients coming in." No more talk of Cecilia. Smart man. "Your job is to greet them, pull their records, and file the charts after I'm done. It'll be super boring, so I hope you brought a book."

"I'll be fine."

"The busier we get, the more I'll have for you to do. This week I'll get you involved with the office stuff. Next week, I'll teach you how to do the billing stuff."

"I can't wait."

My eyes drifted to the snowflakes cascading against the windshield. "I'm happy to have you working with me," he said. "Gives us a chance to know more about one another. And I can keep an eye on you."

His concern was unnecessary, "I already told you, I'm not getting into any more trouble."

He nodded, "I know. This just gives me peace of mind."

We pulled up to the office. I waited for Aaron to unlock the door before I braved the cold to run inside. Lights on. I scanned the beautiful, white desk area where I would be stationed. My tall, black high-backed office chair looked out of place among the bright blue, green, and red colored chairs in the lobby.

"My dad picked out all the furniture, didn't he?"

Aaron sighed, "It doesn't match, I know. When it warms up, your mom's coming in to make some changes."

He went to his office and put on his white coat over his button-down shirt and slacks. I leaned against the doorframe and took a peek into his world. There were several awards on his walls. And his various degrees. Cecilia always had a thing for doctors and dentists. However, Aaron had to be by far the youngest.

"How long did it take you to get your M.D.?"

He chuckled. "Forever." His hands smoothed out his hair, and he grabbed a paper or two from his desk. Now we were on the move back to the reception area. "Didn't actually start practicing medicine until two years ago."

"How old are you?"

"Twenty-eight. I graduated early by taking extra credits before I got into medical school."

He didn't look twenty-eight. I bet Aaron got more speculation about who he was than I did. Gifted, super young. Most people figured we were just really driven. Truth is, his school work probably just clicked for him in the same manner it did for me. Maybe we did have something in common. "You really are a doctor, aren't you?" I said with amusement.

He laughed, "Yes, I am."

"Do you ever get scared that you'll make a mistake or misdiagnose a patient?"

He picked up a few charts from my desk and then looked back at me, "No."

"I see."

Aaron sat in my chair, "Don't get me wrong, I know I'll make mistakes. I'm human. But I believe that if I hurt someone, I can fix it."

"Good to know. I wonder how your patients feel…"

He opened a chart, "Take Mr. Johnson for instance. He's sixty-eight and has a history of tobacco use for almost forty years. We're seeing him today because he has a pain in his chest…"

"He has lung cancer," I said.

"Maybe. Or it could be heart or stress-related. I won't know until I talk with him and run some tests." The chart was placed down, "You see, I can't fix him until I know what's wrong. I won't know what's wrong with him until I talk to him and get evidence of his illness."

"Yeah, but what if you're wrong? What if you're so sure he's got one thing, and he's got something different? He could die because of you."

"See, that's the thing. I'm not worried about being wrong before I even see my patients. If I felt that way, I wouldn't be a doctor."

Good answer. Thought provoking. I looked down, "What if all the evidence is wrong?"

"What do you mean?"

"What if the evidence says it's a heart attack, and he actually has cancer? You just wasted all your time treating a disease that wasn't even there."

"Well, that's easy. Cancer and heart attacks are diagnosed and treated differently. I'd be completely negligent if I made that mistake." His confidence entertained me.

"What if it's both?"

"I'll be lucky, because I'll catch it. I examine all my patients…thoroughly," He paused before smirking, "You have no faith in me. And this is not about my patient, is it?"

Great catch, Aaron. But I hadn't come up with a point to all my questions yet. How to tie everything back to his brother. "No, not at all. You're probably a good doctor."

"So, you're trying to figure something out, huh?"

"No. I'm just asking questions."

"Any questions about my brother?"

Stay calm. He was pressing. One missed step, and I'd regret it. "No, you shared enough about him."

Aaron got up from my chair and motioned for me to sit down. When I did, he pushed it in, "Catalina, I hope this job helps with your confidence and self-esteem."

"Why would you say that?"

He came around to the front of the desk and looked at me, "Because you're gonna need it. With Molly's attack comes more complications. And if we're gonna work together to take down my brother, I need you to be strong."

"What's going on with Porter? I mean, Molly was attacked by mistake, right?" I moistened my lips. "I mean, if he sent someone there to shoot up the place, it wouldn't be to hurt Molly, right?"

"I don't know. My brother isn't answering his phone."

"Maybe he's not answering because he's planning on coming here?" I said.

He put his hand on mine. I moved back, "Catalina, he's not gonna hurt you. He has no reason to."

For a minute, I didn't say anything. "Let's focus on saving Mr. Johnson from his chest pain," I said.

He let go of my hand, "Mr. Johnson has had pneumonia, a kidney stone, and the flu in the last year," Aaron said with a smile, "And I've saved him every single time."

"Great!" I sat up straight and laced my fingers on the desk. "Wait, you haven't been here for that long. How is that…"

"He's been my patient since I was finishing up my residency in Anders. I have tons of patients who moved here for me. That's why your father hired me."

If this was a show to win points, he had received a few from me. My assumptions about Porter's leverage over him were pretty accurate. Get back into Settlement Island and keep tabs on everything. That's exactly what Porter wanted Aaron to do. Unfortunately, Dad gave him the perfect opportunity. "Well, thank God you're their doctor."

"Okay, then." He pointed to the door, "We open at seven. If you need me, you can either find me in my office or in the exam rooms at the end of the hall. If I'm with a patient, please knock before coming in."

I nodded, "Got it. Greet the patients, give you their chart, and file it when you give it back to me. I have it down."

"Awesome," he smiled, "I'll be in the back if you want anything." He walked toward his office and turned back to me, "Oh, and Cecilia's coming over to see me sometime today."

Of course.

༄

The first four hours went by pretty fast. After greeting the patients and getting their files ready for Aaron, a lot of them socialized with me while they waited. Everyone had something nice to say about Dad being their doctor. I found that strange since they were in to see Aaron.

As Aaron guided his eleven o'clock patient back, he told me that I could go to lunch after I greeted his noon patient. For the next several minutes, I sat back, reading a mystery. Normally mysteries weren't my thing, but I had grown to like them. Plus, they served as a learning tool for me regarding my situation with Gavin. I contemplated his whereabouts, wondering if he had made any headway on the Porter front.

The door chimed, disrupting my thoughts. My jaw dropped. Ronda. She approached the desk, and neither one of us said anything. Now face-to-face with her, I mentally pointed out the major difference between us.

Her skin and hair were oily. Smudged dark eye makeup. The light jeans and black jacket were too small for her body. Dead, glossy eyes. What in the hell was Gavin thinking? How could he be close to a lifeless person like her? How could he give her his body?

Knowing that she was more than likely plotting my demise, I quickly got up and went to Aaron's office. He was still seeing his previous patient in one of the exam rooms, so I closed the door and tried to regroup. I searched my mind for the best way to deal with her.

Someone knocked on the door and opened it. It was Aaron. He came in and went straight to his desk.

"Did you get tired of your desk already? Taking over my job?"

I shook my head and tried to hide my panic, "No, I just wanted to make a private phone call."

He sat down, "Okay. Is my noon patient here?"

I nodded weakly, "Yep. I'll get you the chart."

"No rush. I'm gonna fill a prescription first. You can just put the file in Exam Room 3, and I'll take it from there. Then go to lunch."

"Okay," I said quietly as I went to the front again.

Ronda had taken a seat. I was petrified. I grabbed her chart and headed for the exam room. But first I had to take a look. She had an ear infection. No STDs, not that it mattered since she and Gavin hadn't been together for a while. And he said he was clean, anyway.

I finished my task and headed back to the lobby for my jacket. Ronda just stared at me. I wasn't going to be an idiot. Moving quickly, I left the office and made my way to the café. Walking fast, I tried to cross the icy and snowy road without my dressy flats slipping out from under me. Should have gone with the boots.

I cursed myself as a rush of pain hit my head. My ponytail was pulled, and a sharp jabbing pain hit my back. I turned toward my assailant. Ronda struck my eyebrow. The burning pain crawled across my entire skull. Another punch across the face sent me stumbling against a building and slipping on the ice.

My head throbbed. My breaths were rapid.

"Get up!" she demanded.

I reached out to the ice and slid my body away. A blow hit my side. The impact of her boot against my rib made me scream.

"Get your ass up!"

I looked around for help, but everyone within helping

distance seemed to have gone missing. "Ronda, please don't do this," I pleaded.

Another kick. I put my hands down, and they absorbed the next blow, leaving my ribs with a lesser amount of pain.

I shook my head and held in my tears, "I'm sorry."

"Too late now!" Out came a knife from her back pocket.

She kicked me again, harder, and demanded that I rise. I was paralyzed. Everything throbbed. I knew I had to try to fight, but I couldn't. Panic overcame me. She sliced a few cuts across my jacket. No blood yet. It was just a warning.

"Get up!" she waved the knife, cutting a line across my hand.

I tucked my head into my arms. A kick hit my head; more pain. My ear drum pounded. Now, back to my ribs and my back; fierce, deadly kicks, with intermittent stops to slice. My hands intercepted most of the blade work, a hard task for her since I had been bleeding so much. Blood was streaming down my hands and into my eyes.

This was it. Warm blood dripped down my jacket and onto the ice below me. I was beyond tired and consumed by constant screaming pains throughout my body. I was done. I was ready to stop fighting.

Ronda's attention flashed away. She was concerned. Lots of yelling came, and she tried to scurry backwards, the slick ice keeping her in place. The knife fell beside me. They went at it, but Ronda was no match. You can't defeat rage with anger, as she was quickly figuring out.

Three punches were all it took for her to be overpowered, but it wasn't enough. She had to even the score, my savior. When Ronda collapsed, I became the focus.

Cecilia was a dream. A phantom from my past as I descended into death.

"Catalina, can you hear me?" James said.

I needed help. Serious help.

"Aaron," I pushed out. I rested on the ice and tried not to breathe. James grabbed my hand and pressed the wound on my head, right below my hairline. His touch was cold and painful. He was pressing too hard.

A crowd huddled around Ronda and me. Almost everyone checked on me instead of her. Things were becoming more and more painful. James screamed for Cecilia to get her boyfriend. His touch became my life line. As long as I could feel him and the pain his fingers radiated into my body, I had a chance.

Just a few blinks later, I saw my sister again. Then Aaron took over for James. He shuddered and stumbled as he shouted out directions to everyone. I didn't cry. No matter how bad it hurt, I wouldn't give Ronda my tears.

"Catalina, do you know where she hit you?" Aaron said. I could only gargle. He hushed me at once and threw some gloves on James. "Keep pressing on her head, while I check her other injuries."

James was very firm with his application of pressure. No bravado or laughter from him. His hands shook. I had the impression that he had never seen someone he cared about in this way. A tear: he wiped it away from his face with the glove, a tiny bit of my blood on his cheek.

I was nervous; had things gotten worse? I felt colder now. Sirens were distant in the background. I closed my eyes.

"Her eyes are closed!" said James.

"Stay with us, Catalina!" It was Aaron.

I counted to three and opened them. Cecilia had grabbed my hand. Her face was stained with black eyeliner and mascara.

I breathed in and the pain intensified. Aaron felt me shudder. "I know it hurts. We're gonna take you to Anders to run some x-rays and see if you need surgery."

The cops had come, pushing the crowd back, and questioning the people closest to me. One officer in particular was paying special attention to Ronda. He demanded that the paramedics treat her, too.

"Get down on the ground!" An officer yelled at my sister.

She lowered herself to the ice. We were barely able to see one another. I mouthed the word "love," hoping she knew that I appreciated her saving my life. They cuffed Cecilia.

"I'm Dr. Aaron White," I heard Aaron say, "I'll be treating her injuries." Aaron's introduction was clean and professional, without any emotion. "We need to get her loaded into that ambulance now!"

Soon, James was relieved of his duties. Three medics gently lifted me, put my body on a stretcher, and put gauze on my bloody wounds. Ronda was being loaded the same way. Needles went into my arm. Aaron ran with the stretcher, and soon we were in the ambulance.

"She's got at least one compound fracture to her ribs, a large laceration on her right temple, multiple cuts on her hands, and blunt force trauma to her face and head. The sooner we can get to Anders General, the better."

He pressed his hand to my forehead, "Catalina, I know it hurts, but you have to be strong and stay focused. Don't think like a victim. You're not defenseless. You have to push past the pain. You're gonna be fine."

I closed my eyes and welcomed the blackness as we sailed forward. Whether I was alive or dead, it didn't matter to me as long as Gavin wasn't by my side.

"Catalina, stay awake!" I heard Aaron's voice.

I didn't.

I focused on the feeling of warm sunrays roasting my skin. Sand massaging my muscles after a long jog on the beach. The salt resting on my tongue, making me thirsty. Then the water rushing against my feet.

Then everything was gone. California. My ocean. And me.

CHAPTER TWENTY-SIX

Almost

A COLD, CLEAN hospital bed. The sheets stuck to my back. Having these feelings let me know I was alive. Yet, I didn't want to be. The waves of pain were too much to bear. Some were enough to wake me up but not for long.

When I was dreaming, I almost forgot how bad things were. I could, at times, step into a place that was warm and vibrant only to find myself back in the sterile bed. I didn't want to go home; being in this near-dead state was not something I wanted to be reminded of while lying in my room. However, my new residence had no books. There was nothing for me in this place…well, except for one thing.

A beautiful face staring at me. "Catalina Payton! You've got us all worried!"

Miguel Peralta. My best friend. He was in Settlement Island with me. My entire body throbbed, so I couldn't give him a hug. "Hi."

He put his finger to his lips and pointed across the

room. Dad and Mother sat in chairs, facing each other. I looked over at them to make out what they were saying.

"The court date is in one week. In the meantime, they're gonna hold her in case she tries to skip town," Dad said.

"And Cecilia?" Mother said.

"No charges. We may want to get a lawyer in case this girl's family tries to go after us for money."

Mother nodded, "Do you think Catalina will have to testify?"

"I don't know. I hope she does, so that girl doesn't get away with this." Dad put his head in his hands and sighed loudly. Mother put her hand on his back, "She seemed to be right about this place."

Mother moved over and hugged him. Dad wiped his eyes. "I know."

I blinked a couple times as I watched them comfort each other. It wasn't their fault. They had been justified in their motives to move, and I didn't blame them for my turn in luck. A hug from me and an apology would put them at ease. That would have to wait.

Aaron came in, no longer wearing his white coat. He looked normal in his black slacks and black sweater, not like the hero doctor that saved me. He noticed me first.

"Catalina?" he said as my parents looked over in my direction.

I gave a tiny wave, "Hi."

"Miguel, why didn't you say anything?" Mother said. He shrugged.

Miguel always had a way of putting some distance

between me and them, allowing me a chance to breathe. He didn't know that his intentions weren't necessary. I happily welcomed my parents in as they shoved him to the side. Mother sat down next to me, being extra careful not to touch my ribs. I appreciated that.

Dad took my hand, "Hi there. How are you feeling?"

I assessed his question. I was tired and disoriented. My mouth was dry, and my entire body hurt. "Fine," I croaked.

"Good. X-rays showed no broken bones, just some bruised ribs. The cut on your head should be all healed up in about two weeks or so. Luke's dad is going to check it later this week to make sure you don't have a scar."

"How long have I been here?" My words were slow.

"Two days," Aaron said. "You've been out most of the time."

I nodded a little but stopped due to the stiches. Mother kissed my forehead, carefully, "Honey, just rest. We're going to have you transported to the house when you're ready."

"Pain killers," I groaned.

Dad smiled, "Now I don't want you turning into a junkie." I sighed, and he laughed, "You're welcome."

"Do you want to talk about what happened?" Aaron said.

"Shouldn't we wait until she feels better?" Miguel replied. Again, he always had my back.

There was so much I wanted to tell Miguel. We had been out of contact for too long. But this was not the time or place to catch up. I felt horrible, realizing the last conversation we had was about Gavin and his murderous plot. Miguel must have been worried out of his mind. Especially now. Hopefully, he didn't express any of his concerns to my parents.

I couldn't worry about that, though. I closed my eyes in hopes they would think I had fallen asleep. "The police want a statement from you," Mother said as she stroked my hair.

I opened my eyes, "Okay."

Dad sat down on the bed, making it crowded, "Catalina, I want you to know that your mom and I are here for you. Whatever you need. That being said, I'm assigning Aaron as your physician while you recover."

I scrunched my eyebrows but not for long. Too much throbbing. "Why not you?"

"Because I want to baby you and be over-cautious which will negatively impact your recovery. You need to work towards getting better, even if it hurts. Aaron can help you with that."

"And I'll be here, too," said Miguel.

"How long?"

Dad explained the arrangement. He had paid Miguel's mother a handsome sum to have him here with me until I went to California for Christmas. He did that…for me. But if my recovery wasn't complete before my trip, Miguel would disappear back home without me. That was incentive enough. Treatment would be manageable if I had him by my side. My hand gripped his. My other hand squeezed my dad's, "Thank you." More throbbing pulsed through my fingers. I had to let go.

Dad smiled, "You're welcome. Now remember to breathe regularly, even if it hurts. You need to rest, but you can't just sit back and impede your body from healing."

"Where's Cecilia?" I had to see her.

"She went to buy coffee." Mother seemed irritated. Miguel sensed it, too.

"Everything okay with you, Ms. Sally?" Miguel said to my mother.

"Cecilia had to get stitches on her hand, which one would think is serious. Does she think so? No! On her way to the hospital, she insisted that the paramedics call me at home to bring her a new outfit because she got blood on hers."

Mother was furious, but I was grateful. I knew my sister better than I thought. Yes, Cecilia was still shallow, but she only drank coffee if she needed to calm her nerves. She was genuinely worried about me.

I smiled, "Did you bring her one?" Mom didn't say anything. Dad nodded.

Aaron laughed, "Mrs. Payton, you know your daughter wasn't going to walk around in bloody jeans."

"Is she in trouble?" I said. "For the fight?"

Dad shook his head, "No, not at all."

I imagined her standing with the handcuffs on. I loved her. My sister, my hero. Everyone turned their attention to the door.

"I think that's Luke." Mother got up. She tended to my visitor, blocking my view. "Can I help you?" Her tone was confused.

"I'm here to see Catalina Payton."

Mother stepped aside so my visitor could walk in. Miguel and Aaron stayed close to my bed. I'd know that voice anywhere. It had been etched into my mind.

Dad approached Gavin, "Thank you for coming, but Catalina's had a long day. Maybe you should come by the house when she's home."

"It's fine," I said. "Give us a minute?"

Mother and Dad kissed my forehead, "We're going back to Aaron's. Miguel, do you want to come with us?" Mother said.

Miguel's face was a combination of anger, intrigue, and bewilderment. I asked Mother to allow him to stay. It would be easier if they met. When they left, Miguel jumped into a verbal assault, throwing together a string of insults in Spanish.

Aaron folded his arms, "What do you want?"

Gavin gave his cold stare, "I'm not here to talk with you."

Aaron marched up to him, "All I have to do is make one phone call, and they'll carry you out in a body bag!"

Gavin smirked, "I'm not bringing the war here, so leave it at the door."

Now Miguel was backing Aaron up. "Look, dick! You've done enough. Now get out before I kick your ass!"

More insults flew around, but no one hit anyone. I wanted to say something. I had to. "I want to talk to him."

"Why?" Aaron scoffed, "He's the reason why you're here."

"Please. I need answers."

The three glared at each other. Aaron was the first to back down. He went to the door, "I'm gonna go find your sister." He vanished, very slowly and without much protest.

I started to sit up straight, and Miguel helped me. It was his turn to leave. He argued his defense, but I was running out of energy. His kinder side came through, and he stopped the battle. He eventually honored my request after receiving several long sighs from me.

Now Gavin and I were alone. My ribs had a tingle of pain over the medication, making me wince. He sat down on the bed. Beautiful eyes examined me. Saying what was in my heart was going to be easier than I could ever imagine.

"Gavin, Ronda tried to kill me, and I think it's because you like me."

"Catalina, that's not what happened."

"Why lie about it?"

"This is a classic Porter move."

No, not true. "She has feelings for you."

Gavin's silence was thoughtful. He was pondering something. No emotions, just what seemed like a couple of important thoughts. "Ronda and I are not close like that. When I say no, she leaves me alone." He paused. "She's not in love with me, like everyone in town thinks. She's just a shitty girl who makes fucked-up decisions."

"But you guys had sex," I hissed. "And she had that Fatal-Attraction look on her face."

"Look, Ronda wouldn't fight you over me. She's not like that."

"So, it was Porter? He sent her?"

"No, it was Kyle. He's been looking for ways to send me a message. First, he almost killed James, then Molly. And now you. He's trying to force my hand."

I had to pace myself, "It always comes back to you." Pause, shallow breath, "He killed all those people because of you. Porter's people. And he almost killed me." His eyes went down. "He almost killed me…" I had to stop myself from crying.

"I need you to understand that I'm doing everything I can to take care of this. Kyle will pay, I promise."

"That's not enough." I caught my breath, "You were supposed to make all this stop. And you're here, in Settlement Island, not stopping Kyle."

"We're in Anders."

"Regardless."

He pulled at his hair, "I know I need to stop him, but it's so fuckin' hard! I should just go, get out of town, so he can think he's won."

"Why don't you go?"

"Because of you!"

It clicked. I could see everything, "This is my fault?" Now he was unhinged and up. A mess of the man I once knew to be strong and aggressive. He was all ready to go, but he didn't say anything. Not at first. This worried me. Was I right? Did all this happen because of something I did to him? "I can't believe you think this is my fault."

"It used to be easy. Shit would get real, we'd back off, and Porter would back off, too. Now, he'll go to whatever lengths possible to cut my ass down, including taking one of my best friends from me and breaking up my crew. He won't stop until I'm dead unless I give him my town. But he's got it all wrong." Gavin could tell I wasn't following. "You're the one thing he has against me. Not Settlement Island. Not my car. Not even my own mother. You."

I carefully cleared my throat. "He's using me as a weapon?" He sat down again.

"I never had anything I cared about before. I never had something that would keep me from fighting him." He licked his lips, "Porter's been trying to find me since The Pines. And every door he's knocked down, I haven't been there. But he must have found out about you."

"How?"

"Any junkie or enemy would gladly give you up if it meant settling a debt."

And that brought in my conclusions about Kyle. A bargaining chip: that's what I was. And maybe Kyle thought he could use me to cash in on his debt. To draw Gavin out and rid himself of his own mortality. "Well, it's nice to know Porter thinks so little of me. That he can just kill me…"

"I love you, Catalina." The words sounded perfect. They made sense. Gavin would put his life and his town in the clutches of Robert Porter for me. And his face told me the story, everything I needed to know about his position. No tears, just hurt, and fear…inescapable fear. "I know I have to leave to save you, but I can't. If I go, I don't know if it'll be enough. He might try to kill you just to spite me. So, what do I do? If I stay, he'll kill you, and if I go, he'll probably kill you, anyway."

This was hard, but he would understand. "Gavin, Porter is Aaron's brother; Aaron can know what he's up to. My sister almost killed Ronda, so that shows her allegiance." More breathing. "Miguel and James will do anything for me, too." And, of course. "Luke likes me, even though I'm a lost cause." He nodded. "I'm safe, especially now. You can go."

He blinked back a few tears, "Catalina, I never meant for any of this to happen to you."

He took my hand, my fingers running over Logan's ring. "I guess you fell in love with the wrong girl," I said. The silence brought strength. "I don't want to die. I know you don't want to die, either. So, just go."

The moment shifted. "I think you can trust Aaron," Gavin said. "Oliver and Mark are willing to step up, too. I'll get the whole town to protect you if I have to. They owe my family for all the service we've given them over the years."

I shivered. "What about you? Where will you go?"

He got into the bed with me, "I haven't decided if I'm going to leave or not."

"Gavin…"

"Catalina, just let it be, for once. You just gotta trust me. I'll do whatever I have to. I'll keep you safe, I promise." If Gavin's goal was to build my confidence, he had fallen incredibly short. He ran his fingertips across my scalp. The touch felt good.

Every surface, from my face to my feet, ached. The last touch I had felt was the violent kicks from Ronda, then James and Aaron trying to put me back together.

Then, my parent's desperate well wishes, and Miguel's smile mixed with the cold sheets wrapped around my body. Now, it was Gavin who comforted me, who touched me. Sweet, soothing, caresses on my skin as he marveled over my broken body and soul. I moved closer to him, planting my head carefully on his shoulder.

He held me. "I'm not gonna let anybody kill me," I said. "So, take the Dare, and go find a life for yourself. An adventure. Just leave me behind and save us both."

Gavin kissed the top of my head. We lay there, just breathing. I could feel his body relax into the bed. After a few moments, I looked up. He was sleeping.

I examined him. I had never seen Gavin sleep before. He seemed so peaceful, completely at rest. I wondered if he had slept since I had been attacked. Probably not.

Is that what you do when you love someone? Draw comfort from being near them and knowing they are okay?

My head went back to his shoulder. I could feel the goodness of his love over the throbbing pain in my body. He loved me. Gavin Scott loved me, he said so himself. And I hadn't returned the favor. I wanted to say it, but I wanted him to sleep. He needed it, and so did I.

I paced his breaths; deep heavy breaths that seemed relieving. Soon, I joined him in sweet, beautiful sleep.

❧

Mother was who I saw next. She was standing next to me. At first, I couldn't understand why she was so alarmed until I realized Gavin was still sleeping, my head on his chest.

She was careful not to wake him up and jostle me. "Is this him?"

"What?" I whispered.

"The boy you love?"

I nodded. "How did you know?"

"I've been your mother for over twenty-one years. And there's been something different about you." Mother grabbed a chair and brought it over. "Tell me about him."

I didn't go into the gruesome murder parts. I told her about how he had seen me once and took me home on my birthday. I told her about the dancing, the pizza, and the kisses. How he had showed me off to his cousin. The concern he had for me. I told her that he loved me.

And she listened. No interruptions to scold me for picking a boy like Gavin or for being awkward about Luke. She just sat there, watching him sleep, and giving me her attention.

When I was done, she said, "He's very handsome." I brushed some of his hair. "He loves you?"

I nodded. "Yeah."

She placed her hands in her lap, "That is a very wonderful thing."

I looked back down at him and then back at her. There was so much more to say. "I'm happy we're here, Mom. In Maine. Not for him, but for us. Being a family, together."

She knew what I meant without me going any further. "Sometimes the greatest tragedies bring the greatest blessings. And if he loves you, like you say he does, I'm happy you found him, and he found you."

My fingertips went through Gavin's hair. He

remained still. Mother just watched me. No more words. I liked her like this.

Aaron threw the door open. "Gavin, Catalina needs her rest." He stopped. "Mrs. Payton?"

Mother had already gotten up and was headed his way. They exchanged words. Pretty soon, she was leaving, and Aaron was fumbling for something to say.

"I'm going to give you another dose of pain meds," he said. "It'll probably put you to sleep."

"Okay."

Aaron didn't have to say it, but I knew another lecture was underway. He glanced down at Gavin. No sharp looks. He administered the dosage and sat in the chair next to me.

"I don't hate him," he said.

"He told me to trust you."

Aaron let that sink in. "I'll make sure my brother doesn't get to him."

"Thank you."

"And I'll make sure my family knows what my brother did to you," said Aaron. He intended to leave without another word, but I didn't let him.

"This thing with your brother…it's personal for me."

No time for an answer. My head was down again, onto Gavin's chest. I wouldn't allow my body to sleep right away. Just one more minute. I almost had the perfect vision of us together like this. And I was close to using Aaron against Porter. Just one more question. But I couldn't do it any longer…stay awake. I wanted to see Gavin in my dreams, because there I knew he'd be safe.

Chapter Twenty-Seven
Avoid

Miguel was more than impressed with our new home. Mother put him up in one of the upstairs bedrooms. Aaron was also staying with us, so he could be close by. No one left me alone for very long. I felt like I was in Fort Knox. Dad and Aaron had returned to work, but they both rearranged their schedules, so they would be home by six every night.

Mother loved this. Her entire family was spending enormous amounts of time together, right before two major holidays. Cecilia took Miguel out a few times, so he could see the snow. They helped Dad, Aaron, and Luke cut down our Christmas tree. It was way too early for that, but the Payton family had a way of being unorthodox when it came to traditions.

Our first Thanksgiving in Settlement Island was a big deal. Luke wanted to do some hunting with Dad and Aaron. Probably his way of showing off his skills to his potential "future" in-laws. He was allowed to come over as much as he wanted, but I kept him at bay. Dad dropped hints about Luke coming to California, and I successfully avoided that conversation.

None of that mattered. The one person who could make that decision was stuck in bed, covered in bruises, and refused to believe "the average dose" of pain killers was what she needed. Aaron received over twenty text messages from me complaining about the pain. And every reply remained the same…no.

He didn't know that I was keeping track of every excruciating minute and plotting my revenge. Some doctor he was.

Mother came to the door. "Luke's here to see you," she whispered.

When Miguel was home, he made sure Luke didn't see me. The swelling on my face had gone down some, but my ego was still very much bruised. If only I had listened to Luke about going into town. If only I had told someone about my encounter with Kyle.

With Mother at the door, I knew Miguel wouldn't be able to save me. He and Cecilia had gone out to fetch me some ice cream. In the heart of winter, they looked at me funny when I made the request. I reminded them that I was the one braving my treacherous injuries. This usually got them out of my hair. But in that moment, I wished I hadn't sent them away.

Time was up—I had to let him see my face. Luke came in with a bouquet of tulips and a few new books for me. I smiled.

"You are so beautiful. How are you doing?" he said.

"I'm bored," I said, sitting up.

I motioned for him to sit in the chaise lounge Mother had bought for my visitors. That's where everyone relaxed as they spent way too much time "checking in" on me. Aaron had a habit of sleeping there, especially after I had fallen asleep.

Luke got comfortable and smiled, "You've been in here for over a week. When do you get to go outside?"

I looked around my room, "Aaron hasn't said yet."

My voice was low. My bravado was gone. I must have looked like a heap of shame and misery. But I was trying to be a good sport. Luke didn't break his glances away from me, his well-known excitement to see me was almost annoying. As an injured person, it was hard to understand how he could be so damn happy.

"You still on for your trip?" he said. That was the plan. And the only thing that kept me going day after day. He sighed, "It's so hard to see you looking so sad."

"I'm not sad," I grinned. It was the most I could do. Laughing had been out of the question for several days now. "I'm bored. Wanna bust me out of here?"

He stood, "Sure." His hand came out. I stared at it.

"I was joking. It's freezing outside."

"You can't stay in here forever."

"I'm sure Aaron would not approve."

Luke tossed his gifts for me onto the chair. With both arms open, he carefully lifted me up and held me close. Not too much followed. "There's something I want you to see." He motioned to his shiny, silver truck on the other side of the window.

"Is it your winter car?" I said.

Back down to the bed I went. I fussed with my comforter quickly, trapping any escaped heat. The cold would have caused me to shiver, which would have been unbearable. My little hamlet was nice. Very me. And the fireplace was lit. Cozy.

"I wanted you to see it," Luke said. "When you're up for it, I'd like to take you out."

"Now! Let's go now!"

Luke dropped down into the chair, "I meant, when you're better." The flowers and books were placed on the edge of my bed, neatly. His elbows went to his knees. "I've been talking with Miguel. He's real excited about taking you back to California next month."

This had to be a staged conversation. He was fishing. Or my parents were trying to get me to ask him to come along on my vacation. As a good concerned friend, he had earned his seat on the plane. But we hadn't crossed that bridge and for good reason. I felt bad for not telling him about my love for Gavin.

Mother hadn't said anything, either. We never talked about it. She kept my secret from Dad and Cecilia, while quietly keeping up the Luke charade. This made things easier.

Gavin was gone, I could feel it. This gave Luke several advantages. Knowing that Gavin loved me was enough to say goodbye. And my love for him was enough to break my heart. Luke gave me grounds to be distracted. So, did the pain.

I contemplated what to tell Luke, "Being away from here will give me a break."

"Everyone's talking about Ronda. She's still in jail."

"Of course, she is. She tried to kill me."

"I still can't believe that. What the hell was her problem?"

I didn't offer any input. "So," I said, "what have you been up to?"

"Gotta make a trip back to The Pines next week to give my statement to some court person."

This was news. No one in my family mentioned the investigation into Rachel's death. "How come they reached out to you and not me?"

Luke's eyebrows furrowed, "They didn't contact you?"

"Not that I know of. I'll have to check in with my parents about it, but I'm sure they would have jumped at the chance to share something like that with me."

We were both quiet. I reached for the books he had brought. Luke met me more than halfway, so I didn't have to move as much. His kindness was good but not enough to keep me entertained.

My reading average was four books a week. I never thought I'd meet the day when books were no longer appetizing to me. My eyes drifted back out to the window—more snow. Maybe one request wouldn't hurt.

"Let's give the porch swing a try."

Luke put my arm over his shoulder. Bad idea. We readjusted, and I sat back down on the bed. He bundled me up in a jacket and an extra-heavy blanket. Stepping out of my bedroom door sent a waft of cinnamon my way. Slow steps, very slow, me using my legs on my own accord for the first time in a long time.

The house was warm. A fire was lit in the living room. Everything was silent. Luke and I reached the outside and got settled into the swing.

His arm went around me. I couldn't help myself from nestling into him. "So beautiful," I said. It was snowing again, weighing everything down in a cascade of white.

"It's overrated," Luke chuckled.

His comment didn't rob me of the moment. A herd of deer grazed across the lawn. I looked at Luke. He seemed to be daydreaming. Maybe about a kiss.

Kissing was off the table. I had very little range of motion in my neck and my face was still ugly. Mother had made an appointment for the following week with his father regarding the scaring on my head. I didn't oppose having him help me. Ronda didn't deserve to have the right to brag about giving me that deep, angry scar. Not that she could say anything, anyway. She was in jail, and I was locked up at home. No more seeing each other, which was fine by me.

"Things are so quiet right now," he said. "Maybe they'll stay this way for a while."

"We need that."

"I've gotta make a trip into town next month for the food drive. A bunch of us country clubbers are dropping off Christmas meals to the needy. I'll admit…I'm freaked out."

I sighed, "Luke, you'll be fine."

He pointed to my head. "Look at you. A day in the office turned into a trip to the E.R. Some stranger attacked you for no reason."

I couldn't deny him the truth anymore. "Luke, Ronda wasn't a stranger. She came after me on purpose."

"Why?"

I took him through the story. There were times when I had to pause and catch my breath. Every detail was hard to recount. Too painful. He appreciated my courage and stopped me about halfway through.

"So, she's connected to that guy Robert Porter, the killer? Why would he come after you?"

Luke didn't need the entire truth. "I think it has something to do with money. Having a rich family."

"What do you need? What can I do to help?"

"I'm fine." On my end, things were on the mend. My hatred toward Ronda was dwindling. She had my family to thank for that.

Cecilia's Jeep pulled up the driveway. Aaron had bought it for her. Miguel scolded Luke the moment his foot hit the porch. Back inside I went.

"It's for your own good," Miguel said as he tightened the blankets around me.

Back to being a prisoner.

Cecilia sat on the lounge chair. "Adrienne wants to come over and say hi." No, I thought. "It'd be nice for you to see her."

"I'm ugly right now."

Luke dropped down at the foot of my bed. "You look great."

Miguel threw huge clumps of ice cream in a bowl and handed Cecilia the carton. Mint chocolate chip. He took the first bite, then fed me some.

"I've met her…she's nothing to phone home about." Miguel sat in Cecilia's lap.

"Luke and Adrienne dated," Cecilia added.

"Bro," Miguel said to Luke, "you can do better."

Luke's sweet smile was directed toward me. I hadn't updated Miguel on my friendship with Luke and how much I appreciated having him here. But I made plans to tell him, soon. My energy was dwindling. Time for everyone to leave me to my third or fourth nap of the day.

Miguel and Cecilia kicked Luke out. He said something about going to the living room and waiting until dinner was ready. Once he was gone, my entourage opened up a floodgate to all the town gossip, which they had been hiding from me for a week.

"So, James is apparently over the whole Kyle situation, and he's gonna pounce on him soon," said Cecilia. Poor word choice. I asked what her plan was with the whole James-Aaron situation. "James has been a darling, but I've gotta stick to where the money is."

Miguel glared at her, "We fought about that in the car. There's no way this is gonna work out. If Aaron's brother is really a psycho killer, you need to dump him, Cecilia."

"You know I can't. Besides, having a foot in each camp helps. I can't have James running in there blind."

Cecilia had brought up a good point. "What exactly is going on with James?" I said.

"He's worried that Kyle's getting numbers," replied Miguel. "Recruiting guys."

"Now that Gavin's gone, he's gotta figure out what to do next. Mark and Oliver are in, but he doesn't have anyone else."

"That's not the weirdest part," Miguel moved in. "Porter's kinda missing."

"Missing? How?" I said.

"James sent him a message through one of his buddies, and there was no answer. No threats, no killings, nothing," Cecilia said.

"Do you think that maybe Kyle killed him?"

They both shrugged.

I never felt threatened by Porter going missing, even though he drove Gavin away. And killed his fair share of people. It was Kyle who worried me the most. He had killed before, and he knew my face. Of course, Porter could figure out what I looked like, if he wanted to. If he lived long enough to entertain the idea. But Kyle was the one doing the bidding for himself and Porter, so… "Cecilia, I'm sure Gavin's thinking of something, wherever he is."

"Catalina, he's out of the picture. Changed his number, left no forwarding address," Cecilia said. "So, if I were you, I'd be scared. James thinks either Porter or Kyle will come after you again."

I rolled my eyes, "Cecilia, I'm stuck inside all the time, surrounded by five people all the time, not to mention the patrol car that's staying close by. I'll be fine." Deep, painful breath. "And, if Kyle's killed Porter, that leaves me out of it. I was Gavin's weakness against Porter, not Kyle. So, with Porter out of the way, maybe Kyle won't need me anymore."

Three knocks hit the door. Aaron emerged from the hallway. Miguel and Cecilia shot a few worried looks back and forth for a beat.

"Time for your evening torture." He kissed Cecilia. I was relieved to see him…more drugs. "Some privacy, you two."

I didn't want them to go, but Aaron was strict with his orders. Checking my blood pressure was first. "Did you have a good day?" he said.

This was standard doctor talk. "Yeah. Luke took me outside."

He wrote down my stats on a chart he had brought over from the office, "Good BP." Out came the stethoscope, "Take a deep breath."

"No."

He folded his arms, "Catalina, it hurts, but you've gotta do it. It's the only way you'll get better."

"I've looked up the possible complications online, and I'm prepared for those."

Aaron climbed into the lounge chair and put his head back, "You know I've been getting up really early, so I can take care of all the piles of charts and paperwork at the office. All so I can be home in time to give you your meds and check your progress."

He wasn't lying. And he had been sweet and attentive lately… "Fine."

He gave me a smile and stood. The stethoscope went

to my back. My first breath was pathetic. Aaron took a deep one, so I would know how to mimic him. He failed to recognize the crawling cuts of pain that came with every breath I took.

Aaron checked his watch. I was stalling. The breath came in like a sharp sword going down my throat. My lungs and bones screamed for me to stop. He asked for another breath. Then another. After five, my face was completely wet.

"You did really good." Aaron helped me lie down and hushed my sobbing. "If you work on breathing normally, you'll be out of this bed by next week."

I didn't celebrate the news. My nails were digging into the arms of his doctor's coat. He gently placed my head on the pillow. The pain will soften, I thought.

It took too many minutes for me to feel safe enough to move. "I hate you," I growled. Aaron wrote down several notes. "Putting down how much of a wimp I am?"

"No, just stating your progress." Then came that long, dreadful, doctor sigh. The sigh that only made you feel anxious and sick. "I really want you to get out of bed, Catalina. But you gotta work on your breathing on your own."

I already did! My rate of healing wasn't up to his standard because his expectations were too high. But he didn't get it. So, what if he was a doctor. He didn't have to pace himself every time he moved. The whole thing was more serious than he was making it.

The pain crept up further. Anger flooded through my body. "Aaron, I'm doing everything…I just want to get out of this damn house." I held on during the pause. He wouldn't see me struggle. "And you don't seem to see any of that."

"So, do more. Fight the pain, breath normally, and put yourself back together." Aaron went to the door and checked to see if anyone was lingering in the hall. Then he was back at my side. "I need you to get out of this bed. We've got work to do."

"I've got worker's comp."

"Have you heard the news about James?"

"Yeah. I heard your brother might be missing, too."

"I'm sure he'll turn up."

"James apparently thinks Kyle killed him."

"Kyle couldn't kill him, even if he tried."

"So, where is he?"

"I don't know. But I called him yesterday, and he didn't answer, which doesn't mean much."

A pause. "Have you found anything else out?" I said. Nothing came from him. "Aaron, is your brother still after me?" I said.

"No. I told him to get Kyle off your back, and he said Kyle had gotten the message. That was some time after Halloween."

Porter was so casual, his dealings with Kyle. Just throwing orders out to end me, like it was another Monday. It was strange to hate a ghost. "So, what now? Are you still going to take him down?"

"I'll handle my brother, Catalina. And that's all you need to know." Aaron walked over to the door. "Just work on getting better, so we can continue with our plan."

"What? What about Kyle? And I thought the whole plan was to take down your brother?"

"Let me do some more digging, and I'll get back to you." Aaron didn't lead me on any longer. He left.

So, I sat there. The next hour went by very slow. I wanted to scream, but that would be too painful. No, I wouldn't give Kyle or Porter my terror. They wouldn't have that power over me. No one did.

A bellow of laughter came from the other side of the house. My happy family. They were carrying on without me. I counted to three very slowly, then I sucked in a full breath and released it normally.

Aaron would be impressed by me. My relentless journey to heal. I had to. No one was going to hurt me. More importantly, I needed to know for sure what was going on with Kyle and Porter myself. No more hiding. No more bed rest. I had work to do.

Another deep breath; this one was for Porter.

One more deep breath; this one was for Kyle.

And a final deep breath; this one was for Gavin. I hated myself for it, but I missed him.

Chapter Twenty-Eight
Thankful

"You have been doing so good!" Miguel said. He jumped into my bed and pulled the covers around us. "Dr. Aaron must be ecstatic."

Some time had passed since Aaron yelled at me or stressed his concerns over my health. Not anymore. I had gotten out of bed earlier in the week. My first trip to the door was on my own. Dad checked everything the moment I sat down at the table. A sigh of relief was my first clue that I was going to be okay.

Today was Thanksgiving, and my debut trip out of the house and into the real world. Miguel picked out a darling purple dress with black fishnet stockings. A beautiful white coat to add. My other coat had been thrown away. Mother didn't know how to get the blood out.

I returned from the closet with a pair of boots—black, angry boots with a sharp heel, "Think these will be a show stopper?"

"Are you trying to turn me on?" he said, mocking me.

The boots were a bit much, but they meant something to me. A symbol of the rebellion I had revived. This time, my family wasn't the target of my aggression. I had been saving this for Porter. No passive aggressiveness…just full-on rage.

I had made him the center of my anger, which felt trivial at times, but it worked. To have so much hate for someone I didn't know wasn't normally my style. Given the circumstances, I had to place blame somewhere, and Ronda wasn't cutting it anymore. So, I was left with the mastermind behind everything. A foolish and deadly hatred, but it gave me power and strength.

I turned my focus to the mirror and brushed my hair. The curls covered my shoulders. The familiar face was welcoming. I liked her: the little survivor I had become. "When are we leaving?" I said to Miguel.

"I'll go check." He scurried out the door.

We were going to the country club's massive Thanksgiving dinner party. Mother had reserved a table for us all. Everyone was going to be there, eyeing my scars and wounds, I was sure. There was no quiet talk about that. Cecilia was the one to let me know.

She heard Adrienne talking to someone about my deadly journey into town that ended with my almost death. And that event changed everything. The town had changed. It was still very quiet. Nothing new in the papers. And after Luke's father did some minor work on my scars, I became the savior. There was talk about my bravery in the situation, and how my tragic attack had cured everything, which was right and wrong.

My role in Porter's vindication plot was minor. Or perhaps, it was the major piece. I had the love of the key player, the glue that tied us all together. Yet, today, I wouldn't think about that.

Back to getting ready and trying to have fun. Mother wouldn't allow Fun Catalina to wear black or purple. And the rebel cause needed me to be more off-limits. I went back to the closet and peeled off my clothes, careful not to upset my bruises. Navy, short cocktail dress, just above the knees. A bundled-up necklace with various blue and green trinkets went around my neck, hiding most of the scars there. The boots were ditched for gold high heels.

"We're leaving in a few," said Miguel as he came in and stopped. "Damn, girl! What happened to Sexy Catalina?"

That was the right reaction. "This creates the perfect diversion. If you want people to think you're fine, you have to pretend to be fine."

"Hide in plain sight, got it," Miguel was so careful placing my white coat on my shoulders. Then I was escorted into the living room. Mother stopped messing with her hair. Dad and Cecilia applauded my success. She headed over to me, her hug was soft, "I knew I'd turn you into a girl one of these days."

I rolled my eyes. No assistance from anyone was needed. I led everyone to the door and out into the blistering cold. My ribs reminded me that we had done so much today. But I pressed through, the front seat being offered to me by Mother.

Snowflakes stuck to the windshield. Miguel closed the passenger door, and Dad jumped in beside me. "The hyenas in the back are going to shout out all sorts of songs they want you to play. I love you, but if you touch the radio, I'll kill you."

He was in a good mood, which made me smile. "Anything for you, Dad."

The road had been plowed, but Dad didn't take any chances. We inched ahead further into The Estates, passing mansions with paved driveways.

Miguel, Cecilia, and Mother were discussing various things, switching topics rapidly. They had seen the marvels around us so many times. The piles of white, flaky snow just sitting on the ground, undisturbed. So clean and pure. I wanted Dad to stop, so I could touch it. Taste it. The snow led to the partially frozen lake surrounded by frosted trees. Everything was new to me.

"Kinda strange, all this snow?" Dad said.

"You like it?"

He bobbed his head around; not quite a no or a yes. I could relate to his indifference, but in another way. That was my go-to response when asked about things not worth mentioning.

I focused on what I'd say to the few brave souls that would venture toward me and ask questions about how I was doing. I could start with a joke. No, that wouldn't work. When we made it to the parking lot of the club, I implored Cecilia for some advice.

"You're thinking about it too much," she said. "You're the victim. Just act like one." Cecilia propped the door open with her back and helped me down.

"But I'm not a victim," I hissed. "I don't want to be seen as a weakling."

"It doesn't matter." We laced arms, and she continued, "You can't control what other people think. So, just be yourself."

A first. Cecilia had never wanted me to be authentic in any way. It warmed my heart. Miguel took my other arm, "Deep breath, shoulders back, and just be fabulous."

We stepped up together, and the Roman gods opened the doors for us. Poor guys had red faces from the cold. I gave them a $50 tip.

Cecilia scampered off toward Adrienne and three other girls, another group of people I hadn't met. Miguel left me in my place to go order us some drinks.

"Are you okay, honey?" said Mother. "Do you need to sit down?"

"No, Mother." I encouraged her to go mingle.

My coat was taken off my body by a waitress. She handed me a ticket. A few people stared as I put the ticket in my dress pocket and took a shallow breath. Miguel needed to come back with that drink.

I went rogue and entered the crowd. They parted as I moved by. Such power I had emulating from my presumed fragile state. These people were afraid of me. All but one.

No stuffy suit or khakis. No cheesy sweater. Just smooth creases, perfect hem lines, and stark gray.

"Luke?" I said with genuine surprise.

He came up and gave me a gentle hug. "Happy Thanksgiving."

Luke smelled nice. And the tightness around us was enough to make me feel safe and warm.

I pulled him away and contemplated his outfit for a second time. "You look really good."

He pointed to mine. "So, do you." He smiled. "Very dark and sexy."

"It's part of the deception. Throw people off their game."

Luke laughed. Miguel approached us with caution. His drink went to Luke. Then he was off again to get another for himself.

"How have you been?" He took a sip, "Sorry I haven't come by lately. It's been busy at the office."

Luke had a job; I had forgotten. I brushed it off with a little nod. "It's okay. I've been in my room, as always."

Someone was headed toward me. A boozy housewife. "She's been begging my dad to look at your scars. Come on," Luke tugged on my hand, and we moved closer to the windows. We remained entangled together as he stayed close to me. My eyes went straight to the look on his face. I couldn't read him, not even a little bit.

"Thanks," I said. "I'm sure everyone wants to know more about my vicious attack."

"The club's been good about keeping the gossip down. Especially for Molly's sake. And yours."

I didn't want to ask, but it was inevitable. "How is she doing?"

"Angry," he said. I tried to keep a straight face, swallowing my own rage. This wasn't about me. "The police have officially given up looking for her attacker."

"Why? It's only been a month since it happened."

Luke pulled me closer to the window. "There's been talk that her parents filed a lawsuit against the police department, and the cops are retaliating." I started to cut him off, "Rumors have been going around that the cops know who attacked her, but they're protecting him. It's a Settler thing, I guess."

I didn't let the tension in my shoulders last for long. Again, this wasn't about me. "I'm sure they'll find the guy soon enough."

His eyebrows scrunched, "Didn't you hear me? The police aren't looking."

"Or maybe they're relying on all this to kinda sort itself out?"

Luke took a step back. "You know something."

"Gavin's gone," I whispered. "And he's on a quest to make all this right."

"He's just a kid, like all of us. This is like a high school slasher movie. It's sad and pathetic."

I shrugged, "It's complicated…"

"No, it's not, Catalina." Luke straightened up. "You gotta do the right thing. For Molly and yourself."

"But what is the right thing?" I pleaded. "People have died, I've been attacked. This Porter guy has made good on all his promises. And I'm sure the police are thinking the same thing. They're probably just as scared as we are."

"So, you're not gonna say anything?" he scoffed.

Disappointment. Luke had never been disappointed in me before. I didn't think his approval mattered to me, but it did.

"Maybe I should say something if they figure something out."

"There's nothing to figure out." He sighed, "If you know something, tell them."

An easy, moral notion for him to share. But there wasn't much to tell, I reminded myself. Yes, I knew what Kyle had done to Molly, and he was long gone by now. And if the rumors about Kyle and Porter were true, Kyle had killed Porter by now, and inserted himself as the kingpin. Or maybe Porter had killed Kyle. I didn't know.

Aaron had refuted my suspicions. Porter was fine, according to him. This revelation gave me reason to pause.

Where was Aaron? I hadn't seen him in the last two days, and Cecilia hadn't mentioned anything about him. Was he with his brother?

"Sometimes, when I talk, I can tell you're not listening," said Luke.

"This is a lot to process." My hand went onto his. "I want to do what's right for me and Molly, but it's bigger than all of us. These guys are just…"

"Scary as hell," he scoffed, again. "I get it."

"It's hard to tell who to trust."

"Do you trust me?"

"Yes!"

Luke stepped up. One small step was all it took for us

to be close enough to kiss. "I know you love Gavin and all, but I'm here for you. Nothing bad is gonna happen to you again. I promise. So, just tell me the truth."

No twitchy eyes. His back was straight. His heart was open. And I accepted him. The protection he would bring me could help everything go back to normal. Plus, he had figured out where my love lied, which made it easier to be honest with him. I took the opportunity and his loyal friendship with a smile.

"I just want to enjoy dinner," I said. "The whole reason why Gavin left was to give me a second chance at some kind of life. And I want that."

He backed off some. "When you're ready to go to the cops, let me know."

I reached out and grabbed his arm as he walked away. "I'll make you a deal: if you agree to become part of my world of fun, I'll figure out a way to tell Molly and her parents what I know."

"Why do you think I wouldn't want to have fun with you?" Luke smiled. "You're like my best friend, remember?"

No, I didn't. Our relationship was still foreign to me. "What about your other friends?"

Luke told me about his life in Anders. He had a network of guys he hung out with. Normal, healthy guys who drank beers, watched sports, and dodged commitments with their girlfriends. There were a few girls, too, but no one worth going into detail about.

"So, you're not going out on dates?"

"I'm just not that interested in dating," he said. "My

dad's helping me learn real estate, so I can buy a house next summer."

"Fancy new car, truck, and house. You're like, adulting."

"Yeah, well, maybe when you finally move out, you'll be adulting, too."

"So, Thanksgiving in Maine." I pointed to the snowy windows. "Kind of a big deal."

"Christmas is gonna be insane. I'll probably come down to stay with my parents for the week, but after that, I'll be in Anders full-time."

"Fun."

"I know you're going on your trip, but you should, uh, come up to Anders when you get back. I'll introduce you to some people."

"No," I shook my head and didn't stop there. "Come with me to California."

He shifted around for a bit, the anxiety crawling up to his eye. Twitch. "What?"

"Why not? I know it's not Maine, but it'll be fun. And you can see my world."

He raked his hair, the darling, beautiful strands going out of order. No backing down, Catalina. This is what I asked for.

"That's a big step."

Good point. "You deserve it." More hesitation. I finally said, "I owe you for all your kindness and patience. This is my way of paying you back." More unsure looks from Luke. He had to be intrigued by now. Yet intrigue is not enough to move a friendship forward. I had to be different, more genuine. "Please, Luke. I wouldn't want to share this experience with anyone but you."

The flicker in his eyes as he stared at me said it all. "I'll go tell my parents."

Now I was at the window, alone. Big gestures weren't my thing, but I felt good about this one. And we would have fun, I hoped.

Cecilia and Miguel were huddled together, judging me. I didn't duck my head in shame. Let them talk. I walked confidently toward them.

"He's a nice boy, Catalina," said Miguel. He sipped on a rum and coke.

My drink had been reduced to water. I placed it down and cupped my hands together. "He's coming to Berkeley with me. As a friend."

Cecilia clapped. "A good choice, little sister."

"Now you don't have to be worried about being alone," Miguel said. "Speaking of being alone, where's Aaron?"

This was good, coming from Miguel and not me. The divine powers of the universe were on my side.

Cecilia peered through the crowd. "He's supposed to be here."

We made a plan to go look for him. I intentionally left them to team up. If I found him first, we would have to talk. We always had to talk. And Aaron would be able to deflect my questions about Porter's relationship with the police if there was an audience. Not that I could bring something like that up in a setting like this. But I'd worry about that once I found him.

I started in the obvious places; the reception room where dinner was taking place, and the ballroom, where most people were gathered. Then I headed back toward the bar. No Aaron. But someone else was there. James grabbed a drink off the bar and chugged it. He wasn't in reaching distance or else I would have grabbed him before he could disappear. He went into the crowd, I followed. No talking to anyone, just a quick jet through a group and onto the next.

I lost him, again.

"The plot thickens," Miguel whispered behind me.

"What do you mean?"

"James is here. He snuck off with Cecilia to the deck."

I kept my composure and headed off after them. The chill made me turn back. I was the only person in the dimly lit dining room. Except for someone. A man. He was staring at me.

Chapter Twenty-Nine
Darkness

"Sorry. I didn't mean to disturb you," I said to him.

He approached me. Tall, very tall. Brown hair, defined jawline. Expensive blue suit. Dark eyes. I felt small. Insignificant. "No trouble at all." He had a bit of an accent. English, I thought.

"I wanted to get some fresh air outside, but it's cold." I smirked, "It's snowing and all."

"Allow me to join you." He asked for my coat ticket. I reluctantly gave it to him.

This wasn't a boy. He was a man. Strong, glorious man. Cecilia would be jealous if she saw us together. I looked around for her. I still couldn't believe she had invited James here. Did she care about what Aaron would say? Obviously, that thought hadn't crossed her mind.

The gentleman came back, dressed in his coat, and put mine on me. No offering, he just took it upon himself to bundle me up. I walked before him, regretting my plans. The windows were frosted completely. It was more than chilly out. My ribs tightened.

The temperature drop wasn't as bad as I had prepared for. My stranger extended his hand out to me. "Ian."

"Catalina." He kissed my hand, a very honorary custom that had been forgotten in our society.

"Are you new to the Club, Ms. Catalina? I don't think I've seen you before."

"I moved here about three months ago. Still getting used to Maine. No lobster yet."

"It's divine. I'd tell you more about it, but I think it's best that you try it yourself," he said. Gavin would have alluded to himself preparing a Maine lobster dinner date for me. However, Ian did no such thing. Instead, he nodded, "So, this is your first holiday with us?" I confirmed. "Thanksgiving has always been my favorite. The food and festivities. Christmas is always good, too. Biggest tree you'll ever see."

"I'm going out of town," I said with a coy smile.

He looked around and then back at me, "Running away from something? Or someone?"

What? Why would he insinuate…I composed myself. "Visiting family." Ian looked at me from eye-to-eye, like he was checking to see if I was lying. "Maybe I should go back inside."

"I'm sorry, Catalina. I don't mean to be bizarre." He looked down and then up, "I've had a little too much to drink."

Relief. "Well, I'm sure you're not the only one."

He motioned for me to take a seat. I sat down in front of him. The furniture was dry. A waitress rushed out and brought two cups of coffee. She asked if we wanted to go inside. Ian gave her a hundred-dollar bill and told her to keep the coffee coming. My ribs tightened again. He wouldn't be able to drink his way through that much money.

"You look young. Are you attending school?" he said. The cold was seeping into my sides. Tingles of pain. "Catalina, are you okay?"

"I think we should probably take the waitress's advice and head in."

"Wasn't it your idea to come outside?"

I couldn't tell him about my true motives. More pain. It was building fast and rapidly out of control. "It just hurts more than I thought." My posture was slightly hunched over, but I straightened up when we made it in.

"Are you injured?"

"I just took a nasty spill on the slopes." I watched him eye the ballroom. "I don't wanna go back in there."

He complied, and we found ourselves back in the dark dining room. "Come with me."

Following him was easy. Ian guided me through the tables and into the darkness. Not what I had in mind. The darkness continued, and I could only find my way by staying close to him. Then we collided. Pain. My hands felt his back. He didn't object as I pressed my hands tightly against him to keep us from falling. A door opened, and we entered into a room. A library.

No lights, just a colossal skylight overhead, slanted to

allow the snow to cascade down to the deck below. It was all the light we needed to find a place to sit. I passed various couches and chairs, blindly keeping close to Ian who seemed to have a directive. He stopped at the fireplace and began preparing it.

"This is beautiful," I said. Snowfall touched most of the skylight, allowing a few fractured sunbeams to come in. By this time, daylight was almost gone. "And the books!" I looked at a few of the titles, many of which I had read or had at home.

He smiled, "I used to play in here when I was a boy." A match exploded and was tossed onto a log. "I would lie on the floor and watch the snow fall, putting out my tongue to taste it," he chuckled. "I wasn't very bright."

He came toward me, pulling his coat off. It landed on a leather chair. I appreciated the help he gave me as I shed my coat, careful not to move fast. "Thank you."

Ian settled down into a leather couch. The fire light cast shadows over his face. He sipped his drink with such grace.

"You're Settlement Island royalty?" I said. "Super-rich like the rest of us?"

"I wouldn't say that. My family's got money…just like everyone else. But I don't spend too much time here anymore. My parents sold their land and business a while ago."

"So, why are you here for the holiday?"

He pondered my question. "I work in Anders. Engineer." I nodded. "The holidays are more fun down here." Ian smiled. There was a refinement about him which seemed out of place. And his insinuating that Settlement Island was 'fun' didn't seem to fit, either. "It seems strange. Coming back to your hometown to spend the holidays with a bunch of strangers."

I braved a quick, "I was just thinking that."

"It's a vacation for me."

What an odd response, I thought. Clearly a man as good-looking and charming as Ian would have a family of his own. "That's kind of a boring vacation," I said as a test.

Ian chuckled, "Depends on what your interests are. I don't get out very often, and when I do, I come here. The lake's beautiful, no matter what season it is."

"Is that a Maine thing? Being outdoors?"

"I suppose so. Where are you from?"

"L.A."

"I've done business there a few times. I prefer Maine, though."

"What type of business?" I said.

"Working on some commercial buildings."

Ian told me a little bit about the math and science that went into his profession. He was excited over the minute details needed to make sure the calculations were correct. A nerd, for sure. Ian was just as much of a nerd as I was.

"It's nice to know that science is no longer a lost art," I said.

"Your generation is so sad, looking for instant gratification."

A slight, none the less. "Not everyone under the age

of forty is a lost cause. I can read four to five books a week, if I have the time."

"What do you like to read?"

My answer was cut short. His phone came out. A finger went up as he rose and walked over to the other side of the room. Eyes still on me. I didn't stare, even though I was curious to know who he was talking to. He then went on to ignore me. But I didn't feel like I needed to leave. My only option was to go back. Then I would have to hunt for James.

Should I ask Ian if he had seen James? A dangerous question that would be followed by me having to explain who James was to me. If I were lucky, Ian would think I was more concerned about the Aaron-James-Cecilia love triangle. If not, he would want to know more about the panicked look on my face. The murders that were always preoccupying my mind. My quest to find James did pose one question: why would he want to spend his holiday sneaking around with my shallow sister? Didn't he have other people to celebrate with? What was Gavin doing today? If we were normal people, in normal circumstances, I would know everything because we would be together. I'd allow myself to give in to him in all ways. Take his hand and be his girlfriend.

We would date for several years…until I was thirty, at least. Then he'd ask me to marry him, and I'd say "no." Too risky. Eventually, he would do something big…offer me something I couldn't resist. An adventure where the two of us would easily enjoy whatever came our way. Then I'd see him differently.

He'd seem different with age…grown up. All the problems of our youth, the chasing and bickering over things that didn't matter, would no longer hold us back. I would feel like I could trust him with my life. Then I could marry him.

"Sorry about that," said Ian, "Questions from the office."

My brows furrowed. "On Thanksgiving?"

"I have a team across the ocean that is working for me. No Thanksgiving for them." He reached over and grabbed his cup, "What do you do for work?"

"I'm a receptionist at the local clinic."

"Hmm." Ian drew in a very slow sip, "That sounds intriguing. Learning everyone's medical secrets."

"I don't peek."

"Unless he's this tall, handsome man with all the enduring qualities that most women swoon for," he said. I blushed. He pointed at me with his cup and said, "You're a swooner, I can tell."

"There's no man out there worthy of my affections."

"But yet in the finest of hours, on the finest of shores, you wait for his ship to dock. He's been gone too long, your heart can't bear that dreadful song, as the minute hand pulls across the clock," he recited. My heart stopped.

I finished the verse. "I'll be standing there, gold feather in my hair, holding his moistened coat. Unable to waiver, from his shaky favor, that I stand and wait for that damn boat."

Ian half-smiled, "I believe I messed up a line."

"That's one of my favorite poems!" Finally, someone who got it. "I read it in college and never forgot it."

"My father wrote it."

I had to hold onto the chair. "Your father is Grover Capshaw White?"

"Guilty," Ian sat back and placed his cup down, "I love reading literature, but I was never able to confess my words on the page like he can."

I couldn't handle the news. My hand went to his arm. "I'm sorry, but I have to touch the son of the greatest poet of the twenty-first century." My hand covered my mouth. "Did your father write that poem about Settlement Island?"

"No," he leaned into me. "He lived on the coast for the longest time. There was this fisherman named Gale. He and my father grew up together. Well, they both were in love with my mother, Meredith. They fought day and night over her, and my mother couldn't choose."

Aaron and James. But they weren't fighting over Cecilia, because she was only in love with James, so the story didn't apply. My feet went under me and the coffee cup warmed my hands.

He continued and walked over to the shelves of books. "My mother came to the conclusion that she would wait until she got a 'sign from the heavens' before she would pick one. This went on for several years until the night of the storm."

"I read about that," I interrupted. "From what I remember, it destroyed most of the town."

Out came a book of his father's work. He placed it in

my hand, our fingers touching, "You're right." He was so warm. "Gale went out to the water to save the boats. His coat was lost among the wreckage. The next morning, my mother found it and wept."

"So," I paused. "That beautiful story about love lost at sea was basically about your mother choosing your father because Gale died? That's depressing."

"Yes and no." Ian gave me this smile. No one had ever smiled at me like that before. "Mother didn't choose Gale, and he didn't die. He lost his jacket after he said, 'To hell with all this! Burn the boats!' Apparently, he was a coward, and he had lost everyone a ton of money due to his fear. My father wrote about it in a poem, and that's all she needed to choose him."

Truly magical. I continued on with more questions. We must have stayed there for over an hour talking. Light, sweet stories about Ian's father and the legacy he had created in my world. Ian thought it was cute. I adored him, just for what his father meant to me.

Ian was interested in learning more about me, too. There wasn't much to say, so I skillfully turned the attention back on him. I learned about his boyhood and what it was like to have Grover as a father. Fond recollections.

His colorful memories brought on a few of my own. I told him about being a child prodigy. My love of the gypsy life.

"I would never assume you to be a gypsy," he replied.

"I've kinda grown out of it."

"Why?"

I tapped my mug. "Things change. People change."

"Well, you are more mature than any twenty-one-year-old I've ever met."

In many ways, I still felt like a child. I didn't ask Ian his age. Instead, I went for something else. "Are you married?"

"No. I've been too busy to settle down yet." He smiled to himself. "Although, I am thirty-two, so time seems to be passing me by."

"I hear forty is the new twenty."

"I believe that only applies to women."

I made a few more jokes about the boozy housewives in The Estates. Ian laughed and shared a few of his own stories regarding a few women who had made complete fools of themselves. Over time, the talking drifted into a direction I didn't want to go. "Settlement Island has changed. It's a shame, really."

My cup was dry. Perfect. "I think I'll get a refill." I could easily walk away before he asked questions about my run in with Ronda.

He got up with me, "Do you spend most of your time here in The Estates?"

We were walking in unison, "Yes, but I work in town." Here it goes, "And I know you probably have more questions about the scar on my head and the girl who attacked me."

Ian stopped. "I don't know what you're referring to."

I had blown it. My lie about the skiing accident had actually worked. Ian had been a good friend to me, so I admitted the truth. And he took it well.

"Thank you for your honesty," he said. "I understand why you lied about the reason for your injuries."

"I'm normally not a liar," I said. "I just didn't want to play the part."

"What part?" He seemed concerned.

"The victim." My eyes went down. "The hero."

"If someone thinks your unfortunate accident makes you a hero, they can screw themselves." I looked up, and he was smiling. "It is very tragic what happened to you. And you shouldn't live your life in any other way because of it." He stopped at the entry way to the ballroom.

My breaths quickened. Time to say goodbye. It was silly, but I was going to miss him.

"There's a movie playing at the theater I'd like to see. Would you like to accompany me?"

I hushed my excitement. "I'm still on house arrest until January."

"But they're letting you out to go to California?" he said. I nodded. "Good for you."

I sensed his disappointment. "I really enjoyed talking with you, though. It's been a long time since I've had someone to share my love of literature with."

"Me, as well. Are you off to the dance floor with some darling country club boy?"

"No, I don't dance."

"Neither do I."

Damn you, Dad and Aaron for demanding that I stay in the house! Ian stood in his place, staring at me. The look of an admirer. "If you talk to your father, tell him I said, 'hello.' And thank you for your hospitality, Ian." I grew another smile. Large, genuine, fulfilling.

"Any time, Catalina." Long silence. "Have a very good Thanksgiving." I turned when Ian spoke my name, again. He was by my side. "Please don't tell anyone you saw me."

"Who would I tell?"

"Anyone."

A peculiar development I had to explore. "But your family has moved on. Who are you afraid of?"

"I lied," he said.

"Oh." No more liars.

"I do have a brother, but I wasn't sure if he was going to be here. I drove down, hoping to meet him, but he never showed up." I was going to make a joke when he said, "If he finds out I was here, he might feel guilty for missing me."

"I'm sorry. That's uncomfortable. Well, who's your brother?"

"I'd rather not say," he teased me slightly, but in an alluring way.

"You don't trust me?" I said back.

A kiss brushed against my cheek. I shuddered. "His name is Julian."

"I don't know any Julians," I muttered.

"Talking with you made all this worthwhile." Another smile. "Take care of yourself. It's not safe out there."

He can be my refuge, I thought. A great distraction. "What about Anders? Do you have tons of violence there?"

"No. You'd like it." Ian didn't turn back again. The Roman gods opened the doors for him, and he was gone.

CHAPTER THIRTY
Puzzles

THANKSGIVING WEEKEND WAS pretty quiet. No leads on Julian, although I suspected he would be pretty hard to find. Aaron was proud of the progress I was making, even though I had overdone it with Miguel on the dance floor. Christmas week was getting closer, which kept my family extremely busy. Dad took Mother and Cecilia into Anders to do some shopping. It was shocking to see them visually upset when I asked for nothing for Christmas. I just wanted to go home to California. That was enough for me.

It didn't take long for me to understand that my family was going to miss me. We had lived apart so much in California, and they had never shown any concern for my absence before. But things had been different now. I was the center of their world, no longer hiding behind their goals and dreams. It felt good. Their love and support kept me on my mission to get my life back.

I had stayed home long enough, nursing my ribs.

Miguel answered to my every beck and call to make up for his requests for me to give dancing another try. Yet my motivations to go outside were dwindling after I failed to conjure up any leads on Ian. Intrigued by finding out more about him, he consumed my thoughts.

These thoughts led to the most peculiar places. What if Ian knew more about who I was than I had led on? What if he had heard about my incident with Ronda, and he was just being polite? The idea of him hiding something like this made me want to interrogate him. Demand that he tell me why he thought I needed to be careful.

Yet that was a silly notion. My imagination had run away with me, again. This was a common occurrence recently. Staying inside, being isolated from other people, will do that to you. I tucked a piece of hair behind my ear and put my book down. A tap on my window told me that he had arrived. I let in the cold air, as Luke climbed through the now open window.

"I still don't understand why you won't let me go through the front door anymore," he said. In his arms were more books and a blueberry pie.

"Because my family will dictate our every move."

Luke was allowed over, yes that was true, but he was an outsider who could possibly seduce me into leaving the house and abandoning both Aaron and my dad's orders. They tried to control my interactions, and that meant visiting hours were cut to a minimum. This reduced our relationship to seeing each other in the late evenings, after everyone else had moved on to other things. He dropped down into the chair next to me.

"Tired?"

He nodded. "I'm taking most of December off, so I have to get everything done before I go on vacation."

Vacation: our trip to California, together. Luke asked a few times if I really wanted him to go. He mentioned wanting to know if I would end up choosing Gavin instead. "Gavin's gone," I explained again when he opened his eyes and brought it up.

"But you like love him and stuff…I'm sure you guys won't be apart for much longer…"

A very good observation, if Gavin and I were like everyone else. And it did hurt, being apart from him. The crawling pain that shot through my sides as I sighed reminded me why he had left. My heart still wanted him gone, too, even though I did miss him.

"Luke," I said, reminding myself to stop zoning out, "if I didn't want you to go, you would know. You're not a charity case, if that's what you're wondering."

His agreement to drop the conversation was not convincing. I didn't linger on the comment. Neither did he. His eyes shut, again. Being well rested, I felt sorry for Luke. After some coaching, I offered him my bed, and he took it without complaint. I left him and went toward the kitchen.

Miguel was on the phone, so I sat down next to Cecilia on the couch. She was looking at wedding arrangements. "Think you're gonna get the ring for Christmas?" I said.

"I better," she leaned into me. "I broke up with James." My reaction probably seemed out of line. I had continuously told her to pick James or Aaron since the beginning of her tainted love affair. She still surprised me. Somewhere inside, I thought she'd pick James. Her reason for going with Aaron was well thought out. "You love Gavin, and you almost got killed. And James is not willing to get out of the life. His loyalty to the crew is more important than anything. So, if he's gonna look out for Number One, so am I."

"Things are quiet. They've been quiet for a while. I think you're okay."

The phone went down. Her gaze went to the fire that was roasting in the living room. "Cat, I have to be real for once. I'm gonna be twenty-five soon. Twenty-five!"

"It's not that old, Cecilia…"

"Look, I want to finally be legit. Make some choices that take me places." She faced me. "I want to start over, be someone Mom and Dad can be proud of."

"And you think Aaron is the right choice for that?"

She smiled, "He loves me. I don't think anyone has ever loved me as much as he does."

I let her have this one. Aaron could love Cecilia, I guess. He'd have to convince me of this. When I asked Cecilia where Aaron was, she said he was working at the office. Some emergency came up.

It was Sunday…a cold, desolate Sunday. Dad made it a point to keep the clinic closed on Sundays, in honor of the Lord's day. Aaron had followed this rule, every Sunday, until now.

I couldn't let on to Cecilia that Aaron had to be lying. Instead, I went back to my room where Luke was sleeping. A few guilty taps later, and he was awake.

"Can you drive me to the clinic?"

"Why?" he sat up straight. "Is something wrong?"

"No...I mean, not in the way you might think."

Luke nodded and proceeded to put his shoes on. I put on another sweater and a jacket to keep out the blistering cold. It was snowing, a lot. Luke opened my window and stepped out. I tipped my body forward, leg over the window sill, and onto the frozen porch.

Luke's truck was not in the driveway; this was also a part of the arrangement. It rested close to the house, but up the road. As we walked, he held my hand. I didn't protest, not wanting to fall on the ice and further damage my broken body. Once inside, the heater came on, but Luke didn't put the truck in drive.

"Why are we going to the clinic?" he said.

"I need to check on something."

He didn't move. "What kind of trouble are we getting into?"

"Trouble?"

"Well, yeah. I mean, it's a Sunday, and you want to go to the clinic...you're being secretive." I didn't protest. "Does this have anything to do with the murders?" I shrugged.

To tell Luke about my suspicions regarding Aaron might cause him to turn back. My motives had to be different. "I think I might have a clue as to why I was attacked. The true motive behind Ronda's reason to come after me."

∽

Bringing up my attack was all Luke needed to get us moving. When we arrived at the clinic, the parking lot was empty. I used a spare key to open the door. Everything was dark, quiet, and cold. The heat was set on low, which gave me the impression that Cecilia was wrong about Aaron's whereabouts. Maybe he had a secret love that she didn't know about.

Luke turned on a light.

"So, what are you looking for?"

I peered around the corner, approaching Aaron's office. I was wrong. Aaron was leaning against his desk, phone to his cheek, staring at me.

A minute went by, and he didn't say anything to me, nor I to him. No communication with the caller, either. Luke was still in the lobby, so I couldn't say much of anything. Whatever came next had to be well planned out.

I knew Aaron wouldn't open up, not with Luke there. This revelation led to a bold move; I closed the door and went back to the lobby.

"Aaron's in his office," I said to Luke, who sat down in one of the lobby chairs.

By this time, Aaron had emerged from his hiding place, smiling at us both. "You just missed my last patient." Lie. Well, probably a lie. "What are you two doing here?"

I couldn't come up with a good lie. My brain racked, looking for something... "I kidnapped Catalina to take her to dinner," Luke offered. "And on the way, she wanted to stop by here to forge a prescription for some pain meds."

Believable...this was believable. Aaron seemed to buy it without a second thought. He lectured me on being out and denied my request for more meds. Then we were shooed out of the clinic.

"I'll take you home," Aaron said. "Come on."

"Hey, man," Luke stepped between us. "I'm still taking her to dinner."

They exchanged looks. I had never seen them have a disagreement before. Luke stood his ground, which wasn't really necessary. My attention went away to my phone. Miguel was screaming at me about being irresponsible and leaving the house. I put it back in my pocket. By the time I was back into the conversation, Aaron had given up on grounding me.

"I guess you owe me dinner," Luke said. His smile was back.

Dinner with Luke wasn't that bad. Being alone together to talk outside the house seemed nice. But was I using him? There wasn't much time needed to consider that. Aaron finally left before I felt comfortable saying anything.

"He's not supposed to be working on Sunday."

"Oh, that..." Luke guided me toward the truck, which was a good thing. The snow was coming down harder. "He's been here every Sunday for the last three weeks."

I got in. Once he was inside, I said, "How do you know?"

Luke pointed to the community center. "I see his car here when I come down to do my volunteer work."

"Every Sunday?"

He nodded. "Every Sunday."

∽

Dinner was at the lobster shack in town. *The Lobster House*. When we got to our table, Luke slid into the booth and didn't say anything to me for a few minutes. His phone came out, and he spent too much time flipping through something. I sank further into my seat.

This was my fault. Being ignored was something I never had to worry about with Luke. My hand went onto his phone. His eyes went up to me.

"Hi," I said.

"Hey." A cool smile, and he was back to it, again.

"So," I said with a long pause. Eyes back up, "is this your place?"

"Have you had Maine lobster yet?" I shook my head. His phone went into his pocket, "Well, this is your chance."

A waitress came, and Luke ordered a beer. I settled for a white wine. The invitation to talk was missed once Luke brought his phone back out.

"Sorry," I said. My hands fiddled with the cloth napkin. Luke peered up at me. "I'm sorry if I used you today."

"Oh, Catalina." Now his attention was on me. "I'm always here to help…but not like this."

"Like what?"

"Gavin's gone, Aaron's being shady, and I know you want some answers." He summed everything up well. "Now, I just have to ask myself what to do with you…"

No, that wasn't fair, but I couldn't protest. It was true, I needed Luke to rescue me, again. "What to do with me? I should be groveling at your feet, but that would be awkward." He smirked. "Luke, you've been a really good friend this whole time. And I've been selfish and self-centered…"

"Aren't those the same thing?"

"Well, yeah," I cracked a small laugh. "The point is, I put you in a compromising situation. I shouldn't have gone to you for help like this."

He sighed. At that moment, the beer and wine were delivered. This was a good thing since Luke seemed to need a big gulp before his next comment. "We're just friends. I gathered that a while ago. But when you got attacked, no one told me. I had to find out through fucking Adrienne," he calmed his voice. "And then you came home, and I had to convince you to let me come over." He gripped the beer bottle tight. "I'm always going out of my way to reach you. To connect with you. And the only time you invite me in is when you need something from me, like a ride or a reason to get away from Gavin. It's never been about you wanting to be with me for me. There's always something on the backend you're hoping your friendship with good, dependable Luke will solve for you."

I slowly released the cloth napkin, so I could quickly remove the tear that was running down my cheek. It was hard, living the truth. Another night, many nights ago, I had felt what Luke felt. I had sat in a booth across from someone who made me feel those exact feelings. He had called me selfish, too, and told me that he would never feel sorry for me. And now, I was on the other side of the exchange, being selfish.

We weren't the same people, me and that man. Luke's story didn't have to lead down a path where I always got what I wanted in return for him having a "promising" friendship with me.

"How do I make it up to you?"

"Just…" he took a swig of his beer, "treat me like a real friend."

"You're the very first person I met when I moved here." My body went back into the booth. "You came up to me and talked to me." I sniffled. "You're the only one who got me something for my birthday."

"Well, I wanted to do something nice for you."

I bit my lip, "You're always doing nice things for me. And saving me. But I have to ask; did you do all these things because you felt sorry for me?"

"No," he chuckled. "I did them because it's what I do. You can ask anyone."

"So, this is the real you?"

The waitress appeared. Luke dove into his menu and picked out a lobster platter for himself. And I…I finally got to order whatever the hell I wanted, for once.

Luke shook his head. "Lobster scampi with roasted potatoes, winter veggies, French fries, and slice of pie?" he said. I laughed. "I don't think all that goes together." He raised his eyebrow.

"It's a freedom thing."

"Speaking of freedom, I have something for you."

Luke put his finger up as I rolled my eyes. He really had to stop bringing me things. "I've had this since I was eight. I found it in the park near my school." More digging. Out came a gold necklace with a shiny arrow charm.

"Why is this for me?" I said slowly, my words a slight whisper.

"I was packing up my room at my dad's house, and I found this in a box. I've held onto it because I wanted to give it to someone who might enjoy it. And since you like adventure, I thought…you know."

The arrow, spun around, pointing the way. Giving me clear direction. I leaned over and kissed him, right there, in front of everyone. And this time, the kiss had meaning and depth. I couldn't help myself. Maybe it was loneliness or the idea of never seeing Gavin again, but at that moment, I wanted to be close to Luke. I needed him, his warmth, his kindness, his kisses. When we parted, Luke still held up the necklace, unsure what to do with it.

"So, you…want it?"

I nodded. My neck came forward, and he put the keepsake around it. The charm rested in my fingers. "No one's ever been so nice to me."

"This will hopefully help you find your way through all this mess. Find some direction in your life."

We started talking, really talking. We spoke about things that were light and refreshing. There was so much I didn't know about Luke. The things he wanted in life were a lot like what I wanted. When we first met, I had misjudged him. Over lobster and various sides, we joked and shared our interests. Everything was easy. Luke was easy.

After dinner, we pulled back up to my house. There, in the dark of the driveway, we leaned over and kissed, long sweet kisses. We were getting good at this. Finally, Luke broke away. "Time to go?" I said.

"Yeah. Gotta work in the morning."

His next move was opening the door for me. I grabbed onto his hand, and he helped me down. Another kiss. Then another. The snow fell on us, big flakes that stuck to our clothes. He brushed them away, dampening his hair.

At the door, Luke gave me another kiss. "Call me tomorrow?" I said.

He shook his head. "You call me for once."

I nodded. Inside, I sauntered to my room. Lights on, my back went against the door, and my hand went over my chest. "What are you doing here? In the dark?"

Aaron threw some charts on my bed and folded his legs. Perched on my lounge chair, he stayed rigid, ready to strike. I knew why he was there, but once he started talking, I was surprised what came out of his mouth.

CHAPTER THIRTY-ONE

Aaron

"You know, I never thought I'd have to have this conversation with you," he started, "but here we are."

"Look, I'm sorry I walked in on you in the clinic…"

"Why are you kissing Luke when you're supposed to be with Gavin? I've gone out of my way to save that greaser for you…for you."

"What?" I tilted my head to the side.

"Gavin and I have never seen eye-to-eye, and frankly, if my brother killed him, I probably wouldn't care. But I care about you, and you care about him, so I've tried to help your boy because he means something to you."

"Aaron," I stammered, "it's…" I came into the room and took the necklace off, placing it on my night stand. "I…"

"When you saw me at the clinic, I was working on this." Aaron handed me the charts. They contained photos of Kyle in some wooded area. Surveillance, no doubt.

"You're having him followed?" Aaron confirmed my next question. "You have a plan, don't you?"

He told me to take a seat. "My brother's been after Gavin for all the shit that has gone down since Gavin's crew killed What's His Face."

"I'm not sure."

"Well, it doesn't matter. The point is, we can save Gavin if we can set Kyle up for my brother."

"I thought you wanted to stay out of that part of it?" I folded my arms.

"I did until my brother called me yesterday."

"So, he's not missing anymore?"

"No, he was out of town on business. Legitimate business," Aaron emphasized. "You see, Kyle's activities have been bad on both sides. And my brother thought Gavin was putting him up to it. So, naturally, my brother put a hit out on Gavin, and we ended up where we are now. However!" Aaron got up, "However, Porter didn't have all the facts. He didn't know that Kyle was operating on his own accord until I told him about the attempt on Gavin at the Halloween party. Kyle went after him, so he could settle the score for all the evil shit he's done for Gavin's crew. And for my brother, any deals that Kyle had worked out with him were no longer valid."

"Why's that?"

"My brother needed Kyle to stay good with Gavin, so he could have a way in. With Kyle out, my brother doesn't want anything to do with him."

This was a good time to tell the other part of the story. I explained to Aaron what happened to me that night. How Kyle's weird behavior had led me to believe that he was going to offer me up to Porter in some type of sacrifice for mercy.

"Unbelievable!" Aaron raked his hair. "My brother would never go after you. He has no reason to."

"What about my attack? Gavin said Porter came after me because he thinks that Gavin loving me would be a good bargaining chip." I leaned forward. "If your brother were to harm me, he would twist Gavin's hand. That's the whole reason he left; he was trying to protect me."

A loud laugh shook Aaron's body. Once he calmed down, his face still had the same amount of glee. "It's cute, really it is." I spoke up in Gavin's defense of his idea. "No, that's not what I mean," Aaron said. "Kyle was clearly following Gavin's dumb logic when he put that little plan together…"

I slowed down all my thoughts. "Kyle?" my hand went to my mouth. My ribs tightened. "Kyle sent Ronda after me without any direction from your brother?"

Aaron stroked his chin. "I thought you knew?"

"Knew what?"

"My brother…would never sic Kyle on you to send a message to Gavin. In fact, my brother would never go after someone innocent for any reason. It brings too much heat." He sat down on the bed. "Porter got a call from Kyle the night of Halloween, and Kyle said that he had failed showing his loyalty, or some shit like that. He told my brother that he had found someone who would be the perfect revenge for all the people Gavin's crew had killed. But Kyle didn't know that my brother's spies had already blamed him for the deaths. So, you were never of any interest to Porter because you didn't have the leverage he needed to bring his drugs back into Settlement Island. That's what my brother's after; more territory."

"That's good to know," I scoffed.

"So, after Kyle was dismissed by Porter, my brother reached out to James to say that he would leave Gavin's crew alone if they cut ties with Kyle. A hit was put out on him. James said he couldn't do anything to cross Gavin, so he didn't bring it up. However, Kyle must have thought that the crew was going to kill him, so he tried to kill you first to make a point."

"With Ronda?"

"He probably needed someone who was dumb enough to do it. Someone who would seem like a likely suspect to attack you." He paused. "Everyone knows about you and Gavin. They know about him and Ronda, too. So, it would make sense."

"Wow," I huffed. "I always thought it was strange that she came after me like that. But I fell for the lie Kyle set, too. I let Gavin go because I thought your brother had eyes on me."

"In the end, you were a warning, but not in the way Kyle intended. A decoy to set the stage to pit Gavin and Porter against one another, so Kyle could get out of the consequences of all the shit he has caused."

My fists balled, cutting my fingernails into my palm. "So, what do we do now?"

There was a knock on the door, which was pointless because Miguel and Cecilia had already come in. Cecilia jumped into Aaron's lap as I shoved the files closed.

"Working?" she said.

"Yeah," I answered for Aaron. "He wants me to come back to the clinic soon, so we can figure some stuff out."

Miguel laid down on my bed. "Was it just me, or did I see you kissing Luke on the porch earlier?" His eyebrow rose. I had forgotten about that. Aaron shot me a look and then went on to giving his girlfriend a kiss on the cheek. "Is it true?" Miguel said.

"Yeah," I confirmed with a weak smile.

Now Miguel and Cecilia were chattering about why Luke was a better fit for me than Gavin. Boring. They used the word boring several times. We didn't stay on this topic for very long. Dad came to the door, mentioning a movie night. Miguel and Cecilia were game, and they insisted that Aaron and I join in, too. I made an excuse to draw a bath instead.

"Don't worry, Catalina," Dad said. "Dinner and a movie are much later." I had an hour to myself before all the festivities started, was his point. There was enough time for me to soak and pull out my phone. As I settled into the water, my heart sank.

I had to tell him. I had to tell Luke the new developments. A big sigh and the phone was chucked onto the bath caddy, almost knocking my book into the water.

Dammit! For once, I had a chance at a good life since I moved to cursed Settlement Island, Maine. And now…and now I had to break the news to Luke that… that I had made a mistake. A selfish mistake. That I had led him on, again, all because I thought I couldn't be with the one I truly loved.

I sat up in the water; why should I let Gavin drag me back into all this just because he was free now? That didn't seem very fair to me. Luke had pointed out something very true. All of my interactions with Luke were driven by my selfish need to be helped. Yet, everything Gavin had done regarding me and our relationship was out of selfishness, too. I huffed a sigh; no, that wasn't true. Gavin left, giving up everything for me.

I had to fix things and make up my mind. If Gavin Scott was able to come back into my life, I had to grow a spine and stand behind him and whatever decision he needed to make. Be there for him and show my allegiance like all the other people who loved him did. And I could do that. I had to.

Feeling empowered, I sat up and rehearsed what I would say to Gavin via text to let him know I was behind him. Afterward, it felt silly to do such a thing. Never, not once, had we ever sent a text. Regardless, this was still symbolic for me. I nodded, reaffirming this fact. Now, on to the love part. I needed to know for sure. Because if I didn't love Gavin, all this was for nothing. Hurting Luke and putting myself back into the line of fire would be for nothing.

Did I really love Gavin? All the work…all the pain he had brought me. And then, when I needed him the most, he left. He skipped out of Settlement Island, leaving everyone and everything behind. So selfish! My heart jolted. I ignored it. Gavin was selfish! Another jolt.

Okay, maybe his leaving his entire life behind for me wasn't selfish. But…he…he…I sank back down into the water. "He loves me," I muttered.

Cecilia knocked on the door and tried the lock. "Dinner's ready!"

I blew out the candles and wrapped myself in a towel. When I opened the door, she was gone. As I put on my PJs, I heard my phone chirp. A text from Luke saying he missed me. I threw my phone on the bed and joined everyone else.

When I woke up the next day, it was still snowing. Dad had called off his appointments due to the icy conditions. So, this meant I had another day to sulk in my room, plagued by my growing predicament. Luke had called, which didn't make matters better.

I'd have to break his heart, I knew it. But what would be the best way to do it?

"California, here you come!" Dad said. He handed me two printed plane tickets: one for Luke and one for me.

"Thanks," I put them on the nightstand.

"Wait a minute," Dad said. "You don't want to go?"

No, it wasn't that. I had forgotten about my trip. I was too focused on everything happening with Gavin and Porter. Dad couldn't know about this. My lips curled into a smile. "Can't wait."

Next, Aaron came to the door. Dad seemed confused when I willingly let him in. Aaron looked at the tickets, primarily the one with Luke's name. I snapped them back.

"Come home with me this week," he said.

"Home?"

"Back to Anders."

"Why?"

"Well," Aaron started pacing the room, which was rather odd given the simplicity of his ask. It should have been an easy answer. However, with Aaron, things didn't always seem to be simple or easy. "There's some research I think we should do."

"What about Kyle and Settlement Island?"

He shook his head. "Things are too quiet here. I think we can get more information elsewhere."

"And," I sighed, "you think Kyle is in Anders?"

"Yeah, I do." Pictures of Kyle were in Aaron's phone. A private investigator had made some hits on him in Anders.

To organize a plan, Aaron wanted to do some more probing around Kyle's usual haunts. His brother was willing to help if Aaron could find a way to set Kyle up without implementing Porter. "This kind of heat could come back on him, and my brother would hold me liable," he said. They were pretty confident that everything would go smoothly, if Aaron followed Porter's instructions. This was the bright side.

"If Kyle catches on…" I told Aaron with a stern tone. "Maybe you should go without me."

"I can't." Aaron stopped moving. "Too many people in Anders know who I am. I need you with me to get into places where I'm sure to get hung up."

Oh, I saw exactly how this was going to play out. And I wasn't going to be a victim or a pawn. I leaned forward slightly, "If we're going to do this, we're gonna do it my way."

"Alright. What does that look like?"

I pulled the covers back. "A plan. Create a real plan that doesn't involve you getting me killed, and you can do whatever it is you want." For the first time, Aaron didn't interrupt me. This was valuable real estate. "Your brother is in Anders, which means you can work with him on some things, and I can work on my own on other things."

"You've never even been to Anders. What can you work on without me?"

I knew one thing. A card I would play soon, but not yet. "Trust goes both ways, Aaron." He shrugged. I had lost him. "There are a few affairs that I need to attend to in Anders. Things I can't tell you about yet," I said.

"Does it help us?" he said. I nodded. "Will it get you killed?"

"Probably not."

"Fine." Now, Aaron was at my closet. My suitcase landed on my bed. "Pack about three-days-worth of clothes. I'm gonna go talk to your dad, then we'll hit the road."

I put plenty of clothes into the case. A few journals and pens went in, too. Then I got dressed and swept my hair into a low ponytail. I put on the necklace, makeup, rings, and bracelets. All I needed to be complete was my purse, phone and charger. My phone—Luke had called, again.

My head went back, my eyes went to the ceiling. I had to tell him. It had to be now, not later.

※

Luke walked up to the porch, keeping eye contact with me as I sat on the porch, pounds of blankets on my body. The smile, his smile, warmed me up. When he sat down beside me, there was distance between us.

"Hi," he said.

"Hi."

Where to start…that was always the hardest for me. Finding the right words to shatter his heart in a kind, friendly way would be impossible. Another smile from him. He noticed the necklace around my neck: the arrow.

"So, you called me over here. How can I be of service, Ms. Catalina Payton?"

My eyebrows scrunched. "Why do you say it like that?"

He leaned back on the swing, putting us in motion. "Because I know you. Last night, I gave you that necklace, and you kissed me in a way that no girl has ever kissed me before." He tapped his knee, "That's when I knew. I put everything together." Impossible! He couldn't know a thing, right? Or had I been too obvious? I nodded for him to continue. "It's too soon," he said.

"What's too soon?"

"Your feelings for me. With everything that's happened, and your pinning love for Gavin, there's no way you could be ready to date me."

"It's not pinning love…" I muttered.

"You don't get it."

"No," I emphasized, "you don't get it." Luke tilted his head to the side. "Look, I meant those kisses I gave you yesterday." Something caught my eye: Miguel and Cecilia at the window. I motioned for them to leave. They ignored me. I swallowed my frustration.

"Catalina, I didn't mean to upset you. I'm sorry, I'm just a pretty straight-forward guy. And I know what you feel for me isn't real. Even if you pretended it was, it'd be a lie."

"It's not you, it's everything. The murders, Gavin, Kyle, this Porter guy, all of it."

"I get it, bad stuff's happened." He sighed. "But I'm not doing this with you anymore. If you love him, fine. But I'm not going to be your reserve boyfriend."

"You're not on reserve, Luke. It's just…I don't know." I slouched down which hurt. "I don't know what I'm doing."

"Yeah, I can see that," he scoffed. "So, I'm making it easy for you. Just pick him, completely, and be with him."

I laughed. "That's where you're wrong." My eyes studied him. "I can't just pick him." Luke asked why not.

It was time to level with him. Tell him the truth, which is why I had called him over. He had to know me, everything about me. I owed Luke an explanation, a long one, full of reasons and excuses for my behavior. He needed to know why I had been drawn to Gavin, why I loved and feared Gavin, and why the carousel kept turning.

Telling Luke started out very slow. After some time, there was an easy dialogue between us. He didn't judge me. When I didn't make sense, he clarified some points. Every word about Gavin was received very well, given the circumstances. In the end, he stared straight ahead, watching the snow dance to the ground.

"You went through all this, and I had no clue." His words were sad. Like he regretted not doing something sooner.

For all I knew, maybe he could have done something. Maybe his role in everything could have made matters better, not worse. I couldn't put that on him. I gave another long explanation why I was afraid to tell him. How he became inaccessible to me the moment he warned me about going into town. This admission of truth was met with a hearty laugh. "What's so funny?" He kept laughing. "Luke!"

"It's just…" he caught his breath. "I gave you that warning because I thought you'd go looking for trouble. Instead, trouble came looking for you." Ironic, yes, but my ordeal and plight did not put me in such a good mood. Luke caught on and his smile turned sincere. "I just wanted to protect you. My approach was probably too extreme, you know?" I agreed. Eyes relaxed, body rigid, Luke looked back at me. "Everything you've told me. The stuff about Gavin and Kyle. It's not over, is it?"

"No, it's not. Aaron wants to take me to Anders, so we can find Kyle and put an end to all this."

Deep sigh. "What do you want me to do?"

I went still. The heart-shattering moment was upon us. "It's not safe for you to know me right now. Not until Aaron and I sort all this out."

"That's not what I mean, Catalina." I closed my eyes at the sound of my name on his lips. For a moment, I thought it was Gavin who had said it. "Do you want my help?"

Eyes open. "No." My hand laced into his. "I'm not a selfish person, even though I've been really selfish with you."

"Okay." His eye twitched. "So, where do we stand as friends?"

"It's not fair," I muttered, then composed myself. "We need a rebirth for our friendship."

"A rebirth?"

"Well, yeah!" I calmed down. "Our friendship has been bandaged together with secrets and awkward lies. I mean, James poisoned you!"

"Yeah…definitely a low point."

Both hands were onto his. "Let me make this right. For you and for me."

If Luke thought I was being dramatic or crazy, he didn't show it. His fingers came to my hair, brushing away a few loose strands. The kiss he gave me was sweet, forgiving. "Sorry, I had to kiss you one last time." Luke was on his feet, "When you're done making this right, let me know." A wink, an intentional eye movement was the last I saw of him before he was gone from the driveway.

I had lost him. Another man had loved me and left, driven away by the consequences of knowing me.

Now, my focus went elsewhere. Everything tensed up. It hurt. I hated him. I hated him enough to make him pay. Kyle would pay the debts that I had to carry.

Chapter Thirty-Two

Anders

Anders was different, much different from Settlement Island. Skyscrapers lined the freeway Aaron took us on. Still, no lighthouses.

"We'll go to the coast, soon!" he said.

"Yeah, right, I don't believe you," Cecilia snapped. Miguel nodded his head in agreement.

They, too, came along on our big adventure. Aaron didn't understand the bond Miguel and I had, nor did he understand the friendship my sister and my best friend had formed. One that came as a surprise to me, too. I welcomed it. Also, having more people in our crew meant better backup, even though Miguel and Cecilia didn't really know what was going on.

"I could live here," Cecilia said. We had just passed a mall.

Miguel wanted to kick off their vacation with dinner at a lobster place. I should have taken him with me and

Luke. The arrow dangling from my neck reminded me why I hadn't.

"Movie or club tonight?" said Cecilia.

Miguel's vote was the same as hers: club. Aaron explained that he and I would have to do some work at the clinic. Cecilia pouted, and Miguel offered up a few of his sightseeing hours to help me out. He was relieved when I declined.

When we finally pulled up to Aaron's house, the snow had stopped. Miguel opened my door and took my bags. Cecilia had a key, so she let us in. The first thing I noticed was the library tucked into a room down the hall. I went there. Aaron wasn't kidding; he did own more books than me. A touch on my shoulder told me that I couldn't hide in here for the rest of the trip.

Aaron and I didn't talk about the plan before we left. There was no time. Once Luke was gone, I was brought into the house to be scolded by Miguel for not running after him. Then Cecilia caught on to Aaron's plans to leave. Her suitcase was packed shortly after. Miguel was packing his as Mother tried to understand why we were off so soon. A kiss on the cheek from all three of us wasn't enough. She didn't let me go until I lied about Christmas shopping. This was her language, the only way to connect with her.

Yet, I felt guilty for not spending the time with her. I would make it up to her when we got back. No one knew this, except Luke, but I had passed on my trip to California to work on this case with Aaron. It was a last-minute decision I made during the ride over. Getting to the bottom of Porter's plan, and saving Gavin from certain death, all rested in Aaron's hands now. So, with Aaron standing before me, it was time to make good on my commitment…I had given up so much to make things right once and for all. Our trip better be fruitful, or I'd kill Aaron for failing me.

I sighed. If we failed, it was my fault, too, really. I came down here, all for what, a hunch? A flimsy piece of truth that I shared with Aaron? Or was it for something else? Someone else. The brush of his lips against mine. To bring him back to me?

"Catalina?" Aaron called. Time to get back to it.

"So, how do we do this?" I said.

"Before we get into that, there's something I want to show you."

∽

We had arrived at a small house on the outskirts of the city. The plan seemed less promising as we drove up. I was expecting Aaron to say something about this being his childhood home, like Gavin had given me the tour of his world in Settlement Island. Quite the opposite.

"This is the dump Kyle gets his drugs from," was Aaron's reply.

"Enchanting." My eyes drifted around the property. "So, are we going to rush in there, unarmed?" Aaron stopped the engine right across the street. In the shade of the trees, we could see them, but whoever they were could not see us. "We wait?"

"We wait."

"For what? Again, we are unarmed!"

Aaron rolled his eyes and pulled out his phone. "You don't need a gun when you got a brother who has an army of willing killers."

"Figures." I hunched down in the seat, careful not to be seen on the outside. Aaron leaned in back and pulled out two fleece blankets: one for him and one for me. "Thanks." The silence got me thinking about Porter. "How did you stay out of your brother's grasp all these years? I mean, I figured that your brother would have put you on the payroll some time ago."

"It never came to that. I had no intention of being a criminal, and Porter always respected my wishes."

"What about him? Has he been a horrible person this whole time?"

Aaron shrugged, pulling the blanket closer to his chin. "Porter's always been bad since I can remember. He just had the sense for crime, you know?"

"What about your parents?"

"My mom never wanted to believe he'd go this far. Even now, she still thinks he's not the person he is. As for my dad, he cut ties with him a long time ago. Same with his dad."

"Different dads…that's right."

"My dad loved Porter like his own. He even tried to get him to come over to the right side. But my brother has a very strong will." Aaron seemed lost in his thinking. "He had every opportunity to go a different way, but he never took any of them. I mean, my parents did everything they could for us both, but it just wasn't enough."

"What did he want?"

"Power."

This made sense. Every move Porter seemed to make was laced in a mirage of power. His parents probably thought it was a good thing, at first, until it wasn't. "What do your parents do, anyway?"

Aaron put his hand up for me to stop. Eyes forward. There was Kyle with some guy. Dark, thick eyebrows. Serious face. He looked to be a little younger than Aaron and in his late twenties.

"Who is that?"

Aaron had produced some binoculars; "Not sure. Never seen him before."

I squinted. "What are they doing?" My phone rang: Cecilia. Silence. "Do you see what they're doing?"

"Not much…" My phone rang again: Miguel. "Turn that off, will ya?" I complied. "No, I don't know who that is. Maybe his dealer?"

"Looks too clean cut to be a drug dealer."

"You'd be surprised." Aaron sent a text out.

"So, we just wait for your brother to save the day?"

"Not quite…" Aaron stayed suspiciously quiet for a few moments.

I watched Kyle as he and the man leaned against a car, in clear view, smoking a cigarette. This was taking too long.

The rear car door opening and closing made me jump.

"Aaron," said the man. "Mrs. Aaron," he said to me.

"She's not my wife," Aaron said with a sigh. "Did you get the text?"

"Yes." The man pulled out his phone. I tried to make out his features in the dark, but he did a good job staying in the shadows. "Porter has sent three to the left and two to the right." What did that mean? "Now," the door opened, "if you'll excuse me." Door closed.

Aaron started the car. "Is that it?" I said. We pulled onto the street, Kyle and his friend remaining where they were. They had to see us; it was inevitable. "All you had to do was make a phone call?"

"I had to know for sure that he'd be there before my brother could make contact."

"You mean kill him?" Aaron scanned the empty road. "I thought you didn't kill people?"

"This is my brother, Catalina!" I bit my lip. He continued with, "I don't enjoy these games, either. Being caught up in my brother's shit. But Kyle brought the heat to my brother's door. And your door. Don't you want this to end as much as I do?"

Yes, I did. But not this way. Not at the hands of a murderer.

"All I have to say is you should think about this carefully. Killing Kyle is something you can't undo."

His hand stroked his face. Game over, I had lost. He wasn't going to give up that easy. But I knew one person who might be able to help me.

When we got back to the house, Cecilia and Miguel were already working on dinner. I knew I could expect this from Miguel, but not my dear sister. Having this new development from her made my next task seem easier. After the chicken went into the oven, I borrowed my sister and relieved her from her mashed potato duties.

"I never thought cooking would actually be fun," she said. The apron flew off her body, landing on the kitchen island. "What's up?" Getting Cecilia to leave the kitchen didn't take long. Aaron did peer around the corner as I guided her over to the living room. I got close to her. "Okay, now you're just acting weird."

"I need to ask you for James's phone number."

Her eyebrows narrowed, "Why?"

What to tell her…Cecilia didn't need to know everything Aaron and I were up to. I couldn't tell her that James was my secret weapon, one I had alluded to in front of Aaron before the trip. Or, maybe I thought she would tell Aaron the truth about my relationship with James, which would put her in a compromising spot. Maybe it wouldn't. Honestly, I couldn't tell how she would react. So, there had to be a line in the sand, somewhere. Judging by her foot tapping the couch, I knew I had to come up with something.

"It has to do with Gavin."

"And Kyle, right?" My head only shook a few times before she caught on to the lie. "I know you're trying to fix all this."

"What do you mean by that?"

"Catalina Rose, I've been there. You want to take

this on yourself. That's probably why you got Aaron to drag us up here to go shopping. However, I can really use some Prada bags for my store."

"Okay, you seem to know more than you let on," I paused.

Her arms folded. "Baby girl, I know everything. Ronda beat you down, Gavin went missing, and Kyle keeps trying to kill James. He told me everything."

"Kyle?"

"James!" she rolled her eyes. "James figured out that Kyle sent Ronda after you. I knew about everything except for your dumbass plan to try and kill Kyle!"

I hushed her rising voice. "I'm trying to keep Aaron and his brother from killing Kyle."

"Is that what you're doing?" Another head shake. "Seriously, Catalina, you gotta let the boys be boys. I gave up James over this mess because he wouldn't walk away. And guess what? My life got pretty fuckin' simple after I did. No more late-night drama and bailing him out." I tried to stop her with no luck, "Look, I'm not givin' you James's number, okay? So just drop it." She was up and headed back to the kitchen before I could catch her.

The smile growing on her face seemed to throw Aaron off. A long, sweet kiss between them caused my attention to case over to Miguel. He was almost done dressing the rest of the food. I retrieved a spoon from the kitchen table and scooped up some mashed potatoes.

"Good, huh?" he said. I nodded. "Chicken with

asparagus will be done soon." Miguel leaned against the counter. "Mi Amor, what's up? You're sad again."

It wasn't sadness he had seen. The doom that was consuming me, that's what stood out. Next, it had to be the anger growing inside. I retreated out of the house and onto the street. The snow fell in tiny, light flakes on my face as I tilted my head back.

"Fuck!" More words of the kind followed. I marched forward, down the sidewalk, no jacket, just a thick gray sweater, flimsy tights, and a bushel of curly hair brushing my ears. If it was cold, I didn't know. Finally, at the end of the street was a small creek with benches lining it. Down I went, my fists striking my ribs as I tucked my arms around myself.

"What am I supposed to do?" I said to the water. "Everything I do, everything I try just gets thrown back into my face! Everyone else gets to have a plan, an agenda for my life about what I shouldn't do!"

I felt a shadow pass behind me. Very subtle. I looked, but unfortunately, my focus went to the wrong place. He sat down on the other side, close.

"Well, you can chalk this one up to another person havin' a plan for your life…and you may not like it too much."

My fingernails dug into my palm. I didn't feel that much next to the gun nudging my aching rib. "Kyle."

"What did you expect? I see a car I don't recognize, and when the plates come back, it's Aaron White, the brother of my former partner, Robert Porter." Kyle pulled one leg over the other. "So, I got an address, came to check it out, and I find you here, alone."

"They're making dinner for me. If I'm not back…"

Kyle grinned, "Don't worry about that. I'm sure they'll figure things out soon."

"And me? What about me?"

Kyle's head tilted up the street. "I've got a nice car with Louisiana plates. We're gonna take a ride and see where the night takes us."

"I don't think that's a good idea."

"Well," he leaned in, his skin warm as his hand touched my face. "Good news is, I don't need any input from you regardin' this matter. Got it all figured out."

"So, what's the plan? Are you going to kill me?"

Kyle looked out to the water. "It's a shame, really. I mean, you just moved here, right?" I bit my lip. "Yeah, ya did. Not a Settler, like me and your boy Gavin."

"Kyle," I started. "You don't have to involve me anymore than I already am."

His eyes, the bluest I had ever seen, seemed kind. "I have to, Catalina. You should know better than me what it feels like to be vulnerable and alone." His lips went to my ear. "You see, Catalina, I'm a desperate man. I've made a lot of mistakes…fucked a lot of shit up, you know?" Kyle pulled away. "And now that I have no one else, I've got to get creative about how I make amends."

I shook my head. "Make amends? With your crew?"

"No," he said plainly, "with myself." His hand grabbed my forearm tight. "Enough dickin' around. Get up!" I didn't have a choice in the matter. Once on my feet, Kyle held my arm and navigated me onto the path. "Beautiful night, isn't it?"

He looked up, which gave me an advantage. Black ice, right on the road. A quick shove, and he was a victim to it. And I ran, fast, feet slipping and ribs burning. Kyle screamed, struggling to catch up. I expected bullets to come sailing toward me, but there were none.

The chase was on, and I had no idea where to go. I had taken a wrong turn, heading away from Aaron's house. To get the leg up, I ducked into the bushes by the creek. Now, led by only moonlight, I tripped over slick leaves and branches. I heard Kyle slow down above me. A light scanned my area, barely missing me. I hunkered down.

He didn't move; he had to know I was close by. Things had taken a bad turn. I needed help, but if I reached for the phone, the light would give away my position. The ground beside me was too loud to walk on. I had to stay right where I was.

"Ca-ta-lee-na?" his call was a song. "Sweetheart, you're comin' with me."

My nerves were giving out. The desperation to call someone was beyond me. His light went close to my head, and I hugged the cold, damp ground. Kyle descended from the walkway above, close but not close enough. I only had a few seconds to make a run for it.

"Ca-ta-lee-na?" his voice was almost next to me.

I pulled out my phone, typed a quick text to Aaron, and tucked the phone close to the leaves and branches, but within sight once the morning light came. When someone would come looking for me. This was the best option, if there was a chance for me to be found alive.

And so, I waited, still and present in the moment, knowing that my abduction would hopefully give Aaron and everyone else the ammo they needed to take Kyle down for good. When his light shined on my face, I took in a deep breath. A nice, deep breath.

My pulse quickened as it did in that moment when I saw Gavin for the first time. My shoulders tensed up; I could feel his hands on me as I danced with him like a statue. And, finally, my breathing stopped. This simple action belonged to Kyle.

All humanity had left his face. The punch across my brow said he meant business.

CHAPTER THIRTY-THREE

Kyle

THE NEXT THING I felt was warmth and soft blankets against my aching brow. Birds chirped back and forth. The slight draft on my leg, something cold, startled me into a sitting position.

"Oh, good," Kyle said. "You're awake."

He was stretched out in a pair of overstuffed chairs by the fire. I lay on the bed behind him. There was a small kitchen with a wood stove and a door leading to a bathroom.

"Where are we?" I said.

"We're on our own little adventure." Kyle sipped a mug of something, "Coffee?" I pulled the blanket off me. On my right ankle was a pair of long cuffs: one end on me and the other on the bed frame. "Yeah, about that…"

"Take these off!"

Another sip. "Can't do that, sweetheart. You'll go off runnin' again." I looked out the windows, but they were covered with curtains. The light and shadows outside told me it was day but that was it. "Catalina, I searched ya and the car for your phone, and I couldn't find it. Where is it?"

"I think I lost it by the creek," I lied.

"Good!" Kyle got up. "Makes everything real easy for me."

"What do you mean by that?" I stammered.

He shrugged. "I don't like bein' interrupted." Over to the kitchen, my eyes followed Kyle as he pulled out a cast iron skillet. "Sausage, eggs, and hash…that's what's for breakfast." Once the skillet was on, he turned toward me. "Hey, did Gavin ever make ya breakfast?"

"No."

He nodded. "He's the best cook I know. I always wondered what he'd chef up for breakfast…it's kinda a hard meal to cook for. Know what I mean?"

I didn't care, but I kept up the conversation as I thought things through. First, I'd have to figure out how to get the cuff off my leg. Then came getting Kyle out of the way. He rambled on about finding cheap produce in town, his back to me now. My fingers traced around the cuff slowly, hunting for a weakness.

I had never been cuffed before, so I didn't even know how they operated. A key…there had to be a key. Once I got that, I could move on to the next part of my plan: safety. Finding a place to hide once I got out of here would be challenging seeing how I had no idea where I was.

Kyle came back to me. "This thing is dramatic, I know." His hand fiddled with the chain linking the two cuffs. "But it's where we're at for the time being. There's enough slack for ya to move around the cottage without my help."

"But I can't run away."

"Nope. I need you here, with me, and I'll do whatever I have to, so ya won't leave." He leaned in, "Whatever I have to."

Point taken. He set the table quickly with some plates and silverware. Two spots: one for him and one for me. As he cooked, he told me about Laura, a girl he had seen a few times. She was sweet; a black-haired girl who worked for the city. Nothing like my fiery sister, he added.

"Cecilia? Why are you bringing her up?"

"I've always had a crush on your sister. I've seen her on TV and stuff." Breakfast was done. Kyle shuffled food onto the plates and motioned for me to come over. I put my feet on the ground, and he pulled a chair out for me. "When I saw her in that café, I almost died." Cecilia, right. He has a crush on Cecilia. "I never got to talk to her, though."

I sat down, "Well, you're not missing out on much." My gaze went to the food. It actually looked good.

"Go ahead and try it. I promise, you'll like it."

As I inspected my food with a fork, Kyle went back to the Laura discussion. Laura never spent the night, and he couldn't tell how she wanted to proceed with the relationship. I ran my finger around the rim of my plate.

These were Kyle's problems now? What about my problems? The murders and midnight car rides with men who were tearing my life from me, thread by thread. Had anyone figured out that I was missing yet? My abrupt departure had to be noticed, right?

Kyle threw more food onto his plate and sat down. I pointed to my plate. "Are we eating breakfast because it's morning?"

"It that your way of trying to figure out what time it is?"

I showed him my wrists. "I don't have a watch."

"And no phone…"

"Correct."

Out came his phone. "7:45am." He took a bite of sausage, "Ya wouldn't know it, but I'm an early riser."

"Well, good for you," I scoffed.

"You need to eat your breakfast."

I put my fork down. Here went nothing. "Kyle, I don't know what you're up to, but this is beyond weird. Why did you take me?" He sat in silence. "I mean…do you plan on killing me?"

He huffed a sigh. "Let's just get through breakfast and see where the day goes, okay?" I recoiled. "Look, just relax for a bit."

"You don't know me, so you have no idea how hard it is for me to relax."

Kyle laughed. "I can imagine." He leaned back in his chair. "Catalina, this is…" he sighed.

"What? This is what?"

His tongue rolled over his teeth. "There's a lot you don't know about me, either." He paused. "And I'd be willin' to tell ya more if you eat." An enticing offer. I nibbled on a sausage; it was good. Soon, I tried the eggs and the hash. Also good. "Now, I'll make ya a deal: if you don't cause any problems for me, I won't cause any problems for you."

"But what's the point? Did you kidnap me, so you could have company? Because Laura stood you up or something?"

He chuckled, pointing his fork at me. "See, this is why Gavin must like ya so damn much." I stopped eating. Kyle got serious and leaned forward. "This situation between you and me is evolving very quickly."

"Situation?"

"Well, yeah. Gavin, James, Porter…everyone wantin' me dead. And then there's you."

"What about me? I'm not trying to kill you."

"I know that," he scoffed. "But every road out of my problems leads back to you."

"Road? What road?"

"The road back to the beginning. Before shit got all twisted."

"Before you killed everyone?"

Kyle picked his teeth with his fork. "Have I killed people? Yes. Did I do it because I had to? Yes."

"What about Molly? Why did you shoot her?"

"That was an accident. I was gunnin' for James and missed."

I nodded. "So, you were trying to kill James? Your own friend?"

"I hate James. And he hates me. So, if we get a chance to kill each other, we will."

"And Gavin?"

"I'd never kill Gavin. And he'd never kill me." Kyle had a fond smile on his face. "Gavin's a real stand-up guy. Honest. I owe him my life, and I could never take anythin' from him."

"Including me." Kyle had gone silent again. "So, you're not going to kill me?" I said.

Other people would have been relieved by this new piece of information. Sane people. For me, a chill came back over my body. If Kyle wasn't going to kill me, what did he want instead?

"There's some old books 'round here," Kyle interrupted. Up again, he was cleaning the table. "I'm goin' out for a bit."

Out? I spied the chain on my leg but didn't make my motivations obvious. My eyes were up in time to see Kyle pull a rifle from the small closet by the door. He smiled, leaving me completely on edge as he left.

Having Kyle gone gave me time to think. Back to the plan. He probably didn't leave a key behind, but maybe he was cocky enough to think I wouldn't try to get free. Every place, every room turned up nothing. No creaky floorboards underneath the bed gave way to a possible hiding place, either.

I moved on to the bed, checking the pillows, tearing off the covers and overturning the mattress. Still, I had nothing, just like when I started. Kyle had made good on his promise to keep me here. There had to be something else; there was always something. But what? I pondered for a few minutes…break the cuffs!

Kyle had to be gone for a long time, yet the hours passed for me quickly. There were no knives or other weapons I could use to pick the lock or break the chain. The fork was no good, either. I kept my spirits up, though. I had his word…he wasn't going to kill me. So, maybe I could talk him down.

The door opened, bringing in some light from the outside and Kyle. It had to be late afternoon. In his hand was a rabbit, skinned and gutted. "Dinner!"

My stomach churned. I sat down at the table. The fire had gone low, so he put a few logs on and went back outside. I got to the window, brushing the curtain aside. There was nothing but snow and ice. And a lake! Settlement Island Lake! I was back home.

This was good! This was really good! I was closer than I could ever hope for. Kyle returned, carrying an arm full of onions, potatoes and carrots. No gun. Smart, Kyle. Very smart.

"Have you ever had rabbit before?" No, and I didn't want to. "It's not as bad as you might think."

"Is that where you went? Hunting?"

"Yeah. We're off the grid here." Convenient. "But don't worry. I've been huntin' since I was a kid. I can shoot anythin'."

"I'll just have veggies."

He shrugged. "More for me."

Kyle was fixing dinner, so preoccupied with stirring and roasting that he didn't feel my eyes peering into him.

Somewhere, on his body, was the key. Thick canvas coat, a tee-shirt, I think, flannel shirt, jeans and boots. The key was there, hiding in some pocket or under a layer.

Seducing him might get his clothes off, but that was Cecilia's style, not mine. So, what was left? How to get his clothes off without losing my virginity in the process… the bathroom. A tub! Get him to take a bath, Catalina! I hid my smile when he turned to me. He had been talking. About what? I had no idea.

"Storm's comin' soon. A Nor'easter." He nodded, "Yeah, we should be fine."

"That's a bad snow storm, right?"

"Pretty much."

"Maybe we should go back to town."

"Settlement Island, you mean? Nah, it's too far away. Besides, they've put a hit on me. Gotta stay out of sight."

"For how long?" No response. "Kyle, you have to give me something. Eventually, my family is going to come looking for me. And we can't stay here forever."

"I live here, Catalina."

Really? This long-forgotten shack in the woods was Kyle's permanent home? No, that couldn't be. He wouldn't be dumb enough to take me to his house, the first place Aaron and Porter would come looking for clues. Besides, nothing about this location gave me the impression that someone could stay here for more than a week, at most.

This was a lie. And if Kyle was lying about the cabin, he could be lying about not killing me. I didn't let this revelation get to me much, because what did Kyle have to gain by killing me? I wasn't his direct enemy. Gavin would never forgive Kyle for killing me, and Kyle knew that. So, what was it? Was it my connection to Porter? No, it couldn't be that. I had never met Porter, and he didn't care much for me. So, what was it, then?

Kyle sat down at the table with a beer. He offered me one. I accepted, even though I didn't drink beer much. This one was for Kyle; a way to get him to open up about his plans. I'd have to be smart, that was for sure. But things weren't hopeless just yet.

"Why do you like my sister?"

"Cecilia?" He shook his head, grinning as he drank his bottle. "She's got this Asian, black, princess look to her. Plus, she's loud and bossy."

"Cecilia is not Asian," I said as a start, "and she thinks she's a princess. Definitely loud and bossy." I warmed a smiled. "Do you like bossy girls?"

"Depends." He shrugged. "A girl who's just bein' a bitch, no. It's the girl who knows what she wants and isn't afraid to take it. Someone you can't control."

"What about me?"

"Sorry, darlin'. You're just too borin' for me." A slight from him meant a compliment to me. "Gavin likes ya a lot. I can tell."

"How?"

"He's different now." Another sip. "Before you came along, he was all business. Like, we would get into it with Porter, and he'd be all over retaliation. Or, if we had cars we needed to sell off, he'd be in the shop, gettin' orders ready. Now, he's more distracted, like he's got somethin' on his mind. He don't come 'round as much. And, he's workin' things out with Porter."

"That doesn't mean I have anything to do with it."

"But it does, sweetheart." He leaned in. "The only time a guy in Settlement Island makes amends like that means he wants to get out of the game. And he'd only do that if he had a reason to."

This provoked a response. "What about you? Are you getting out of the game?" He looked down. "Kyle, you have to tell me things."

"I can't make amends with anyone on any side. Gavin said that my allegiance has created too much division with the crew. My attempt on James and Porter have put my brothers at odds, and I got Logan and some of the others killed. I thought blood-for-blood would be enough, but Porter gave Gavin an ultimatum. He dies or you die. Twisted shit, but fair. And so far, Gavin hasn't made good on his promise to hold up his end of the bargain for the truce."

"Yeah, cuz he doesn't know where you are…" I scoffed.

Kyle got up, slowly. He went to the front door and opened it. When he stood in the doorway, just staring at me, I took this as a sign to get up. I joined him and looked outside. Sitting, just off the dirt driveway was Gavin's Nova. My hand went to my mouth.

"Is he here?" I said. Kyle shook his head. I grabbed his jacket and pulled him close. "What did you do to him?"

Kyle tossed the door shut, keeping the snow from

coming in. "I didn't do anythin' to him. He knows I have the car, and he knows I'm here."

"Wha..." deep breath, "What is going on?"

Kyle stirred his rabbit stew slowly, painfully taking his time, even though he had to know that I was completely unhinged. Back at the table, we sat down, together. His nails dug into his hands. My eyes went to the window, hoping to see Gavin or someone, anyone.

"It's hard..." Kyle said. The rest of his beer was finished. "I sent Ronda after you to settle the score with the family, mainly Gavin and James. Tryin' to get some points with Porter, too. It was easy, really. She hated you, and she needed the money. And I would be able to put my brothers in line. Show 'em how far I'd go if they fucked with me." I tried to butt in and tell him about my pain. He just put a hand up. "After the attack, Gavin came to me, ready to kill me. Not just over you, but for everything. And I was gonna let him, because I didn't want to live like this anymore. But, he didn't do it. He kicked my ass, threatened me, but once the gun was at my head, he didn't pull the trigger. He held it there for over a minute, but he never could do it."

"Gavin's not a killer," I said. Now, I knew this for sure. Even when Gavin himself told me, I never believed him. But, with Kyle in my midst, I knew for sure that Gavin couldn't kill anyone. A small, contrite smile pressed against my lips. "So, you have his car?"

"He let me go. Just got into the car and left. It took me some time to find him in Anders, but I did. We had a talk..." his throat cleared. "Gavin knew that he would never kill me, and I could kill anyone without feelin' the slightest bit upset. So, we knew we had to come up with our own agreement. An unspoken one, if you will."

"Okay?"

"He'd keep my brothers from comin' after me, and I'd stay on the outside until I could make other plans."

No, that wasn't possible. "So, you've been talking to him?"

"Yeah, this morning while you were out cold. I told him I'd be back at the cabin and out of the way for a while."

"So, he knows I'm here?"

"Why would I tell him that?"

I gestured to the door. "You have his car, which means he gave it to you! That's probably how we got here!" Kyle laughed. "What's so funny, Kyle? Huh?"

"The Nova's rear-wheel drive. It can't handle the snow. Gavin had me tow it up here, so Porter couldn't find it."

My brows came together. "Why would Porter care about the Nova?"

"Because Gavin's a ghost right now, Catalina. I'm not dead, he's not dead, and for us to stay that way, he's gotta look gone."

I leaned back in the chair. "He made it look like he cut ties on purpose. With his car gone and his absence, it looks like he left Settlement Island."

"You're smart," said Kyle with another smile. "Gavin always said you were smart."

"But what about me? Why take me?"

"Because of Aaron White. He saw me, which would mean I'm alive. So, all he has to do is tell his brother, and Porter will know that Gavin hasn't killed me."

"So, why not go after Aaron?"

Kyle's eyes were somber. "Because he wouldn't be the best leverage for my life."

The stew boiled over, so Kyle got up while I pondered his words. The best leverage for his life, huh? Porter would do anything to protect Aaron; he was his brother. So, Aaron would have been the better bet. I almost brought this up when another thought came to mind. Gavin was supposed to kill Kyle. And with Kyle alive, this meant that Gavin would have to explain to Porter his actions. Why he had come up short.

My limbs went weak. If Aaron knew Kyle took me, and he would if he got my text, he would tell his brother. Porter would then reach out to Gavin. With everything coming together for them both, Gavin would have no choice but to kill Kyle or be killed himself. A tear ran down my face. This was my fault.

Kyle whistled while he got our dinner ready. He seemed relaxed, maybe even unsure that I had figured out his motive. I had played into the plan perfectly. Kyle knew I was the most valuable piece to the game, and I let him use me, willingly.

I was the leverage Kyle needed to force Gavin's hand. Either Gavin turned himself over to Porter or Kyle would kill me.

Chapter Thirty-Four
Barter

IF ONLY I had minded my own damn business, like Cecilia had told me to! By helping in the situation, I became insurance for Kyle's life. Pretty damn good insurance. Kyle asked me what was wrong as he sat my plate down.

"Nothing. Just feeling bad."

"About what?" he sat down with his stew and dived in.

I picked at the vegetables. "Just my family. They're probably really worried about me."

He nodded. "You come from a nice family?"

"Something like that."

"Yeah, my family's a joke." Another bite. "Both of my parents were drunks."

If sympathy was what Kyle was looking for, I had none to give. And I didn't care much to learn more about him. Yet, he was eager to tell everything he could. He went on, telling me about his childhood and being a Settler. Apparently, Kyle has always been a drunk, himself.

He started drinking at thirteen. A few drugs here and there, but drinking has always been his thing.

This was right in line with what Adrienne had told me. And judging by her comments and his behaviors, I knew I had a plan.

"...so, that's why I'll never get out of Settlement Island for good," he said. His meal was done, and I hadn't even started mine.

"You'll never leave because you're trapped?" I guessed. He motioned for me to try the stew. I nibbled on a few vegetables. Kyle watched me eat until I took a bite of the rabbit. I was done at that point. "You're trapped, right?"

His eyebrows went together. "Trapped? No, not at all. I love Settlement Island. I'd never leave here, if I had a choice." He opened another bottle. "What about you?"

"I'm not from here, so I don't know."

"Yeah, but you're from somewhere. The great Los Angeles!" he chuckled. "Is there any pride over there?"

"I've got some loyalty to my hometown," I stated, "but it's the ocean I miss most."

"I've never been to the coast."

"Not even here?" He shook his head. "How is that possible? I mean, it's like just right there," I teased.

Kyle leaned in, "I'm scared of sharks."

I rolled my eyes. "First of all, sharks rarely attack humans. And second, I don't think sharks are swimming around up here, looking for victims. The water's probably too cold."

"Say what you want, Ms. Catalina, but I ain't goin' to no beach to be eaten by no shark." Closed-minded. He nudged me again to keep eating. "Rabbit doesn't keep very well in the fridge."

"Right."

"Have you ever been hunting?" I told him no. "I'll have to take ya out some time. Teach ya how to fend for yourself."

"You want to give me a gun?" I drew back. "Someone as clumsy as me? Not to mention, I am technically your prisoner."

"Sure, why not? After all, I've killed more people than you have." A slow drink from his beer, his eyes on me.

I understood his implication. I had to keep my nerves. "Why are you being so nice to me?" This question seemed to take him aback, which was a happy accident. I reached down and tugged on the chain. "Except for maybe this thing."

"I have no reason to be a dick to you."

"So, it's like a respect thing?" He looked at me sideways. "I'm just trying to figure out…"

"If I'm going to kill you?" He jabbed at the beer label. "I already told you: if you don't cause problems for me, I won't cause problems for you." Kyle lit up. "There was this time huntin' where we were stalkin' this moose: big son-of-a-bitch! It was me, Gavin, Mark, my friend Nick, and Earl, I think. Well, we were comin' up on this thing…"

"I'm sorry," I interrupted, "Gavin goes hunting?"

"It's a Maine thing." He shook me. "Anyway, I was sayin'. We came up on this thing…" I huffed a sigh and tuned him out.

I didn't know Kyle liked to talk so much. Maybe he was lonely. My first impressions of him and from what everyone had told me, Kyle was the quiet, brooding type. A guy with a chip on his shoulder, a terrible personality, and an all-around monster. Somewhere in all that was a guy who seemed to really want to entertain me.

As time went on, he started asking me questions about my life. Surface stuff that I really didn't care to talk about. But I humored Kyle and gave him a few key points about my life. Beer after beer, he was becoming more unsteady in his chair. He blamed it on being tired, which I could agree with.

After kidnapping me, Kyle braved the snow and brought us back to this location, which took about four hours. Then, he stayed awake, making sure I was "safely" brought into the cabin, and we had enough wood and supplies for the upcoming time. How much time, he still didn't say. Apparently, he didn't sleep, since I had the bed.

"You could have taken a nap at any time," I offered.

"Nah," Kyle said. "I was havin' too much fun huntin' and stuff to slow down." He pulled out a vile from his coat pocket, "Plus, I have this."

"Gross."

"You've never tried it?"

"Nope. I don't do drugs."

"Wow," he chuckled. "The shit we've done, I mean, I'm surprised Mark and James are still alive."

"What about Gavin?"

He shook his head. "Nah. Never been into the hard stuff." He looked up. "Never even tried it, I don't think. He smokes weed, but not very often. I've only seen him high maybe a couple of times in my life. Doesn't really drink, either. Probably has something to do with his mom." My glance went down, "You don't drink, huh?"

"I'm a wine drinker, I'll have you know. Maybe too much wine at times."

Kyle laughed. "I bet you have this big, expensive wine cellar at home, huh?"

"Mother has a really nice collection. She's been collecting wine since I was a kid."

He nodded. "I always wanted to get into wine, ya know. Be all sophisticated." Kyle opened the vile and tapped some powder onto his hand. I stopped him. "I'm gettin' tired."

"There's nothing wrong with that."

Kyle laughed. "I don't want the night to end." A strong sniff, and he tilted his head back. "It's harsh," he coughed and cleared his throat. "But, it gets the job done."

I huffed a sigh. More time with Kyle, awake, telling stories, keeping us together. He grabbed another beer and got me one, too. The rabbit stew was mostly gone from my bowl, so he took it back to the sink. He looked outside. "It's white like snow!" he said with a giggle.

"Tell me about it," I muttered, pulling my legs up to my chest.

It was getting cold. Kyle threw more logs on the fire.

He came back to the table, chewing his lip while his head bobbed around.

"Does Gavin yell at you about chewing your lip?"

"Yeah, always has. Has somethin' to do with his mom."

"How long have you actually known Gavin?"

Kyle chuckled a little. He downed his beer. "Focus!" I realized he was talking to himself. "I've known Gavin since…" more laughing. I told him to get on with it. "Since we were kids. We always clicked." He snapped his finger in my face. "In a snap!"

"You're useless," I said.

Kyle rolled back in his chair, "I'm sorry." Another beer was retrieved, "I'll come down a bit, soon. Promise." I glared at him. He smiled, "You should try some. Then, we'll be at the same level."

I motioned in his direction. "Yeah, cuz that looks like a lot of fun."

Kyle chuckled, "I know why he likes you so much." Some sniffing and drinking. I just stared at him, gauging the likelihood of him passing out soon. He entertained himself with a muttered conversation with his beer bottle. "Ya know," Kyle looked at me, blood-red eyes. Getting tired, I hoped. "You know, I think Gavin would have finally gotten up the balls to kill me because of you."

"But he didn't, so here we are."

Kyle started singing to himself, some song about lumberjacks and outback pride. And I continued to watch. The high came down enough for him to retrieve enough words for a conversation. The vile came out again. I was quick in taking it.

"Alright!"

I threw it on the bed. "Kyle, you really need to get some sleep. It's probably late."

He pulled out his phone, "One. Yeah, sorta late."

"I'm not tired, so you can have the bed."

Kyle put his hand in the air. Up he went, not to the bed, but the door. A stark chill frosted the room as he went outside. "Shit, it's cold out here!"

I realized why he had left when he came back in, zipping up his fly. Door shut, he dropped down across from me. "Hey, there's somethin' I thought we could do."

"Yeah, what's that?"

Kyle leaned in, "Well, it's cold outside…and the fire can only keep us warm for so long…"

"And?"

"And you're cute in your own way." Sex is what Kyle wanted. I shook my head. "Look, it's just a one-time thing. I haven't had sex in a while, and I'm sure you haven't had sex in a while, so let's do it."

"No, Kyle."

"I don't have any condoms, but I can always…"

"No, Kyle!" my voice strained. "I'm not losing my virginity to you!"

He leaned back, "A virgin, huh? Well, alright then." Kyle went out of his way not to touch me as he sat down. One more beer.

My current sexual status seemed to shut him up for over ten minutes. He avoided eye contact with me. Even the vile didn't peak his interests. We sat in silence, drinking our beers, having nothing to say. I thought about every story he had told me, every comment he had made. The many times I tried to get him to be quiet and leave me alone. And all it took was the most embarrassing feature regarding my life to get him to finally comply.

I laughed, I had to. A deep, bellowing laugh that I couldn't control. It felt good to get it out, to break the silence with a contribution from my end for once. Kyle laughed a bit, too. His laugh wasn't as robust, but it was there.

"I'd never take that from you," he quieted down, "unless you wanted me to."

I shook my head, "I don't."

He pointed his index finger at me, his thumb was up, making his hand into a gun. "Good call."

Exhaustion was taking Kyle. No more talking, just a slight slouch forward onto the table as he held his beer. Everything was catching up to him. He kept his eyes on me, closing them for longer periods of time. I didn't want to ruin this.

"You know, Kyle," I said, in an effort to notice that the conversation had officially died, "I've thought about it, and this is the most rustic Maine experience I've had since I've been here."

"I'm..." he slouched forward a bit, holding himself up on his forearms. "I'm...glad."

I got up. "Time for bed." He swatted my hands away, just like Luke had when James drugged him. "Come on," I said in a soft, sweet tone. He didn't resist. When he got up on his feet, he toppled over on to the bed, me pinned underneath.

His face went to mine. "Are you sure you don't want it?"

"Positive."

"I can make it all romantic, you know."

"Goodnight, Kyle."

I pushed against his chest and down his stomach, feeling his phone in his jean pocket. He rolled over onto his back, blue eyes looking at me. Boots still on, jacket and everything, he didn't make any effort to get up and take anything off. I searched the bed and found the vile, putting it on the table, so he could see it. "I'm gonna need that in the morning," he muttered. I told him I wouldn't take any. "Watcha gonna do?" I pointed to the small stack of books sitting on the kitchen counter. "Good."

Kyle still watched me pick up around the cabin, putting dishes in the sink and throwing another log on the fire. He needed more coaching to fall asleep. I sat down next to him on the bed and patted my lap. He inched his way toward me, his head falling onto my legs. I touched his hair, wondering how I could speed up the process. A song; a song would do.

There was a fairytale Mother used to tell me when I was too sick to read books. She put together a story about a girl and a dragon. In the tale, this dragon had captured the girl, not to harm her, but to have someone to talk to. Eventually, they became quite the pair. They would go on adventures together, travelling across the high seas, down to the valleys beneath the mountains.

They searched for treasure, for gold. And over time, they found something more enduring; a friendship, a bond that was never broken.

Mother somehow managed to turn it into a sweet melody. I sang for Kyle, letting my voice be a soft whisper. His skin was hot and slightly red. I felt his heaviness as he relaxed more. A couple of rounds of the song, and he started snoring.

I didn't move right away, for fear of waking him. But I needed to get to his phone. I rubbed his back, which startled him some. As I rubbed, my hand went to his pocket. I could feel the phone. A few deep breaths and I relaxed. My fingers slipped inside as my other hand continued rubbing. With very little effort, the phone was out.

There were several text messages from various people. I clicked the home button, but it asked for a passcode. Back to the lock screen, I scrolled down until I got to Gavin. I clicked on the message and typed in a reply for him to call me, "Kyle." It didn't take long for his name to come up on the Caller ID.

"Whatever it is, it better be fuckin' good." His voice, though fierce, brought me joy, and tears, and sadness. He was alive…and moody, as always. I wiped my face, still unable to say something. "Kyle!"

"Hey," was all I could get out. My chest was on fire and my throat dry.

"Catalina?"

"Yeah," now the tears were uncontrollable. I shook my head, breathing some to get my mind straight. In it all, I stayed quiet, still worried that Kyle would wake.

"Are you with Kyle?"

"Yeah."

There were pauses. "Where are you?"

"At his cabin in the woods. Where your Nova is."

"Are you okay?"

"For now."

He sighed over and over. It sounded like he was walking on snow. "Listen to me, Catalina. Kyle's not going to hurt you, okay?"

"Okay."

"I'm coming to get you. There's a huge Nor'easter coming, and I gotta get you out of there before it hits."

"Where are you?"

"I'm in Anders at Brianna's." Brianna, my dear friend. She belonged to a life I no longer seemed to have. "Listen to me, Catalina. It's going to take some time for me to get to the cabin. I need you to stay calm and don't do anything stupid, okay?" An insult, nonetheless. "Catalina?"

"I hear you," I snapped.

There was more crunching on his end. "There's so much I need to tell you…" He sighed. "I…"

"Tell me now," I said. "Give me something to pass the time while I wait…for you."

I could hear Gavin get into a truck. It was mean, just like the Nova. "I can't…not yet."

I was disappointed, but I kept my voice even. "Then, I'll just wait for you, I guess."

"Trust me, Catalina, it'll be better in person."

Kyle moved. "Gotta go." I hung up and tossed the

phone on the bed. Kyle shifted his weight, eyes shut, still snoring.

I rubbed my face, again, ridding myself of whatever tears were left. He was coming; Gavin was coming for me. And when he got here, I'd do whatever it took to keep him alive.

Chapter Thirty-Five

Settler

Waiting for Gavin to arrive was easier than I thought. I fell asleep shortly after our conversation, no longer apprehensive about my situation. Gavin was coming for me, and I knew I could trust his word. He always kept his promises. When I woke the next day, Kyle sitting up on the bed was the first thing I saw.

"Mornin' there," he said, shuffling into a sitting pose.

I returned the pleasantry, and stretched, too. Kyle rolled off the bed, collecting various items, one of which was his phone. This move was a slow reach across the bed and me, eyes on me, looking to see my expression. I stayed as blank as possible. Lucky for me, Kyle had other things consuming the same side of the bed. These included a knife, a lighter, and a bandana. How they got there, I didn't ask.

"Nor'easter's comin' today, so we gotta get ready."

"How do we get ready?" I said.

The plan was simple. Kyle only had a few supplies to

get us through the next day or two. It wasn't enough. He would go out hunting for something bigger, and I needed to make sure all the windows and crevices were sealed. But first, Kyle wanted to "wash" the night away. A bath!

He was smart, smarter than me on this topic. Inside the bathroom, he shed his clothes, and ran the water. While he was gone, I had a very spirited conversation with myself about not taking the keys last night, when I had a chance. My concentration had been elsewhere; on help, on Gavin. Waiting may have been the better move.

I tugged on the cuff: what should I do about this problem? I had to get him to release me on his own accord. This act of faith would set the stage to build trust with him. And it would make it easier on me to gather whatever supplies I needed, in case I had to leave the cabin before Gavin's arrival.

Not a survivalist, I didn't know what I should be spying. A jacket: that would be the first thing since I didn't have one. Maybe a lighter to make a fire, if I could ever figure that out. Finally, some food which seemed in very short supply. Kyle only had what he needed on hand: enough for about a week. With a hearty breakfast under my belt, I might be able to brave the cold without needing anything else long enough to get to Settlement Island or Gavin.

These were good things to consider, but there were still the angry clouds growing outside. The wind had become more vocal since the night. This was our first Nor'easter of the year, my first one ever. And unlike everyone else, I had spent most of the winter stuck in my room. I hadn't acclimated to the blistery cold. But sheer willpower, and the need to get away, would be enough for me. I had to make it enough.

Sneaking around was even more difficult now, seeing that the cabin was so small, and the mood had changed so much with the coming day.

Kyle seemed suspicious regarding our events last night. I could tell by the slow uneasiness he had around me. Almost like he expected me to attack him. The vile still sat on the table; no morning boost. Kyle wanted to be alert, he explained, and uninhibited in case I tried something stupid.

The cabin was still clean of weapons and keys. Everything I needed for freedom sat in that room, with him. My spirits couldn't be broken by this. I had to stay sharp and in the moment with him. Get him to make the keys and phone vulnerable for me to take.

There was one thing he wanted, something that I could give him that would get his clothing within my reach and away from him. I rebuked myself for even considering the act at all. I was desperate, but not that desperate.

When Kyle did return from the bath, he had fresh clothes on. Where his other clothes had gone, I didn't know.

"Your turn," he said as he brushed his wet hair. Things had turned, and I had become the vulnerable one. He sensed this and said, "Don't worry. I remember our chat about your virgin hood. I'm not gonna try anythin'."

"How do I know for sure?"

"Well, I'm not high, and you're not Cecilia, so..."

Got it. I grabbed the vile for insurance. "Just in case you feel the urge for a pick-me-up."

"Nah, none for me today. We got a lot of shit to do, or we'll be sorry come nightfall if we don't get to it." He went to the closet and pulled out a pair of jeans, a thick red flannel shirt, and a heavy brown canvass jacket. "Take a hot bath and put these on. They'll keep you warm."

No clean underwear. "What about the chain?"

"Chain stays on," he replied with a bit of attitude. "Can't have you runnin' around, ya know?" I nodded which probably didn't seem convincing. "Catalina, the temperature's droppin' fast. Don't get any bright ideas 'bout tryin' to escape. One or two hours in the cold without me, and you'll be dead."

A fair warning since I had never been in a snowstorm of any kind. I gave Kyle this one and closed the door as much as I could. The chain blocked the door jam, so I didn't have enough privacy. This didn't matter. I heard the front door shut immediately.

"Kyle?" Nothing. As the water ran, I watched the steam rise in thick clouds. It was cold outside, and I needed to do a good job sealing up the windows. I could see the frost on the inside. Better get a move on. Next to the tub was a new towel, shampoo, bar of soap, some lotion, and a package of underwear. "What is with this guy?" I said. Had he thought of everything?

I opened the cabinet and found a few more replicas

of everything he had laid out for me. He did plan on us being here for a while. Secretly, I was thankful for Kyle's attention to detail in the matter. The privacy he had given me, the respect for my wishes. It was almost as if he wanted me to be happy here, with him.

The tub was full, and I got in. Soaking for a few minutes, I closed my eyes. I just needed a moment to think. But what to think about? Gavin was supposed to be on the way, and my captor had become more tolerable. I was fine, for the time being. The wind kicked up against the side of the cabin. The trees scrapped violently against the roof. Time was dwindling.

I scrubbed the events from the previous days off, leaving my hair untouched. As the water drained from the tub, I quickly dried off, and slathered some lotion on. New underwear, such a welcomed change. Kyle's clothes fit me well, which would be expected since he was slender, just like me. On the sink, below the mirror was a face cloth, a brush, and a pink toothbrush. Mine, I presumed.

Clean face, teeth, and untangled hair, I left the bathroom feeling better. Kyle hadn't returned, so I made the bed and went back to the windows to check the frost which was growing rapidly. To solve this problem, Kyle had left a few rolls of masking tape. Several tape jobs later, Kyle had returned with a big grin.

"Got one!"

"Got one what?"

"Moose! A big fucker, 'bout a half mile from here."

He went on to tell me the story about how he'd been tracking the poor fellow since yesterday. And how his new "big game" rifle was the winning ticket to the whole ordeal. Not knowing what that meant, I nodded, and congratulated him on his score.

"After breakfast, I'm gonna need your help gettin' him cut up and stored." Nope, not happening. I expressed this to Kyle, making sure he knew that I probably wouldn't get on board regarding the matter. "If you want to survive the winter, you'll have to change your mind."

"It sounds like a lot of work."

"It is a lot of work. But two skinny kids like us can eat off this thing for months."

"So, is that your plan? Are you going to keep me here with you for the long-haul? Do you plan on us getting married and having a little wilderness family?" Kyle looked at me blankly. "Kyle, you know I want to go home, right?"

"I'm pretty sure you do."

"Look, I've been nothing but patient with you and this whole thing. But, I don't want to do this anymore. I want my life back."

"That's not part of the deal," he said sternly. "You put yourself in this position because of your ties to Aaron White. Porter knows I'm alive, which means Gavin's gonna have to come cash in my ticket, and I'm not ready to die right now. So, if you want to keep Gavin alive, you're gonna have to stick around with me until I come up with a better plan."

"Just leave."

"I already told ya," Kyle hissed, "Settlement Island is my home. I ain't goin' nowhere."

"Why not?" my voice was softer. I wanted to reason with him, in a way that he could understand. "Kyle, if you left for some time, I'm sure things would blow over." He shook his head. "Come on, Kyle," I put my hand on his arm. "Don't you want to see the world? Or at least more of Maine?"

"Catalina," he said softly, "all my family's here. Everyone I've ever known lives here. My granddaddy built this place with his daddy when he was a boy. He lived in here with his ma and his siblings. Half of my family tree is buried out back in the forest. I can't go nowhere."

Kyle retrieved his arm from me and muttered something about breakfast. I sat down at the table, contemplating my thoughts, and the evidence I had gathered in this short time. Here I was thinking Kyle had orchestrated this whole thing to get back at Porter or set up Gavin. Yet, it was quite the opposite. Kyle couldn't leave because he truly didn't have anywhere to go.

He had no friends, family, or ties outside of here. Gavin and the crew were his brothers. The division in their family meant Kyle no longer had anyone. He had told me, sometime last night, that his parents had died of alcoholism and drug overdoses. I was sure they were out back in the forest somewhere, too. And he couldn't leave them, even though they were only a memory in his mind. But in order to stay in Settlement Island, Kyle had to be smart, bold, and desperate.

This move to take me wasn't about power…it was personal. A way to twist Gavin's hand and make him forgive Kyle? That would probably never happen. However, if it came down to it, Kyle only had one choice. I shook my head, realizing what Kyle was actually up to...

"You don't want to kill Gavin because you don't want to lose your brother, do you?"

Kyle had started cutting up more potatoes with a pocket knife. He stopped. "No, I don't. He's all I got left, really."

"So, you took me because you want to give him a reason not to kill you?"

"Again, it had nothin' to do with Gavin," he went back to chopping. "Gavin and I had a truce, remember?" That I did. "Well, Gavin would have never told Porter about me. You did, by workin' with Aaron. If I get you out of the picture, Aaron and Porter would no longer have leverage over the deal Gavin and I made."

"Why is that?"

"If I disappear, and you disappear, then there's no one to say that Gavin didn't kill me after I killed you."

"Of course," I said while leaning back in the chair. Gavin said that Kyle wouldn't hurt me; now I knew why. "You wanted to create the stage, make it look like Gavin had done his job. And in return, you would be able to live here for the rest of your life, with your dead family."

"Gavin's good at keepin' secrets, I'm sure you know." Yeah, I did. "So, he would never say anythin' that would lead people on. Plus, I have a few friends on the outside of the crew who wouldn't say anythin'. That guy you saw me with, Blake, he's my dealer. He hates Porter's crew more than Gavin and I do. He's been keepin' everythin' on the down low, too."

"So, what about Gavin knowing about me? Are you going to tell him?"

"I can't. If I do, he'll want to rescue ya because he wouldn't let me keep ya here knowin' you wanted to leave."

Tread very softly, Catalina. "And if he found out?" Kyle muttered some things to himself. It sounded like he was making a list of things to do and in what order. "I should have just listened to Cecilia," I said to get his attention.

"Why, what did she say?" I told him about my last conversation with my sister. He nodded, "Yeah, ya should've stayed out of it."

There was still one question. "If you had everything figured out, why did Gavin leave Settlement Island?"

"He never did." Kyle threw the potatoes into the pan and started on the sausages. "Gavin's dad's side of the family is direct descendants of Joseph Settler, the guy who built all this up. The old Settler cottage is like three miles up the road from here. It's tough terrain, can't get back there without four-wheel drive. That's why I have the Nova. Gavin brought it out here, but he can't take it up the road, so it's close by."

"So, he's been living in his family's cabin?"

"Yeah, since the last time he saw you. No one knows about that place but me. And I wouldn't have known about it if his grandpa didn't get stuck comin' up to the cabin one summer. Me and Gavin were like ten at the time. It was just after his dad left. His grandpa was doing some work on the old Settler cabin." He smiled. "Gavin was a quiet kid then, real shy. I started playin' with him while his grandpa worked. Then his grandpa made us help, which wasn't so bad."

"And you became friends?"

"We was brothers because I didn't have no siblings and neither did he. I was just this poor hick kid, and he was smart, real smart. And good-lookin'. When school started, everyone used to pick on us. Then, Gavin learned how to fight, and we got our crew together, and he got popular. But the whole time, he never told anyone about the cabin. I didn't, neither."

"I wonder why."

Kyle stopped cooking. "When you do what we do, run with the people we run with, you gotta keep the things you love most a secret. But he did tell me about you."

"That's how you know so much about me...how he feels about me."

"He's got a weakness to talk when he's calm and unbothered, which doesn't happen very often. I mean, he's not an anxious guy, but he's always on-guard."

"Tell me about it," I scoffed. "I've never seen him really laid back or peaceful, except for maybe once or twice." I told Kyle about Gavin's insomnia and his constant worrying about their battles with Porter.

"Yeah, he's not like the rest of us. We drink and smoke to get through all that. And he's not one for partyin', except when things are really bad. Like lately." Kyle laughed, "I managed to get him high last week and it was relaxin' for me, too. Just sittin' there with him, not havin' to talk about makin' amends or what I'd done wrong. After smokin', he just laid back and contemplated life. Talkin' about the stuff that was on his mind. And it was you for a long time there."

Kyle sighed. "It was hard, knowin' that what I did to you hurt him so much. I felt bad for hurtin' you, and him, but I couldn't say nothin'." The silence allowed me to inventory the sadness in Kyle's words. "But I'll make amends in my own way, to you both." His mood shifted. "You should see his place." Kyle giggled, "It's so much nicer than this…" He went on to describe the inside.

While Kyle went off on a tangent, I tried to keep my emotions even. Not scold myself for what I had done by calling Gavin. Yet, I had to ask, "Kyle, do you think Gavin will figure out that you took me?"

"No, he won't," Kyle made that point very clear. "We hang out, some, but we keep our distance in case someone gets smart about our plans. You see, that would complicate things. And if he knew I had a hand in your disappearance, he would take that the wrong way."

Like he had. "What do you think he'd do?"

Kyle paused on everything, talking and cooking. I impatiently waited for his answer. "Guess it would be the end of us."

"The death of you both?"

Kyle didn't seem to think too much about my questioning. He checked the windows for the storm. Plotting and planning, I had seen this before with Aaron. We thought we were so smart, Aaron and me. But Kyle had bested us. "What did Gavin tell you about me?"

"He didn't talk about you much," which was the truth. "Everything always came back to the murders, James, and your thing with Porter. I didn't know you two were so close. I don't think anyone out there does."

"Good. That means I still have a chance to make my amends with him, if he were to find out about you. We still have our bond."

"Will it be enough, though?" I had a thought. "If Gavin finds out about me, and he takes it the wrong way, you wouldn't have anywhere to go. Nothing to do."

"Look, I trust Gavin, Catalina." Kyle wasn't angry, but rather passionate. "We're brothers, and we'll always be brothers. And if he comes here to make amends, we'll do it together. If he comes here to kill me, we'll just have to kill each other. It's the only way."

No more questions. Kyle put breakfast on the plates and changed the subject back to prepping the deer. "Moose, Catalina, not a deer," he reminded me.

I smiled at my oversight, even though I still wasn't paying attention. Defeat had bested me, yet again. The more I learned, the more helpless my situation became. The storm was stirring, bringing more angry wind and frosty air. I could relate.

But I couldn't tell Kyle the truth. I could warn him again, but that would put me in a dangerous position. If you don't cause any trouble for me, I won't cause any trouble for you.

Well, trouble was coming, and with it came at least three murders in tow, mine being one of them. I had to find a way to get to Gavin before he got to me.

Chapter Thirty-Six

The Killing

Our next task after breakfast was prepping the moose. I had to help, Kyle made that very clear. Now, there was the matter of the cuffs. Kyle hesitated to take them off and tried to find a way to attach us together. That move would have been lunacy, which he figured out rather quickly. With a sigh, he said, "I guess I'll just have to trust you."

Kyle's trust in me was not a bad move. I had no plans to go anywhere. How could I? My attempt to get help from Gavin led him right into a trap that I had set for them both. Even if it were unintentional, I felt guilty. Two brothers, killing each other, because I had misread the situation. Dammit, Catalina!

Kyle told me to be excited because this was a huge deal! Bagging a moose, as he called it, was time for celebration! There was so much he wanted to do with the meat. Recipes from past hunters in his family had been comprised into a journal. "It's a great day!" he raved.

The key, which Kyle had kept in his boot, unlatched my leg. "Yes, it is a great day," I said, moving my ankle around. I was free. I rejoiced by calling myself a slew of names I didn't want to say outside my mind. Kyle picked up on my absenteeism from our conversation and threw another jacket around my shoulders. Then he handed me some gloves and a hat.

Another question came from him about what was bugging me. "I don't want to do this," was my answer. "It's cold, and the moose is going to be heavy…"

"That's all city stuff, Catalina!" he howled. "We've gotta get on it before the storm's here. Once that happens, we won't be able to leave the house until everythin' let's up. It could be a day or longer." Now, Kyle was crouched down in front of me like a father giving his kid a peep talk. "This is not your thing, but it's a good skill for you to have. And I'd be honored to teach it to ya."

His excitement and soft-hearted approach won me over. I nodded, no longer protesting the task. To my surprise, Kyle grabbed the rifle. "Never go out into the woods without a gun, got it?" When I asked where my gun was, he laughed. "I don't trust you that much." Smart man.

⤚

When we got to the kill site, there was blood across most of the snow. I held my stomach as Kyle laughed at my sickness over the sight. The moose, giant and very much dead, sat on top of some branches, flakes starting to cover him or her.

"It's a he," Kyle informed me. "Okay, Catalina, here's what we're gonna do." He looked up at the sky. "We're gonna do the gutless method with this guy." I didn't have to ask what that meant. "We're cutting off the best parts, leaving the guts and carcass behind. That way we'll save time, and we don't have to worry too much with losing the good meat."

"Okay," I said while holding my hand to my mouth and nose.

"It's not that bad, I promise." Kyle laughed, "Trust me, when we're having steak later, you'll be happy we got this guy."

"You got him, not me."

"Now, now, this is a team win. You bein' at the cabin, gettin' the frost out gave me some extra time to be out here with him." Kyle's inclusion made me smile. His gloves clapped together with a slight thud. "Let's get into this…"

The lesson started with some key highlights: start with taking off the legs. This was Kyle's job with some help from me. A knife, a big one, was his weapon of choice. My job was to pull the leg away from the body while he sawed, and sawed, and sawed. It was a hard tug, pulling the heavy appendage with my gloves. I didn't watch long enough to see where he cut exactly. Each leg took some time. Once they were done, Kyle and I drug them under a tree and packed them with snow. An orange ribbon was tied to a low-hanging branch.

Orange, a color I had forgotten, but seemed fitting for the occasion. The dress I wore in the café, the day long ago that ultimately led me and my curiosity here.

"If the snow lets up," he explained, "we'll come back for these." Judging by the consistent snowfall, I figured that would be almost impossible. "There's tons of meat on here! Don't want it to go to waste." This wasn't much of a concern since it was below freezing, meaning the meat would be good for a while.

After getting my help with the other legs, Kyle went in for the "really good stuff." This consisted of the backstraps: perfect tender meat along the spine that was fifty to sixty pounds of premium meat. Kyle took these off with the big knife, cutting carefully. Once done, he wrapped the large loins in a bag, with my help.

I did well, he said. To congratulate me on my success, he put one of the smaller loins around my neck. Blood ran down to my clothes. Then, on my face, he wiped a line of blood under each eye. As he laughed, I freed myself, throwing the loin onto the pile with the others.

"Kyle!" Blood still dripped over my jackets and threatened to go down my back and underneath to my shirt and jeans. "Kyle!" He didn't stop laughing.

"It's tradition for your first kill. My granddaddy did it to my dad and my dad did it to me. It shows you're a man now…or a woman."

Kyle kept laughing, leaving the rest of the meat to sit untouched as he enjoyed the mortified look that was morphing into a smile of my own. Eventually, I joined him, realizing that I had to look a mess. This poor city girl helping a gleeful Kyle get his score back to the cabin, so we could dine like kings. Kyle got back to work, sawing more parts of the moose and adding to our pile.

Then, we had to make our way back. This activity took a lot longer than I expected on account of the snow and the weight of the load.

In the end, we took six trips total, pulling a sled behind us. We got everything, legs and all. Kyle was impressed by the sheer amount of now frozen meat sitting in his driveway. Everything worked out perfectly.

By the time we were done, the sky was looking especially threatening. Kyle gave me directions to help him lift the legs into coolers outside the garage. Next task was pushing the Nova into the garage and out of the fast falling snow. It was a two-man job, and since I was the first "man" to come by in a while, I had to do. With this task done, it was time to feast.

One of the loins made it back into the cabin. I opted for another bath while Kyle cut steaks and pieces for stews and jerky. "Months, Catalina! We can eat off this thing for months!" he said.

I nodded to myself, pulling the wet, bloody clothes off. We had done good.

The bath drew steam up to the mirror. My fingers, still stained with blood, grazed the top of the water to check the temperature. Warm, sweet bath. I had certainly earned my keep today.

My legs went in first, then my back, then my head. Under the water, I let the blood release from my hair. I could hear the wind kicking up when my head came to the surface. Kyle shouted something about the storm being the worst one in a while. I could only agree, having no point of reference.

After my bath, I put on more of Kyle's clothes and went back to the main room. "It never snows in L.A."

"Yeah, probably not. No huntin', either?"

"Maybe. If there was, I wouldn't know."

I joined him at the table, hair wrapped in a towel. He threw another two logs onto the fire for my sake. I smiled at this.

"You did good," he said. "We've got so much off this thing!"

I actually felt accomplished. As I went to the fridge, I had a thought. Maybe one that I shouldn't have. "Killing things is easy for you, huh?"

"I don't know what you mean." Kyle worked with his knife on his meat.

"The moose. Do you regret killing it?"

"I suppose not." He took the beer I handed him and opened it on the edge of the table. I tried, and it didn't work. Kyle took my beer and flicked it against the table, opening it quickly. "Does this have to do with the murders?" he said when he handed it to me.

That wasn't the first thing on my mind, but it was where I wanted the conversation to go. "I guess so."

"I didn't want to kill no one," he said, not looking at me or drinking his beer. He was intent on fixing his meat, cutting it into perfect uniform sizes. "Hard to understand, I know, but it's where I'm at." He stayed focused, all my other questions regarding the murders being met with mumbles and grunts.

"What are you making?" I said.

"Jerky." He fiddled with the meat. "I only killed those people because they were going to kill me."

"So, if you could have gotten away without killing them, you would have left them alive?"

He was silent. "Yeah."

It wasn't convincing. But I didn't press the issue. Another thought came to mind. "How long would it take you to get to the cabin from Anders?"

Kyle peeked out the window. The sun was almost gone, and the wind was howling against the cabin at full blast. Instead of scrapping against the trees, the wind was now pushing them down, forcefully against the roof and side walls. "With the Nor'easter? Hours."

This explained Gavin's absence, yet I had forgotten he was coming until now. Kyle finished his meat cuts and went to the bathroom. Out came the vile.

"Kyle…"

The door opened, and he threw it outside, bringing in a flash of snow and wind with his decision.

"Now, back to more pressing things." More pressing things meant steaks for dinner. I asked him why he had thrown out his drugs. "Well, I need to slow down. Don't want to be tempted to overdo it in the storm." Then, he smiled and looked at me. "And, maybe I don't want to be that guy right now."

"That guy?"

"I do what I want, when I want, and I don't want to be high tonight. Or maybe for a while."

"Okay," I said with a head nod. I also noticed that

his beer had been left unattended. "So, what can I do to help?"

Kyle wanted a hearty dinner of biscuits, steaks, gravy, and veggies. I had never made biscuits before, and he was a good teacher. There was so much more to Kyle than most people would know. He wasn't an amazing cook, like Gavin, but he was really good at it.

And over dinner, we actually had a good conversation. Kyle wasn't much into reading, but preferred art. Out came some paintings he did. They were good. "Spending time in the cabin, stuck here during the harsh winter days alone, gives you a talent for almost anything," according to Kyle.

We put another log on the fire and sat on the bed, next to each other, just talking.

"So, this is the Maine life?" I said.

"Uncomplicated. Unfamiliar to people like you, of course."

"People like me?"

"Yeah. You big-city folks who think what we do here is old-fashioned or stupid."

I shook my head. "I never said any of those things."

"No, you didn't," he chuckled, "but I'm sure you're thinkin' it."

No, I wasn't. "Actually," I said. "This is the most peace I've had since I moved here." I looked over at Kyle. "When I came to Settlement Island, I learned real quick about the murders; your war with Porter. Then I met Gavin, and I thought he had killed Chris."

"Gavin didn't kill Chris, Porter did," Kyle interrupted me.

"I know that now. However," I paused, moving onto my back. "From the moment Gavin saw me in that café, I've been fighting for my life. Losing sleep at night. Living in fear, every second of the day. Being afraid of Gavin, Porter, and, well, you." I stared at the ceiling, listening to the wind hurl everything around. "And now, for the first time in months, I'm not afraid of anything or anyone." My eyebrows came together. "I feel safe and in control." My eyes flickered. "And it's sad, really. Why couldn't I create this peace on my own? Why did I have to get kidnapped to finally have what I always wanted?"

"Maybe it's the uncomplicated part, ya know?" Kyle nodded. "I've fucked shit up, I know that. But being out here, in the simple life, has taught me that you don't have to try hard to find peace. You can find peace inside, if you try to."

"But all those people died," I said with a few tears not yet coming down my face. "That's pretty complicated, Kyle."

"I know you don't know this yet, Catalina," He looked at me. "But I hope you can understand why I have peace." Kyle put his hands on his chest. "I killed people, and the good Lord is gonna have his way with me when I'm said and done with this life. But for the time bein', all I can do is try to make things right. I gotta stay out of the way, keep my brothers safe, and ask for atonement for what I've done." I shook my head. He took my hands in his. "Soldiers go to war every day, fightin' for freedom.

They shoot people to protect their families and people they don't even know. And they get called heroes…"

"You think you're a hero?" I said beneath all the tears.

He shook his head, "No, sweetheart, I don't. I was a coward, and I took those men's lives because it was easier than puttin' myself on the line." He looked down. "But," his eyes came back up, "I did what I did, not because I was tryin' to prove a point or I was tryin' to get rid of 'em. I did it because I didn't know what else to do."

"What?" I yanked my hands back. "That's a horrible way to look at it."

"That's probably so. But I swear on my mama's grave, I'll let the good Lord choose my punishment."

"You can turn yourself in," I said. "Do something to give the town and everyone some peace. The whole town's scared because I, a Clubber, was attacked by Ronda, a Settler. There's a division that you've created that has everyone fearing for their lives. But, Kyle, if you turn yourself in, you can be the bigger person. You can actually make all this go away."

He nodded, "It might come to that. But I'll be safe, and Gavin and my brothers will be dead for my sins. That's not on 'em. Everything I've done is on me." Kyle smiled, but this time it was different. A sad, melancholy smile. "Catalina, I have peace because I've had the most fun with you in the last couple of days than I've had in years. Huntin', teachin' you how to be a Settler; these things bring me joy, real happiness. So, if I have to cash in my ticket for all that I've done, I can because

I have peace." My hands were in his again. "Thank you for reminding me who I am. And I hope you find who you're supposed to be, too."

"I know who I am, Kyle." I wiped my face. "Always have and always will."

"I don't think you do, not yet." His hand went to my cheek, brushing away the last bit of tears. "You can't know who you are until you have peace with who you are. Until you can look at yourself in the mirror, with all that you've done, and know that all those things were you. The good, the bad, the things you would never tell another soul, they were all you."

He laid back on his back, staring up at the ceiling. Sober, peaceful Kyle Workman. I laced my fingers in his, feeling his warmth, a reminder that I hadn't imagined this conversation. And I laid there, his fingers loosely around mine, searching my mind on who I thought I was, who I could be. I could feel it, what Kyle had been talking about.

In every moment I had, every second that I was inside my body, I never really knew who I was. Yet, it was the kindness of the beast, co-existing with the monster under the bed, that had changed me. The killer lurking in the shadows who brought the light.

True peace…so much more alluring than true love. A love affair that I must have with myself before anyone else. It was funny, really…what had I been doing with all my time alone? Reading books, fretting over things that had come to pass? I had told my parents that when we moved here, I wanted to explore. And Cecilia, she took it as invitation and need for me to know myself better. She was right.

Then, holding up my glass of champagne, I had lied. I had no intention of finding something that had never truly been lost to me. Yet, the lie was never on them, but on me. Maybe it was God who had brought this revelation to Kyle and then to me. The good Lord knowing Catalina Rose Payton better than I ever could.

The remaining tears were brushed from my face. That was what I needed to silence the last bits of fear.

We lay there undisturbed for a long time. Not asleep, yet not quite awake, either. When I did come to, my eyes went to the door that had opened. I didn't recognize him at first. The hair, tucked under a hat, was silvery blond and brown. Black jacket, boots, his hands free, one holding the vintage gun he had held to Chris while making the boy contemplate his decisions.

Kyle didn't move. No advancement from him, even though there were plenty of guns to choose from. It was almost as if he wanted to be shot, to get it over with. And that was it; his last admission to me. Kyle wouldn't fight back, not now. The peace on him, staring at the gunman, was undeniable. His ticket would be cashed.

I don't know how long it took for me to get off the bed, but it was an eternity. I ran, my eyes on Gavin, even though he didn't look at me. The coldness of his jacket told me I had arrived in time. I wrapped my arms around him, my lips going to his ear. "Please don't kill him."

I didn't let go, afraid to look. This wasn't it. This wasn't how I could find peace or be brave. I took some steps back from Gavin, moving out of his reach. The gun still stood in front of him. And I, I went in front, creating a barrier between him and Kyle.

If this was Kyle's time, it would be mine, too.

Chapter Thirty-Seven
Sanctuary

"Get out of the way, Catalina," Gavin said flatly.

"I can't do that, Gavin." My eyes didn't leave his. I could tell he was getting impatient, but I couldn't let that get to me. "Please," I said.

Gavin shook his head. "This crosses the line. Our truce is done."

"But it's not," I moved close to him. "Kyle told me about what happened between you and Porter. I know you had to do everything you did because it was the only way for you to stay alive. But none of this is Kyle's fault." The gun didn't move. "I put Kyle in this position the moment I stupidly helped Aaron…"

"Aaron?" Gavin put his eyebrows together. "You told Aaron?"

"We were working together to bring Kyle down, so that Porter could…"

Gavin put up his hand for me to stop. "So, you really

did do this?" I nodded. "Catalina, do you even have the slightest idea how fucked we are now?"

"I tried to tell her," Kyle muttered.

I turned to him, "You're not helping."

Gavin lowered his gun. Around me he went. "Why didn't you tell me you took her?"

Kyle motioned to the gun, "Thought you'd take it as a misunderstanding, which you did."

Back to me. "How could you be so stupid, Catalina?" Gavin raked his hair.

"It wasn't her fault, brother. Curiosity got the best of her, I guess."

I appreciated Kyle's help in the matter, but Gavin didn't show any signs of calming down. Back and forth, he marched through the tiny cabin. I took a seat next to Kyle on the bed. Now, he didn't look so forlorn. He put his hand on my shoulder.

"It's not your fault," Kyle said to me. "Whatever it is, we'll work it out."

"He seems really mad at me, though," I said.

"Nah," Kyle smiled. "This is Desperate Gavin, not Killer Gavin."

Gavin stopped. "This is fuckin' funny to you two?" He approached me. "What, you don't want to go home anymore? Are you and Kyle a couple now?"

"Nope, he's got a thing for Cecilia," I said. Kyle tilted his head in agreement. "Besides, Gavin, it seems like Kyle covered his tracks. And your tracks. We're gonna make it look like you killed him because he killed me, and Kyle's going to stay off the map for a while."

"Bagged me a moose today."

"I helped."

Gavin's thick eyebrows came together tightly. "Un-fuckin-believable."

Seeing Gavin this way, the beautiful man I had lusted after for so long, completely unraveled before me, was such a sight. Gone were my apprehensions and my fears. Now, I could see him as he truly was: just a person. The mystery and the myth were no longer holding me. All my months of worry were completely forgotten.

Kyle got up and grabbed a beer. When he popped the cap, he handed it to Gavin. He sat down next to me, clearly noticing my confused look. "What?"

"None for you?" I said.

"I told ya, I'm slowin' down for a bit."

I smiled at him. Gavin dropped down into a chair, drinking his beer slowly. "I battled snow, lots of snow. I put my life on the line…" He shook his head. "I thought you were in danger," he said.

I shrugged, "It was all a misunderstanding."

More beer went down his throat. "Kyle's killed people."

"Yeah, we talked about that." I looked at Kyle. "And we're working that part out."

"You see, it's all about havin' peace, brother. After the moose kill, Catalina and I had a real heart-to-heart…"

Gavin threw his head back. "Kyle, shut up. Catalina, this is not some vacation." His head came back down. "This idiot's fucked shit up real bad for my crew."

"So, have I," I said.

"And?" Gavin said.

"And…" I licked my lip instead of biting it, "I can't undo what has already been done. Kyle needs to sort out his debts. But I'm gonna stay out of it from now on. No more hiding in lofts or trying to bring anyone down."

Kyle put his hand on mine. "I'd appreciate that, sincerely."

"I mean it, too."

Gavin slammed his beer bottle down. "It's like you two are one fuckin' person now." I looked at Kyle, smiling. The peace thing was really working. Gavin got up and grabbed another beer. He didn't say anything else. Kyle and I just looked at him, drinking his beer angrily before he got another.

The silence was unusual. Kyle talked a lot, which is something he didn't apparently do around Gavin. In actuality, the entire mood and energy of the cabin changed with his arrival. It was dark and disturbed. A bad omen intruding on an understanding that was working well for us.

I motioned for Kyle to meet me in the bathroom. Gavin didn't seem to notice us leave and close the door.

"He's really mad, isn't he?"

Kyle leaned against the tub. "Nah, this is something else." He stroked his chin.

"And you're not saying much, either."

"Well, Gavin's the boss. Whatever he wants, he gets." Kyle dug his nail into his palm. "Best to stay in line."

"You can't stay in line with this. He's completely lost it."

Kyle shook his head. "We're the ones who look like we've lost it, and for good reason. Gavin bein' here means that one of us ain't gonna live through the experience." He opened the cabinet door and pulled out a pistol. I shook my head. "Catalina, I have to prepare myself in case Gavin decides to turn on me."

The door kicked open, and Gavin stood in the doorway. "Keepin' secrets from me now?"

"What happened to you?" I whispered.

"Well, I came out here to rescue you from your so-called captor. And when I get here, you are defending him. Throwing yourself in front of me to keep him safe." He took another swig from his beer. Slightly unsteady on his feet, Gavin got close to my face. "What happened to you?"

"To me?" I took a step back. "I already told you. I made a mistake and…"

"No, that's not what I mean." He paused. "You… you have no idea what you've done."

Kyle put me behind him. "Gavin, this has nothin' to do with her."

Gavin got close to Kyle's chest. "Porter's gonna kill us, you and me." He sighed. "Yeah, we're dead. Aaron told him about Catalina missing and you taking her." He tilted his head to the side, "Thanks for your help, Catalina." Back to the fridge and another beer.

Kyle turned to me. "Catalina, Gavin's a mean drunk…"

"I can see that," I muttered.

"And he's right about Porter." Kyle sighed. "He must

have cashed Gavin's ticket, which means that he and I are gonna have to fight it out. Porter was clear: Gavin kills me or he dies for not keeping up his end of the bargain. Our only way out now is to decide who gets to live."

"You can't do that, Kyle."

"You…" said Gavin, "don't do anything, Catalina." He slouched in his seat. "Oh, this is goin' to be fuckin' fantastic." His head went to his hands as he leaned forward.

Kyle's expression was very low. "This is really bad," he said to me. "Gavin doesn't drink this much." He approached him, "Brother, what did Porter tell you?"

Gavin's head went up, and he laughed, not a hearty laugh. "Ticket's cashed, brother, like you said. Nor'easter comes, and we'll be dead shortly after." Gavin put his beer down and threw himself back against the wall. "Are ya gonna kill me, Kyle? Cuz you know I can't kill you."

"Nah," Kyle sat down on the bed, the gun grazing his back. "What if I go away?"

"Too late for that. I didn't kill you, so I'm dead either way for lying to Porter."

"But that's not fair," I said.

"Yeah?" Gavin pulled himself up to his feet, coming toward me. I didn't move. "Life isn't fair for people like me and Kyle. But you wouldn't know that, would you, Catalina?"

"Hey, Gavin, lay off her, okay?"

Gavin looked me in the eyes. "No, Kyle, I got this one," I said. There was no more hiding. "I'm disappointed in you, Gavin."

"Are you now?"

"Well, yeah." I blinked a few times. "I'm sorry for everything I've done, but you don't have to make it worse."

Gavin grabbed me, pushing me up against the wall. Kyle touched his back, and Gavin punched him, hard. Now I was afraid. I went to get away, but Gavin grabbed me, putting me against the wall again.

"I love you," he said. "I would never hurt you." He was sober. I could see the concern in his eyes. "I need to get you out of here."

"Why?" I whispered.

"Because Kyle's right," he muttered. "It's either him or me, and I don't want you to die in the crossfire."

The grip around my arms was loose. Kyle didn't see this. I leaned in closer, "And Kyle?"

"I don't want to, but…" he whispered.

Kyle rolled over and groaned.

Gavin grabbed my arm and pushed me onto the bed, softly. "Sit there and think about your decisions."

Back to the act. He was good, real good. I put two and two together. There was no alcohol on his breath. He needed me to keep up my part of the ruse, even though I had no idea where the plan would lead us. Kyle sat up. Another punch, and he was down. "Don't worry, he'll be fine."

"Why did you knock him out?" I said.

"I need time to think. To calm down."

Gavin sat down at the table. I checked on Kyle, but he didn't move. Back to Gavin. He didn't look at me, but rather out into space. This was our first time together since the last time I saw him. Our first time alone. I was completely out of practice with our relationship, feeling like an outsider to what he needed.

I went to the edge of the bed, just letting the quiet surround us.

"You got a moose?" he said after some time.

"Kyle did," I said, my head dancing around. "I just helped." A pause. "Gavin, what are you going to do?"

"You look good," he nodded.

"Thanks. Now answer my question."

"Just give me a minute, okay?" He sighed. "By the way, you seem to handle yourself well with him," Gavin nodded more. "I haven't seen him sober and calm in years."

I didn't know what to say. "He likes it out here. Said it's not complicated. He can slow down." I paused. "How did you know Kyle wasn't going to hurt me?"

"Because he's actually a nice person," he said simply. "And he knew that after the shit he pulled with Ronda, if he tried to hurt you again, I'd have to kill him."

Yeah, there was that. Gavin's shoulders tensed; he hadn't really forgiven Kyle for that. "He told me about how you guys met," I said to lighten his mood. Gavin slightly grinned. "He told me a lot of things about you. I didn't know you were a descendant of Joseph Settler."

"Yeah."

"He also said that you have to keep your life a secret. The things you love most."

"That's true." Gavin sighed, looking up. "He told

you about our arrangement?" I nodded. "Yeah, I, um, took off, came to the cabin, and just stayed there."

I folded my legs. "What did you do?"

"Well," he settled into his chair, "I cooked a lot, did some hunting with Kyle when he wasn't high and out of his mind, and read about three books a week. Mostly some history stuff that James had leant me."

"That sounds wonderful," I said with a genuine smile. "Sounds like you had a lot of peace."

"No, I didn't." Gavin shook his head, "It was hard leaving you in town to deal with everything that I had done. But the only way I could keep you safe was by standing by and doing nothing."

A hard sentiment, I was sure. And I didn't have any regrets for his absence. Instead, I had a life. I told him about it, what I had been up to. The complications with Luke and the friendship I had made with my sister. I told him about Aaron's foiled plans, and how he and I had been civil. And finally, I told him that I had made peace with everything, finding a place inside myself to be comfortable and safe.

"What about me?" he said. "Did you think about me?"

Every day. My eyes went down. "This liking each other thing is hard, isn't it?"

Gavin nodded. "I'm not good at it," he laughed.

"Me, neither," my eyes went up. We looked at each other. "So, now what do we do?"

Gavin looked down at Kyle and then back up to me. "Catalina," long pause, "I'm probably not gonna make it through this. Porter's cashed my ticket, Kyle will try to fight me, and there's no way out." He blinked a few times. "I wish I could find another way, but I can't. The only thing I can do is save you."

Gavin had an idea of how it would go down. Porter had people on the way to Settlement Island to find Kyle and Gavin. It would take some time, but with the right amount of patience, they would find the cabin. Nothing could be done tonight, not with the Nor'easter bearing down on us. In the morning, after the snow had settled and the wind had quieted down, Gavin would take me back to my parents. Then, he'd go face his judgment.

I shook my head. "That's a stupid idea."

"Catalina…"

"Just leave." He tried to cut in, but I kept going, "I'll send you to my Aunt Eloise's house in Berkeley. You can work with Irving, her boyfriend, at his shop."

"Catalina, Settlement Island is my home."

I shrugged. "So, what? You and Kyle have got to get over this homeland pride that you have. If you got out of here, and actually saw the world, you'd see how small all these problems are." I got up. "There are people out there who live lives that have nothing to do with drugs, or gangs, or stealing cars or murder! They're normal people."

Now, he was up, pulling me to him. "You think you have it figured out. But Catalina, if I leave, it's gonna create more problems than it will solve. No one else will push the drugs out of Settlement Island. More people will die, and I can't run from that. But, I'm tired. I'm tired of fighting, too. And eventually, I'm gonna get caught." He sighed. "Remember when we first met, and you asked me what my fate was? What would I choose?"

"You chose death…"

"…because it's inevitable." His hand went down my shoulder, his fingertips brushing down my sleeve. "But at least I got to fall in love." I sighed. "And I got to be loved, too."

A few breaths and I controlled myself. "You really want your life to end in tragedy?"

"Death won't be that bad, I think," Gavin joked. "Tell me something real. Stop talking like a textbook…"

"What am I supposed to say? Beg you to live? For me? If you can't live for yourself, no one else will keep you alive."

"Nah," he shook his head, "now you sound like a self-help book." His eyes leveled with mine. "Be real, Catalina."

"I am being real!"

"No, you're not. It's like you're just saying stuff for the sake of saying it. There's no real heart or…"

"I lied!" I shook my head. "I don't want you to die! I want you to live for me because I love you too much to lose you again!" My hands thrusted against his chest. "Gavin, I can't…" I took in a few breaths, "I can't do this anymore, either. I'm tired, too. But no matter where I go in my dreams, you are there, haunting me." Now his face was serious, calm. "Darkness has become me, Gavin. Your darkness. I'm consumed by you. So, you have to live, so you can bring me some light. I need your light because I can't do this alone. So, please, don't leave me in the dark alone." I gasped and everything I felt came to me. "I don't want to do this alone," I whispered.

There were no tears, but a torrent of emotions taking over me. I dropped down to the floor next to Kyle, afraid to let all my feelings in. For if I did, they would be the death of me. He touched my back, but I moved his hand away. "I'm gonna have to do this alone," I muttered.

Gavin sat down. He pulled me into him. By now, I couldn't breathe. I battled the wave coming over me, while holding onto him. "I'm not as strong as you. I can't be brave on my own. I've tried, and I can't do it. Please don't make me…"

He stroked my hair, holding me in his warmth. "I won't leave you, Catalina," he said.

I don't know how long I cried. Wrapped in his warmth, in his love, I felt safe enough to just let the feelings overtake me. I let them all in: fear, love, joy, hate, anger, and peace. Real peace, not this fairytale that Kyle had dreamed up with me.

Gavin kissed my forehead. "I'll never leave you again, I promise."

It was a somber promise that came with consequences. I knew this now. I felt it. And with that thought, and the warmth growing in my heart, I fell asleep.

Chapter Thirty-Eight
Storm

HE SMELLED GOOD in the morning, like rain after a violent storm. I hadn't moved from my position, my head on his lap. Gavin was still leaning against the bed, his eyes on me. "Insomnia?" I said. He nodded. "Did you sleep at all?"

"Yeah."

I sat up next to him. The only person missing in our trio was Kyle who had gotten up sometime during the night and taken the bed. With Kyle still asleep, Gavin put his finger to his lips.

"Change of plans," he said. "The storm's let up, so we can probably start making our way back into town."

"Then what?"

"I'll talk to Porter; try to get him to spare my life."

"What about Kyle?"

"He stays here."

I nodded. "Your decision or his?"

"After you fell asleep, I had some time to think about

what you said. About finding another way. Well, death is inevitable, and that hasn't changed. However, Kyle and I don't have to fight each other." Gavin sighed. "If one of us talks to Porter, the other one could live. And if Porter kills one of us right off the bat, the other person gets to live automatically. So, we drew straws…"

"Really?"

Gavin smirked. "No, we didn't. However, we both agreed that I would negotiate, since I'm the one who made the truce with Porter. I offered to take care of Kyle for him, so he wouldn't have to lose more guys. Besides, Kyle was more of Porter's problem than mine by that point, so I earned some merit with Porter. He thought I was doing him a favor by tearing up my own family to make things right between him and me. So, if I come to Porter first, he will be less likely to kill me. Deep down, he wants Kyle's blood, not mine." This was a smart decision in his mind, even though it still seemed pretty stupid. Leaving him open without backup, walking into the fire, didn't work for me. But Gavin was adamant that I was wrong. He'd find a way to live…he promised. My next question had to do with us. "What do you mean?" he said.

"Are you going to drop me off at home and do this alone?"

"I planned on it."

I vigorously shook my head no. "I'm going with you!"

"Well, it's settled then." He got up and I joined him. "I can't stop you from coming with me, so I guess you're coming."

No fights or arguments. It was never this easy with Gavin. Truth was, he probably wanted me there, but it would have been selfish for him to ask. And I would go with him, because I was selfish, and maybe there was something I could do to help.

A few shifts on the bed and Kyle was awake. "Morning," I said.

Kyle rubbed his face. "Breakfast?" Gavin nodded. "Coffee?" Another nod. "Alright, I'm up." He retreated to the bathroom.

"Answer something for me," I said. "Last night, why did you knock Kyle out instead of just dragging me out of here?"

Gavin sat down on the bed. "Kyle's a survivalist. He'll always look for a chance to weasel out of things. And I had to make him believe that I was off the rails, so he wouldn't try to get the jump on me."

"He would do that?"

"He's killed five or six people, Catalina."

I scrunched my eyebrows. "You've known Kyle longer than I have, but I think he actually seems to be a different person now."

Kyle emerged from the bathroom. "You can never know what a desperate man will do," Gavin muttered to me.

Kyle pulled on a new shirt and smiled at me. Same breakfast as always: sausage, eggs, and biscuits. I would miss his cooking. "Snow's lookin' good, brother. Should be an easy ride out." Now his attention was on me. "I got everythin' ready if you want to get cleaned up before you go."

I hadn't thought about it, but a bath and some fresh clothes would make me feel better. Kyle laid out another pair of jeans, another plaid shirt, and more neatly wrapped undergarments for me. This prompted Gavin to put his hand to his mouth, like he was contemplating our arrangement.

"Kyle's a good host," I said.

Kyle nodded. "If you get your bath in now, you'll be out in time for breakfast."

I closed the door and drew the water. I could hear chairs moving into position. They didn't do anything to hide their conversation from me.

"Tell him I'm done with all this," said Kyle. "I've had atonement, and you've spared me because I had paid my debts."

"What are you going to pay?" Gavin said.

"I've got ten and a few other things. If he wants blood, I'll be willing to take a shot."

"To the face?" Gavin laughed.

Kyle laughed, too. "Arms, legs, or non-lethals. You?"

"I don't want to get shot."

"What's your leverage?"

There was silence. "Not sure. I was gonna just have Porter bring down my sentence, but Catalina doesn't want me to die."

"Hmm," said Kyle. "You gotta live for you, brother. No one else but you."

"I got the talk last night," he said. "Guess I lost sight of what's important. You know, making a life that has nothing to do with this shit."

"Talk to Porter, finish this, marry Catalina, and live in the cabin." They both chuckled. "It was a pleasure knowing you, Gavin Scott. I'm gonna miss you."

I could hear them pat each other. "Kyle, for what it's worth, I'll always have your back."

"Take care of our girl, okay? She's good people. It's hard to find those these days."

"Tell me about it." I shut off the water and got in the tub. There was a knock on the door. "Hurry up, we gotta go."

Charming, wonderful Gavin Scott, always in a hurry. I soaked in the water, letting it rinse away my fears and defeat. Once we left the cabin, things would be different. Harder, I believed. I'd have to do my best to keep Gavin alive, but I had no leverage to offer. Another knock told me bath time was over.

I toweled off, threw on Kyle's clothes, and rejoined the boys. A plate of hot food was put into my hands. "Thanks, Kyle."

"Can't send ya off without a proper meal."

Gavin went to the closet and grabbed a toothbrush. Such an odd thing to do given the circumstances. While he brushed his teeth, Kyle sipped his coffee and just looked at me. He was making a memory, I could tell. Like we would never see each other again.

I reached out for his hand and held it. There's more I wanted to say, but I couldn't. Kyle, I forgive you for what you did to me. The pain and terror you had caused me. And I don't regret meeting you. Each moment over the last couple days changed my life, truly. To stare the devil, a killer, in the face and see only compassion and care. Out of everyone, you were the nicest to me, Kyle. The strength you showed me that is within myself. I'm finally able to go knowing that I had changed you and you had changed me.

Kyle cleared his throat. "Live your life, Catalina." He smiled. "Live a happy, beautiful life."

"You, too."

A squeeze, and we parted. I finished my breakfast just as Gavin finished fixing his hair. Not that he needed it. We got bundled up in gloves and hats, two more jackets for me. My original clothes were placed in a plastic bag. I thanked Kyle.

When the door opened, everything was covered in white, sparkling snow. Gavin put me to work scrapping the snow and ice from his massive, lifted truck. Black, tinted windows, and big black tires. Typical Gavin. While I worked, he checked fluids, poured in some gas, and started her up. Angry, loud, just like the Nova.

"When will you get your other car back?" I said.

"Spring, after the snow melts."

After our ride was seaworthy, Gavin didn't waste any time hopping in. I stayed for a moment, just looking at Kyle standing in the doorway, sipping coffee. The look he had, I couldn't quite place it. It reminded me of a poem that had not been written yet. Perhaps we'd write it together, if we ever saw each other again.

The chill and ice pushed me into the truck, next to Gavin. He had shed some layers, only wearing a black sweater and a gray beanie.

"Is black your favorite color?"

He shook his head. "Orange."

※

We crunched through the snow quietly for the first leg of our trip. I peered out the window at the vast landscape of green trees standing above white. To my right was the lake, sheets of ice encasing it. I couldn't see Settlement Island, but I was sure it had to be there, somewhere.

"This side of the lake was the original land Joseph Settler owned," Gavin said. "He built his cabin and just lived out here, alone. Eventually, he powered across the lake and set up shop right under Green Post Bluffs."

"And so the legend of Settlement Island was born."

"Come summer, I might move back into the cabin."

"Yeah? Found a reason to live, have you?"

He smiled. "This girl talked me into it." Eyes on the road. "Besides, if I manage to live through all this, I'm gonna need some time to sort some other things out. Find my way again and maybe become a normal person."

"Who will take care of Paula?"

"Brianna's family," he smiled. "Your dad wants her to go to Anders for some really good physical therapy. She'd have to stay there full-time, and my aunt and uncle are more than happy to take her in."

"What about the house? Are you gonna have to sell it?"

"Nah. I'm working something out with my dad." His dad? "Don't worry," he said moving toward me, "I won't leave you, I promise."

He must have misread the look on my face. I passed on the dad talk. "Sounds like things are working out for you."

"You said something yesterday…" I said a lot of things, some of which I never wanted to say again. "You made me think about my life. My future. And the future of Settlement Island."

"What's on your mind?"

Gavin shifted in his seat, his finger grazing his lip. "I shouldn't give up on being normal just yet. And I should stop playing Russian roulette with my life. Because, I actually have more control over my death than I think." Again with the death talk. "If I get out of this life, and stay out of it, then I can just live here. Just have friends, drink beers, and have fun."

"Yeah, what an idea," I scoffed. "Maybe try some common sense for once."

"That may be true for someone like you, but those things were never in the cards for me. But, maybe I can do it. I create a plan for my life and get the hell out of here. Get Porter to reach a permanent deal, so he'll leave me alone forever. James has stopped selling in Anders, so he's willing to give Porter all his business there. If Porter leaves Settlement Island for good, we'll leave him alone. No more drugs, murders, kidnappings. Clean slates for everyone."

"Why does Porter want the streets of Settlement Island so bad, anyway?"

"He's running out of territory. He's got some competition in Anders that's beefing up. New dealers coming into his turf, and he's running out of guys. So, here, he can sell as much as he wants because James doesn't let anyone sell in Settlement Island, not even himself. Thinks it's bad karma, or something like that."

"Do you really think he's gonna go for the deal? Porter, I mean."

"I don't know." He tapped his lip. "If I can figure out a way to get Porter to leave Settlement Island and not kill me or my crew, I don't care what I have to do. I just need the right leverage," he muttered.

This led to more silence. We still had about an hour to go before we'd reach the town limits. Neither one of us was in a hurry to get anywhere. Gavin had set up the meeting place for the turn off by the country club. This was nostalgic. I peered over at the ring on his finger: Logan's ring.

If he were to die there, he'd die in the same place that started this whole thing. And I'd be close to home, I guess. I could run to safety there. Yet, going home to my parents' house seemed foreign to me. A long-ago place that belonged to a long-ago girl. Eventually, I would have to reach out to my family and let them know I was okay. But not now. There was still time for someone to kill me, so I didn't want to get their hopes up.

"When we get there," Gavin said, "stay behind me. He has no reason to hurt you."

"Do you think he'll have backup?"

"Probably. Porter's a paranoid guy. And he would never trust me." I nodded to this. "But seriously, Catalina, he won't hurt you. He'll probably let you go. And when he does, take the chance. Don't wait for me."

"You need your crew."

"No. I've gotta face this one without them."

"And die alone?" He didn't respond. "Gavin, I just don't get you."

"It's a noble way to go."

Now he was the one being dramatic. "If he won't hurt me, I'm staying. That way I can tell everyone what your last wishes were…and how dumb you are."

"My last wishes…" He seemed entertained by this. "Here lies Gavin Christopher Scott, born July 23rd. He had killer hair, a good-looking car, and a good-looking woman who desperately loved him in a cheesy, romance-novel kind of way." He winked.

"Or, here lies Gavin Christopher Scott, lover of Catalina Rose Scott, the one woman who knocked some sense into his pretty little head, so he didn't die today. He didn't listen, so guess she was right, like always."

"Catalina Scott?"

It had slipped out, even though I had never thought about it. "Don't read too much into that."

He nodded.

We hit the town limits sign. Only a few minutes, and we would be there. I chewed my lip but stopped before he could see. Gavin stayed in his position, arm against the window, finger on his lip. He was contemplating something, I could tell.

The lot across from the turn-off looked abandoned. We were the first to arrive. Gavin pulled the truck around, facing the road. "Truth or Dare, Catalina," he said as he killed the engine.

"You really want to play right now?"

"Truth or Dare?"

I rolled my eyes. "Truth."

"If I asked you to be my girlfriend, would you say yes?"

I shook my head. "That's what you're thinking about?" He motioned for me to answer. "Yes, probably... I don't know! Love is hard!" He laughed. "Truth or Dare, Gavin?"

"Truth."

"If you had only one wish, what would it be?" I leaned in. "Make it a good one."

This required a lot of thinking from him. Too much thinking, if you asked me. "Be a real man, create a real life. And I want to share it with you."

"That compliments the dare I reserved."

His fingers laced into mine. "Well, I guess I'm taking you up on your dare, then. If I live through this, we're getting out of Maine and having an adventure, just like you wanted. I'll make it worth it, too. Breakfast in bed, long walks on the beach, if that's your thing."

"Totally my thing."

He smiled. "I do want to grow old, and have some grandkids, take care of them like my grandpa did for me. Honestly, I want to be a man he would be proud of."

"You already are."

The kiss, our first one in so long, was perfect. It was layered with passion and desire for each other. He wasn't forceful or needy; I was the one searching for more from him. When we broke, sometime later, he pulled me into him, wrapping his arms around me.

"There's no one else I'd rather have here with me, right now."

"Ditto," I said.

Tires could be heard on the snow close to the road. A black SUV, followed by another one pulled off, circling behind us. Gavin looked at me one more time, a small smile on his lips for a brief moment. This kiss, the final one, lasted long. I let him lead. To my surprise, he just kissed me softly.

His door opened. So, did mine. We walked around to the back of truck, meeting each other in the middle. We reached for each other's hand, lacing our fingers together.

"I love you," he said.

"I love you, too."

The SUVs stood there, just watching us. Gavin didn't move, so neither did I. The chill came back on, bringing shivers my way. Finally, the passenger door opened to one of the vehicles. And when I saw him, I couldn't believe what he had done.

Chapter Thirty-Nine

Truce

"Aaron, what are you doing here?" I said. He walked up, carrying my phone in his hand. A quick toss, and Gavin caught it. They eyed each other, slow at first. Was this a good or a bad thing, I honestly didn't know. "Aaron?"

"Well, Gavin, you found her." Aaron's attention went away from Gavin and onto me. "Catalina, how are you feeling?" Saying I was fine wasn't enough. Aaron jumped into doctor mode. I fought him, but he took me through the assessment, anyway. Knowing I was fine, he went back to Gavin. "So, here we are, Gavin."

"Aaron. I see you switched sides." Gavin watched Aaron look around and then back. "So, what is it? Your brother sent you out here to settle his affairs?"

"I asked to come. Not for you, but for her." Aaron motioned in my direction. "I came to rescue you, Catalina."

"I made a mistake by texting you, Aaron." I paused. "Well, I found out later that it was a mistake."

Aaron shook his head. "You did the right thing." Back to his adversary. "Where's Kyle?"

"I'm not turning Kyle over to you or your brother."

Aaron folded his arms. "Well, we're gonna have a pretty big problem, then."

"There has to be another way," I said. I looked at Gavin. "You can make a deal, right? I mean, Porter sent his brother here. That's pretty messed up."

Aaron sighed. "Gavin already made arrangements with my brother. If he turned over Kyle, he would live. But I don't see any Kyle, so…"

"So, you're gonna kill him?" I said.

"Catalina…"

"No, Aaron," I stepped in front of Gavin. "You can't do that. You're a doctor. You said you don't hurt people."

"I don't hurt people!" he said. I didn't back down. "I volunteered to come here, so my brother wouldn't see your face. He wouldn't know you existed."

"Your brother would never hurt me."

"Catalina, you are a debt now. No Kyle means that you had a hand in keeping him from Porter. Gavin has to settle his debts, and you'll have one to settle, too."

"Don't you get it?" I searched his eyes. "Aaron, you volunteered to come here, but your brother wanted you to do this all along." I shook my head. "If Porter really wanted Gavin dead, he would have come here himself. But he didn't. He sent you because he knew you would never kill anyone."

"Catalina, this is between me and him, okay?"

I grabbed his arm. "Aaron, we exposed Kyle and

Gavin's failed attempt at settling the truce with Porter. You and me. He wanted them to kill each other, and they didn't. Porter found that out through you. And now, he sent you here, because if you tried to kill Gavin or Kyle, Kyle would probably kill you…" My breaths were shallow. "Your brother was willing to send you to your death because you failed him."

Aaron shook his head. "Catalina, this is old-feud business. Things were good until Gavin and his pack of shitheads let my brother get back into town." He walked around me. "You made me a deal, Gavin, and you've let me down, twice." I didn't have to ask, Aaron elaborated. "Gavin and I go way back, Catalina. When I left, I told him I'd keep my brother off his back if he kept his deal with me. And he didn't."

Gavin folded his arms. "It's true. Aaron did come to me to keep Porter in check, and we did put together some sort of truce…"

"And then you got lazy, and Kyle killed a bunch of Porter's people, and now he has to pay. Either you get Kyle down here or you get in the car."

"No!" I said. "Aaron, you wanted to stop your brother. How are you going to do that by giving him what he wants?"

"Because I put two and two together." Aaron counted on his fingers. "My brother will calm down if the other half of the equation is gone. Makes sense, doesn't it?"

"But you can't do that." Aaron rolled his eyes. "Because eventually, your brother will not stop until everybody is out the way, including you."

"Don't you want to be free? This is your chance. Just let Gavin go and get on with your life."

"I'm not gonna do that, Aaron." I grabbed his hand. "Please, I know you have your orders, but you have to talk to him, okay? Because if you don't, this will never be over. He could slaughter all of Settlement Island, and it will never be enough. And you know it."

"What's wrong with you?" Aaron tilted his head to the side. "You would do this? Put your life on the line for what? A greaser? A nobody?"

"He's a Settler and this is his home. And he'll die for it, if he has to. He's got pride and loyalty, and he doesn't switch sides just because it's convenient. That makes Gavin so much more of a man than you will ever be. He's not the nobody, you are."

Aaron just looked at Gavin for a moment and then went back to me. "Catalina, Porter is a person of balance, an eye for an eye…"

"I meant what I said."

He took a step back and pulled out his phone. "You know what? I'm not doing this anymore." A long text and the phone went back into his pocket. "Catalina, I love you cuz you're my family now. But I'm not gonna turn you over because of him. Gavin's had too many lives, and I'm not letting you take his ticket."

"Catalina," Gavin's hand was on my shoulder. "It's okay."

Aaron nodded. "Then, it's done." His phone came back out. "Hey, I've got Gavin here…"

There was no time left. Aaron was serious. I grabbed

the phone, "My name is Catalina Payton," I said, rushing out of the hands of both Gavin and Aaron. "I know Gavin owes you for all the debts and murders that he's caused," I said as I evaded them.

"But, it's not all his fault. I helped Kyle stay hidden, and I convinced them both to defy you. I hear you're a man of honor and you want justice. So, listen to me. I'm willing to make things right and pay the price for what I've done as long as you spare their lives. Gavin and Kyle are done crossing you. All they want is their town back. And I know you want atonement for everything they've done, so I'll make you a deal for them.

I'm willing to do whatever it takes to keep you in the clear and make sure that no harm comes to your business. Gavin and his crew will not bring heat to your door anymore, and Kyle will stop killing your people. And in return, if anyone from Settlement Island retaliates against you because of Gavin and Kyle, I'll let you take out your vengeance on me. Because everything they did was for me." Gavin narrowed his eyebrows at me. "Well, lately, everything they've done was because of me. So, that's the deal. I take their place and offer you my word that you can replace Gavin's life with mine."

Aaron reached for the phone, but I kept it from him. "You're not worth that much to Porter, Catalina. Trust me, the price on their heads is worth way more than yours…"

"I come from a rich family. We've got millions of dollars." I paused. "You can have me and my share of the family money." Aaron laughed. "Gavin loves me,

Porter. And I love him. And I'll do anything to keep him alive. So, please, I won't hide. If any harm comes to you because of him, I'll give you everything."

"Your word is your bond?" Porter said on the phone. His voice was low, deep, very stern and without emotion.

A deep breath. "My word is my bond."

"Catalina Payton, if that is the arrangement, so be it." The line went dead.

Aaron took the phone back. "All this for him…"

My eyes went to Gavin. Sorrow was on his face. An irrational, selfless act of love was bound to be my greatest mistake. However, I regretted nothing. If Porter wanted me, he could come and get me.

CHAPTER FORTY

The Beginning

A HERO'S DINNER, is what Dad called it. Christmas had come, and everyone was incredibly happy to have me home. Miguel convinced his mother to let him stay until after the New Year. I had to pay for that. She expected me to spend my entire vacation, which would probably come during the summer, slaving away in her kitchen to pay for keeping her son. I didn't mind.

The snow was falling fast. Not another Nor'easter, but another storm to say the least. I looked out the window, watching various cars pull into the driveway. Luke and his parents had come for the festivities. Dad and Mother had invited a few others, too.

Smiles, seas of smiles, as they braved the icy conditions for dinner at the rich doctor's house. Mother loved this. It was her dream. Having people over while Miguel impressed them with his cooking skills made her look good. Cecilia and Dad helped. I was asked to stay away from the kitchen the moment I burned the second batch of macaroni and cheese.

"You'll learn one of these days," Miguel had said with a smile.

When Luke came to my door, I was almost ready. No knocks, just an entrance that told me this wouldn't take long.

The hug was sweet. "Happy to have you home," he said.

"My very first Maine Christmas."

He nodded. "I'll see ya out there." No lingering. According to Miguel, Cecilia told Luke to give up on me. But I wouldn't let it go with this.

My arms went back around his shoulders. "Thank you for everything, Luke."

"No problem." He was gone quickly. Another grab at his shoulder.

"I'm really glad we get to spend Christmas together, here."

He eyed the golden arrow necklace sitting on my desk. "You love him, and he loves you. But sometimes, love doesn't last forever, if it's not real." He smirked. "Keep it," he said, referring to the necklace. "I can wait." This was enough for him to leave.

Luke was probably the better choice, yet I had made mine. Porter hadn't come for me yet, but Aaron made sure I knew that he would come one day. And there was nothing he could do to protect me.

As we prepared for the holidays, I found out that today, Christmas, was Aaron's birthday. My gift to him was a quick, meaningful conversation. I told him that I understood why he did what he had done, and I would keep up my end of the bargain with his brother.

In return, Aaron gave me a sigh and said a few simple words. "I would never let him kill you, Catalina." Since this conversation, I hadn't seen much of him today. Cecilia said he had gone out to the office for something, an emergency visit with one of his patients. But I knew the truth. As selfish as Aaron may have seemed to me, I knew he would do anything to help me.

In the end, I was glad to be rid of the fear of the unknown. I would deal with Porter, when I had to. Until then, I wouldn't fret. I had other things to worry about, anyway.

There were lights in the driveway. I smiled. My hair was in perfect curls, thanks to Mother's help. The dress was simple, white with a black belt. Mother told me not to wear it, but it was my choice. Pink heels, holding me up.

A tap on the door, and he came in. Perfect hair, sculpted eyebrows. Blue undershirt hiding behind a gray sweater and blue jacket with brown trim. Black pants and boots. In his hand was a small, silver box.

"I didn't get you anything," I said.

He walked in, "You don't even know what it is yet."

I smiled. He heard my dad first. The box went hidden as Dad came into the room. "Gavin, so happy you could make it! Thank you so much for saving our beloved Catalina."

"It was my pleasure."

"What are ya drinking? Beer? Scotch? Brandy? Bourbon?"

"Whatever you want, Dr. Payton." Dad nodded at this and reminded us to be ready to eat in ten minutes. Once he was gone, the box came back out. "This might not be as beautiful as you are, but I tried." I closed the door and took the box. I went to kiss him, but he blocked me, motioning to the box. Upon opening it, I saw the silver necklace with a small charm. A book. "This is to remind you of who you are."

My eyebrows creased. "How so?"

"Well, you love to read. And you've had a storybook life, so far. No matter what happens in the future, Catalina, make sure you don't lose the storybook."

He turned me around and put the necklace on my neck. A soft kiss on my shoulder was all I needed to accept his wonderful offer. When he went in for the kiss, I dodged it. I couldn't let him go that easy. My mind needed a second to come up with the perfect gift for him. Something symbolic and thoughtful, too. I pulled out the book of sonnets that Luke had given me. Finding the page didn't take very long.

I looked at Gavin for a moment. Yes, this was the right one. The right gift to give. I tore the page from the book and handed it to him.

"It's my favorite poem."

The Lost, The Forgotten

Before you go, you must know, the hunted will soon fall

And in my heart, I've been torn apart, I must heed the call

Destiny's broken, my love has spoken, it's all that I know

The lost has wandered, the forgotten has been laundered, and you'll never let me go

After he read it, he folded it up and put it in his pocket. "I'll carry it with me, always."

Now, we gave into the kiss. His warmth, his beauty, the invitation into his world. I felt the cold on his jacket as he warmed up next to me. And when we parted, we smiled at one another. I loved him, and he loved me.

We laced our fingers together, ready to follow our destiny, come what may.

Don't miss the next book in the

RIDING WITH DARKNESS SERIES…

DARKNESS IN THE LION'S DEN

Available December 2021

Read on for a preview…

Chapter One

Promises

The cool morning air touched my face as I hunted, longing to find what I was looking for. It soothed my nerves. I had never done this before, but I hoped it would work out. It had to work out. My sandals crunched on the grass beneath me as I stalked back and forth, making a memory of what looked good and what I could do without. I could be good at this, if I tried. If I gave the whole thing a chance. Not be impatient for once.

I turned a corner, and a woman smiled in my direction. A sweet, gentle smile. She must have known that I was out of my element. But I did have help. Miguel had made the list and texted it over before I went out. He had a confidence in me that was both enduring and aggravating. However, he was the chef, and he knew exactly what my capabilities were. Above all, he loved me, and he knew how important all this was to me.

I set my basket down and looked over some wines. Instead of picking from here, I would go through

Mother's cellar and find one. Back on the trail, I looked in other people's baskets to get an idea for anything I had missed. Fruit. Strawberries dipped in chocolate. Sweet, bitter, wonderful chocolate. I could taste it as easily as I could taste his lips. What a fantastic duo. Another smile, this time from me to the other patrons of the Settlement Island Farmer's Market.

My trip had lasted over an hour, as there was so much to see and do. It reminded me of the various markets back home. Telegraph Avenue never ceased to amaze me with its endless varieties of daily staples and oddities. Today, I wasn't after strange and peculiar things. I needed food, a cornucopia of food, to prove once and for all that I, Catalina Rose Payton, could make something other than cereal for dinner.

Ever since that long-ago October day, the day I learned of his story, he teased me and overdid every single meal we ate together. That's the hard part when dealing with a boyfriend who is perfect at everything: it means you fall incredibly short in every attempt you try to make. But not tonight. This was my night.

The basket was getting heavy. Maybe I had overdone it. Maybe I was being overzealous. I set it down. Yet, there were a few other items…

"You know, I'm flattered. Really, I am. But you don't have to do this," he said.

I smirked, "You started it."

Gavin's perfect blue-gray eyes ran over the apples and oranges stacked up in front of him and between us. The summer sun had escaped him as he stood under the umbrella in a plain white tee-shirt, blue jeans, and boots. Always boots, even on the hottest days. Sculpted hair: I knew in the summer he had to put a light sheen of hairspray on, so the humidity wouldn't deflate his most prized contribution to the world. I am overdoing it, of course. But he is beautiful to me.

"You look good," he said.

Yes, my summer transformation had taken him aback when I started dressing in sun dresses, sandals, and hats. He always looked good, and I felt gorgeous next to him, for once. Mother actually gave me the idea. She was by far the most beautiful woman in Settlement Island, and I wanted to be her. Or at least look like her. And he gave me a reason to.

"Thank you, kind sir. Now," I started walking and so did he, "you're not allergic to anything, are you?"

"No...except your cooking."

"Ouch," I went back for my basket and returned, the long table still between us. "In my defense, no one ever taught me."

"Fair enough," Gavin picked up some kale and a bunch of cauliflower. Did he know where I was going with our dinner plans? Probably. I was rather predicable, he told me. "What about dessert?"

This was a Cecilia and Dad specialty. They had started baking on the weekends as a way to de-stress and spend time together. Dad and I still worked at the office, so he didn't feel the need to go beyond our current arrangement. I could resent him for picking Cecilia over me, but I chose not to. Besides, I was a terrible cook, dancer, conversationalist, golfer, everything. We were better off as we were: co-workers.

"Well, I'm excited," Gavin came around the table and took the basket from me.

"No, you're not." My eyes met his, and I had to take a moment to look at my boyfriend. He rolled his eyes and kissed me softly. Gavin hated it when I just stared at him. At least now, when I marveled at him, it was because I loved him. Before, I was always calculating his next move, afraid of what he would do to me if I divulged his secrets. He thought we no longer had any secrets, because now he told me everything. But today, he did have one more secret that I already knew.

"Truth or Dare, Catalina," he said.

"Dare," I wrapped my arm around his. As we walked, the other market-goers made way for us.

"You're going with a dare?" I nodded. "Well, I wasn't ready for that one."

"You know so much about me. It was only a matter of time until I picked Dare."

"Okay," Gavin looked over the rest of the produce. "I dare you to keep an open mind tonight."

"Why?"

"Because, for once, I'm not going to spoil you and give you whatever you want."

I laughed. "You never spoil me, Gavin. You still deny me the one thing I want from you."

He grinned. "Well, Ms. Payton, I didn't know you only wanted one thing from me."

"It's the only one that matters," I said. Gavin stopped

at the wine table and picked out a red. "I'm sure my mother has something you'll like better."

Gavin shook his head. "I'd like to eat local-only tonight." We continued on.

"Truth or Dare, Gavin."

"Today is my birthday," he said.

"I know." I smirked. He stopped and was silent, angry that I had bested him with his only remaining secret. "James told me the other day. How he found out is a total mystery to me."

"I got arrested on my 21st birthday, and he bailed me out of jail. I had to give him my birthdate, so he could make arrangements." He paused. "Is that why you are attempting to cook me dinner?" I hid my smile. "So, you're going to kill me on my birthday?"

"You're a cruel man, Gavin Christopher Scott."

"It's the truth. I'm sorry if it hurts."

Gavin took me by my house, so I could get my things together. We would have dinner and spend the night at his family's cabin in the woods. Dad had put Gavin's cake in a box, which helped me keep yet another secret safe. Gavin and my dad were close, so asking him to leave my boyfriend alone on his birthday had become a chore. You see, it was only a matter of time before Dad hurled my requests for him to keep quiet aside, so he could make a scene. Making a scene was his specialty. I braced myself, ready to shush him into oblivion. Finding the house empty gave me the impression that someone had distracted him, giving me a hand, no doubt. Mother had left a bottle of wine next to the cake. She was the do-gooder. Gavin examined the bottle with a smirk.

"Okay, hers is better."

I got ready quickly and grabbed my bag. Gavin had already packed the truck. When I got in, he sat there and just stared at the lake.

"What is it?" I said.

He leaned back in his seat. This seemed to happen a lot lately. Gavin would seem to get lost in his thoughts, unaware of the world around him. No moving, shallow breathing, and lots of staring. I slid over next to him.

"Gavin?"

A few seconds went by, and he came back to me, a smile on his face. We headed out of the country club and up the rugged road to the cabin. About halfway up, Gavin took a turn I didn't know existed. We travelled about a quarter of a mile before the trees parted in the middle of a meadow of grass and flowers.

Gavin opened his door and helped me out of the truck. Out came a blanket, and we walked into the center of the meadow. We laid down, him pulling me into his arms as my head rested on his shoulder. The clouds threatened rain, but there was too much sun to ruin our moment.

My head came up and I looked at him. The sun and shadows on his face. He was mine. This beautiful, complicated man was mine. I leaned into him and kissed him, his lips warm and soft against mine. Another kiss and then another. Our breaths became deep as I leaned my body onto his. It was easy for him to put me back on the blanket and prop himself up on one side.

"Catalina, we talked about this."

"All we do is talk about it." Sexy grin. "Less talk and more action."

Gavin shook his head. "You already have me. There's no need to move too fast."

"Move too fast?" I laughed. "Gavin, I'm the only twenty-one-year-old virgin in the world. It's embarrassing." I paused. "Unless you're a virgin, too."

"Definitely not."

He chuckled as he wrestled me down to the blanket. I wasn't amused. "Why not?"

Gavin's face turned serious. "Catalina, I'm a realist. Always have been. And I don't want to take something from you that I'll regret later. Remember, I'm not sure if I'm the guy for you."

"You're not taking anything if I'm willing." My arms crossed. "How long has it been since you last had sex?"

"An eternity," he scoffed. Then he realized I wanted a real answer. "This is uncomfortable."

"Why?"

"Because that was all meaningless sex. I didn't love them. Hell, I didn't really like them, to be honest. They were just available." Now, I recoiled. He put his hands on mine. "Catalina, keep an open mind." My face turned up in disgust. "Okay, that was the wrong thing to say," he gave a hearty laugh. "I've had sex before. I can't take that back. But what I have with you is way better than what I had with those girls."

"Better than sex?"

He paused. "Look, I was just a guy who met a few girls who thought I was hot. And that was it."

"Did they even know your name?"

He tilted his head. "We all can't have self-control like you do."

If only it were that easy. "Can't have sex when no one notices you," I muttered as I traced the blanket's faint lines.

His hands went to my face. "Don't think too much about it. I was very selective, even when I gave in to the temptation. And I'm safe, remember?"

"That's not helping."

He nodded. "What I'm trying to say is, sex meant nothing to me then. I had it occasionally with a few girls I met."

"And Ronda."

"This thing with me and Ronda." Gavin cleared his throat. "Everyone in town has it wrong. I only slept with Ronda a few times over the course of like eight years."

"But Molly and the other girls said you guys were always together. That she went where you went."

"Yeah, fucking Molly thinks she knows everything," he scoffed. "But she was wrong. Ronda and I were not close. We just knew each other from school and town. I only slept with her because she was there. And now I hate her." He tensed up. I put my hand on his. "Look, I don't know what to tell you, really. I can't change my past, and Ronda was a complete waste of time."

"Because you didn't date."

"Because I didn't believe I could fall in love until I met you." He took a deep breath. "Catalina, there was no point in having a girlfriend if I was gonna end up dead by twenty-one. Or twenty-two. Get it?"

I did. But it didn't make me any less sad. It wasn't his past that bothered me, but rather the fact that by being the chosen one, I was denied the one thing he had given away so freely before. My back went to the blanket, and I smiled at him to show that I was over it. I would give him this one. I would deny my desires and make sure he got what he wanted on his birthday. After all, it was a miracle that he had made it to twenty-five.

When we got back to the cabin, I put my stuff in his room, and headed off to the kitchen to start on dinner. Miguel was available to Facetime me, so I wouldn't miss a beat. Gavin was in the shower, which gave me a chance to stumble through the beginning on my own until I got into a rhythm. His kisses on my neck reminded me that I was no longer alone.

Gavin pulled a knife from the block and began cutting vegetables. I shooed him away and demanded that he start a fire in the living room where we would be dining. When he returned, he inspected all my work and made some adjustments to enhance the flavor of everything. "You're gonna love it," he said.

"No, you're gonna love it," I corrected him. He didn't believe me, but at least I had something to be proud of.

Dinner was oven-roasted chicken breast, cauliflower

puree, kale salad with homemade dressing, and a medley of roasted vegetables. Gavin plated everything nicely as I poured the wine. We sat at the table and dined on our dinner while chatting on our newest favorite topic: philosophy. Over the summer, Gavin had started challenging my intellect as a way to "catch up" to me. Our debates were fun and one of the only times I could best him at something.

After dinner, it was time for me to give him a gift. My heart beat fast as I looked at the plain white box that was hidden under the coffee table. We settled into the couch before the fire. He looked at me with amusement. I took his hands to keep mine from shaking.

His eyebrows creased together. "What's wrong, Catalina?"

I took a few deep breaths. "Before I give you this gift, I figured I would explain it first."

"Why? Doesn't that defeat the whole point of it being a surprise?"

"Well," I said slowly, "I'm not sure how you're gonna take it."

"Try me." His response wasn't a challenge but rather a playful invitation.

"Last week, when Dad and I visited Paula for her therapy, she had me help her pack up some stuff in her room. As we were going along, she found something that she thought you might want for your birthday. So, this is from her, not me."

I placed the box on his lap. Gavin opened it carefully and pulled out the framed picture of his grandfather and him. "She said that was taken about a month before he died."

"It was," he said as he continued to look at the picture. After a pause, he looked at me. "Why are you so nervous?"

"There's more." I retrieved a small, long box from my purse and sat down. He opened it with caution. His silence warranted an explanation. "Your grandmother told me that your dad and your father didn't get along after they took custody of you. And he wasn't allowed in the house because he had a habit of stealing things to buy heroin, so they thought it was gone. But we found it. Apparently, your grandmother hid it and forgot where it was until now."

Gavin ran his fingers over the knife blade and the handle that held his grandfather's initials. "I took it into a blacksmith's shop in Anders and had him restore it." Now, he was back in his trance again, quiet and in a far-off place. I looked out at the fire that consumed the logs, much like this moment had consumed my heart. "Paula says you always wanted it, and you never believed your dad when he said he didn't take it. And he never did. It was just lost."

He placed the photo and the knife down on the table and turned toward me. His eyes blinked quickly, threatening to show the slightest sense of vulnerability. Then he got up and sat down next to the fire on the bear skin rug. I always told him that rug was cheesy, and I had a mind that he kept it to spite me, until I sat down next to him. It was, indeed, soft and comforting. Gavin's arms went around me as he looked at the fire. We stayed this way, not talking, until he sighed.

"Thank you," he said. "Thank you for these beautiful gifts."

"I can't take credit. It was all Paula."

"So, you didn't get me anything?"

I had brought the knife with me to the rug. I turned over the handle, so he could see the initials on the other side: G.C.S. "I thought it would be nice to have your initials on it, too. It's yours now."

He laughed. "You have millions of dollars at your disposal, and an arsenal full of my secret desires for inspiration, and this is what you give me for my birthday?" Gavin smiled. "You are the only person in the world who really knows me."

I smiled. "This was technically Paula's gift, not mine."

Gavin pointed to some small etchings close to where his initials were. "When I was ten, I tried to cut my initials into the knife handle. My grandfather told me I needed better tools to do it. So, he took me to the hardware store to buy all the stuff we needed to get my name on there. When we got back, my dad had breezed into town for a visit. My grandfather sent me into the house with the knife while he dealt with my dad. As they got into it, Paula sent me to my room, and I left the knife on the table. Then, it went missing, and I assumed my dad took it…"

"But Paula took it and hid it instead, and you didn't know."

"We never talked about it. I felt guilty because it was my responsibility. And my dad ended up staying in town for a week and started causing more trouble for my grandparents. He kept coming by, trying to get into the house. We were all so stressed out dealing with him that we had forgotten about the knife until after my grandfather got sick. Before he died, I apologized for losing it. He told me not to worry about it..."

"And you never thought to ask Paula." He shook his head. "So, you've been holding this guilt for over thirteen years?"

"I never thought I'd see it again." Gavin took in a deep breath. "Catalina, did you know any of this before I told you?"

"No," I said. "I had no idea all that took place. Paula gave it to me, and I just thought it would be nice to have your name on it."

Gavin put the knife down. "This means more to me than anything in the world. Well, almost anything." He went into his pocket and pulled out the poem I had given him for Christmas.

The Lost, The Forgotten

Before you go, you must know, the hunted will soon fall

And in my heart, I've been torn apart, I must heed the call

Destiny's broken, my love has spoken, it's all that I know

The lost has wandered, the forgotten has been laundered, and you'll never let me go

"I carry this in my wallet. And with this knife, now I have two things from the most important people to me."

"It's kinda fitting, in a way. The poem and the knife." I nestled in closer to him. "You thought the knife was lost and forgotten to you. But the knife never let you go. It was always there, right within reach."

"Undiscovered until you came along." Gavin looked at me. "I love you, Catalina Payton. And you love me, which is a fucking miracle." More pondering. "We've lost each other, over and over. We've hunted each other and tried to let go, but we've never been able to." He laid down next to me. "I've never been a part of a love story before. I've always been the villain, never the hero. Never the one the girl should long for, but rather the monster she should stay away from."

"Well, you've had a lifetime of problems, so I don't blame you for finding it strange that I like you, let alone love you." I smirked. "I've never been a part of a love story, so I don't know how all this works, either. My life was painfully predictable before I met you. And now that I know Gavin Scott, the monster, I have to say that I'm glad I was wrong about you. I'm glad I was brave enough to be your friend and the object of your admiration."

"You sound like a novel."

I laughed. "As do you, my friend. It's all those philosophy debates, I guess." Now, to be serious. "Truth is, Gavin, you have a whole life ahead of you that should be discovered. A whole mess of opportunities and living that you need to do. And, if you'll let me, I'd like to do some of that living with you."

Gavin stayed still, only his chest moving. My eyes stayed with his until he leaned in and kissed me. I held onto him, feeling loved and adored. His hands moved to the floor as he pulled himself on top of me, kissing me heavier. My fingers grazed the skin underneath his shirt. Within an instant, I was on top of him, kissing him as my hands rested on his stomach, wandering toward his chest. Off came his shirt, both our doing.

His skin was warm and soft as the fire cast shadows on his face. Gavin unzipped my dress, exposing me to him for the first time. I had a mind to hide, but there was no time. More kissing and feeling across his back as his kisses went to my neck. Soon enough, through the constant distraction of kisses and seeing each other for the first time, we were completely naked. I paused, looking at him. My hand went across his bare chest and my eyes looked over everything else. I nodded to him, and he placed me on the ground, his kisses never-ending.

The moment he was inside me, I felt different. Twenty-one years of innocence and frustration were replaced with a longing for acceptance and love from him. I closed my eyes, feeling him, his passion and desire for me and mine for him in return. No matter what happened for the rest of the night, or all eternity, I was so thankful to know every part of him. To see Gavin Scott for who he was and to show him every part of me was bliss. I loved and needed him and now he finally knew how deep my desires for him truly went.

About the Author

Tara Majuta is a published author, book coach, whale saver, and lover of life. Riding with Darkness is her second published book. Her first book, The Fascinating Files of Claudia, is being reprinted with an available date of December 2021. Her love of writing comes from wanting to be a princess at the age of 10. She began writing in September 2007. Since then, she has drafted over 30 books to be published in the upcoming years. Currently, she teaches aspiring authors how to write fiction books. Check out brilliantbookscoaching.com to learn more.

Made in the USA
Columbia, SC
13 February 2023